THE CHOSEN QUEEN

Joanna Courtney has wanted to be a writer ever since she could read. As a child she was rarely seen without her head in a book. After spending endless hours entertaining her siblings with made-up stories, it came as no surprise when Joanna pursued her passion for books during her time at Cambridge University – where she combined her love of English and History by specializing in Medieval Literature.

Joanna continued to write through her first years of work and then, once married and living in Derbyshire, in the sparse hours available between raising four children. She has written over 200 stories and serials published in women's magazines, some of which have been broadcast on BBC radio. Joanna has also won several fiction prizes and written and directed an award-winning play. She teaches creative writing across the country and for the Open University.

Joanna is fascinated by defining moments in history, of which the Battle of Hastings is certainly one. The outcome of that momentous day is one of the big 'what-ifs?' of England's past and she has loved being able to immerse herself in the world of the Anglo-Saxons, Normans and Vikings whilst writing The Queen's of the Conquest trilogy.

Praise for *The Chosen Queen*

'An absorbing and emotional debut novel'   *Candis*

'A beautifully written multi-layered tale with a tremendously authentic sense of place and time . . . an epic feel . . . highly recommended'   Liz Loves Books

'Gripping, intriguing, romantic'   Tracy Bloom, author of
No-one Ever Has Sex on a Tuesday

'*The Chosen Queen* is an epic read . . . Rich plots, fascinating characters and detailed historical events'   Compelling Reads

'A glorious, rich, epic story of love, friendship and sacrifice which will sweep you up and transport you to another time. I absolutely loved this and can't wait for the next book in the series'   Rachael Lucas, author of
Sealed With A Kiss and *Coming Up Roses*

'Wonderful, mesmerizing storytelling that had me hooked from page one, keeping me engrossed throughout the entire novel and still left desperate for more'   Reviewed the Book

'The story reaches a heart-rending climax. A must read. I loved it'   Freda Lightfoot,
author of *The Amber Keeper*

'An atmospheric, vividly written book that took me on a fascinating journey into the past, so much so, that even after I finished the book, I am still wondering about the characters and their world. I simply cannot wait for the next book. I am hooked!'   Sh... B..k Blog

THE CHOSEN QUEEN

JOANNA
COURTNEY

PAN BOOKS

First published 2015 by Pan Books
an imprint of Pan Macmillan
20 New Wharf Road, London N1 9RR
Associated companies throughout the world
www.panmacmillan.com

ISBN 978-1-4472-8078-1

3 5 7 9 8 6 4 2

A CIP catalogue record for this book is available from the British Library.

Typeset by Palimpsest Book Production Ltd, Falkirk, Stirlingshire
Printed and bound by CPI Group (UK) Ltd, Croydon, CR0 4YY

*For my husband Stuart
who's always believed in me.*

ENGLAND
1066

SCOTLAND

GODFRED

NORTHUMBRIA

Stamford
Bridge

York ○ ○
○ Fulford
Riccal ○

Rhuddlan

Caernarvon ○

Gwynedd

Chester ○

MERCIA

Powys

Billingsley ○
Coventry ○

EAST ANGLIA

St.
Davids
○

WALES

Deheubarth

Hereford ○

Glamorgan

Gloucester ○

Nazeing ○

London ○

WESSEX

Wilton
Abbey ○

Winchester ○

Senlac Field ○

Britford ○

Bosham ○

Hastings ○

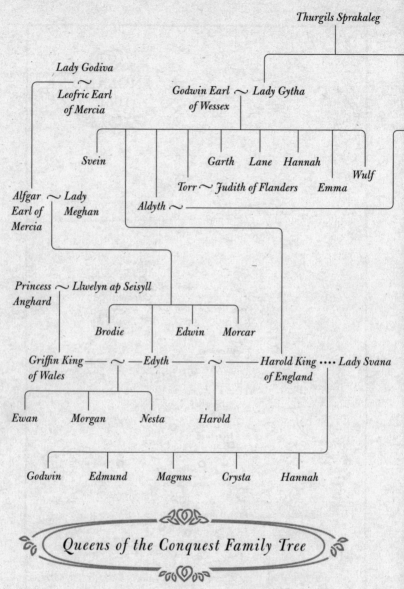

Thurgils Sprakaleg

Lady Godiva ~ Leofric Earl of Mercia

Godwin Earl ~ Lady Gytha of Wessex

Svein

Garth   Lane   Hannah

Wulf

Torr ~ Judith of Flanders   Emma

Alfgar ~ Lady Earl of Meghan Mercia

Aldyth ~

Princess ~ Llwelyn ap Seisyll Anghard

Brodie   Edwin   Morcar

Griffin King —— ~ —— Edyth —— ~ —— Harold King •••• Lady Svana of Wales   of England

Ewan   Morgan   Nesta   Harold

Godwin   Edmund   Magnus   Crysta   Hannah

Queens of the Conquest Family Tree

Note: A dotted line indicates a handfast marriage

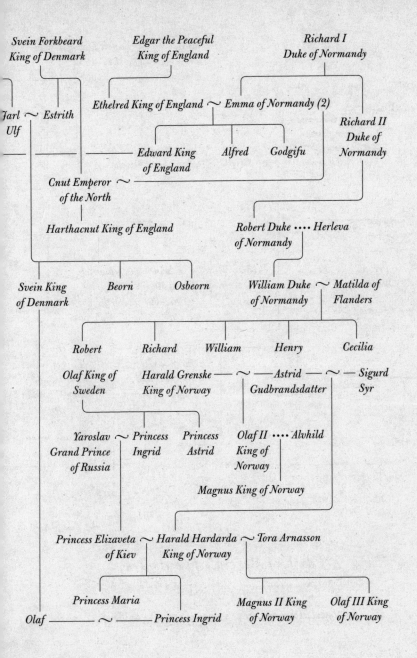

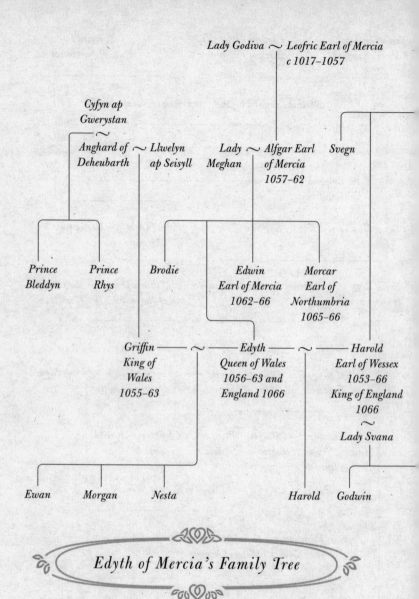

Lady Godiva ～ Leofric Earl of Mercia
c 1017–1057

Cyfyn ap
Gwerystan
～
Anghard of ～ Llwelyn   Lady ～ Alfgar Earl   Svegn
Deheubarth   ap Seisyll   Meghan   of Mercia
                                    1057–62

Prince   Prince   Brodie   Edwin   Morcar
Bleddyn   Rhys   Earl of Mercia   Earl of
                                      1062–66   Northumbria
                                                   1065–66

Griffin ——— ～ ——— Edyth ——— ～ ——— Harold
King of   Queen of Wales   Earl of Wessex
Wales   1056–63 and   1053–66
1055–63   England 1066   King of England
                                           1066
                                           ～
                                           Lady Svana

Ewan   Morgan   Nesta   Harold   Godwin

Edyth of Mercia's Family Tree

Note: Dates shown are a duration of a reign as earl/king

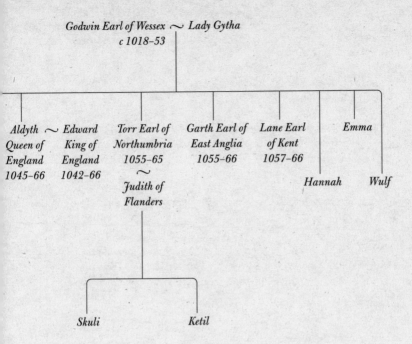

Godwin Earl of Wessex ∼ Lady Gytha
c 1018–53

Aldyth ∼ Edward
Queen of   King of
England   England
1045–66   1042–66

Torr Earl of
Northumbria
1055–65
∼
Judith of
Flanders

Garth Earl of
East Anglia
1055–66

Lane Earl
of Kent
1057–66

Emma

Hannah   Wulf

Skuli   Ketil

Edmund   Magnus   Crysta   Hannah

THE
CHOSEN
QUEEN

PROLOGUE

Sometimes when she closes her eyes and pictures that night, Edyth cannot tell where memories end and dreams begin. She wonders if she was enchanted. She was only eight after all, her mind still shifting in and out of made-up worlds, but something about that night, played out in firelight beneath a million stars, still feels so solid, so very real as if, rather than being befuddled by it, her mind became truly clear for the first time.

He looked like a king that day, Harold. Even in a simple bride-groom's tunic of darkest green he looked like royalty as he stepped up to take the Lady Svana's hand. There was no gold in sight, just flowers; no parade of bishops, just a smiling monk in a sack-robe and bare feet. There was no betrothal contract, no formal prayers, no exchange of lands or elaborate gifts, just the linking of hands joining two people for a year and a day.

'No longer?' Edyth had asked. Marriage was forever, everyone knew that – grumbled about it, jested about it, accepted it.

'Only if we wish it,' Lady Svana had told her. 'Ours is a marriage of hearts, not of laws. If we cease to love, it ends.' Edyth must have looked shocked because Svana had laughed and said, 'Fear not, this union will last to the grave – love prefers to be free.'

Those are the words Edyth still hears, like a fiddler's tune played over that whole night: 'love prefers to be free', and they colour her memories a thousand glorious shades. There had been feasting,

3

on long tables stretched out across the meadow. Then, as the sun dropped, myriad lanterns had been lit in the trees and there had been dancing. Guests had whirled, maypole-mad, around a giant fire that turned them into tumbling shadows and sent sparks of joy into the night sky until, finally, they'd kindled the dawn and it had all been over.

The next day Edyth had wandered, dazed. Her father had been scornful, covering up a sore head and any memory of the self he had briefly become – a self that had danced with his wife beneath the stars, his daughter on his broad shoulders and his sons glee-fully circling. Perhaps he had been enchanted too? If so, the magic had fled with the light of day.

'Ridiculous paganism,' he'd muttered. 'What would the Pope say?'

Edyth hadn't cared. She'd never meet the Pope, far, far away in some mystical city across the seas, but Earl Harold was here and despite being high up in the king's council where all was tangled rules and debates, he'd been content to stand on a hillside, head bared, and marry for love.

'Fool,' her mother had said. 'What connections does she have? What influence does she yield? What use is she to him?'

Edyth had said nothing but it had seemed to her then that Harold glowed when he was with his handfast wife and that it was that glow, more than any gold or land or title, that drew people to him. 'Love prefers to be free,' Svana had said and Edyth had carried that with her ever since. It had been her ideal, lit up by firelight and scented with meadow grass, and now, on the brink of womanhood, she craved such a passion for herself.

PART ONE

CHAPTER ONE

Westminster, March 1055

Dusk was sneaking up the swirling eddies of the Thames, calling the men and women of King Edward's England to their beds. Inside Westminster's great hall, however, no one was listening, least of all Edyth Alfgarsdottir. In a clatter of platters and trestles the formal part of the mid-Lent gathering was being dismantled and for the first time she was to remain until the feast danced itself into bed. Anticipation spiked in her stomach and she pressed herself against a pillar, her fingers nervously tracing the intricate carvings in the wood as she took in every glorious detail of the unravelling court.

The royal hall was old and nearly as ramshackle as the abbey church beyond but tonight the fading rays of the spring sun were pouring into the vast space, making it shine. The light tumbled through the open doors at either end of the room, pooling around the small window openings and sneaking between the thatch above. It caught in the gold trim of the highly painted shields along the walls and danced in the copious jewellery adorning England's wealthiest men and women so that the whole space seemed to Edyth to shimmer with hazy promise.

All around, conversation was rising and twisting as fast as the smoke from the central hearth. The formal bows and hand-shakes of earlier were loosening into clutched arms and shared laughter. Ladies tugged demurely on fat, corn-blonde plaits or plucked at headdresses, pulling them back discreetly to let a pretty wisp of hair show. Gentlemen tucked eating knives into patterned leather belts, swept back their hair and ran calloused warrior's hands over their moustaches. Edyth searched for a group to join but they were shifting and changing like mice in a barn and she dared not step in.

She glanced awkwardly back along the edge of the hall where the elderly and the infirm, whose limbs were too swollen, twisted or sword-savaged to bear them for long, huddled on stiff wooden benches and looked hopefully out of the open doors towards the low sun. It hung reluctantly over the rolling Thames just beyond the hall, but very soon it would drop into the dark water. Then the invalids and children would be able to retire to their beds. Here in the hall, though, the rush lights around the tapestry-hung walls would be lit to keep the evening alive and she, Edyth, would be a part of it all.

Drawing in a breath rich with meat-smoke and spiced apple mead, she forced herself to step out towards the central hearth. The remains of the stag, lowered over the fire to crisp, were spitting fat and a careful space had cleared around it. Through the swirl of mingled smoke and light Edyth spotted her friends waving her eagerly over. Instinctively she moved towards them but then ducked away, wiping a ghost speck of ash from her eye. She wasn't in the mood for prattle tonight. She'd longed for so many years to be part of the late-night life of the court but now she was here she felt edgy and unsettled, slightly apart from the easy gossip. Maybe she'd caught her father's mood – with the great council on the morrow he'd been as nervy as an unhooded hawk all day – or maybe this restlessness was all her own.

'Would you like to dance?'

Edyth jumped and stared at the man bowing low before her, the jewel-studded hem of his fine blue tunic sparking in the jumbled light. He straightened, holding out his hand imperiously, and the flash from his amber eyes sent the shining royal hall into tumbling shadows.

'With you?' Edyth stuttered.

He took a mock look around the carousing crowd before returning his gaze to her.

'I'm not in the habit of asking beautiful women to dance with other men.'

Edyth flushed and glanced guiltily around. Lord Tostig of Hereford was part of the Godwinson family, all-powerful in the south of England, and, as such, hated with a fierce and determined passion by her father, Earl Alfgar. Being seen consorting with any of them would be tantamount to treason in his eyes. She faltered.

'Do you not wish to dance?' Torr pulled his hand back a little and instinctively Edyth reached up to take it. 'You do? Excellent. I am not a bad dancer, you know – you can trust me not to tread on your feet.'

'It is not my feet I am concerned for,' she shot back and he laughed.

'Do not believe all you hear around the court, Lady Edyth.'

Edyth blushed and looked to the rush-strewn floor. Lord Tostig was known to all as Torr, or Tower, for reasons that seemed to cause much giggling in the ladies' bower, and was reputed to hunt down the prettiest ladies of the court as efficiently as he hunted wild boar. Was he hunting her now?

'If I believed even half,' she managed, 'I would have cause to be cautious, would I not?'

He laughed again.

'That might be true, but caution, Lady Edyth, is much over-rated. Now, shall we?'

His richly ringed fingers clasped tightly around hers as he led her through the tangle of guests around the fire and down to the rear of the hall. The gleemen were tuning up on a raised dais, servants were clearing back the scented rushes from the floor, and all around young men were luring partners forward.

Edyth felt, as much as heard, the buzz of flirtatious chatter and glanced around to see her friends nudging and pointing. She swallowed and drew herself up as tall as she could, willing the other dancers not to question her right to join them. Her gown, a deep russet, cut expensively tight to reveal her growing curves and with indulgently wide sleeves to show off her slim arms, was as grand as any, but still she felt uncertain of her place amongst so many ladies of the court. Lord Torr, however, seemed to see nothing strange in his choice of partner and whisked her confidently into the central line.

'Trust me,' he whispered, his lips brushing her ear.

Edyth swallowed. Trust was not something the young lord inspired, though she wasn't sure exactly why. She was finding the mysteries of adult relations irritatingly hard to fathom. She'd tried asking her elder brother Brodie about it when he'd been sneaking mead from their father's barrel. He'd flushed scarlet and told her she'd find out on her wedding night. But she was only fourteen; her wedding might be three or four years in the making and she wanted to know now.

She hadn't dared ask her mother, the purse-lipped Lady Meghan, for she would just say – as she so often said – that Edyth wasn't seemly and the other girls were just full of made-up stories and half-truths. Lord Torr, she knew instinctively, would answer all her questions if she so wished but suddenly such knowledge felt dangerous. She tried, again, to pull back but the gleemen had struck up and the dance was being led out. The sixteen couples looked to the lead pair – Torr's lively younger brother Lord Garth and their sister, Queen Aldyth – for the pattern of the dance and for a little while Edyth was forced to concentrate. Lord Torr, however, proved to be the strong dancer he had claimed and had soon mastered the steps.

'So, Lady Edyth,' he said, leading her confidently across the set, 'are you ready for what the morrow may bring?'

Edyth jumped. At the royal council on the morrow a new Earl of Northumbria would be chosen and her father, currently earl of lowly East Anglia, was determined that the appointment would be his. The anticipation was making him in turns excitable and irascible and, reminded of her treacherous choice of partner, Edyth looked nervously around for him. The crush of the crowd was protecting her, but for how long? Torr pulled her close.

'Who but God can ever know what the morrow will bring, my lord?' she responded, struggling to breathe.

He chuckled.

'Very good, Lady Edyth. Earl Alfgar has made quite a politician of you.'

'My father is a gracious man.'

'But is he a wise one?'

'My lord?!'

Again the chuckle.

'You need not answer that. I would not like my own boys to comment on myself or my wife.' He smiled easily, seeming to find nothing strange in talking about the slim and stately Judith of Flanders whilst his fingers whispered caresses across her own. 'And we must all seek advancement. I, for one, lag forever behind my smooth-tongued older brother.'

'Earl Harold?'

Edyth frowned. Ever since his faerie wedding she'd had a quiet liking for the easy, affable Earl Harold of Wessex. She'd noticed him at court Crownwearings and seen how men were drawn to him, how they looked up to him. Women, too, flocked to his side but, though he was always polite, she had never once seen him charming them, as Torr was surely charming her now. Earl Harold's favours, even after all these years of marriage, were kept for his slim, ethereal handfast wife and Edyth loved to see them together when the Lady Svana joined him at court.

The soft-faced lady often smiled at her, even waved, but with her father grumbling about the Godwinsons Edyth had never quite dared approach, preferring to watch from afar. Even Earl Alfgar, though, had been heard to grudgingly call Harold 'the best of the Godwin bunch', so surely Torr was reading his brother wrong? Yet his eyes had clouded and his steps had slowed and, given how she had suffered at the hands of her own patronising elder brother, she felt suddenly sorry for him.

'Maybe you will be granted East Anglia tomorrow?' she suggested as they paused at the top of the dance and to her delight his eyes sparked alight.

'You think so?' She nodded keenly and he smiled, a slow, fox's smile. 'But is that not your father's earldom, my lady? Is he, then, planning on going elsewhere?'

Edyth's gut twisted; he'd trapped her.

'No! I mean, who knows. Maybe, in the fullness of time, God willing . . .'

Confused, she glanced around the packed hall. Some politician she was! She suddenly caught sight of her father, his wide back thankfully turned as he talked earnestly with a handful of other men at the fire. Her skin flared as if it was she who were so close to the flames and she willed him not to look until she'd moved down the dance. Thankfully Torr spun her away.

'Worry not, Edyth, this conversation is for our ears alone. Such a shame, is it not, that Earl Ward's son, Osbeorn, was lost in battle and could not inherit his earldom?'

'Indeed,' she agreed, grateful for the change of subject. It was the death of the legendary northern warrior, Earl Ward of Northumbria, that had brought the council together to choose his successor. 'To die at the hand of the Scots is a terrible thing.'

'A dreadful necessity, I fear.'

'Necessity, my lord?'

'King Edward is very keen that young Prince Malcolm should reclaim his throne from the traitor Macbeth and as Earl Ward fostered him in his exile, he and Osbeorn were eager to fight. It is good that Lord Malcolm has been nurtured by Englishmen, do you not think? An ally over the border will be of great value to the crown, you know, and to the new Earl of Northumbria, whoever he may be.' He pushed her away again but his fingers never left hers and barely had she stepped from the line than he was pulling her back in. 'I am very well acquainted with Lord Malcolm. I was also fostered by Earl Ward for my training, so spent several years with him. A smart young man, keen to negotiate – with the right people.'

His words seemed to Edyth like snakes, whipping dangerously around her feet, too slippery to grasp, and now she regretted eschewing her friends. The dance was turning faster and faster and as Torr spun her expertly, the rush lights on the walls flickered at the edges of her vision, multiplying dizzily as they caught in the highly polished bosses of the shields hung all around.

'I could introduce you if you like,' Torr purred. 'He's quite a handsome man, Lord Malcolm, athletic too, and he'll be in need of a wife.'

'I think I can trust my father to find me a suitable husband, thank you.'

'Of course, of course, but you are an important asset to England, Lady Edyth. Does your father know Malcolm as I do? He's well on his way to reclaiming his throne you know, *well* on his way. You could be Queen of Scotland, Edyth. You'd like that, I'll wager. You'd be grateful, wouldn't you?'

His hand dropped, slinking down from her waist to pick out the curve of her buttocks. Edyth felt a thrill rush straight between her legs and hated herself for it.

'I would rather be Queen of England,' she retorted stiffly, pulling away.

'Would you now? I think you are a little late for that.'

'I did not mean . . .'

'My wife's niece has beaten you to it.'

Edyth stopped, shocked.

'The Lady Matilda? But she is wed to Duke William of Normandy, is she not?'

'Indeed she is. Duke William, who has been promised the throne of England.'

'Nonsense.'

Surprise had made her blunt and she bit at her tongue but Torr just laughed, then leaned further forward so his mouth was close to her ear.

'It's true, Edyth. He came to England and it was promised to him. He was here. Four years ago, in 1051, he was here for Christ's mass. Do you not remember?'

Edyth shifted uneasily as the other dancers wound around her. She'd been young then, just ten, but she *did* remember. It had been a strange Yuletide, stiff and formal, the sharp-nosed Normans stifling the usual exuberance of the Saxon celebrations, but there'd been no promise surely? No ceremony?

'You do remember,' Torr pushed, seeing her face. 'I don't

14

though. I wasn't here. None of my family were. We were in exile.' He shook his head. 'Forced into exile by bitter men.' He ran a finger down her cheek, flaming her skin. 'It's desperate in exile, Edyth, far away from all you know and love. No wonder Malcolm wanted to fight for Scotland.'

Edyth blinked. This whole conversation was still twisting like an adder and she felt caught in its coils.

'No one concerns themselves with Duke William now,' she managed as Torr steered her into the dance once more. 'Whatever was said, it is past. No one thinks he is King Edward's heir.'

Torr smiled, a slow, lazy smile that tore at her guts.

'Duke William does. And tell me, who else is fit for the throne? Harald Hardrada, King of the Vikings, perhaps? There's certainly no one from the lauded English line of Cerdic. The king has no children, Edyth, no nephews even, just some distant cousin trapped in darkest Hungary. If Edward dies, England is wide open – *wide* open!'

Edyth jerked away, stepping off the dance floor and onto the piled rushes at the edges.

'You should not talk like that, my lord. It's not right. The king isn't going to die and even if he does we won't have a Norman duke in his place. No one would allow it.'

'Of course not.' He followed her so closely that she backed into the timber wall and felt her head clang against a shield edge. She put up a hand to ward away both the pain and her partner but Lord Torr was not so easily rebuffed. 'Hush now, sweetheart,' he said softly. 'Do you want your father to hear such talk on your lips?' He pressed a finger lightly against her mouth. 'You should not fret. Let's leave politics and think more of . . . pleasure.'

He dipped his finger so that the tip grazed Edyth's tongue and she felt the contact like a touch paper to a deep well of kindling somewhere uncomfortably low inside her. She fought to make sense of it but could not think with him standing so close over her. It was much darker against the wall than out on the floor and with the whirl of dancers separating them from the others of the court they were all but alone.

'Pleasure, I am told,' she managed, though her voice was annoyingly husky, 'is a transient thing.'

He leaned a hand against the wall above her, curving his hips towards hers.

'Mayhap you are right, Edyth. Better, I am sure, to find love – real love.'

'Like Earl Harold and the Lady Svana?'

'Like Harold and his little handfast woman, yes, but then my brother is the steadfast type. Loyalty comes naturally to him along with responsibility and duty and all those boring traits.'

Despite herself Edyth giggled.

'You cannot say such things – you're a lord.'

'For now.' Torr's eyes flicked briefly over his shoulder to the packed hall then shot straight back to her. 'But you are polit-icking again and it is a waste. What is life without pleasure, Edyth Alfgarsdottir?'

His amber eyes met hers and Edyth felt herself pulled towards him. Her head swam. She felt as giddy as if she were still dancing and as blind as if it were the depths of night but then a low growl caught her ears and with horror she recognised the rumble of her father's ever-ready temper nearby. Tearing herself away, Edyth stepped firmly sideways.

'I have taken too much of your time, my lord,' she said, curtseying. 'Your wife will, I am sure, be missing you and my father looks for me.'

For a moment Lord Torr looked angry and the heat in Edyth's belly turned to ice, but then he chuckled.

'You are a dutiful daughter, Lady Edyth, that is good. You will need to support your father tomorrow.'

'What do you mean?' she demanded. Alfgar was pushing between the dancers and was nearly upon them. 'What do you mean, my lord?'

But, with a low bow and wicked wink, Torr was gone, leaving Edyth alone as her father descended with the force of a Viking fury, seizing her arm and yanking her sideways.

'What on earth are you doing, young lady?'

'Dancing, Father,' she stuttered out, trying to extricate herself.

'Dancing? Parading yourself like a hoyden, more like – and with *him*.'

Alfgar's face was wine-red and his hand raked through his hair in a gesture she knew all too well; it meant the rise of his fiery temper.

'Lord Torr was very courteous,' she said nervously.

Alfgar spat into the rushes.

'I'll wager he was and I know why too.'

Edyth opened her mouth to protest but for once she caught herself.

'Why, Father?' she asked instead, widening her eyes.

'Why?' Alfgar looked startled, then flushed an all-new shade of red. His voice softened. 'Never you mind, just stay clear of him. Now, what did he say to you of Northumbria?'

'Northumbria?' she stammered. 'Not much.'

'Not much? What does that mean? He did say something. Tell me!'

Edyth felt tears prickle. Her beautiful amber-studded brooches were heavy on her shoulders and her eyes stung with the smoke from the fire and the tang of mead on her father's heavy breath. She scrabbled for answers but could find only snake scales – whispers of inheritance and exile.

'He just said I was to, to support you tomorrow.'

'Support me? What does that mean? What's he insinuating?'

'I don't know, Father, truly.'

And now the tears came. She brushed one furiously away but it was enough. Her father loosened his grip on her arm.

'Ah there now, Edie, do not cry. I'm sorry. You are young, a girl yet – which is all the more reason why that oaf Torr should not . . .'

'No, I – I'm not, Father.' He was looking around for her mother. He was going to send her to bed like a baby and she couldn't allow that. Forcing the tears down, she pushed her shoulders back and straightened her neck. 'I think we need to watch him, Father. I can help you with that.'

He shook his head indulgently but his eyes returned to her face; she had his attention.

'You do not know what you would get yourself into, child.'

It was true but no use saying so now.

'I could cope with it, Father. For you I could cope with anything.'

She smiled up at him and, with a soft chuckle, he swept her into his arms, suffocating her with the mingled scents of wool and mead and sweat.

'I could dance with *you*, Father?' she suggested sweetly.

'Oh no!' Alfgar backed away as she had known he would. 'No, your old man is too stiff for dancing these days, Edyth. Find yourself someone younger, but not – *not*, do you hear me – a Godwinson.'

'Yes, Father.'

She dropped a swift curtsey and escaped. The rest of the evening was hers; let the morrow worry about itself.

CHAPTER TWO

$\mathscr{E}$dyth reached up for the next branch, cursing her clumsy skirts for slowing her down. She'd be late for the council at this rate. She scrambled higher up the tree then paused to glance guiltily back through the branches to King Edward's Westminster compound, little more than a hundred paces away on Thorney Island. People were backed up at the wooden bridge over the bubbling Tyburn river, eager to enter in good time for the great meeting. Horses pawed beneath impatient masters, cart-drivers jostled with each other to be first in line, and the air sang with barely suppressed fury. The vast stretch of the Thames rolled carelessly past to the right of the road, safe in its own dangerous currents, but the Chelsea meadowlands on the left were teeming with muddy servants. No one, at least, was looking her way and she glanced back into the woods.

She'd been coming back from Chelsea market behind the rest of her family when she'd seen Lord Torr slipping into the bushes with a servant girl. Curiosity still sparking after last night's encounter on the dance floor, she'd been quick to follow. She'd lost the unlikely pair briefly but now there were noises coming from the other side of the bramble thicket – a rough mingling of breaths which she longed to understand – and she had pulled herself into a tree to follow them.

Edyth glanced guiltily again towards the royal compound where gaudy pavilion roofs peeped over the palisade fencing, the flags of all the great families of the land flapping proudly in the light breeze, taunting those not yet inside. Catching sight of her own father's black and gold banner, she shuddered. The council was still a turn of the glass away but he would already be pacing like a caged bear. She had to hurry. Reaching up for a lichen-encrusted branch, she heaved her slender body higher and suddenly there they were.

'Oh!'

She clasped a hand over her mouth to contain her surprise and nearly lost her balance. It was like nothing she'd imagined. The girl was on her knees, rough brown skirts rucked up so that her most intimate area was exposed whilst Torr, his own trews around his ankles, clasped her roughly back against him.

As Edyth watched, he reached one hand out to grab at the girl's hair, arching her back and making her cry out his name, and this time Edyth was too slow to catch her own gasp. Torr looked up. He saw her immediately and far from rushing to hide, locked Edyth in his gaze. For a long moment she was caught, then finally she yanked her eyes away and began to scramble down, half-climbing, half-tumbling through the dense branches of the oak.

Her hair tugged, her skirts caught, but she dared not stop. She had to get out of there. Nearly at the bottom, her foot slipped and she fell. She screamed as the ground rushed up to meet her but at the last minute two strong arms caught her and lowered her easily. Terrified that Lord Torr had come to claim her, she fought to free herself.

'Steady on now. You're quite safe.'

The voice was soft and gentle and Edyth dared to look.

'Oh, thank God.'

It was not the dark-eyed Torr but his brother, Earl Harold.

He was looking at her so kindly that she longed to collapse into his arms but just in time she remembered her father's displeasure and pulled away.

'Are you quite well, Lady Edyth?' Harold asked. 'You're as white as a sheet.'

'I . . . I fell.'

'So I saw and I'm not surprised. You were coming down that tree like a hound after quarry.'

'I'm late for the council,' Edyth said weakly. 'Mama will kill me.'

'She will when she sees your dress. What were you doing up there?'

Edyth tugged miserably at the rips in her woollen overgown, her thoughts racing.

'I thought I saw a falcon.'

'Really? Where?'

Harold was instantly alert, scanning the trees, and Edyth cursed under her breath.

'I was mistaken. It was just a . . . a robin.'

'You mistook a robin for a falcon? Come now, Lady Edyth, with a hawkhouse as fine as your father's I find that hard to believe. What were you really up to?'

Edyth glanced uneasily at the trees; someone was coming their way, she was sure of it.

'I have to get back,' she said desperately, and tried to turn up the road towards the royal compound.

At that moment, however, the bushes parted just ahead of them and Harold grabbed Edyth's shoulder as the serving girl emerged, still straightening her gown. The poor girl stared at the richly clothed pair, her eyes widening in horror, then she bobbed a hasty curtsey, turned, and ran.

'Some falcon, young lady,' Harold said darkly to Edyth. 'Come on, we'd better return you to your mother.'

'No, please . . .'

But Harold's hand tightened on her shoulder and Edyth was forced to trot alongside him as he strode back towards Westminster.

'Earl Harold,' she begged, 'please don't tell my mother. I heard noises. I was just . . . curious.'

'Curious? I'd say. And did you find out what you wanted to know?'

Edyth blushed as she pictured Lord Torr's naked buttocks and, more frightening still, the look in his wolf's eyes as he'd caught sight of her. The image tingled inside her with a nauseating mixture of excitement and revulsion.

'I . . .' she started. Harold's fingers were digging into her shoulder and one knee was aching where it must have hit a branch as she fell. Her stomach was churning and suddenly she just wanted to crawl into bed and hide. 'I . . .' she tried again but could manage no more.

Harold stopped, halting Edyth with him. She stared at the rough road, tracing the cart-tracks in a desperate attempt to fight back tears.

'I'm sorry,' she stuttered.

'You're shocked.' He held out a linen square and she snatched gratefully at it, scrubbing at her stupid, leaky eyes. 'Fret not. All will be well.'

His voice was kind and she was almost ready to believe him when, from behind, she heard a jaunty whistle and approaching footsteps. She tensed, her skin prickling.

'Oh no,' Harold said, more of a growl than speech. 'Not you? She didn't see *you*?'

Edyth kept her face hidden in the linen but even blinded she could sense Lord Torr's brooding presence as he sauntered past, so close he almost brushed against her. Her body pulsed and she bit hard on her lip, fighting the sensation.

'I'll talk to you later,' she heard Harold say.

'I'll look forward to it,' came the easy reply and then, thank the Lord, he was gone.

Silence fell, punctuated only by the thud of Edyth's own blood in her ears. Then she heard Harold sigh.

'I think,' he said, prising the linen from her fingers and offering his broad arm, 'that we had better go and see Svana.'

Edyth stared nervously at the soft canvas doorway, extravagantly trimmed with gold thread so that it seemed to shimmer in the low March sunshine. She'd cherished the Lady Svana's smiles and waves but, with her father standing a growling guard, had never dared speak to her since that far-off faerie wedding. She'd heard tell that she practised magic – ancient eastern magic. The ladies in the bower said that she'd inherited her East Anglian lands from a line of wizards and kept great secrets. They whispered that she was a hundred years old but kept her youth and beauty with potions and spells, and that she could only ever stay at court for a few short weeks before she shrivelled back to her real self. They claimed she had bewitched Harold into loving her and that she could make her womb quicken at will and – worst of all – that she would not share these amazing secrets with other women.

To Edyth's relief, her mother, Lady Meghan, said it was all nonsense but Earl Alfgar still muttered about 'pagan leanings' and, despite him having ruled East Anglia for the last three years, he had not let his family onto Svana's lands since the long-ago wedding that Edyth still held so fondly in her heart. Many times she had ridden to the edges of Svana's estate at Nazeing, peering across it for signs of enchantment, but she had never seen anything more than sheep and pigs and workers in the fields – though they did seem to whistle more merrily than most.

Her heart juddered and she glanced around the royal compound, buzzing with people. Those still queuing anxiously on the bridge had parted like churned butter as Earl Harold had approached and she had sailed through on his arm feeling like a true lady. Inside, however, all was a-scramble as servants hastily erected pavilions for late arrivals, their lordly masters fretting to get inside and change out of travel-stained clothes into their council finery. No one was paying any attention to them. No one would know if she went inside with Earl Harold or, indeed, if she came out.

Only last night, Brodie had told her that when returning from the great hall he'd seen this very pavilion shimmering with a strange light. Edyth had scoffed at him. He was useless at holding his ale and, besides, he was always making things up to scare her, but suddenly, now, all the stories seemed to pour into her mind and harden into a painful rock of fear.

'Perhaps,' she stuttered out, 'I would be better returning to my own pavilion?'

Harold tipped his head on one side and smiled lightly.

'If that's what you would rather. I shall take you there.'

'No! I mean, no thank you, my lord, I can manage by myself.'

He looked down at her, not cruelly but with a flint-like determination.

'You know I cannot allow that. We need to talk about what happened to you today and we can either do that over there with your parents,' he gestured across the compound to her father's stocky black, white and gold camp, 'or here, with my wife.'

Edyth looked again at his pavilion. Was the Lady Svana really inside? She still remembered their brief conversation at the wedding but that had been a special day, a free day; dared she speak to her here at court? On the other hand, dared she face her parents' ranting disappointment? And so close to her father's big moment.

'I thought so,' Harold said with a smile. He went up to the door flap, nodding to the serving boy on guard. 'Morning, Avery.'

'Good morning, my lord, my lady.'

His bondsman bowed low then whipped back the door flap and Harold ducked inside. Edyth hovered nervously. Would there be pagan images inside? Bones? Runes, maybe? She'd heard tell that you could curse yourself just by reading them if you did not know what you were doing. She didn't remember any such horrors at the wedding but, then again, she *could* have been enchanted. Harold's head poked out.

'Come on in, Edyth, and quickly before your father sees you.'

He winked and, stunned, Edyth forced her feet to carry her within. She hardly dared look but when she finally forced her eyes upwards, it was with amazement and relief. The red and gold pavilion walls were lined with the palest yellow gauze and hung with delicate tapestries of nothing more pagan than flowers and trees. The floor was strewn with furs that felt soft through the thin soles of her boots and the few furnishings were of simple, light wood.

An oil lamp hung from the centre pole, surrounded by a pale green glass that cast shimmering patterns around the linen room and the oil had clearly been scented with herbs for the air within smelled fresh and sweet after the more earthy odours of the compound. It was nothing like her own family's dark pavilion – all heavy tapestries and displays of shields and weaponry – and Edyth gazed around her in wonder until her eyes fell on her hostess and she suddenly felt giddy with nerves.

Lady Svana had risen from her chair and stood a head taller than Edyth. She wore a flowing robe of spring green, clasped at the waist with a simple band of amber beads, and her hair, the colour of ripe hazels, was as loose as a maid's. Edyth dropped into a deep curtsey but Lady Svana clasped her hand, drawing her up and forward in one easy motion. Edyth caught the scent of her – lavender and meadow grass and rosemary – and drew in a deep breath.

'Lady Edyth, is it not?' her hostess said, her voice soft but perfectly mortal. 'How lovely to meet you properly at last.'

Edyth attempted a smile but it wobbled slightly at the edges.

'But you look troubled, my dear,' Svana went on. 'Come, take a seat with me.'

She gestured Edyth towards a beautiful willow-basket chair padded with a soft sheepskin but Edyth, looking from the near-white wool to her tattered, bark-stained gown, shook her head.

'I'd better not, my lady.'

'Why don't you remove that dress then, if it's making you so uncomfortable?'

Edyth panicked. Is this where the pagan rituals started? Had she escaped the cooking pot just to be thrown into the fire?

'Behind here.' Lady Svana opened out a fretwork screen. 'You can wear my bedrobe for now and my maid can sew up these little rips whilst we talk.'

Edyth breathed again and glanced at her tattered skirt.

'Little rips?'

'Great big holes if you prefer, my dear, but either way the council opens soon and you'll be in less trouble with your parents if they're not there. Elaine has very neat stitching.'

An older lady with grey hair and kindly eyes came forward, nodding confidently. Edyth glanced at the mess of her skirts and pictured Meghan's fury if she turned up for the most important event of her father's political career this way.

'I wouldn't want to be a bother,' she said.

'No bother, lass,' Elaine said. 'I mended many such a tear in my lady's dresses when she was your age, and most of them without her dear mother's knowledge. Tree climbing, was it? Well now, no harm done, hey? If you'll just . . .'

She indicated the screen and, unwilling to protest further, Edyth slid behind it and removed her dress. It was one of her better ones, made from a rich green wool her mother had bought from a Flemish trader for a 'pretty penny', so she could imagine the fuss if Lady Meghan saw it like this. Meekly she passed it out to Elaine and in return was handed a light robe of soft lilac. It went on, as far as she could tell, not over the head as normal, but from behind, wrapping around her and tying with a silk cord. It was far too long and she had to bunch it up in her hands to step forward but it felt wonderful.

'This is so beautiful,' she said to Svana as she emerged, her shyness forgotten in the joy of the garment. 'What's it made of?'

'Ottoman silk. Harold brought me it from his last travels. He feels guilty when he's away a long time so he brings me beautiful gifts to make up for it.'

'And to be sure she'll have me back,' Harold added, clasping her round her slender waist and kissing her. 'Always I fear she will tire of me.'

'And never she does,' Svana retorted softly.

Their eyes met and they smiled at each other. '*Love prefers to be free*' sang the eternal words in Edyth's head but since the sights she'd seen this morning that idea didn't seem quite so simple. All her life her mother had talked of the great husband that, like a fine gift, would one day be hers but now she understood what that entailed – not just grand halls and beautiful gowns and fine horses but the guttural, exposed ritual of the marriage bed. She shifted uneasily and Svana sprang away from Harold and drew her firmly into the chair.

'You still look pale,' she said. 'Warm wine should help. Harold!'

Harold nodded and, to Edyth's amazement, strode to a side table, poured wine from a jug and ambled off with it, presumably to warm it over one of the compound braziers.

'But . . . but he's an earl,' Edyth protested.

'He's a man, Edyth. He needs to feel useful.'

Edyth processed this new information. Is that what men needed to feel? Is that what drove them to . . . ?

'Edyth? Sweetheart? What did you see from your tree?'

Svana was studying her face, not as her mother might for specks of dirt or telltale traces of guilt, but with genuine concern. Still, though, Edyth felt uneasy.

'Nothing.'

Svana raised one elegant eyebrow.

'You don't trust me.'

It was not an accusation but Edyth longed to merit the woman's kindness and the lure of answers was strong. She glanced around. Harold was still absent, Avery was outside the door, and Elaine had her grey head down over her needle. They were as alone as it was possible to be at court.

'There was a man,' she managed.

'Any particular man?'

'Lord Torr.' She flushed as she said it; even the name sounded wanton now.

'Oh. Oh, I see.'

'You do?'

'I take it he was not alone?' Edyth shook her head. 'With a girl perhaps? Were they naked, Edyth?'

She said it so simply that Edyth was surprised into answering directly.

'Sort of. He had no trews on and his tunic was hitched up and she . . . she . . .'

'Had her skirts around her waist?'

'Yes,' Edyth agreed though her throat felt dry and the word snagged. 'But she was . . . She was . . .' She closed her eyes and forced herself to say it, 'kneeling.'

She fumbled for more words but Svana rescued her.

'You wish to know, perhaps, if that is normal?' Edyth nodded mutely but Svana did not seem embarrassed at all. 'Normal is such a restrictive word, is it not? And the human body is such a wonderfully unrestrictive thing. A man and a woman can make love in any way they choose.'

'They can?'

'Of course, as long as they *do* choose – *both* of them. Never let a man force you to do anything you do not wish, Edyth.'

'Even if he is my husband?'

'*Especially* if he is your husband!'

Svana's tone was playful now and Edyth looked up to see that Harold had re-entered with her wine. She felt heat flood through her body and fumbled for the goblet he held out. For years now her mother had been impressing on her that a husband was to be obeyed in all things; she would be horrified if she heard such talk. Edyth glanced guiltily to the door but Harold's laugh drew her eyes back inside.

'Don't let her fill your head with nonsense,' he said lightly, catching Svana around the waist again as if his hands were drawn to her of their own accord. 'She's eastern – thinks it means she can do as she likes.'

He looked down at his wife and Edyth saw his eyes darken as Lord Torr's had done in the forest. She felt all her new knowledge and awareness collecting behind her eyes, heavy and itchy, and put her hands up to try and rub it away. Svana instantly leaned forward.

'You're tired, sweetheart?'

'No!'

'Confused?'

'A little.'

'That's as it should be. It takes time to become an adult.'

Edyth sipped at her wine.

'I think the girl was willing.'

'Then all is well,' Svana said firmly.

'Even if they're not married?'

'Better to be married.'

'Like you two?'

'Exactly.'

'But you're not properly married, are you?'

It was something her father had told her a hundred times but her words seemed to hit Svana like arrows.

'More "properly" than any priest can offer,' she snapped.

Edyth flinched, horrified, and Harold stepped hastily forward.

'A handfast marriage binds the hearts, Edyth. That, surely, is worth more than land-contracts and church threats?'

'Yes,' she stuttered, looking helplessly past him to Svana, whose supple body was rigid. 'Yes, yes, I see. I'm sorry. I'm so sorry. I didn't mean . . .'

But just as swiftly as Svana had tensed she recovered, visibly shaking herself free of whatever fury had held her in its clutches.

'Nay, Edyth, *I* am sorry. Handfast marriages are my people's custom and I forget that others do not see them as completely as we do. I just ask one thing of you: as you become a woman, try not to rely on others' judgements. Do you see?'

Edyth nodded, awkwardly aware that most of her judgements, if such they were, were more her father's than her own. Earl Alfgar had always been most free with his opinions and she had never thought to question them but if they could wound a lovely lady like Svana, maybe she should?

'Don't fret,' Svana said, seeing her face. 'There's time enough for that too. Ah, Elaine, thank you.'

Edyth turned gratefully to the mended gown and perused it disbelievingly – the rich fabric was nigh-on as good as new. She looked at Elaine's fingers and back to the gown.

'Are you magic?' she asked uncertainly.

'Nay, lass,' Elaine laughed. 'Just well practised.'

Svana placed a gentle hand on Edyth's arm.

'There is no magic, you know, Edyth, whatever they say – save, perhaps, the magic we make ourselves. Shall I help you on with the dress?'

'I can manage, thank you.'

Edyth scrambled behind the screen, senses whirling. She was reluctant to surrender Svana's luscious robe but out in the compound the creaking abbey bell was sounding to call people to the council and her mother would be furious at her absence. Her father too. Swiftly, she changed, folding Svana's slippery gown as carefully as she could.

'I must go.'

'Indeed. Thank you so much for coming by.'

Svana made it sound as if this had been nothing more than a polite social call and Edyth was grateful but Harold . . . ? She glanced at him. He wasn't the tallest of men but he held his shoulders strongly and seemed to have extra height in his commanding eyes. He was handsome, she supposed. His eyes were a striking midnight blue, his sand-blond hair richly curled, and his arms so broad and long they looked as if they'd wrap around you twice. What did he look like when he was . . . ? She shook the wanton thought away. She couldn't go around assessing every man like this just because of one glimpsed moment.

'Will you tell my mother?' she asked nervously.

Harold looked to Svana, and Edyth saw her shake her head. She held her breath.

'Not this time,' Harold confirmed, 'but, Edyth, take care. The tree might throw you harder to the ground next time.'

Remembering Torr's challenging stare, Edyth knew what he meant and shook her head against the rogue memories now firmly embedded in her mind. Taking her leave of Harold and Svana, she stepped cautiously outside and immediately caught sight of her father's black cloak down one of the rough walkways between the pavilions. Heart beating, she ducked out of sight, crossing round behind a series of smaller tents so that she came out behind him.

'Father.'

'Edyth, about time! Your mother's clucking like a bantam. Where in God's name have you been?'

Edyth stared up at him. She'd never lied to her father before; never had to. She'd been the victim of his ready temper many times but on the whole, whilst he was tough on her three brothers, he'd ever been indulgent to her. Now though . . . Fumbling in her pocket, still thankfully attached to her belt, she drew out the ribbons she'd bought at market and held them sheepishly up. For a moment he looked suspicious and then he grinned.

'Really, Edie my love, only you could spend so long over ribbons! Still . . .' He leaned in, an almost childish smile playing across his lips, 'we've all had to make an effort today.'

He patted his tunic, a new one in expensive dark blue which stretched paler across his belly, then nodded ruefully to the matching bindings around his trews.

'You look very handsome, Father,' Edyth provided.

'Thank you, Edie, and I'm sure your ribbons are lovely; it's important you look your best if you are to be the Earl of Northumbria's daughter.'

'Father . . . !'

'Tush, 'tis a formality, that's all. Before long everyone will

know. Come now, though, let me take you through to the moot-
point – your mother has been waiting on the benches for ages
and I must join the rest of the council.'

He straightened and, contorting his face into a look of
studied gravity, offered her his arm. Edyth took it cautiously,
worried he might sense the Earl of Wessex's previous escort,
but Alfgar seemed oblivious and, as the great and good of
England gathered for the spectacle of government, Edyth was
left to keep that uneasy association to herself.

CHAPTER THREE

'*E*dyth! At last. Have you no conception of politeness? Where in the name of all the saints have you been?'

'Sorry,' Edyth muttered. 'I lost track of time.'

Her mother, Lady Meghan, was sat on one of the front benches, frothed up in a new dress and three strands of amber beads and fuming with righteous anger. Edyth ducked around her and slipped in between her two younger brothers, cheeks burning at the smirks from those sat behind them.

'You've been naughty, Edie,' nine-year-old Morcar said gleefully.

'Very naughty,' Brodie agreed smugly from Meghan's other side. 'Some people just have no idea about decorum, do they, Mother?'

Edyth resisted the urge to stick her tongue out at her elder brother and instead looked around her at the gathering crowds. The council was to be held, as always, on the stretch of Thorney Island between the crumbling Westminster Abbey and the low shingle beach down to the great River Thames. Servants had been working since dawn to erect a wooden dais some twenty paces long and now Edyth looked up to the two huge thrones sitting upon it, carved backs to the river, and willed the king and queen to take their places and start the meeting before her mother could complain further.

'We've been here for ages,' little Morcar told her. 'My bum's sore from sitting.'

'Ssh, Marc.' Edwin, two years older than Morcar but at least five years more serious, frowned crossly at his brother. 'You can't say words like that in public.'

'Words like what? Bum?!'

Edwin raised a hand and Edyth quickly sat forward and dived in her pocket for the remains of the marchpane she'd bought at the market. She divided it between the boys and, for the moment at least, peace was restored. She gave a small sigh of relief and settled herself. She was in plenty of time, whatever her mother said. The eighteen councillors had not yet taken their places on the elegant seats below the dais and many of the lords and ladies were still filing onto the semi-circles of benches facing them. Mind you, with the earldom of Northumbria up for appointment, every last noble seemed to have made the journey to Westminster and Edyth realised her mother must have been here for some time to secure her prime position at the front. No wonder she was grouchy.

'Not you too!' she heard her mother mutter now and Edyth looked up, hiding a smile as her grandmother, the stately Lady Godiva of Mercia, slid graciously into a slim stretch of bench next to her.

'Thank you, my dear,' Godiva said to her, settling her beautiful golden-coloured skirts and tweaking the richly laced sleeves of her undertunic so that they made a discreet appearance at her still slim wrists.

'You're late,' Meghan hissed.

Godiva glanced lazily at her daughter-by-marriage.

'On the contrary; I am perfectly timed, my dear. I'm far too old to be waiting around for those lazy councillors to show their faces.'

Edyth giggled but at last the 'lazy' councillors – all the highest men of England – were emerging from the abbey precinct and making their way through the crowds and, in a panic, late-comers were crushing into seats all around.

'Must you push so?' Edyth's mother said now, turning indignantly to an ample woman trying to squeeze onto the end of their bench.

'Yes I must,' the woman fired back. 'I can't sit on the floor like a commoner, can I?'

She gestured superciliously to the mass of folk settled quite happily on the scrubland before the abbey's domestic buildings to their left. They had arrived, as they always did, with rugs and sacks and straw bales to sit on and with baskets full of food to feed the mass of children who played around them. The councils were a fine spectacle and no one within walking distance wanted to miss the chance to eye up the fine clothing and see the theatre of government in action.

Edyth sometimes thought it looked like far more fun in the rough-and-tumble crowd but it wasn't, so she was told, 'dignified' and clearly the pushy woman felt the same. As the king and queen emerged to huge cheers the latecomer again tried to plant her bottom on the woefully inadequate space beside a horrified Brodie, but Lady Meghan was having none of it.

'There's no room here,' she said icily. 'Perhaps, if a seat was so important to you, you should have arrived earlier?'

She fluffed up her skirts, planting her feet firmly beneath them, and the woman was forced to back away. Lady Godiva leaned forward.

'Quite right, Meghan, my dear. Who does she think she is, sailing in at this late hour?'

Edyth peered up at her grandmother who winked at her but Meghan just sniffed and said, 'Some people need to learn how to comport themselves. I need space. I'm wife of the Earl of East Anglia after all and very soon to be . . .'

'Mother! Nothing is decided yet.'

'Yes but . . .'

'Hush! Look, the king is speaking.'

Edyth gestured gratefully to the dais as an expectant silence fell across the mass of humanity crammed onto the island. Queen Aldyth seated herself on her throne, her slim figure straight and elegant and her head held high beneath an intricate crown, whilst King Edward stepped forward to address his people. As thin as his wife, but tall and straight-shouldered in a rich cloak of deepest purple and a jewel-encrusted crown, he was regal to the core. Edyth remembered Torr talking so casually last night of his lack of heirs and suddenly she noticed how white the king's hair was, how gnarled his hands as he raised them to the crowd, and how stooped his shoulders beneath his heavy garments. She shuddered, then swiftly reminded herself that the queen was young yet and very pretty. There was time, plenty of time. Torr had no business talking that way.

Despite herself, her eyes looked round for the arrogant lord and found him sat at Earl Harold's side, looking ominously smug. Or perhaps he was always like that? Edyth hadn't paid him much attention before but now he seemed hard to avoid. He sat rigidly straight in a tunic so stiff with gold it looked almost solid and he glimmered in the low sun like a peacock next to his more sombre falcon of a brother. His cloak was embroidered with his emblem – a sharpened spear – and he stroked it lightly, a small smile playing on his full lips. Was he remembering his serving girl, she wondered, and then felt a spike of disgust at her own thoughts and whipped her eyes away from Torr and back to the king.

'Councillors,' he was saying, 'honoured guests, lords, ladies and all my people – welcome.'

His hands swept wide and everyone craned forward. With

the spring rains in full flood, the River Tyburn was gurgling and frothing against its banks, making it hard to hear. The king raised his voice.

'We are here today,' he intoned, 'to mourn the passing of a great man. Earl Ward held the earldom of Northumbria for thirty-two years with great wisdom and strength.'

A ripple of affection ran around the crowd. Earl Ward had been a bear of a man, eloquent on the battlefield if rather less so in court society. A straight talker who had come to power when the Vikings continually threatened weak King Ethelred's shores, he'd had a clear and simple view of life and had lived to keep his people safe. He'd been a stalwart of the council and his huge shoes would be hard to fill.

Edyth found herself seeking out her father – the man who so hoped to do so. He was sitting to the king's left next to his own father, Earl Leofric of Mercia, and Edyth could see his knees twitching and his thick fingers clacking nervously through the rosary on his belt. Already his new tunic looked askew and one of the bindings on his trews had come loose and was flapping free in the breeze. Edyth glanced nervously at Meghan but her mother's face was set dead ahead and she had no choice but to listen once more to the king.

'Archbishop Eldred will lead a memorial service after this council,' she caught and felt Morcar tugging at her sleeve.

'Do we have to go to that too, Edie?'

She placed a quick hand over his mouth to muffle his piping voice.

'Yes, Marc.'

He rolled his tawny eyes.

'But it'll be so boring.'

'It's respectful.'

'Boring.'

It was like an echo of Torr's words last night and Edyth

shifted again but this was no time to think of such things. On her other side Edwin was fixed on the king and Brodie was twitching nearly as much as their father. Between them she could see Meghan's nails digging into her palms as if she might carve her husband's advancement from her own flesh.

'But first we have a solemn legal duty to fulfil,' King Edward said.

Edyth tensed. Lord Torr was quietly adjusting his cloak back from his feet as if, she could swear, he were preparing to rise. To their right Lady Judith, Torr's skinny wife, stiffened her back even more than usual and Edyth heard Lady Godiva, ever astute, sigh quietly. Suddenly she longed for the king to go back to extolling the previous earl's virtues. She closed her eyes.

'Northumbria is a vast and challenging earldom. Its ruler protects this realm and all its people from our enemies – the wild Scots in the north and Hardrada's ferocious Vikings to the east. It is a grave duty and I have dwelled long and hard on my choice.'

Edyth felt her own nails digging into her palms and was grateful when Morcar's little hand sank into hers, forcing her to stop. She opened her eyes and the moot-point swam for a moment before settling. Every man, woman and child in the arena and beyond was silent, focused. Only the rivers tumbled carelessly past and she fixed on a small log bobbing its way down the Tyburn towards the open Thames.

'I need a fearless, authoritative and determined man for the role and I believe I have found him. From henceforth the earldom of Northumbria will be held in trust to the crown by . . .'

The log hit the surge of the tide and was momentarily sucked beneath the surface.

'Lord Tostig Godwinson.'

Around Edyth the crowd erupted but she was fixed on the log. Where was it? Had it been dragged down by the vicious Thames undercurrents? Everything seemed suspended as she stared into the churning water but suddenly there it was, popping exuberantly up from a white-laced eddy and heading merrily downstream. Edyth almost raised a hand in farewell but as she moved to do so she felt Morcar's clammy grasp and sense rushed in.

'No,' Meghan was moaning. 'No, no, no.'

Brodie was clutching her tight, but his arm looked so slender around her shaking shoulders and was surely not enough to keep his sensitive mother safe from the gossip already buzzing all around them.

'Why is Mama crying?' Morcar asked Edyth.

'Because we aren't going to Northumberland.'

'The "vast and challenging" place?' Edwin queried, 'with all the enemies?'

Edyth nodded.

'You listened well, Edwin.'

'But why would we want to go there anyway?' Morcar again. 'It sounds horrid.'

Edwin tutted.

'It's an honour, Marc.'

'It still sounds horrid.'

'It is horrid,' Godiva said briskly, 'but your father wanted it anyway and he has never been one to take a slight lightly. He needs to stay calm now.'

Her sharp eyes were trained on her son, like a hawkmaster on his bird, and Edyth turned nervously to look at Earl Alfgar. He had half-risen from his bench and was raking his hands through his thick hair in a way that she recognised all too well.

Sit down, Father, she willed him, *please sit down*. But Alfgar was not in a temper to pick up even the most ardently sent thoughts. As Lord Torr flicked his cloak back to let his golden tunic shine, Alfgar rose too.

'Mama,' Edyth warned urgently, reaching over Edwin to shake Meghan's knee.

Meghan paled.

'Alfgar,' she murmured, 'Alfgar, no.' But her husband did not even look their way.

'Why?' he demanded loudly.

The crowd silenced in an instant. Someone tittered. Everyone strained forward.

'Why?' the king asked coldly. 'Do you question my judgement, my lord?'

'Is that not a councillor's role, Sire?'

The crowd sucked in its breath but Edward simply dipped his head.

'In the privacy of the chamber, yes.'

'But this matter was not debated in the privacy of the chamber.'

'Because, Earl Alfgar, the decision was between myself and God.'

'And God chose this . . . this trumped-up youngster to rule all Northumbria?'

'Leo,' Godiva muttered urgently under her breath and, as if hearing his wife across the arena, Earl Leofric rose to try and tug his son back. Alfgar, however, had stepped closer to his king and was not within his father's reach. Edward looked down at him.

'Do you believe, my lord, that you better understand God's wishes for my kingdom than I, his anointed representative?'

Alfgar faltered.

'No, Sire, of course not, but I just wonder if you've considered this fully. An earl owes a duty of care to his people and it takes time and wisdom to understand that. Lord Torr is young and untried whereas I have served you for many years and have proved myself a fine leader in East Anglia.'

'As I hope you will continue to do.'

Edward's voice was tight with warning. The crowd licked its lips.

'But . . .'

'Take your seat, Earl Alfgar. You are disrupting council business. Your birthright is in Mercia and you will serve the crown – and, as an only son, your family – best in central England. Lord Torr was fostered to Earl Ward for several years and knows the lands well. I am confident he will rule them wisely.'

He lifted a hand to where Torr was stood, feet planted wide and handsome head held high. Alfgar looked across. Behind him Earl Leofric reached out but, as if stung by his father's touch, Alfgar sprang away with a strangled roar.

'Time and again I am slighted.' He paced the dais, glaring at his fellow councillors. 'Time and again I am set aside for that family.'

He spat into the dust at Torr's feet and the crowd below him ooh-ed encouragement. Edyth felt Lady Godiva quiver beside her and a chill crept up through her feet. She clutched at the warmth of Morcar's hand and sneaked an arm around Edwin's back. They'd all seen their father like this. His temper was roused by the slightest matter and the best thing to do was to hunker down and wait for it to blow itself out. The king, however, did not know that and neither, Edyth was certain, would he care.

'I was only made Earl of East Anglia when that upstart . . .' Alfgar swung round to point wildly at Harold, 'was exiled and as soon as he came back – came back, note you, at sword point!' He drew his sword from its scabbard and the crowd gasped. 'I was ordered to give it back.'

'Perhaps rightly so, my lord, if you know not how to respect responsibility.'

It was Torr, his voice rigidly calm as he indicated the flailing sword. Only councillors were allowed to enter the moot-point armed and that was expressly for the purpose of defending the king's person. Placing himself deliberately before Edward, Torr reached out for Alfgar's weapon but Alfgar, incensed to new heights, sprang away, pointing it straight at his rival. To Edyth's left her mother was moaning again, a low, keening sound that tore at Edyth's heart. She wanted to leap up and call out to her father to stop but she knew it would do no good. He would not hear her through the roar of his own rage; he would not hear anyone.

'Earl Alfgar!' Edward's voice rang round the hushed crowd. 'Lay down your weapon immediately.'

He doesn't know, Edyth thought. The king did not know that her father was deaf to reason. How could he? And now he was moving forward and Alfgar was turning his sword tip instinctively away from Torr and towards . . .

Instantly the councillors were on their feet. Swords flashed from scabbards and in a heartbeat Alfgar was surrounded. He looked about, fury turning to bewilderment, and Edyth felt her heart bleed as surely as if her father had slashed it through himself. Someone – Earl Harold, Edyth thought – took her father's sword gently from his now limp hand and he stood, defenceless and hunched, before his king.

'Earl Alfgar, turning a sword on the king is treason.'

'Sire, I didn't mean . . .'

'Treason. There can be no mercy. You must consider yourself *nithing*.'

'Nithing. Nithing!' The crowd of common folk took up the word with vicious glee, delighted to have been party to such a dramatic spectacle. 'Nithing.' Nothing; below notice in law.

The king raised his hands and spoke above their hissed chorus:

'You and your family must leave this land until such time as you are deemed fit to hold office once more.'

'Sire?'

Alfgar looked as confused as an old man rattled from sleep and the king placed a hand on his shoulder.

'You must think, my lord. You must dwell on what it is to rule, to hold men's lives in your hands.'

'I will. I will, Sire.' Alfgar was gabbling now. 'I can do that, truly. I will retreat to my lands in East Anglia and . . .'

'Alfgar, you have no lands. You are nithing.'

Again the echo and now even the lords and ladies were on their feet and pressing forward to hear the final judgement.

'No!' Edyth clutched her brothers tighter as her father fell to his knees. 'No, please.'

'This gives me no pleasure, Alfgar, but I cannot let such behaviour pass. You are exiled.'

The word fell like a hammer blow on Edyth's head and she rocked beneath it. Exiled? What had Torr said last night? *It's desperate in exile, far away from all you know and love.* Had he known what would happen here? Had he looked for it?

Her eyes found him, stood slightly aside and to her horror she saw that he was looking straight at her. She felt his hand on her waist as surely as if he had stretched out across the crowd to draw her in and let everyone know she had been party to this humiliation.

'We must go.' She tore herself away and reached for her older brother. 'We must go, Brodie – now!'

'Quite right, my dear,' Lady Godiva said calmly, then she leaned close and added, 'Stay safe, Edyth – and stay strong. I know you, at least, can do that.'

Edyth looked at her grandmother in surprise but nodded

gratefully and then turned as Brodie also drew himself up tall. Clutching their mother to him, he began to fight his way out of the arena but the large woman Meghan had earlier denied seating space stood in his way.

'Decided to let someone else have your place?' she taunted. 'How kind.' Around them people cackled and, encouraged, the woman added: 'Some people need to learn how to comport themselves.'

More laughter.

'Keep going, Brodie,' Edyth urged but it was as if everyone was pressing in on them, prodding them, testing them like apple-pickers seeking rot. All her innards crawled beneath their touch but she pushed her head up and fought on.

'I would not be so quick to judge,' she challenged. 'Fortune turns fast.'

'Too fast, indeed, for mortals,' a deep voice agreed. 'Let them through please, let them through. Show mercy in God's eyes.'

The crowds parted as if Moses himself had spoken and Edyth saw Harold Godwinson step forward as she shepherded her family through the welcome gap.

'God bless you, my lord,' she said when they reached him.

'And you, Lady Edyth. We will escort you.'

He turned a little and the Lady Svana stepped up at his side. She was dressed in a soft grey gown that swirled like mist as she walked but she was as solid as rock at Edyth's side as they made for the compound gates.

'Where will we go?' Edyth asked her.

'I know not, but your father will keep you safe.'

'As he has done this morning?' Edyth caught herself. 'He will. I know it. I'm just . . .' She dropped her voice. 'Fearful.'

'Of course you are. I was so fearful when Harold was exiled that I was sick for weeks.'

'Truly?'

'Truly, but it was well in the end.'

They reached the bridge leading off the island and Harold stopped.

'You must see your brother invested,' Edyth said carefully to him.

He bowed.

'It brings me little pleasure.'

Edyth started but already Harold was stepping back, his eyes wary, and she grabbed at Svana's arm.

'How long?' she asked urgently. 'How long did it take for him to return?'

Svana swallowed.

'A year.'

'A year? A whole year? What will I do for that long?'

Svana leaned forward and whispered a kiss across her forehead.

'Write to me.'

'You wouldn't want . . .'

'Write to me, Edyth, really. Now, look there.'

Edyth turned to where she pointed and saw her father between two guards, his knees dipped and his head low.

'Papa!'

All else forgotten, she ran to him, bundling the sheepish guards aside. 'You will need to support your father,' Lord Torr – Earl Torr now – had said to her last night and the words swirled tauntingly in her head. How dare he? How dare he ever assume, for even a moment, that she would not?

'I'm so sorry,' Alfgar said, pulling them all into his shaking arms. 'I'm so, so sorry.'

'No matter,' Edyth told him. 'We will make things well, Father. We will make things well together. Now come.'

Lady Godiva had said she could be strong and she would

prove it. Setting her chin, she took Alfgar's arm and led her family away from Westminster, away from the crowds, and away from the court.

CHAPTER FOUR

North Wales, May 1055

'Here we will rebuild our power, Edyth.' Alfgar let go of his reins to throw his hands wide. 'Here we will be safe.'

'Safe,' Edyth echoed obediently, though in truth it was not the word that sprang to mind.

They had been riding for days and she was tired and saddle-sore. Morcar had complained most of the way, tugging on his hazel curls and blinking up at the maids, becoming increasingly cross when, for once, his sparkling eyes did not get him his own way. Edwin in contrast had become more and more silent, retreating behind his blond hair and barely even eating enough to sustain his skinny frame. This morning he had not spoken a single word, but then none of them had found much to talk about until now.

'Safe,' she said again, testing the validity of the word; it still didn't ring true.

She scanned the vast landscape before them. They were on the ridge of a considerable hill and could look out across rolling grasslands, dotted with endless sheep, and on down to the distant sea. And what a sea! Brought up in her grandfather's central province of Mercia, Edyth was used to tumbling streams and stretching lakes but not this vast expanse of ocean. Even after her father had been made Earl of East Anglia they had kept to the inland areas around Thetford and Nazeing and avoided the exposed eastern coast. She knew the tidal Thames of course, and she'd sometimes ridden out to Southampton from court gatherings at Winchester, but the sea there was narrow and tame compared to this rugged Welsh water.

It was spring. That much was clear in the green of the grass and the buttery yellow of the daffodils trumpeting joy from every verge. Yet the young rays of the sun did not seem able to penetrate the determined chill of the sea breeze or to draw any colour into the choppy waves. To Edyth, shivering in her saddle, this sea looked like a hunk of raw iron enclosing the helpless land like a vice. A flotilla of long, dark boats was at anchor just offshore but other than that the water was a relentless stretch of nothing. Her father was staring eagerly at her, as if he had provided some sort of banquet, but it was hard to respond.

'It does not look all that safe to me, Father,' she finally admitted.

'Pah!' He tossed his head and she felt the stab of his disappointment. 'This is Rhuddlan, girl, palace of the Red Devil himself, King Griffin of Wales. Believe me it is very safe – as long as you are on his side!'

He laughed heartily at his own jest and Edyth glanced across to Brodie. Her gangly older brother was grinding his teeth as he always did when he was afraid and that made her bolder.

'And *are* we on his side, Father?'

'Of course, of course. What d'you think I am, a simpleton? I have tracked King Griffin's rise to power these last ten years. I first took notice when we were residing in Mercia but even from East Anglia' – his chin went up at the thought of his lost earldom – 'I have had friends stay close to him.'

'Spies, Father?'

'*Friends*, Edie. A man needs alliances if he is to stay afloat at court. I have worked to make them and now that work is coming to fruition. Griffin is but newly returned from a great victory in south Wales and will be looking for ways to further his political stability. *I* am one of those ways.'

'You are a loving and careful husband and father, Alfgar, my dear,' Meghan said.

Edyth looked to Brodie once more and this time he caught her eye and she saw her own raw disbelief reflected in his. There had been nothing careful about Alfgar's outburst at the council, not that either of them would dare say so.

'I try.' Alfgar smiled. 'King Griffin is ruler of all Wales – the first man ever to achieve domination over all four territories and at barely past his fortieth year. He has done it, Edie, by political intelligence, battlefield daring and, I am told, unending energy and charisma.'

'By which,' Brodie said in a low voice to Edyth, 'we can understand that the Red Devil is cunning, ruthless and merciless.'

'And our host,' Edyth added nervously.

'If he so chooses,' Brodie threw back.

Edyth shivered and looked out across the rugged landscape once more. Down below them, at the heart of the valley, stood what she took to be the Welsh king's palace. It was much like a classic English compound, enclosed by a sharp-tipped palisade fence and boasting the normal run of thatched wooden buildings – a great hall, dormitories, animal sheds, kitchens and latrines – but unlike most English palaces it stood alone in the bleak landscape. There was no town below it, no smaller village compounds nearby, and no sense of any human life beyond the king's fence.

'Are we entering, Father?'

'Of course, Edyth, of course.'

Alfgar beamed at her just a little too widely and Edyth realised with a sickening jolt that he was nervous too.

'Is the king expecting us?'

'Oh yes. I sent letters ahead. Obviously there's been no chance to secure a reply, with us being on the move and with him newly back from battle, but I am confident we will be welcome.'

Still, though, he hesitated. Down below, Edyth's sharp eyes noted the great gates of Rhuddlan opening. Two men on horseback emerged, fully armoured and with swords aloft.

'Er, Father . . .'

'Not so impatient, child. I'll just check in the baggage train for a suitable gift to present to Griffin when we arrive.'

'Father, look!'

Brodie, too, had seen the men and tugged on his father's arm. Alfgar paled. He glanced around at his family and for a moment Edyth thought he was going to order them to flee towards the dark, jagged mountains on the eastern horizon, but then he squared his shoulders.

'You stay here. I will go and greet these men.'

He dug his spurs into his horse but clearly with insufficient conviction to persuade the beast to move. Cursing, he dug again and now the animal jolted forward and he had to clutch at the reins to stay seated. Meghan sank down over her own horse's neck.

'He's going to be killed,' she moaned, 'and before us all.'

At this, Morcar started to cry and Edyth swiftly checked her horse round to her littlest brother's side.

'Nonsense, Mama,' she said brusquely. 'He will not kill visitors who come in peace. He is a king.'

'A Welsh king,' Meghan said darkly and Morcar whimpered again.

'Mama,' Edyth admonished. 'We must be strong, as my revered grandmother said.'

'Yes, well, your revered grandmother is not stuck in the wilds of Wales, hoping for hospitality from some devil of a king.'

'Mama!' Morcar was crying louder now and Edwin was as white as the sheep surrounding them. Edyth reached out hands to both of her younger brothers. 'All will be well, boys. Truly.'

Morcar nodded obediently but Edwin just glared at her as, down the valley, Alfgar reached the armed men. The exchange was brief but swords were lowered and then heads bowed and suddenly Alfgar was turning to hulloo heartily up the valley and wave them forward.

'See,' Edyth said to Edwin, 'I told you all would be well.'

Still Edwin stayed silent, his pale eyes stormy beneath his wind-teased hair, and there was nothing left but to spur their horses down to the apparent safety of the Palace of Rhuddlan.

'Is that the king?' Morcar whispered, tugging on Edyth's skirt.

She reached surreptitiously down to try and stop him. She'd changed out of her muddy travelling gown into the rich green one she had worn to the council and she did not want Elaine's so far unnoticed stitching to be pulled loose.

'Of course it is, stupid,' Edwin answered for her, his voice released by warmth and food. 'He's wearing a crown.'

'But he's so . . . so . . .'

Morcar struggled for an apt word and as Edyth looked across the packed hall, she could see why. King Griffin was stood at the huge central hearth with her parents, some ten paces from where she and the boys waited nervously to be introduced. Although level with his subjects he seemed to stand high above them, his lean bulk at once magnificent and terrifying. Almost as tall and broad as the legendary Earl Ward, his size was made all the more striking by a mane of dark hair run through with a rich copper and topped by a plain gold diadem that marked out both his majesty and his warrior status.

Despite the chill, he wore a short-sleeved tunic in a heavy red fabric and great coils of gold snaked up both his arms, twining in the thick and equally coppery hair that dusted them like rust. His legs were also bare save for a pair of beautifully worked leather boots which came all the way up to his knees. The leather was cut with intricate Celtic knots, picked out in blue. To his belt was strapped a matching scabbard holding a sword whose solid, un-jewelled hilt sat like an obedient hound within quick reach of his big hand.

He looked, indeed, like the red devil he was known as, and yet his face was handsome and his eyes – the pale blue of aquamarines – shone with understanding, even intelligence. As Alfgar beckoned Edyth forward and the crowds split curiously to let them through, those eyes turned her way and she felt as if he was absorbing every single thing about her, as if she were naked before him. Unbidden, a thrill chased through her body like an arrow flying to the very heart of her physical being. The king smiled as if he had seen it – indeed, as if he had sent it – and as she drew close she found herself smiling back.

Her father was trying to speak but Griffin stepped forward, cutting him off.

'This must be the Lady Edyth.'

Alfgar swiftly gathered himself.

'This is my daughter, Sire, yes.'

Edyth dropped into a deep curtsey and heard Griffin laugh, a rich, musical sound.

'She has been brought up well. Such pretty English manners.'

He put out a big hand and Edyth gratefully reached for it to be raised from her supplication but he was too quick for her and instead clasped her chin. His fingers were warm and surprisingly delicate, though his touch, as he lifted her face, was insistent. Edyth's lips felt suddenly dry and she put out her tongue to lick them. Griffin's eyes flickered.

'I am honoured to be here in your beautiful palace, Sire,' she managed, painfully aware of the Welsh courtiers – a rough-edged gang of soldiers and their pretty, dark-haired wives – crowding round.

'You are,' he agreed with a slow smile, 'and I shall be very pleased to have you.'

He placed strange emphasis on the word 'have' and Edyth, still caught in a curtsey before him, felt it judder in her blood. Behind her, her mother shifted and prodded at her but what could she do? The king was looking straight at her, his fingers still beneath her chin and his eyes drilling into her own.

'I hope we will not trouble you, Sire,' she stuttered out.

'Trouble me?' Finally, thank goodness, he raised her to her feet. 'I think maybe, Edyth Alfgarsdottir, you will trouble me greatly.'

Now her father was laughing too, a rough, awkward sound, more like a donkey than a man. Edyth was horrified.

'Sire, I do not mean to . . .'

'Hush, Lady Edyth. Do not fret. I like trouble, do I not, men?'

He let go of her at last and turned to his courtiers who laughed too and called back. They spoke in their own language, though even with the lyrical inflection there was little doubting the bawdy tone. Edyth forced herself to look modestly down but inside her blood was throbbing. The boys were introduced, even Morcar bowing low and earning himself a hearty pat on his little back, and then Griffin suddenly turned.

'Lady Edyth, Lady Meghan, meet the Lady Gwyneth.'

The king reached back and, as if playing some sorcerer's trick, produced a woman from the crowd behind him. She jerked forward, staggering a little, and glared at the king as she righted

herself and faced the newcomers. Looking at the lines around
her eyes and across the hand she lifted reluctantly towards them,
Edyth hazarded she must be about her own mother's age, but
life had clearly not been as kind to her. Where Meghan's pretti-
ness was fleshed out with good eating and fine lotions, Lady
Gwyneth was slender to the point of skinniness and her face,
although striking, was gaunt and strained. Edyth could not help
herself looking back at the king glowing with health and vitality
and wondering why he kept this woman so poorly.

'You think I do not feed her,' Griffin said.

Edyth jumped. Had she spoken aloud?

'Of course not, Sire.'

'I am forever telling her to eat but she defies me!'

Lady Gwyneth rounded on him, hands flying to her thin
hips.

'I am not yours to command.'

'So you persist in believing.' The king grinned at Edyth.
'Lady Gwyneth cherishes her anger.'

'Lady Gwyneth,' the lady spat out, 'has much to be angry
about.'

Edyth looked from one to the other, amazed at such a raucous
exchange. There were arguments aplenty at the English court
but always behind walls. Thin walls perhaps – certainly not
thick enough to keep determined gossips away – but walls all
the same. She looked around at Griffin's court openly enjoying
the lively exchange and felt dangerous laughter begin to build
inside her as the royal couple squared up to each other.

'Perhaps, my lady, you would rather I had married you?'

Edyth saw her mother's eyes widen and had to fight to
smother her own surprise. Gwyneth, however, thrust out her
bony hips and glared at the king from near-black eyes.

'Perhaps, my lord, I would not have married you in a million
years.'

'Strange – you came eagerly enough to my bed.'

Several of the men cheered and Meghan put her hand to her head as if she might faint. Edyth saw Alfgar slip an arm around his wife's waist, but his own eyes were alight with amusement and she found time to wonder if here, in a country clearly unbound by tedious conventions, her father had found a place where he could thrive.

'I had little choice!' Gwyneth shrieked.

At this, though, Griffin held up a large hand.

'That is not true, my lady. I have never forced a woman into my bed.'

'Never needed to,' someone called from the crowd and Griffin smirked and waved, as if acknowledging a great compliment.

'Perhaps because I am King of all Wales!'

At this, cheers rang out all around the great hall, the men roaring approval of their leader's newly acquired status. Edyth looked around in wonder. Brodie had escaped their exposed central group and sidled over towards a gang of lads and Edyth saw him beam as one of them clapped him hard but apparently welcomingly on the back. Meghan, meanwhile, had also taken the chance to detach herself from her husband and usher the two wide-eyed younger boys towards the big doors where their nursery maid was cowering fearfully. The maid grabbed the boys and hustled them gratefully away and Edyth saw her mother take a few steps to follow before forcing herself back inside.

She returned her eyes to Griffin. He stood tall and proud, absorbing the adulation of his people as his right and Edyth had to admit that, gracious as King Edward always appeared, this was a man who truly looked like a monarch. As she watched, he caught her eye and smiled.

'You will think us very wild, Lady Edyth.'

'Nay, Sire, you have won a great victory and should celebrate.'

'You are right. How should we do that?'

The room was quietening now and Edyth was horribly aware of many eyes turning her way again.

'With feasting?' she suggested awkwardly. 'And, and dancing?'

'Dancing – yes!' Griffin bowed low. 'And you, Edyth Alfgarsdottir, our most welcome guest, will do me the honour.'

Edyth glanced to her father who nodded her forward.

'The honour would be all mine, Sire.'

Edyth took Griffin's proffered hand and more cheers rang out as the king waved his courtiers back to clear a dance space around the hearth. Joy sang through her. The king, the sparkling, rough-cut ruby of a king, liked her. Perhaps exile would not be such a bad thing after all?

A turn of the hour-glass later, as Edyth was slammed into the wall of the ladies' latrine, she wasn't so certain of herself.

'What do you think you're doing, young lady?'

Meghan had one hand on her curvaceous hip and one pinning Edyth to the cold wooden wall and was clearly boiling with rage.

'Mama, what's wrong?'

'You know exactly what's wrong. You're not old enough for these sorts of games.'

'What sorts of games?'

'Making eyes at King Griffin. He's forty-two – more than twice your age – and one hundred times more experienced.'

'How d'you mean?'

Edyth widened her eyes but Meghan was not as easily fooled as her husband by her daughter's innocence.

'You know what I mean. I've been making enquiries and they say the king will never marry. He has no need to; he ruts any girl that catches his eye.'

'Mama!'

'Don't you "Mama" me, Edyth. You need to know. Can you imagine King Edward behaving this way? Or what he would say if he saw us caught up in such wantonness? Now, you listen to me, you've had your flux for a year now and the last thing this family needs if it's going to claw its way back into decent English society is a Welsh bastard in your belly.'

'Sssh, Mama!'

Edyth looked around, horrified. They were the only ones in the latrine but the walls were thin and anyone walking beyond would be able to hear.

'Don't you sssh me.' Meghan was even more riled now, though she did drop her voice to a strained hiss. 'Do you think I chose to come here? Do you think I like living at the mercy of some strange king who believes he's God just because he's conquered a handful of rebellious Celts?'

Edyth bit her lip. There was a manic look in Meghan's shadowed eyes and her normally immaculate hair was creeping out of her headdress in wild wisps. Edyth hadn't realised how tightly her mother must have been holding herself together on the long ride west, nor how close she was to losing control now.

'All will be well,' she soothed. 'Don't fret, Mama. I was just trying to be nice to the king so he does not send us away. You don't want to be sent away, do you? Not now. Not with us all so tired.'

She put out a tentative hand to touch Meghan's arm and felt her mother stagger, then Meghan's arms flew round her.

'You are right, Edyth. Of course you are right. You're a clever girl, far cleverer than me, I know that. Your father knows it too.'

'Nonsense, Mama.'

'Nay, Edie, if we are to speak the truth let's do it properly.

You are a clever girl and you will be a clever woman but not if you let yourself be bedded now, even by a king.'

'I will be careful,' Edyth promised. 'I will be very careful, Mama.'

CHAPTER FIVE

Nazeing, June 1055

Lady Svana,

You very graciously granted that I might write to you from my exile so I am taking the liberty of doing so. I know you must be very busy tending your farmlands and minding your children and being wife to Earl Harold, so I will not trespass long on your time.

I am well. We have been welcomed by King Griffin of Wales who is a kind host and a fascinating man. He is the first ever King of all Wales and from what I have seen of his warlike guard that must have been a hard title to win.

He has a consort here, a Lady Gwyneth, but she is not his wife. She is a crabby thing so I cannot think why he bothers but he pays her little attention, preferring to dance, would you believe it, with me. Their dances are very wild and very fast – even Lord Garth would struggle to keep up – but the king knows them all and is big and strong enough to guide even a stupid novice around the floor. I am learning fast.

It is very beautiful here. I ride out to the sea most days and you can travel the coast for miles. King Griffin says there are many hidden coves he will show me when the weather is warmer. I look forward to that time for it is still chill here,

*though Easter is long past. It is as if the wind is iced by the
grey sea and not fully warmed until it reaches all the way to
you in the east.*

    *I send my love with this letter on the tail of that wind and
hope that it, at least, is still warm when it finds you.*

    With duty and affection,

    Edyth Alfgarsdottir

Svana looked up from the letter and frowned. It was a sweet
missive but something about it disturbed her. Tucking it into
the pocket attached to her belt, she let herself out of her bower
and into the central farmyard. Outside, she put up a hand as
if to catch the love Edyth claimed to have sent on the breeze
and clasped it to her breast. She liked the girl. She had fire
and curiosity. She was open to the world and that, Svana hoped,
would gain her great riches in her life. But it also made her
very vulnerable.

    She strode forward, clucking absently to the chickens that
massed around her, and out into the grasslands beyond. Her
eyes scanned the flat pastures for Harold. He had escaped
court duties for three precious weeks to be with her and the
children and she sent up a prayer of thanks that he was here
to consult on Edyth's letter. Having inherited her lands many
years ago, Svana had long been used to commanding her farm
and her people, but this was different. Something about the
young lady of Mercia had touched her heart. The girl's bright,
fierce approach to life reminded her keenly of her younger self,
though at fourteen she had been safely sequestered on her
family farm, not adrift in a foreign court. Svana was worried
for Edyth, worried for them all. For this wasn't just Edyth's
innocence at stake, but a potentially volatile political situation
and for that she needed her husband.

    'Everything in order, milady?'

She turned to see Joseph, the farm's hugely capable steward and her maid Elaine's husband of many years. They had both been invaluable to her as she'd learned to run this farm and now he stood, cap deferentially doffed but eyes bright with enquiry. She encouraged her servants to deal openly with her, despising the long chains of spurious respect with which so many lords seemed to tangle up their affairs, and she met his eye directly.

'Everything is well. I was just looking for Harold.'

'The earl rode out with his falcon some time back, milady, and I believe he took young Godwin with him. Said it was time he started his training.'

Svana smiled. Harold had mentioned something of the sort to their eldest last night and she was pleased to see he'd stuck to his word. Godwin would be beside himself with delight; she just hoped he managed to stay calm. Harold was a patient man, but a man all the same, and if his son did not show due deference to the birds that were his passion, there would be trouble.

'I might ride out and join them,' she said. 'Which way did they travel?'

'Over to Old Hooky.' Joseph pointed to the little copse just visible on the horizon. 'Apparently the birds like it there.'

Svana stifled a smile at his tone. Her steward loved all God's creatures but there was no doubt that he preferred them with their feet – preferably four of them – firmly on the ground.

'Thank you, Joseph.'

'I'll fetch Spirit for you.'

He rushed off to the stables for her horse and Svana watched him go with a fond smile. She could never live at court where all was jostling for petty power and privileges. Harold would like her with him in the king's entourage more often, but it crushed her soul to travel endlessly, living forever in pavilions, and eating every night in a great hall with suspicious lords and ladies. Harold did not like it much more than she, but he had been brought up to it by the great politician Earl Godwin, their own son's namesake, so he was more at ease at court. And he could always come here to recover.

In her turn, she would like Harold here more often but they had learned to compromise. Most people thought their marriage strange, nay, thought *her* strange for not following her high-born husband everywhere he went. The women in particular resented her for inheriting her father's lands, a privilege only granted in the freethinking Eastern Danelaw. Elsewhere women could hold dower lands, gifted to them within their lifetime, but they were rarely on single estates. Svana sometimes thought the court ladies saw her farmlands as a personal slight and did not seem to understand how keenly she felt the precious duties of an estate that had been in her family for nigh on a century. They often griped about her lack of commitment to Harold and some had even tried to lure him away from her; she knew because he laughed about it with her.

'I am yours,' he would whisper, when the lights were blown out and their bodies were entwined beneath the sheets. 'I am yours forever, not because a priest tells me so but because my heart does.'

'*Dear Harold,*' she thought. She knew he, too, found her 'eastern ways' strange at times. The Danelaw had been separated out from his Wessex heartlands by a noble treaty between the great King Alfred and the invading Vikings nearly two hundred years ago and had kept its own laws ever since. Svana treasured the independence they gave her as a woman and also as a free spirit beneath God's skies. She was as good a Christian as any in England but Roman bonds choked her and she preferred a more natural worship. Harold, a staunch tradition-alist, did not truly understand her opposition to priests and she was, therefore, even more touched that he had been happy to marry her beneath the skies.

Now she sent up a murmured prayer towards the soft clouds above as Joseph brought up her dappled grey, Spirit, and handed her into the saddle. Smiling her thanks, she kicked the horse into a canter and headed up the hill towards the copse, giving Spirit her head and enjoying the feel of the wind through her hair. At the top her heart leaped as she caught a glimpse of Harold's new orange tunic amongst the foliage.

'Harold!' she called but he did not hear her and suddenly she was glad of it, for it offered her the chance to watch him unseen.

He was bending solicitously over seven-year-old Godwin who stood, solemnly rigid, his arms outstretched and every fibre of his being tuned into his father. Harold brought his prized falcon, Artemis, down towards him and Svana found herself holding her breath as his broad arm met his son's. For a moment everything seemed to still and then, with studied nonchalance, the bird hopped across from man to boy. Instantly Harold moved his other hand to steady Godwin but the child did not falter and even from a distance Svana saw Harold's shoulders roll back and sensed his smile.

She clicked Spirit forward and Godwin, his hearing sharper than his father's, turned and saw her. His hand flickered as if to wave, but he resisted and Svana felt tears well ridiculously in her eyes at the sight of her baby so grown up.

'See, my lady,' Harold called, 'how fine a falconer our son is.'

'I see,' Svana agreed, slipping off Spirit and throwing the reins over a branch. 'I had not realised he was such a man already.'

Godwin held his arm even stiffer, though his face was turning pink with the effort. Harold bent again to take Artemis back and, released, the young boy ran to Svana.

'I did it, Mama. I did it all by myself.'

'You did, Winnie, you did.'

He pulled back.

'Nay, Mama, you should not call me that now. It is a baby name.'

'But you *are* my baby.'

'No.' Godwin shook his head firmly then considered. 'Well, maybe sometimes.'

'Bedtimes?' Svana suggested.

'Bedtimes,' he agreed, kissing her before remembering himself again and struggling to be put down. 'But it isn't bedtime yet and I am busy with Papa.'

Svana let him go.

'I'm afraid I need to speak to Papa, Godwin, just for a moment.'

Harold stepped swiftly forward.

'Maybe you could fetch Artemis' hood and jesses, son? That would be very helpful.'

'Yes, Papa.'

Godwin raced over to Avery to fetch the falconer's kit and Harold caught Svana around the waist and kissed her.

'All well?'

She looked up into his eyes, a soft, dark blue, ringed with a delicious amber you could see only if you were close – very close.

'Very well,' she said, kissing him. 'It's so lovely having you here, but Harold, I've had a letter.'

'Not from the king?'

'No. No, you are safe yet. From Edyth.'

'Edyth Alfgarsdottir? That's good. How is she? *Where* is she?'

'At Rhuddlan with King Griffin.'

'Ye gods!' Harold rolled his eyes. 'I don't suppose we should be surprised. Alfgar's had his eye on the Red Devil for years. I suppose this means we must shore up defences in the west.'

Svana batted at his arm.

'Stop your politicking for one moment, will you, and think of Edyth.'

'Why? Is she in trouble?'

'I'm not sure. She writes that the king dances with her.'

'I'll wager he does. Word is that man . . . Oh. Oh, I see.'

'She's fourteen, Harold.'

'Plenty old enough to be wed, my love.'

'In the eyes of the law, maybe, but in truth she is yet a child.'

'And a curious one at that, but her mother is there, Svana.'

'I suppose that should count for something.'

'You doubt the Lady Meghan's influence over her daughter?'

'No.'

Harold laughed.

'We're not at court now, sweeting. This is me, remember?'

Svana reached up and kissed him.

'It is you,' she agreed softly, 'and I am glad of it, but I would say nothing bad of Lady Meghan. She is just, perhaps, a little weak.'

'A fair assessment,' Harold agreed, 'but a protective mother all the same and Lord Alfgar will not want his daughter deflowered. If nothing else it would greatly lessen her value at court.'

'Harold!'

'Well, it would. Come now, my love, what would you have me do?'

Svana shook herself.

'I know not. Just, well . . . the sooner Alfgar is pardoned and back in East Anglia the better for his daughter.'

'If not for England.'

'Alfgar does well enough as an earl.'

'Praise indeed.'

'Please, Harold – for the girl.'

'Very well. I'll talk to the king and I'll send forces to Hereford. Griffin will look to attack, I'm sure, and once he does we can meet them and peace can be arranged.'

'Could we not just arrange peace now?'

Harold laughed.

'It does not work that way, Svana.'

'Why not?'

'Why not? I don't know. There needs to be a show of force, I suppose, so both sides can be judged.'

'My fighting man,' Svana breathed softly, an allusion to the emblem he bore so proudly on his cloak and shield.

Her own was a laden vine and she much preferred its delicacy to Harold's tough, dark figure but she believed everyone had the right to be their own person and she had to remember that now.

'*Your* fighting man,' Harold agreed, just as softly, pulling her close, but at that moment the clink of jesses heralded Godwin's eager return. Svana bowed graciously away.

'I shall leave you to it and ride back to help Elaine create a fine feast for my falconers.'

'Oh, good,' Godwin said. 'I'm starving. Can it be just us? Not Edmund and Magnus?'

'Are your brothers not allowed to eat?'

'They can, but in the nursery.'

'How then will you tell them of your success with Artemis?'

Svana watched Godwin struggle with this conundrum and smiled at Harold over his little head. She was glad to see her husband had relaxed again and reminded herself not to touch further on matters of war. Harold was here too rarely to spoil their time with quarrels.

'I suppose they can come,' Godwin conceded now, 'but I get served first.'

'We'll see,' Svana said lightly and kissed him and Harold before heading back to Spirit.

She would order luncheon and afterwards she would reply to Edyth and urge her to caution until such time as she could be safely brought back to England.

CHAPTER SIX

Rhuddlan, July 1055

My dearest Lady Edyth,

I am touched and honoured that you have written to me and would happily give my time to however many words you would be kind enough to send. I am glad you are well and being made welcome at Rhuddlan. I hope you enjoy your time in King Griffin's court but hope too that you will soon be returned to us in England.

I am certain any overtures your father might make to King Edward would be welcome. If you could persuade him to prostrate himself you could soon be back in East Anglia and could, perhaps, come and stay on my estate? Harold is often away on the king's business and I would greatly value your company if your mother could spare you. We live simply here but you would be well cared for.

I trust you are safe in Wales. I am sure there is much to learn and to experience but do not rush, I beg of you. Be wary of the price of gifts, for I would see you home not too much changed from the Edyth who rode forth. King Griffin is a brave king but, perhaps, a dangerous man. Do take care, my sweet.

With very fond wishes,
Svana

'God's truth,' Edyth muttered to herself, 'what do they all think I'm going to do – besiege his bed?'

She tossed her head indignantly, trying to ignore the sneaking awareness that the idea was far from unpleasant to her. She had been in Wales for three months now and Griffin had remained flatteringly attentive. She had come to enjoy the aching tug of his touch in a dance and sometimes, when she lay in bed with her younger brothers sleeping soundly on pallets either side, she pulled a pillow down the length of her body and imagined how it would be if it was Griffin against her. Once or twice she had even kissed it, but so? It was to practise, that's all; it didn't mean she was going to actually do anything, not with him. He was just so very easy to dream about with his strong arms and his piercing eyes and his lilting, knowing voice.

'Safe,' Svana had said in her letter, the same word her father had used, as if they were colluding in some dull set of rules. That didn't surprise her from her father but she'd thought Svana was more liberal. '*Love needs to be free,*' she'd told her, had she not?

'*This isn't love,*' a voice said in her head and she grimaced at the truth of it. Everyone in the rough Rhuddlan court said the king would never marry and besides, he was talking of riding out to battle soon so that would be an end to any flirtation. Edyth's body flickered in disappointment but she ignored it. Svana had said she could go and stay with her once they were returned to England, so that was something to look forward to. She would reply as soon as she could but for now she had to dress for dinner.

Placing the letter carefully into a leather pouch she tucked it under the bed and summoned her maid. Alfgar had been unable to bring a full staff into exile so Griffin had assigned a girl to Edyth. Becca spoke only Welsh but Edyth was learning

and she needed to practise, for tonight she planned to test her
new language skills on Griffin.

'*Ma' fe'n anrhydedd i ddawnsio gyda chi*,' she said over and
over as Becca arranged her hair into honeyed braids – I am
honoured to dance with you.

He would like that she was sure and as soon as she was
ready she made for the great hall, keen to find out. Barely had
she entered, however, than someone tucked a hand under her
elbow and she found Lady Gwyneth at her side.

'Lady Edyth, yes?' she asked in slightly broken English.

Edyth pushed her shoulders back and swallowed.

'*Fi'n Edyth*,' she responded carefully – I am Edyth.

The woman raised an eyebrow.

'You speak Welsh?'

'I am learning.'

'And why is that?'

'It seemed polite to be able to address my kind host in his
own tongue.'

Gwyneth snorted.

'It is not the only tongue he speaks,' she said, curving her
bony hips suggestively.

'Indeed,' Edyth agreed smoothly, ignoring the older woman's
insinuations, 'his English is impeccable.' Gwyneth clearly
didn't understand the last word and Edyth felt suddenly mean.
'You are very kind to let us stay here, my lady.'

'Oh, it is none of my doing. I am little more than a guest
myself.'

'But you are the king's . . .'

'*Putain*? Whore?'

'Consort.'

'I prefer my own term, in either language.' Gwyneth laughed
bitterly. 'Do not be fooled by the glaze of civilisation, my lady.
This is not England. We do not pander to Roman niceties

71

here. If a man wants a woman and is strong enough to take her then he will.'

Edyth looked nervously around the packed hall. Most of Griffin's court were here, making free with the local honeyed ale, but the king had not yet arrived. It was a warm night at last and the great doors stood open at either end to show the magnificent views. To the back, the far-off mountains looked, for once, more blue than black and at the front the iron sea had allowed the sinking sun to coat its softly rippled surface with pinks and apricots. The court had picked up the softer mood and was whispering and giggling easily together. Edyth drew a deep breath and leaned in towards Gwyneth.

'You are not married to King Griffin?'

'No. Clearly. I am not queen, am I?' Gwyneth's lip curled. 'I was married to Lord Huw of Deheubarth, the territory I grew up in and where my family live still. Griffin wanted Deheubarth for himself and, after several attempts, he killed my husband and took it – and me with it.'

She spoke with an almost unearthly calm that unnerved Edyth.

'I'm so sorry,' she said. 'Did you love Huw?'

'Love?!'

'It is not such a stupid idea. My parents love each other, I believe. My grandparents certainly do.'

'Then your grandparents are lucky, child, or lying. I did not have the luxury of loving Huw but he was my husband and I had a respected place in his court. I was more than just a spoil of war as I am here.'

'Has King Griffin not been . . . kind to you?'

'Kind?' Gwyneth spat into the rushes. 'Kindness is not a virtue we prize in Wales, Edyth. Griffin is strong and powerful and lusty.'

'Lusty?'

'Oh yes. That man gave me more fun between the sheets than Huw ever did.'

'Gave?'

'*Gives.* I may be older than you and less . . .' her eyes wandered out of the great doors to the wanton sunset beyond, ' . . . less rosy, but Griffin wants me still.'

'I doubt it not, my lady. I am but fourteen – a child yet.'

Gwyneth grasped at her arm.

'Then act like one or you will regret it. Men are easy to control, Lady Edyth, as long as you do not offer false promises. I shall show you, shall I?'

'Show me . . . ?' Edyth began but now the king was stepping into the hall and Gwyneth was whipping past to greet him.

'My lord.'

He bowed tightly.

'Lady Gwyneth.'

'You look well tonight, Sire, lusty.'

She ran a slow finger down his tunic, curling up to him and blocking Edyth out.

'As I recall, my lady,' he responded instantly, 'you like me best that way.'

'Ripe for battle – yes.'

Her hand crept lower and Edyth turned away. How could Gwyneth behave like this in front of everyone?

'Then make sure you eat well,' Griffin laughed, loud enough for all who chose to hear, 'for you will need all your energy tonight. Shall we?'

He offered her his arm and Gwyneth took it and sailed past Edyth with a mocking wink. All night she monopolised the king, engaging him with intimate conversation in sing-song Welsh and touching him with her clearly expert hands. By the time the minstrels were called, Griffin had pulled her onto his lap and was plainly in no mood for the dance floor. Indeed, barely was the first jig over before he leaped to his feet and, announcing to the entire hall that he had 'a battle to fight with this lady', departed the company, Gwyneth in triumphant tow.

Edyth watched them go to raucous cheers and wondered what she was meant to feel. Jealousy – is that what Lady Gwyneth had intended? Because it wasn't that. Pity came closer, with scorn hot on its heels. To be treated like that in front of everyone was shaming. There was no way any man would do that to her, be he the king of all Christendom. And yet, much of the joy had gone out of the evening and, with the habitual Welsh chill creeping back into the night air, people soon peeled off to their beds.

Edyth was glad to go and burrowed down into the welcome warmth of her covers. Listening to the soft snuffles of her younger brothers either side, she tried to be grateful that King Griffin was not subjecting her to his lust. Yet her mind refused to shut down and kept snaking off to the bed, somewhere in this isolated palace, where, right at this moment, he was doing 'battle' with Lady Gwyneth. If his dancing was anything to go by it would be wild and rough and that thought sparked memories of Earl Torr in the woods. Edyth pulled her pillow over her head, trying to muffle out her damned curiosity but she knew, already, that she would sleep little tonight.

She woke from an uneasy slumber next morning to find the bedchamber empty of all but Becca, sewing in the corner. Sunlight was slanting in through the cracks in the wooden window shutters and noises from beyond suggested that the men were already at their training. She leaped up and ran to look out onto the central courtyard below. The bedchamber she shared with Edwin and Morcar was on the second floor above the commander's rooms and offered a fine view of the yard. The main palace buildings were positioned around four

sides of a square, tighter in design than their English counterparts. This was presumably to create shelter from the bitter
sea winds but Edyth liked the feeling of intimacy and privacy
it created once within and today it looked magnificent.

The sun was casting an already warm glow onto most of the
rough central square so that many of the knights had thrown
off their outer tunics and were fighting in their thin linen
undershirts and trews. Edyth watched, entranced, as Griffin's
commander led them in a series of punishing drills, swords
flashing in the sunlight and clanging alarmingly as they sparred
in pairs.

There was no rest for the king's militia. Griffin had explained
to her that Rhuddlan was ever under threat from possible
invasions by rival Welsh factions or the barbaric Irish. Dublin
remained closely linked to the roaming Vikings and with the
voracious warrior Harald Hardrada on the Norwegian throne,
the seas were more threat than protection. There were rumours
the Scandinavian king had aspirations to be an Emperor of the
North like the legendary King Cnut and Wales would be a
useful back door into coveted England to help him achieve
that goal. No one was fool enough to believe the locals would
be spared on the way through so it was vital, Griffin had assured
Edyth, that the men stayed sharp.

Now she could see the intense concentration in everyone's
eyes as they wielded their blades – blunted training pieces but
impressive all the same. She could see the way they bit down
against the pain in their muscles and even, in those closest, the
ripple of the muscle itself. It made her own body ache restlessly.

'*Yn olygfa bendigedig*,' her maid suggested shyly, coming over
– a splendid sight.

'*Bendigedig*,' Edyth confirmed with a smile.

'*Gweld dy frawd*?' – see your brother?

Edyth looked where the girl pointed and saw Brodie deep

in training. He was working his blade with the same intensity as the rest and, as far as she could tell, he was doing well. She glanced at Becca and saw a misty look in her maid's eyes.

'*Ydych chi'n hoffi fy mrawd?*' – do you like my brother?

Becca flushed and shook her head fiercely, pointing instead to Brodie's sparring partner, a young Welsh guard.

'*Pwy yw e?*' – who is he?

'Lewys,' she admitted, flushing even more deeply and adding a thickly accented, 'dress?' as she scuttled to Edyth's gown chest.

Edyth took the hint and dropped the subject.

'I shall go riding,' she said. 'I shall go and see the sea - *y môr*.'

Becca reached gratefully for her dark green everyday gown.

'*Gyda phwy?*' she asked – who with?

Edyth frowned. It was a good question. Brodie was clearly busy and her father was also labouring his way through the drills. He'd found himself a white-haired opponent but still seemed to be struggling to keep pace. It was comical to watch here in the sunny palace yard but Edyth was uncomfortably aware that this was preparation for real battle where not just Alfgar's dignity but his life would be on the line. He needed all the practice he could manage.

'My mother maybe – *fy mam?*'

Becca nodded encouragingly and so, her laces swiftly tied, Edyth drew in a deep breath and went through to the neighbouring chamber to find Meghan.

'Morning, Mama.'

Meghan looked up from her sewing.

'Morning indeed. You are quite the slug-a-bed, Edyth.'

'Can I help it if no one wakes me?'

'No one wakes you?! Heavens, the noise the boys were making this morning would have woken your ancestors' spirits.'

'I had trouble getting to sleep last night.'

'You did? Are you well?'

'Quite well, thank you. Lacking exercise, I think. Would you ride out with me?'

'Ride? Out?'

'Yes, Mama.'

'Out where?'

'Down to the coast perhaps. It is very pretty and . . .'

'And very dangerous I am sure. Those cliffs are so steep. One false move and . . .'

She plunged her hand downwards and slapped it violently onto the wooden floor. Edyth jumped but swiftly recovered herself.

'We can stay away from the cliffs, Mama. Oh, do say you'll come. It's so boring inside.'

'Where's your sewing?'

Edyth rolled her eyes. 'You can sew when it's raining,' she pointed out. 'And it does that often enough for anyone here.'

'That much is true.' Meghan sighed heavily. 'Oh Edie, I do so want to go home. I miss the markets, I miss the company, I miss the court. Heavens, I even miss your grandmother!'

She looked so small suddenly, hunched over her tapestry, that Edyth darted forward and kissed her.

'And we will, Mama – soon. The men are preparing to ride forth any day now.'

'To fight?'

'If they must, yes.'

'Alfgar with them?'

'Of course.'

'And Brodie too. My little Brodie.'

Edyth patted Meghan's knee helplessly.

'He's not so little now, Mama. Have you seen him out there with his sword?'

'No. I have not seen him and nor do I wish to. I cannot bear to send him to war.'

'But Father must fight to regain his earldom so you can go home.'

Meghan stabbed unhappily at her tapestry as if she would draw blood from the poor fabric.

'Why can he not just go and talk to the king – say sorry?'

Edyth thought of Svana's letter, hidden beneath her bed. '*If you father would prostrate himself* . . .' Is that what her mother was suggesting too? It would never happen.

'Men need to fight,' she said, 'or they grow bored, like I am bored. Oh, do come riding, Mama – it will make you feel so much better.'

Meghan, however, shook her head stubbornly.

'I'm not going out there. I'm not going near that vicious sea. I don't like it.'

Edyth edged to the window. Still beautiful.

'Well I do,' she said, 'so I shall go.'

'Not alone.'

'But you will not come.'

'Not alone,' Meghan repeated. 'Who knows what brigands live abroad? Find someone to accompany you or you must not go at all.'

Edyth gave up.

'Yes, Mama,' she agreed as meekly as she could manage and then fled the chamber.

Her body felt restless and wild and she knew that on this glorious morning she would rather climb the terrifying Eryri mountains than stay cooped up in the bower. Somehow, some-where, she had to find someone to ride out with her.

CHAPTER SEVEN

Skirts bunched in her hands to free up her impatient legs, Edyth made for the stables on the far side of the courtyard. As she edged round the training men to reach the entrance, she spotted Edwin and Morcar, wooden swords clutched tight in their little hands.

'Going to battle?' she teased them as she passed.

'Yes,' Edwin retorted fiercely and Morcar chopped out at her leg with his miniature weapon.

'May God be with you then, brave warriors,' Edyth laughed, dodging the blow, and ducking into the stables.

It was quieter inside the long low building with just the soft breathing of the many horses in the stalls along either side. Most of them were the stocky Welsh cobs who, the king had told her, were hardy, fast and skilled at negotiating the hilly terrain of the black mountains. He'd taken her to the door of the great hall one night to look out across the silvery sky to the dark jagged teeth against the horizon, revelling in her fear of them.

'Why *black* mountains?' she'd dared to ask.

'Because your fate has to be black to lead you in there,' he'd shot back then chuckled at the look on her face. 'Not really, Edyth. The Eryri – the Highlands – are beautiful and are simply called black after the dark stone at their heart. They are the safest place in the world if you know them well, for no foreign enemy would follow you up their craggy sides.'

Edyth hadn't been much cheered by this glowing testimony and felt little compulsion to see them any closer, but she liked the horses with their broad backs and sturdy feet and now she murmured to them as she passed, searching for a groom she could persuade out on a trek. There seemed, however, to be no one about and she reached her own mare at the far end without seeing a soul. Leaning over the stall, she stroked the bay's neck tenderly, though she couldn't help noticing that she looked a delicate thing beside her Welsh counterparts. Small too. Edyth could swear she'd not been able to see over her fine back before arriving in Wales three months ago.

'It seems you have outgrown your pony.'

The deep voice echoed her own thoughts so perfectly it was as if God had spoken, but when Edyth spun round it was the king she saw stood before her. Where had he come from? And so silently? She dropped into a curtsey but he caught at both her hands and pulled her straight back up.

'This isn't England, Edyth – we don't waste time with niceties here. Besides, you are far prettier stood tall.'

He had not let go of her hands and Edyth felt her heart start to pound. With no one else in the stable, she was alone with the king.

'As you wish, Sire,' she managed.

He smiled.

'Oh, I can think of far nicer ways I'd wish to see you, Edyth Alfgarsdottir, but I can bide my time.' He looked her up and down. 'You must not be afraid.'

'I am not.'

'I see your heart beating – here.' He touched her neck where the blood pulsed. 'And here.' Now he traced his finger downwards across her breast, pressing just hard enough to leave a trail of fire across her skin. She flinched.

'I trust you won your battle last night,' she flung at him.

'Of course,' he answered, unabashed. 'I always win my battles.'

'That is good if you are to ride forth with my father.'

'I am. When his band of mercenaries arrives we will go but fret not, Edyth, I will bring him to victory and then I may just have to claim a prize.'

He had stepped closer again and she was aware of his body all but surrounding her own. She forced her shoulders back.

'Prize, Sire? From the Lady Gwyneth perhaps?'

His eyes sparkled knowingly but all he said was: 'No, not from her.'

He reached up and took hold of Edyth's long blonde plait. Lifting it, he curled it slowly, sinuously around his fingers then, leaning in, he whispered a kiss across her neck. The movement took her by surprise and she had no time to be shocked. A moan escaped her lips and she felt his grip on her hair tighten but then, with a soft sigh, he released her.

'Now, what shall we do about this pony?'

'Sire?' Edyth stuttered, thrown.

'You are grown too big for her, sweet as she is. You need a woman's mount now.' He grinned and grabbed her hand. 'Come. I have just the thing.'

He set off down the stables and Edyth, her body still spinning from his touch, had to trot to keep up. Then, just as swiftly, he stopped before a stall and she ran into him.

'Steady now.' He caught her slim waist. 'See here.'

He pointed into the stall and Edyth stepped up to look over the wooden gate at the most beautiful mare she had ever seen. Pure black, save for a white blaze down her nose, she had some of the muscular build of the Welsh cobs but was far finer-boned.

'She's a cross-breed,' Griffin told her. 'I put a pretty English mare to stud with my own Welsh stallion and this beauty is the result. She's yours.'

'Oh no, Sire. I couldn't possibly accept such a gift.'

'Do you defy me, Edyth?'

'No. Oh no, Sire, I'm sorry. I just . . .' She dared to look up and saw he was smiling. She took a deep breath. 'I simply mean that she is too good for me.'

'Ah, Edyth Alfgarsdottir, nothing is too good for you. Learn that and you will do well in life. Now, let's saddle her up for you.'

He clapped loudly and a stablehand came running. Edyth could only watch in disbelief as the mare was fitted with an exquisite leather saddle and led out of her stall. She eyed her nervously.

'You ride well?' Griffin questioned.

Edyth's head shot up.

'I do.'

'I thought as much. Go on – mount. She's broken in and she's a biddable thing if you show her you're boss.'

Edyth put her foot in the stirrup. The stablehand rushed to assist but it was the king who gripped her ankle and steadied her as she mounted. The mare skittered but instinctively Edyth grasped the reins and she stilled.

'She likes you,' Griffin said.

'What's her name?'

'Môrgwynt. It means . . .'

'Sea wind.'

'It does.' He looked at her curiously. 'You are learning Welsh, Edyth. Why?'

'For you,' she answered instinctively.

'For me?' For the briefest moment Edyth thought she saw the hint of a blush creep up the king's neck but he swiftly collected himself. 'I am glad to hear it. Well, off you go then – she's yours to ride.'

Edyth shifted awkwardly on Môrgwynt's back.

'My mother will not let me ride alone, Sire,' she admitted.

'Of course not. You are – as I think I have mentioned already – too great a prize to be put at risk on these wild cliffs. I shall ride with you.'

'*You?* I mean, you, Sire?'

Môrgwynt was picking up her hooves, eager to stretch her long legs, and Edyth felt her strength and longed to test it but with the king? Alone?

'You think *I* am the risk?' Griffin suggested, clicking his fingers to have his own stallion brought forth. 'You think you will be in danger with the Red Devil? Oh yes, I know they call me that, Edyth. I know everything, including that you are right to be concerned, but I can control myself – for now. Come, let's ride!'

It was a glorious morning. The king's guards let them out of the small back gates that led directly onto a track towards the sea and Môrgwynt flew over the rough turf, as keen to ride free as Edyth. She was quick and responsive and by the time they reached the coast Edyth had the mastery of her.

'You were made for each other,' Griffin said as they pulled up at the cliff's edge.

'Indeed, I feel as if I have been riding her for years,' Edyth agreed eagerly, the joy of the ride loosening her tongue.

'And will for many to come, I hope.'

'I . . .' Edyth stuttered foolishly, the idea of a future beyond this strange time of exile catching like a loomhook on her tongue.

Griffin brushed aside her hesitation.

'Let me take you down onto the sand,' he said. 'The tide is

low so we can gallop along the sea's edge and I can show you my ships.'

She looked down at the longboats bobbing gently on the swell. There were five of them, of plain wood with little of the ornamentation the English fleet favoured, but, like all of Griffin's goods, they looked solid and strong. Edyth had watched the men sailing them on fine days and she was curious to see them closer. She peered over the cliff. A precarious footpath wound down between the rocks but the horses would never manage it.

'How do we gain the beach?' she asked.

'Follow me.'

Griffin spurred his horse back inland and led Edyth into a curving dip which twisted down the hillside and eventually opened out as if unveiling the shoreline for their personal pleasure. Môrgwynt faltered at the feel of the soft sand but Edyth urged her gently forward and she soon picked up pace again.

The sky was clear with just a few juvenile clouds chasing each other across the horizon. The sun, high now, flung its rays out across the water with seeming abandon and the water threw them back in a thousand nuggets of gold. Birds wheeled on the breeze, calling out their joy to each other and teasing the horses to greater speed. The bay was long and as the horses hit the harder sand at the water's edge they moved into an easy gallop, sending water flying either side. It caught at Edyth's skirts but she did not care. Griffin kept behind her and she gave Môrgwynt her head, scarcely noticing that her hair was blowing loose from her demure plait or that her cheeks were pinkening with the sun and the speed of the ride until, all too soon, she reached the craggy rocks at the far end and had to pull up.

She turned back to see Griffin pounding towards her, copper-streaked hair flowing out behind him, muscles flexing as one with his stallion. Her own body rippled in response as if the sun had dappled all its power across her as he came to a halt in a spray of sand.

'Is it not glorious?'

'Glorious,' Edyth agreed. 'I love it.'

'I can see that and I am glad of it. There is not much for you to do in the palace, I fear.'

'Only sewing.'

Edyth wrinkled up her nose and Griffin laughed.

'You do not like sewing?'

'No. I know I should but it is so slow.'

'Unlike Môrgwynt.'

'Yes.' She stroked the mare's long neck. 'And I do so love being outside. It is so much less stifling than the bower.'

'I am sure you are right. One of the great benefits of being a man is avoiding the bower.'

Edyth giggled.

'But you do have to go to war,' she pointed out.

He sobered.

'We do. I fear a sword pricks harder than a needle but in truth, Edyth, whilst I deplore the waste of life, I love a good battle.'

He looked out to his boats, riding the sea, and Edyth watched him.

'You will do battle alongside my father – why?'

'Why? Why not? The battle is there to be fought and alliances are useful. Land is useful, especially the fertile border-lands of the Marches. Besides, if I do not push at the edges of England, England will push at me and I cannot have that. I have all Wales to protect now.'

'What *is* all Wales?'

'What indeed.' He smiled. 'Wales is four territories, Edyth, split apart by mountains. Gwynedd, up here in the north-west, is my heartland, my birthright – though my bastard uncle stole it from me for too long.'

'What happened to him?'

'Nothing he didn't deserve. Anyway, it's mine now and it's beautiful.'

Edyth swallowed but pushed on.

'And Powys? Your half-brother holds that for you?'

'Bleddyn, yes. My mother lives there with her second husband and my younger brother, Rhys.'

'And in the south?'

'The south!' Griffin spat, his eyes darkening. 'God save us from the south.'

'Where the Lady Gwyneth comes from?'

'Indeed. She's from Deheubarth and the whole place is as troublesome as she. Her nephew, Prince Huw, is ever grumbling against me, though he dares do no more. Prince Caradog in Glamorgan is just as bad and I have to watch them all the time – hence my soldiers, and my ships.'

He gestured proudly to the fleet. From here Edyth could see the sleek lines of the vessels, the long oars and the smartly furled sails. She could also see padlocked caskets of weapons and barrels of provisions already stacked on board.

'You are ready to sail?'

'Always. You can never be too careful. Attacks can come out of nowhere.'

'And with these you can escape.'

'With these, Edyth, I can regroup and mount a renewed assault.'

'I see.'

Griffin laughed.

'Do not look so uneasy, my little English lady. The southerners avoid me, and I them.'

'Your court does not, then, move around?'

'Move around? Oh, as King Edward does. God bless you, no. It would be like sleeping in an adder's den. Now that I have conquered the south my men will collect my dues each month and I will hold court there twice a year.'

'Do the people not want to see their king?'

'Strung up maybe.'

'Oh.'

'I'm sorry, Edyth – Wales is not like England, nor ever will be. My people admire my strength and respect my will. They accept my rule but they do not like it. They would not line the streets to see me as they do the saintly King Edward.'

'I'm sorry – you must think me very foolish.'

'I think you wonderfully fresh and untainted by the world. Your innocence does me good.'

Edyth blushed.

'You must be proud to have conquered all the territories.'

'I am, Edyth. I truly am. It was my father's dream.'

'That you should be King of all Wales?'

'That *he* should be. He used to tell me about it when I was a child, describe how it would be.'

His bright eyes had taken on a lost look and Edyth felt a breathless sense of intimacy.

'And how *would* it be?'

'Glorious, of course. All would bow before him and he would have a new crown fashioned with four great rubies for the four quarters of his country. He used to describe it so vividly that I can almost see it now.'

Edyth looked at the crown Griffin wore – a rich but simple diadem.

'You have not had it made?'

He shook his head fiercely.

'It does not feel right. The jewels were the dream. The reality is wars and spies and man turning against man. The Welsh are not, I'm afraid, a naturally united people. Our land is scythed into sections by the mountains that divide them and we cleave more readily to local lords than national ones. My father was murdered.'

'Murdered?!'

'Don't look so shocked. It is the way for kings.'

'Not in England.'

He snorted.

'Nay, perhaps not in England – though you've had your share – but here it is to be expected. *I* expect it. Every day I expect it.'

'And yet you live so . . .'

'Recklessly?'

'Fully.'

He smiled.

'It's amazing how alive you feel in proximity to your own death. I could be king for another twenty years, Edyth, or for just a few more hours. It is best, I find, to make the most of all this wonderful life offers.'

'But are you not afraid?'

'Of course, but you cannot let fear stop you.' He slipped off his stallion's back and Edyth hastened to join him. 'What really scares me,' he admitted, 'is that I will lose it – the hunger. My father died when I was just ten. He was my god, Edyth, my world. I grew up with his dreams woven through me and all my life I have fought to achieve them for him. It hasn't been pretty. I have had to be ruthless – it is the only way – but I have done it. I am King of all Wales at last.'

'So why be afraid?'

'Because what do I do now?'

She shrugged.

'You have to keep it.'

'I have to keep it.' He nodded slowly. 'You are right, of

course.' Suddenly he caught her in his arms and whirled her round. 'You are right, Edyth Alfgarsdottir; you are wise indeed.'

His arms were tight around her, his face close to her own, but his eyes were still on the sea and on the dreams he must see imprinted across the waves. He stilled.

'Will you help me?' He held her so that her feet dangled like a child's, though her heart was beating a more adult tune. 'Will you help me, Edyth?'

'I will try,' she whispered and now his eyes met hers.

'You are a very special woman.'

He set her gently on her feet and pushed her hair back from her face, cupping her chin in his big hands. Then, very carefully, he leaned down and touched his lips to hers. Edyth ran her hands around his neck, meeting his kiss eagerly and Griffin moaned and pulled her against him. She felt the contained warmth of his body and the soft touch of his mouth melting her, but as she began to truly enjoy the caress he prised himself away.

'Nay, Edyth – you will undo me.'

She blinked up at him, confused.

'I am too young for you? Too inexperienced?'

'No! But I would not dishonour you, nor your father, for anything. If you will consent, Edyth, I will ask your father for your hand.'

Edyth felt the world start to spin.

'You want me as your wife?'

'Wife and queen, yes. Yes I do.'

'But they say you will never marry,' she stuttered.

'They do? Then they are wrong – with your consent.'

Edyth looked up at the great man and saw his wise eyes searching her own, as vulnerable as a child's. She tried to think of England with its elegant, mannered courts and its peaceful countryside and Svana's invitation to stay on her enchanted estate, but it all seemed terribly far away with the Welsh sea throwing itself at her feet, the Welsh birds circling her head and the Welsh king looking down at her with such tenderness.

'I consent,' she whispered and now he pulled her fiercely against him.

'You will be a great queen, Edyth,' he promised, his lips whispering the words against her own. 'You *deserve* to be a great queen – greater, perhaps, than a rough king like myself can offer.'

'No, Griffin, you—'

But he put up a finger to silence her.

'No matter, cariad. It will be my honour to see you to your throne.'

And then his mouth covered hers and, for a sea-wisp of time, crowns and thrones and titles seemed as nothing.

They rode back towards the palace at a more sedate pace, newly shy with one another despite the intimacy of their promises. Griffin had kissed her only briefly, then handed her back onto her horse before his 'baser self' took hold. Even so, Edyth felt as if he had stripped her naked there on the sand, so acutely did she feel his want, and she was sure every man and woman of the court would see it too. She had no idea how she would face her mother without her reading all that had passed, but when she finally reached her, Meghan was too distracted to so much as look at her.

'They will ride to battle, Edie.'

'I know.'

'On the morrow.'

'The morrow?!'

Edyth thought of Griffin's words that any day might easily be his last and felt fear grip her. He had said nothing of riding out so soon, only that she should not speak of their marriage until he had asked her father.

'How do you know?' she demanded.

'Your father's mercenaries have arrived and apparently they are too expensive to keep here so the king's commander has ruled that they will ride immediately.'

Edyth ran to the window and looked out and sure enough the pasture behind the palace was teeming with men pitching rough soldiers' tents and lighting campfires.

'There must be a thousand of them,' she exclaimed.

'Two thousand,' Meghan sniffed. 'They cost a fortune but your father insists it must be done to prove . . . oh, I don't know what to prove but he seems very certain.'

Edyth watched the ant-like mass of fighting men and felt her stomach curdle. She and Griffin had ridden in through the small gates on the seaward side where all was still waving grass and rippling water and romance but here, before her now, was the reality of Griffin's life as king. Not dreams and crowns and queens, but conflict and battle.

'They ride on the morrow?' she repeated, chilled to her bones despite the heat of what had seemed such a beautiful day.

'It is hard, I know, but if God is with us – as I'm sure he is – we will be able to go home.'

'To England?'

'To England, yes, Edyth. Where else?'

But to that, Edyth had no reply.

CHAPTER EIGHT

Bosham, October 1055

Lady Svana,

I was so pleased to receive your kind reply, though I fear you worry too much about me. Rest assured I am safe, nay, honoured here and am living most comfortably. I must confess, though, that it is rather dull now the men are gone to war. It is not so much that I delight in their company, as that life is so much livelier when they are in court. Now there seems to be little more to do than sew and sing and stop my brothers getting into mischief and my mother weeping for home.

Already, it seems, the days are tipping over into autumn. I am sure you must be very busy on your farmlands but for myself I cannot believe I have passed a whole summer in Wales. Not that it is not a very beautiful country and not that I would not mind staying longer, just that so much has happened since the mid-Lent council when last I saw you in such unhappy circumstances.

My one consolation is my horse. The king gifted her to me and she is the most beautiful creature in the world. She is called Môrgwynt which means sea wind and some days it seems as if she is, indeed, at one with the air. I ride her

*whenever I can persuade a companion out with me which,
with the men gone, is not nearly often enough.*

*I pray this wretched battle will soon be over and peace
concluded and that I will, one day, see you to talk over all
that has happened here in Wales.*

With very best wishes and love,

Edyth

Svana looked over the letter twice until, to her horror, a tear
plopped onto it, sending the ink scudding wildly across the
vellum. What on earth was she crying for? It must be the new
child stirring in her womb. She put her hand to her stomach
and felt it pushing against her.

'Hello in there, trouble,' she whispered.

This babe felt different from the last three. Perhaps it was
because she was older but it was making her so tired and so
wretchedly sick. She had tried all the remedies she knew – mint,
lavender, thyme and even an infusion of very expensive oriental
ginger – but to no avail. She'd even agreed to join Harold,
entertaining the court at his favourite manor of Bosham in his
Wessex heartlands, in the hope that the sea air would aid her
nausea. The sniping and gossiping in the ladies' bower, however, counteracted any health benefits nature offered.

'Just settle down, will you,' she pleaded softly and felt a small
but determined kick in response.

A girl – it had to be. She stifled the thought swiftly, not
daring to give it room to breathe in case it was not so. She
longed for a daughter but until she was so blessed she couldn't
suppress a tender, almost maternal feeling for Edyth, and the
careful lines of the girl's letter worried her.

'Why has the king gifted her a horse?' she asked her bump
but no answer was forthcoming, save the stirrings of Svana's
own common sense.

Why did men ever gift women anything? Even dear Harold, who brought her presents mainly to see the happiness on her face when she unwrapped them, definitely enjoyed the earthier expressions of gratitude once the lights were blown out. She grimaced at herself. Perhaps she was growing cynical with age? Perhaps the Welsh king just liked displaying his wealth? Perhaps he was courting Alfgar, not Edyth, with his gift? Perhaps, perhaps, perhaps . . . Svana sighed.

'Heavens, my love, not weeping again?'

She looked up to see Harold ducking into their plush chamber and brushed the tears hastily away.

'It's Edyth, poor girl.' She waved the letter. 'Heaven knows how long this has taken to find me down here; it's dated over a month ago.'

'How does she fare?'

'Well, she says. Bored of ladies' company but I don't blame her for that.'

Harold laughed.

'Well, my love, you will be glad to know that I can release you back to your lands.'

'Oh no, Harold. I'm sorry. I didn't mean it that way. I am quite happy here with you.'

'When you are with me, yes, but I know the rest is a trial and I love you for it. In truth, though, the court will be moving on in a day or two.'

'It will? Why, Harry? What's happened?'

'It's to do with your young correspondent or, rather, her father.'

'Oh no. Don't tell me you have to ride out to war?' He looked to the ground, so like one of the boys caught doing mischief that for a moment Svana wanted to laugh, but this mischief was deadly serious. 'Why you? I thought Earl Ralf was leading the defences in the west?'

'He was.'

'He's dead?'

'No, no. He's well enough. A little red-faced perhaps.' Harold sank onto a stool beside Svana and took her hands. 'As you know, Alfgar and Griffin have been besieging Hereford. All Ralf needed to do was to hold out for a few more weeks and winter would have driven them to sue for peace but, oh no – the impatient fool decided to meet them in the field. Not only that but he took his men out as cavalry.'

'Cavalry? Into battle?'

Harold shrugged.

'What can I say? He's a Norman by blood and I suppose, despite what we've taught him, he still believed it was the best way. Maybe he wanted to prove that to us – to me.'

'It didn't work?'

'You could say that. The horses were churned up in the Welsh mud within minutes. Griffin's forces were all over them. They had to retreat but the city was vulnerable. I am told the Welsh have done much damage. They have secured not just a victory but a jest at our expense.'

Svana saw Harold's jaw tighten and knew the wound ran deeper than his light tone was letting on. She clasped his hands tightly.

'I'm sorry.'

He looked at her and puffed out his breath.

'It is no great matter. If looking foolish is the worst that we suffer we should count ourselves fortunate but we cannot let it go at that. The king's honour is at stake.'

The babe rolled suddenly in Svana's stomach as if, like its mother, it was scornful of such ideas. Definitely a girl then. Svana's hand closed protectively over it and Harold placed his own on top.

'It quickens?' he asked and Svana nodded. 'Perhaps, then, it will stop making you so sick?'

'I hope so, though now fear for you will take its place.'

He looked reproachfully at her.

'Nay, Svana, fear not for me. I know what I am about on the field and I train hard. I am well fed.' He patted his belly ruefully. 'And I have the best armour. It is late in the year so this cannot go on long. I will return to you for Christ's mass, I swear.'

'At Nazeing?'

'Svana . . .'

'I know, I know. Christ's mass is at Gloucester. Always has been and always will be.'

'You will come? The boys too?'

'If I am well enough.'

'You are angry with me.'

She looked deep into his eyes and saw the faint amber rings glowing like fire around the soft pupils. She sighed.

'Not with you, my love, just with all this . . . this war-mongering. It seems so pointless.'

'Maybe it is, Svana, but what can we do? England is a rich and prosperous land. Others covet it and if they attack we must surely defend ourselves?'

'My fighting man,' Svana said, stroking his face, and he smiled ruefully. 'We cannot let foreigners prey on our land or our people, I suppose, but why must it always be *you* who does the defending?'

Harold shrugged.

'The king seems to think I am the best for the job.'

He looked so very bashful, sat there before her with his skilful warrior's hands clasped softly over her belly, that Svana could argue no further. She wound her hands around his neck and kissed him fervently.

'You *are* the best, Harold – the best for England and the best for me.'

He kissed her back.

'Don't tell anyone,' he whispered, 'but I prefer you.'

She felt her loins stir.

'It is just a shame, then, that England is so very demanding. Do you have time to come to bed?'

His eyes darkened and he pulled her up into his arms.

'I do, my love. I most definitely do. England can wait that long.'

Afterwards, as they lay in a tangle of blankets, Svana curled against him, trying to imprint every finger space of him onto her flesh to last her in the lonely weeks ahead.

'You will be quick?' she asked.

'As quick as I safely can.'

She stuck her tongue out at him.

'And you will broker a peace between King Edward and Lord Alfgar?'

'I will do my very best.'

'And you will bring Edyth safely home?'

'Why would I not?'

'I don't know.' Svana sat up and fumbled for the letter. It took her a minute to find it amongst the hastily discarded clothing but at last it emerged from beneath Harold's trews. 'She says "*I hope to see you one day*".'

'As I'm sure she will.'

'But why "one day", Harold? Why not soon? And why does she talk of "all that has happened"?'

'Girls prattle, my love. She is bored, you said so yourself.'

'So why does she not write more?'

'Perhaps vellum is scarce in Wales?'

'Hardly, Harry. If the king can gift her a horse, he can afford a few sheets of vellum.'

'A horse?'

'Yes, a beautiful creature, Edyth says.'

'But why . . . ? Oh, honestly, Svana, you have me questioning now. Look, the girl is in deepest Wales with her mother and King Griffin is at Hereford, knocking down walls and doubtless making free with the local girls. Things may have grown flirtatious but that is over. I will ride forth and I will bring them to the table and we will all see you in Gloucester for Christ's mass.'

'Promise?'

'That's not fair,' he objected, kissing her.

Svana sighed.

'So little is,' she said wistfully but Harold stoppered her words with his lips and she gave in to his renewed caresses whilst she could.

CHAPTER NINE

Billingsley, December 1055

Edyth,

I pray this missive does not take as long to reach you as I fear yours did to reach me and apologise deeply for the delay. My dear husband has been chasing the king around the country, I chasing him, and your letter, I fear, chasing us both. I wish I could send one of Harold's falcons straight to you with my words tied to his leg but until he can be trained to seek Rhuddlan we shall have to content ourselves with the slow progress of horses and men.

I hope this finds you still well. My babe has quickened and is due in the spring by which time I very much hope you will be back in East Anglia. Perhaps, if God wills it born safely, you would do us the honour of standing as godmother? Harold likes to see the children offered to God and as I defy the poor man on so much it seems only fair to grant him this small favour, especially when it secures them loving and inspiring mentors – something I know you will be for this dear child.

Harold has ridden forth to meet your father's forces. It does not please me that such a clash should occur. I wish men could settle their disputes without swords and I pray for a

year of peace but perhaps such a year is for women and until
they hold the reins of power it will not come. I can only hope
and trust that neither side here truly wishes harm to the other
and that a peaceful settlement can be reached and we can
meet in Gloucester for the Yuletide court. I wish you all good
cheer and desperately hope to see you soon.
  With love,
  Svana

Edyth folded the letter carefully. It was creased and stained
from too many readings but it had kept her comforted on the
cold road into England, not least because she was certain Svana
would be delighted to hear she was riding to peace talks. A
letter had come from Griffin a few days back inviting them to
join him at Billingsley, just over the English border. Meghan
had hailed the news with almost ferocious joy and they had
ridden out as soon as the chests could be packed.

Becca had begged to accompany Edyth 'for her comfort'
and, noting young Lewys in the guard, Edyth had consented
with a smile. She had been glad of the company for it had been
a hard, impatient ride but now she could see a line of tents on
the horizon and knew they must be close to the Welsh camp.
She tucked Svana's letter carefully into her pocket and drew
tighter on Môrgwynt's reins.

'*Y ddraig!*' came a sudden cry – the dragon.

Edyth followed the guard's eager pointing and saw Griffin's
rampant dragon pawing the bright air as his standard snapped
in the sharp December breeze. Her breath caught and Môrgwynt
skittered sideways. She had not seen the Welsh king for five
months. She had told no one, not even her mother, of her
tentative engagement and it had begun to feel as if she had
imagined it. Her hands shook on the reins. If her marriage

were to happen she would not see Svana, or any of the English court, at Yuletide, nor any time soon after.

'Come, Edyth,' Meghan said jauntily, throwing her fur-lined cloak over her shoulder, 'let us ride in to your father.'

Her head high and her face glowing, Meghan led them up to the edge of the Welsh camp. They were sighted from afar and by the time they approached the first tents, a rough guard had been hastily assembled. They rode carefully up the line and then, suddenly, there he was – King Griffin. Framed in the doorway of his deep scarlet pavilion, he stood taller and stronger and far, far more handsome than Edyth had dared to remember. His hair was fox-red in the low sunlight and his eyes, as he fixed them upon her, bluer than the winter skies. He might be closer to her father's age than her own but he radiated an energy and lust for life that set her heart crackling.

'Lady Edyth. May I?'

He held out a hand to help her from Môrgwynt's back and she slid from the horse and into his arms. He steadied her, his hand light but firm around her waist, and for a moment it was as if no one was there bar him.

'I have missed you,' he murmured.

'And I you, Sire.'

It was true suddenly and becoming more so with every moment he stood over her.

'You are, then, still willing . . . ?'

She watched his lips form the words and longed to kiss away the unbelievable uncertainty in them. She could feel herself growing with every moment at his side, as if she were a plant that had withered, unnoticed, and was now greedily sucking up spring rains.

'I am yours to command, Sire.'

'Oh, Edyth.' Griffin's voice dropped a tone. 'I'd forgotten how you excite me.'

'Then I am glad I am come to remind you.'

He groaned softly and Edyth felt a tingle of power but now Alfgar was upon them and they had to pull apart and face the world.

'My dear girl, you are grown fully a woman. I am so glad you are here to share our triumph. King Griffin and I have fought such a campaign!'

Edyth caught Griffin grinning at her over Alfgar's shoulder and she had to bite on her lip to stop herself laughing with him at her father's enthusiasm. One glance at her mother's face, however, killed all her amusement.

'Alfgar?' Lady Meghan asked sternly, her eyes boring into Griffin's hand, sat lightly but firmly around Edyth's waist.

Alfgar grinned and tugged her keenly forward.

'See our dear daughter, wife.'

'I most certainly do. She appears very . . . comfortable with our host.'

'As she should be, my sweet, for they are to be wed.' Edyth saw Meghan's eyes widen and shifted awkwardly. 'It will be a match of great honour,' Alfgar hastened on, 'for she will be Queen of Wales.'

Meghan rounded on her daughter, urgent fury in her eyes that she had not been party to this secret, but the Red Devil was towering over them, awaiting congratulations.

'How wonderful,' Meghan stuttered.

Griffin roared with laughter.

'Fear not, dear lady, I shall take care of your daughter for she is very precious to me. On this great match a wonderful peace will be founded.'

'And will, I hope, last,' Meghan said primly but she was already swelling with the import of the moment and, no doubt, the thought of all the new gowns that would need to be ordered.

'When do we talk peace?' Edyth asked hastily.

Alfgar rolled his eyes.

'We have been talking peace for days, Edie. Peace, it turns out, is a complicated business.'

'Poor Father. You have never liked formalities.'

'True, true, but I am learning patience.'

Edyth reached up and kissed him.

'I am glad of it.'

'And we are nearly through, I think. Harold niggles away about the tiniest details but Griffin is standing firm.'

'Harold?' Edyth's heart jolted. She glanced at Griffin. 'The Earl of Wessex is here?'

'For King Edward, yes. You know him?'

'Oh, a little.' Edyth could feel her heart pounding and put her hand to her neck to try and hide it from the watchful king. Griffin's bright eyes narrowed.

'How?' he demanded.

'How? Just, just because I know his wife, the Lady Svana. She holds lands in East Anglia near my father's soon-to-be-recovered estates, is that not right, Father?'

'It is,' Alfgar agreed but Edyth could sense Griffin watching her intently.

'Come within,' he said now – an order. 'I am sure your father wishes to settle your mother and the boys in their pavilion but perhaps then they will join us for a glass of wine? I am getting quite a taste for the drink.'

He smiled but his hand was under Edyth's elbow and his intent was clear to all. Meghan started forward but Alfgar steered her away, contenting himself with a guarded, 'We will not be long', before leaving his daughter to Griffin's mercies. As soon as they were inside the pavilion Griffin pulled Edyth roughly against him.

'What is Earl Harold to you?'

'Nothing, Sire, truly.'

'Nonsense. I saw your eyes. You are hiding something.'

'But not from you.' Edyth quivered in his iron grasp. She had no idea what to do now, could see no way out of his jealousy, save the truth. 'He caught me once, a while back.'

'Caught you? If he—'

'Griffin, listen, please.' He started at her use of his name and she pressed her advantage. 'He caught me up a tree. I was watching something – two people. They were . . .'

To her relief she saw a smile creep into Griffin's eyes and his grasp relaxed.

'They were what, Edyth? Tell me.'

'They were, were rutting, Sire.'

'Rutting?!' Griffin threw back his head in laughter then clutched her in against him. 'Rutting? And did you like the look of it, cariad?'

'It surprised me, Sire.'

'Griffin. Call me Griffin again. What surprised you?'

Edyth shut her eyes.

'How big he was.'

'Oh, my love. Oh, Edyth!' He buried his head in her neck, pressing his lips against her skin. 'Do not worry,' he said throatily. 'I will not disappoint you there.'

Edyth pictured Lord Torr lazily stroking his member. She pictured the girl, bottom thrust eagerly upwards, begging for him to enter her. She tried to imagine herself like that but felt revulsion nudge up against excitement in her gut. And still Griffin kissed her.

'Sire, please, I . . . I'm afeared.'

He pulled back and looked down at her curiously.

'Afeared? There now, you need not be. I will look after you. I am going to give you such pleasure, Edyth. Such pleasure.'

'*What is life without pleasure, Edyth Alfgarsdottir?*' Torr's voice said, shivering up her spine, but now Griffin was taking her hand and, turning it palm upwards, placing the gentlest of kisses into the curve of her fingers.

'Trust me,' he said softly. 'Tomorrow I shall wrap up the peace talks. Let Earl Harold have his petty parcels of border-land for I have my prize and I want to take her home and enjoy her as she, I swear, will enjoy me.'

The town of Billingsley was of middling size – maybe a hundred occupants – and the lord's great hall was not so very great. It was, at best, twenty paces long and was already bursting with people when Alfgar and Griffin led their party into the nego-tiations next morning. Griffin had insisted Edyth be included in the deputation and Alfgar, flushed with the raucous welcome the king's betrothal announcement had received in their camp last night, had readily agreed. Edyth would have gladly stayed in her father's gloomy pavilion – and even taken up a needle – rather than face Earl Harold in negotiations but Lady Meghan was so delighted to be back over Offa's Dyke and on English soil again that she was agreeing to anything.

'Oh yes,' Edyth had heard her telling two local ladies earlier. 'I'm delighted at my daughter's match. Rhuddlan is very grand and the countryside very beautiful and King Griffin is the first man to rule the whole of Wales ever – is that not impressive?' Edyth had stepped pointedly up to her mother's side but Meghan hadn't even flinched. 'It's so much more civilised there than you'd imagine but, then, the king is so very wealthy and so very, very strong.'

Edyth had not quite been able to see her mother's face but could have sworn she'd winked and certainly the two ladies had giggled lasciviously.

'And your daughter to be queen. You must be so proud.'

'So proud,' Meghan had confirmed, patting Edyth's head absently. 'Such an honour.'

And now they were walking into the hall and, despite the chill of the day, Edyth felt hot all over. Her arm was resting on Griffin's and he was holding his own as stiffly as any English courtier but he might as well have been gripping her waist for the clear implications of her appearance at his side. '*It's not just an appearance*,' she told herself sternly as the English rose and bowed, '*it's fact. You are betrothed to this man and you are proud of it.*' Even so, she could not meet Harold's eyes as he stepped forward.

'My lords – ladies. You honour us with your presence.' First he kissed Meghan's hand and then turned to Edyth. 'You are much grown, Lady Edyth, since we saw you last. You look well.'

'I *am* well, thank you, my lord.' Edyth could feel Griffin's eyes tight upon her and still dared not look at Harold. 'I have been kept most kindly at Rhuddlan.'

She glanced at Griffin who clasped his other hand over hers.

'Lady Edyth has graced my palace with her presence. So much so, indeed, that I have asked for her as wife and her father has been pleased to consent.'

The assembled men gasped. Alfgar shifted awkwardly but jutted out his chin.

'It is an alliance, I am sure, that will serve us all well,' Alfgar said stiffly. 'Our two countries have enough enemies beyond our seas without fighting each other.'

Edyth blinked at her father's sudden eloquence. How long had he been deliberating over this little speech? He sounded defiant, defensive even, as if expecting opposition, but Harold just stood frozen to the spot staring at Edyth.

'Which is why,' Griffin prompted, 'we should conclude the terms of our peace.'

Harold nodded but did not move. Edyth kept her eyes firmly on the floor and after a moment he clicked his teeth, as if to a recalcitrant horse, and wheeled away. Griffin escorted Edyth into a seat next to him, Alfgar slid in on her other side and together they faced a now steely Harold.

'Redistribution of land,' he said crisply and reeled off a list of estates from a paper before him.

A lively debate ensued. Edyth knew she should pay attention but she was mesmerised by the sight of Harold in action. This was a man she had seen joking with his wife, fetching wine, chatting with courtiers. Even at council he had always seemed calm and jovial, yet here he was, deeply serious, commanding his men with an iron certainty and a cold, driving will.

This was Harold the soldier, fighting for his country's rights, and suddenly Edyth wished she hadn't come, hadn't had to see this. It was as if some of the magic of Svana's glorious husband was being sucked away and yet, at the same time, she could not help but be awed by his ruthless determination. They scythed through the many points at speed, each side now apparently keen to conclude, until finally Harold drew in a deep breath.

'And finally – Billingsley.' He looked around as if to take in the town itself. At the far end of the hall, on the public benches, the local lords shifted uneasily. 'You wish this town as your own, King Griffin?'

'I do.'

'Yet the town itself would choose to remain English.'

'What has it to do with the town?'

A murmuring began at the back of the hall and Harold cleared his throat.

'In England we respect the opinions of our people,' he said.

'In Wales our people respect the opinions of their king.'

Harold frowned and Edyth drove her fingers into the folds of her gown, willing this to be over.

'We have conceded to your other demands, Sire,' Harold

growled, 'but granting you Billingsley would extend the border further into the Marches than ever before.'

'As seems only proper given our superior performance on the battlefield.'

'There was no battlefield.'

'Only because your Hereford cavalry turned tail.'

'And you retreated into the hills.'

'A man should always fight from a vantage point.'

'But not usually from a cave.'

Harold's voice was low and venomous and his men were looking at him with an ill-disguised horror that suggested this was not his usual style of negotiation. His eyes met Edyth's and he held them for a long moment, then suddenly he rose.

'May I propose a solution?' he asked.

Griffin inclined his head.

'I shall make a gift of this good town to your betrothed. May the Lady Edyth take it as a wedding token and hold it as part of her dower lands to the honour of us both.'

'What?'

The word burst from Edyth's mouth before she could stop it and she coloured furiously at her own lack of grace. Griffin smiled indulgently as he rose and faced Harold. A stumble behind, Alfgar shot to his feet too.

'On behalf of my wife-to-be, I accept.'

Someone on the back benches cheered and, after a moment, his fellows joined in. Griffin stepped out to the fireside and Harold joined him. The two men clasped hands as Alfgar hovered next to them.

'Look after her,' Edyth heard Harold say, soldier-fierce, before he clapped Griffin on the back. After announcing the peace was concluded, he was suddenly all courtier's smiles once more.

In an instant the tables were pushed back, the fire stoked

and a great joint of pre-cooked boar hoisted over it to crisp. Barrels were rolled forth from the kitchen and the mood relaxed. The party had begun and somehow, in the midst of it all, Edyth had become owner of a town – this town. She just had time to hear her mother say, 'Well done, my sweet' before Griffin tugged her forward.

'Come, let us dance!'

He whirled her into his arms, kicking up his feet in the sort of Welsh jig she had thrilled to dance back in Rhuddlan. Here, though, with the English thegns watching in bemused ben-evolence and Harold stalking the dance floor as if he might whip out his hunter's arrows at any moment, it was hard to recapture the mood. She was glad when, at long last, she could retire, but even in the pavilion there was little rest.

'Edwin says you are not coming home with us,' Morcar whispered into the darkness.

Edyth swallowed.

'Edwin is right.'

'Why, Edie?'

She felt her covers lift and Morcar's slender little body crawl in next to her. She clasped him tight.

'Because I must return to Wales with King Griffin.'

'Why?'

'Because she's going to be his wife, silly. Like Mama and Papa.'

The covers lifted on the other side and Edwin crept in too.

'Oh.' Morcar thought about this. 'Will I see you again, Edie?'

Edyth stared into the darkness, pressing her eyelids as wide apart as they would go, willing the tears not to creep out and betray her.

'Of course you will, Marc. You can visit me, I expect, and I will come to Gloucester at Yuletide.'

'If the peace lasts.'

Shocked, Edyth turned her head in Edwin's direction. It

was too dark to see his face even this close up but Edyth could imagine his serious expression perfectly.

'Why do you say that, Edwin?'

'The Red Devil likes to fight.'

'He does.'

'And Earl Harold doesn't like him very much.'

'Well no, maybe not.'

'So . . .'

'So,' Edyth said firmly, 'it's up to me to keep them friends.'

'Like you keep me and Edwin friends?' Morcar suggested.

Edyth thought of her brothers' endless squabbling and sparring.

'Yes,' she said wearily, 'just like that. Now, sleep.'

CHAPTER TEN

Gloucester, Yuletide 1055

*H*arold approached Gloucester cold to his very bones and more tired than he could ever remember being before. He must be getting old. Either that or something about these negotiations had taken more out of him than usual. His hand went to his tunic and patted at the sealed roll safe beneath it.

'Could you give this to Lady Svana?' Edyth had asked him as they had parted.

She'd been pale and tearful and he'd had to remind himself sternly that any girl might look that way when parting from her family for the first time. This wasn't any girl though – this was Edyth. What on earth would Svana say when he told her?

'*Bring Edyth safely home,*' she had exhorted him when he'd left on this godforsaken mission and that was the one thing he had not done. In all other respects the encounter had been a success but his wife would not see it that way. She'd taken Edyth Alfgarsdottir to her heart and was looking forward to having her nearby in East Anglia and, in truth, Harold wished it could be so himself. He knew Svana grew lonely without him. He knew she hated him being away so often and could not see the tricky lines he had to tread with the king to secure even the time he did with her and the children. And now with the new babe on the way it would be harder than ever.

He looked to the skies. They were grey and heavy with snow and seemed lower on his head than usual, as if God himself was pressing down upon him. Should he have married Svana? He had defied his father to do so. Earl Godwin had brought Harold and all his siblings up indulgently. He had bought them the best clothes, the best education and the greatest honours but with those had come expectations and Harold knew that, in marrying Svana, he had disappointed the great Earl. In his darker moments he sometimes even wondered if it had hastened his death. Not only that but he had stood against the court and even against the church and that pained him, though far less than it would have pained him to live without her.

'A man like you, Harold,' his mother had railed at him, 'does not marry for love.'

She'd spat the word out as if it was a poisonous bug and Harold had known she was right but he was not just a man like him – he *was* him and he loved her. It had seemed enough at the time. It still did. He was just weary, not seeing straight. A hot drink would go a long way to soothing this ridiculous self-pity.

He pushed his horse up to the city gates, forcing himself to smile graciously at the scraping guards who let him through. He was glad to be here at last. Gloucester was his favourite of the three royal compounds. It was not as stuffy as Winchester and it was considerably more spacious than run-down Westminster. They were a week short of Christ's mass but already a number of pavilions huddled together in the grey cold. Harold looked eagerly around, but could see no 'fighting man' standard to proclaim his family's safe arrival. He shuddered and slipped from his horse, passing his treasured beast to young Avery without a second glance. A cluster of young men, bundled up in furs and drinking mugs of spiced wine, were bunched around a brazier and he moved instinctively towards the warmth. The lads parted hastily, bowing low.

'Nay, huddle in,' he urged. 'It is too cold for ceremony.'

With a grateful sigh they closed in again. One of them produced a rough goblet and poured the earl wine from a large flagon tucked beneath the brazier. Another lifted a poker from the flames and plunged it into the liquid. It hissed and a cloud of scented steam rose into Harold's face, tingling blissfully across his frozen skin.

'Thank you.'

He took a careful sip and felt the wine ease down his throat, trailing warmth behind it. He took another and another and only as he started to thaw did he notice all the lads staring at him.

'How did you fare in Wales, my lord?' one of them dared to ask and Harold suddenly realised how eager they must be for news.

'Well,' he assured them. 'Very well. Peace is made and Earl Alfgar will return to East Anglia.'

'Brodie with him?'

Harold sought out the questioner, clearly a friend of Alfgar's eldest son.

'Brodie with him. He fought well.'

'He fought?'

There was envy in the voice and it caught at Harold's heart; Svana hated fighting.

'You will have your time,' he snapped, 'and believe me, when you are face down in the mire with horses' hooves a finger space from your head and dead men's blood splattered over you, you will not think it such a fine fate.'

'My lord?'

Their eyes were wide in the gloom and Harold shook himself.

'Don't mind me, lads. I'm travel weary, that's all. I need rest.'

'And the comfort of your wife's arms, my lord?'

'If only!'

'But the Lady Svana is here.'

'She is?'

'She arrived two days ago, my lord, with all your brave sons. Your eldest was riding his own pony like a proper little man.'

Harold glanced wildly around the compound but still he could not see his standard. The light grew ever dimmer and now a few flakes of snow were starting to form.

'Where is she?' he demanded.

'The king has housed them in the guesthouse, my lord, with your wife's condition and all.'

'She is unwell?'

'No more so, I believe, than is usual in pregnancy.'

'Of course. Of course, thank you. Thank you so much.'

To the lad's great surprise, Harold clasped his hand, pumping it enthusiastically before he strode off towards the guesthouse. The guard huddled in the doorway scuttled to attention and Harold, heart pounding like a minstrel's drum on parade, stepped inside. The lower floor of the guesthouse was empty but Harold could hear voices from above and recognised the excited squeals of his sons.

'Hello!' he called, leaping for the carved wooden staircase. 'Hello? Are there any handsome young men up there?'

'Papa!'

He reached the top just in time to be knocked sideways by a tumble of children. He gathered Godwin, Edmund and Magnus into his big arms and pushed forward, seeking his wife. She was sitting on the bed, wearing a thick woollen dress of a beautiful blue, pulled tight across her now straining belly. Her hazel hair was caught up in a fur-trimmed hood and she looked unbelievably beautiful.

'"Tis the Virgin Mary herself,' he breathed, moving towards her, his boys still attached.

'Hardly,' Svana smiled, rising. 'I think you took care of my virginity a long time back.'

Harold stood before her, drinking her in.

'Are you sure?' he said softly.

'Perhaps not. Best if you make certain tonight. Oh Harold, I've missed you so.'

Harold plunged forward and clasped her to him.

'And I you. How did you manage the journey with these horrors and this one?'

He put his hand to her belly but Svana just smiled.

'This one, as you call her—'

'Her?'

'Maybe. Anyway, this one is being good as gold. I feel better than ever and she gives me no trouble. Not that I can say the same for the boys!' She reached up to tickle them and they squirmed delightedly. 'Though in truth they have been good too.'

'It's too cold not to be,' Godwin muttered.

'Really?' Harold said, swinging his eldest boy round to face him. 'Because I heard tell that you rode your own pony into Gloucester like a man.'

Godwin beamed.

'I did. I did, Papa, and all the way from Nazeing too. Well, nearly. I only went in the carriage one day when it was raining and that only because Mama made me.'

'Mama was quite right. You must be well for Yuletide.'

At this the boys started jabbering excitedly. Harold rolled his eyes at his wife though already the rough tumble of his family was warming him far more than any spiced wine could ever do. But then Svana asked: 'How were the negotiations?' and he froze.

'Mixed,' he said cautiously. Her eyes narrowed and his gut twisted. 'Peace was negotiated successfully and Alfgar returns to East Anglia. He and his family will be here on the morrow.' He looked to the rafters. 'That is, most of his family will be here.'

'Harold?'

Harold set the boys down and, perhaps sensing their father's change of mood, they ran off to play.

'It is Edyth, my love. She is to be wed.'

'To King Griffin?'

'Yes.'

'I knew it! Did you not stop this madness, Harold?'

'How, Svana? I would have if I could but it was all arranged between the king and Edyth's father. It was not my place to object.'

'Surely you could have raised some political obstacles?'

'Whilst concluding a treaty between our two countries? Hardly. The match, I'm afraid, was most fitting.'

'Most fitting?!'

'Not for me, Svana, but for the general mood.'

She huffed and he didn't blame her; it sounded useless even to him.

'And Edyth herself?' she demanded. 'How fares she?'

Harold considered.

'She seemed a little tearful when we left but not unhappy. Truly, Svana, I think she likes him and I think he is a good man – mainly. Certainly he seems to dote on her. That is good, is it not?'

Svana tossed her head.

'It will only last until he's bedded her.'

'Not necessarily. I still dote on you.'

Svana closed her eyes and Harold stood waiting fearfully

but when she finally opened them he saw resignation in their grey depths.

'I feared this from her letters but perhaps, as you say, it is not all bad. She's just so young.'

'Not any more, my love. She has grown up fast this year.'

'And will grow up faster yet before it is out.'

Harold nodded. He kissed his wife.

'I am told,' he said softly, 'by too many to doubt it, that the Red Devil is very proficient.'

'Harold!' she protested but a giggle escaped her lips and Harold knew the worst had passed.

'I will keep an eye on her, Svana, I promise. Oh, and she gave me a letter for you. Here.'

He reached into his tunic and produced the roll of vellum he had kept with care. Svana glanced at the boys, still playing happily, then sunk onto the bed. Harold sat beside her and placed an arm tight around her precious shoulders and, together, they read Edyth's words.

My Dear Svana,

Harold will have told you my news by now. Do not blame him. It was my fault. I wanted the king to like me and he does and, Svana, I like him too. I know he is big and fierce and a bit wild at times but he is tender-hearted underneath. I have seen it. He wants me to help him hold Wales. I don't know if I can do that but I want to try. I shall miss my family and I shall miss you but I have given him my promise and must keep to it.

I am so very sorry I cannot come and visit you and I will understand if you do not wish your beautiful babe – for I am very sure it will be beautiful – to have a godmother stuck the other side of Offa's Dyke so I release you from that request, though I will always cherish your asking.

I hope this is not the end of our friendship for it is dear to me. Griffin must return to Rhuddlan to celebrate this Christ's mass after so long away on campaign, but perhaps next year I can join the court at Gloucester. We will be wed in the spring though I confess, my lady, that I may be wife sooner than that.

I cannot believe I am to be a queen and I fear that beneath the crown I will remain the foolish girl you knew. I hope you may write again when you are free and please believe that, whether you can or no, I will think of you often and with love.

Yours until we may meet again,
Edyth Alfgarsdottir

PART TWO

CHAPTER ELEVEN

Rhuddlan, December 1055

Rhuddlan was white. The whole of the royal compound was hunkered down beneath the snow as if in hibernation. The only sign of life was a dark wisp of smoke rising up through the thatch of the great hall but even that was thin and unwelcoming. Edyth stared forlornly at it and wondered if she would ever again be warm. The distant sea was grey and flat, even its spirit subdued by the endless snowfall, and though she tried to picture the glorious day when she and Griffin had chased along its shore, it felt too far away to grasp. She shivered and huddled into Môrgwynt's great neck, seeking relief from the battering western winter. Right now she couldn't see much joy in being Queen of Wales.

'Fret not, cariad.' Griffin rode up beside her and leaned over to place a great arm around her shoulders. 'We will soon be home.'

Home! This was her home now – this wild little outpost, four hard, cold days' ride from England. She tried to smile at her betrothed but her lips were too cracked and frozen to curve as they should. Griffin leaned in and kissed them hard.

'I will warm you, Edyth.'

Her insides flared, making her skin feel even icier. Maybe

another day's ride would not trouble her too greatly – nay, another week's?

'Don't be afeared, cariad. I will be gentle.'

'I thought you liked to battle between the sheets.'

The words shot out before she could hold them, but Griffin simply smiled.

'I *can* battle, Edyth – between the sheets as elsewhere – but I do not choose to. Do you intend to fight me?'

'No! Oh no, Sire.'

'Griffin. And good. That is good. I will treat you well, cariad, fear not. Now come, there are too many cold toes and empty bellies to linger on snowy hillsides. We ride for home!'

'My lords and ladies, let me present to you my queen – *your* queen!'

Griffin pulled Edyth to her feet, holding her hand aloft like a victorious fighter and almost yanking her feet from the ground in his enthusiasm. Musical cheers rang around the great hall and Edyth felt herself flush with delight at such a welcome.

The feast was well under way. The fires were high, the food rich and the ale plentiful. A hundred rush lamps burned around the walls throwing heady golden patterns off the shields hung between them and the leaden white of the snow was shut firmly away. Most of Griffin's small winter court would sleep here tonight rather than brave their own frozen quarters but the king's chamber had been prepared for him with no less than four carefully tended braziers. Edyth knew because he had shown her on the way to dinner.

'See, cariad – we will be in comfort tonight.'

'But we're not yet married,' she'd dared to protest.

He'd just laughed.

'Who's to know out here? No Roman priest will brave Welsh roads until spring so why wait? Believe me, Edyth, you will be glad of it before the sun rises again.' She'd nodded dumbly and he'd caught her up in his arms and spun her round. 'You are so sweet, Edyth. God, I'd take you now if I could.'

'You would?'

Edyth had almost hoped he might – at least then it would be done.

'No, the anticipation will make it all the sweeter. Come – our subjects await!'

And now those subjects were here, roaring their approval and all she could think was that every one of them knew exactly what would happen to her tonight. Her stomach churned and she wished she hadn't eaten the eels but now Griffin was waving his great hands for hush and his steward, John, was approaching bearing a beautiful wooden casket. Edyth stared at it.

'I have a gift for you, Edyth Alfgarsdottir.'

Griffin reached out to the casket and the whole hall stilled in anticipation. He lifted the lid and reached inside, pausing expertly for the crowd before drawing forth a crown – a beautiful, highly jewelled crown. Edyth gasped.

'Is it not exquisite?' Griffin lifted it high to show his lords and ladies before turning to Edyth. 'Just like you.' A tear burst on her eyelid and she brushed it away. Griffin smiled and leaned down to kiss her. 'I ordered it made before we left for battle. Do you like it?'

Edyth tried to focus through the mist of her foolish eyes. She took in the delicate Celtic patterns in the gold, the beautifully cut amethysts and aquamarines around the base and the four great square rubies standing proud on swirling points.

'It is your father's crown.'

'It is and now, my love, it is yours.'

With that, he bent and placed it on her head. It fitted perfectly and had been thoughtfully made with a rabbit-fur lining so it was soft on her head. Edyth put up a hand to touch it.

'Does it suit me?' she whispered, awed.

'It does,' Griffin said. 'You look perfect.' Then he leaned in closer and whispered, 'And will look even better when it is all you are wearing.'

'Griffin!'

'Edyth. You are mine – all mine. Come.'

'Now?'

'Now.'

He leaped up and swung her into his arms, carrying her down the length of the great hall to raucous cheers. Edyth hid her face in his broad shoulder and was grateful, despite the sting of the iced air, when they left the court's knowing jibes. Within moments, however, they had reached the bedchamber and her whole body seemed to flare with the heat of the fires and with her own pulsing awareness. Griffin sent his brazier-men scuttling away and set her gently down.

'We are alone at last, cariad. Nay, don't speak. Don't speak and don't think – just feel. It is time for pleasure.'

What is life without pleasure, Edyth Alfgarsdottir?

Earl Torr's words drifted across Edyth's mind as Griffin pulled back her headdress and lowered his lips to her neck, but she pushed them aside. She was here, in Wales, and must look forward not back. Griffin's kisses whispered across her skin and, despite her nerves, she felt her blood rise to meet them. She sighed gently and he kissed harder, moving his lips down to the dip between her breasts. His fingers found her laces and expertly untied them, loosening her overgown so he could tease the neckline downwards.

Edyth's body began to pulse. Griffin's lips never stopped moving, pushing across the curve of her breast as if following the rising beat of her heart. She gasped at the thrill and buried her hands in his hair and now Griffin began to flick his tongue across her nipple before tweaking at it with his teeth.

'Griffin, I—'

'Don't speak,' he said huskily, 'not this time. Don't speak, don't think, just—'

'Feel,' Edyth whispered.

'Beautiful girl.'

He stepped back, bent and lifted the hem of her overdress, peeling it effortlessly over her head so that she stood in just her shift. He smiled then swung her into his arms and placed her on the bed, kneeling up at her feet. He licked his lips and bent slowly, taking one of her feet in his great hands to slide off her shoe and kiss her ankle. Edyth swallowed. In all the conversations she'd listened into in the bower over the years no one had ever said anything about ankles.

'Feel,' he murmured and now he began to move upwards, lingering over each leg in turn, rolling the hem of her shift higher and higher. Edyth felt sensations rushing down her thighs and back up again – all the way up. Desire pooled between her legs as he moved closer and closer and suddenly his tongue – his tongue! – was there and she cried out with pleasure. Now she knew why the serving girl had pushed herself so eagerly towards Torr. Her body felt as if it was cracking at the edges, opening up beneath his touch, and she wanted more. Much more.

When he stopped, she longed to grab at him and pull him back. She squirmed on the bed and he smiled wickedly.

'Don't fret – I'm not done with you yet. Your shift . . .'

He went to remove it but Edyth was there first, ripping it over her head so that she was naked before him. She felt no shyness, no nerves, just desperate anticipation.

'Ah, cariad!'

Griffin's voice was rich with appreciation. He was shedding his own clothes now and Edyth watched in awe as his great body was unveiled to her. It was firm and hard. His chest bulged with muscle but his waist was as slim as an arrowhead, pointing down. Edyth's eyes widened but now he was over her again, kissing her lips, her eyelids, nibbling at her ears and her body was falling apart beneath him.

'Now,' he murmured.

She felt his hands on her thighs, gently parting them and then he was inside her and a sharp tear of pain unfolded into waves of pleasure.

'Harder,' she said.

He chuckled and obliged and she felt the waves build until she had no control over herself and could only buck against him. Vaguely she was aware of herself crying out and Griffin responding. Vaguely she felt him pulse inside her and realised he must be releasing his seed but that seemed as nothing to the sheer joy of his touch.

Eventually he shifted off her and lay at her side. She curled against him.

'Good?' he asked.

'So good.' She raised herself up and looked at him, suddenly anxious. 'Did I do it right?'

'Oh Edyth, you were perfect.'

'Really?'

'Really.'

'Thank heavens. Can we do it again?'

Griffin groaned but his smile was splitting his face apart.

'Soon,' he agreed, kissing her, 'but first I want to see you in your crown.'

'Of course. I am, after all, yours to command.'

Griffin groaned again.

'Why does it feel as if that is not going to be true?' he said as Edyth, giggling, rose to retrieve her beautiful crown from the floor.

CHAPTER TWELVE

Rhuddlan, September 1056

My dearest Edyth,

Thank you for your latest letter. I am so glad the summer has been warm and hope that you are seeing as beautiful an autumn on your western shore of our island as we are in the east. The vines are laden here and the corn piled high in the barns and we all grow fat.

Our ram, devil that he is, got in amongst the sheep and God has chosen to bless the poor creatures with winter lambs. They look most bemused. Just last night a ewe, a mother many times over, struggled and I had to pull not one but three lambs from her womb. All were hale and on their feet in moments and though it was fully dark I felt blessed to have been with her for the birthing. However many times I see a new life come into the world it still feels like a miracle.

I am so pleased to hear that you have your own miracle on the way and that the begetting of it has not proved too arduous. As we discussed once before, so very long ago as it now feels, the act of love can be a wonderful thing and I am pleased the king treats you so tenderly.

Edyth paused in her reading and grinned. The king was not always, these days, as tender as those first times and, Lord forgive her, she encouraged him in his delicious devilry. It had grown tougher as her belly had swollen but they had managed.

As the summer sun had shone on the fields, however, it had seemed that the newly green grass needed soaking in blood and Griffin had ridden to war. He'd been gone almost two months and she was aching for him. Being with child seemed, if anything, to have increased her appetite and now, as she grew near to her time, she felt itchy and cranky. Shaking herself, she turned back to Svana's welcome letter.

I was so sorry to miss your wedding, though your father has talked of it so much I feel almost as if I were there. The Whitsun court rang with tales of your beauty and your gowns and your crown. I hear it is magnificent, as is only right. I must practise my curtseys before I see you and your little prince or princess.

My own blessed daughter grows fast and I am quite hopelessly smitten with her. We have called her Crysta, after Harold's mother, and she is the sweetest thing – so small compared to her brothers and not nearly as demanding. She wants but one thing, a godmother, but Harold and I agree that must wait until you are visiting as I will have no one else but you for my baby girl. Harold dotes on her already and I can see that she will have him wrapped around her little finger. I fear I am no longer the first woman in his life but I am content.

Or I would be, but he is gone. Off fighting, as men will insist on doing. What would happen, I wonder, if they all just stayed at home with their wives? Would the world stop? Would the crops not grow and the babies not be born? Would the land change shape? Men, it seems, are obsessed by borders and the one between our countries seems the most enchanting

*of all. I can only pray our husbands will not kill each other
and trust, my dear friend, to our charms to lure them home
to us unscathed.*

Your ever loving,
Svana

Edyth read Svana's last line over and over. The barely
suppressed melancholy contained within it spoke to her own
and was both an irritation and a balm. Griffin had left her in
command of his palace but it was a command that was proving
hard to assert. The courtiers who had paid such respect to her
when the king was at her side treated her with contempt in
his absence. It was only the support of old John the steward
that was keeping her afloat. For the rest – the women – it was
like trying to control haybarn cats. Only this morning John
had come to her complaining that his supplies of beeswax were
being run too low.

'It's Lady Gwyneth,' he'd confided. 'She's asking for new
candles every day. The king is due home any moment but at
this rate he will return to dark evenings and we'll all have to
be a-bed the moment the sun dips.'

Edyth had thought that sounded perfect but John had clearly
been in distress at the prospect and she'd forced herself to put
her sulky, demanding body aside.

'I will talk to her,' she'd promised but she'd been stalling all
morning. Svana's letter had provided a welcome excuse to
duck the confrontation but she had read it several times now
and she knew she had to go and find Gwyneth.

'*You're the queen,*' she told herself sternly, reaching for her
crown. '*You're in command – Griffin said so.*'

Griffin, however, was not here and everything seemed so
much harder without him, especially his supercilious ex-mistress.
As if sensing her distaste for the task, the babe kicked out,

sudden and strong, and Edyth put her hand to her belly. She could actually feel the shape of its determined little foot and she stroked it softly. She was the queen and she was carrying the king's child, so Gwyneth and her caterwauling women could learn to do as she said.

Decided, she let herself out of her elaborate bower and crossed the courtyard to Gwyneth's far humbler rooms in the cold western corner of the compound. The guard on the door bowed low but the women were slow to rise and even slower to curtsey. Edyth strode forward to where Gwyneth was seated on a grand chair, almost a throne. She stood before her in silence and eventually the lady curtseyed but, like those of her maids, it was the briefest of dips, more an insult than a courtesy.

'John tells me you are running our supply of candles dangerously low, my lady,' Edyth said in her now-perfect Welsh.

'John is a fool.'

'John is a skilled steward and one of the king's most trusted servants.'

'The king is not here.'

'No. He is fighting for the honour and wealth of our country.'

'*Our* country?'

The mutiny was low but Edyth's sharp ears caught it. She turned to the speaker, a sultry, dark-eyed young lady.

'If you have a problem with Wales, Lady Alwen, I'm sure we can arrange for you to live somewhere else. Ireland perhaps . . .' The girl's berry-stained cheeks paled; everyone knew the Welsh court was a picture of civilisation compared to the barbarous Irish one. Edyth smiled grimly. 'As I was saying, the king, my husband, is fighting for our country and will not wish to return to a dark hall. John says we can afford twenty candles a week for the bowers, of which ten are for my own. That seems fair.'

'Fair? There are more of us here.'

That much was true. Most of the time Edyth only had her

maid, Becca, for company whereas Gwyneth's bower was bustling with ladies, gossiping and sniping and, as far as Edyth could see, living off the royal purse for no service in return.

'You are right,' she said coolly, 'perhaps some of you should return to your own estates.'

'You can't tell us what to do.'

Edyth put a quiet hand to her crown.

'I am not seeking to do so, simply suggesting that your husbands will be disappointed if they return from war to find their farmlands poorly tended for your want of attention.'

'That's what stewards are for,' Gwyneth spat.

Edyth kept her face straight.

'Quite right, my lady, and *our* steward says ten candles. See he is obeyed, please.'

She turned to leave before any of them could challenge her further but as she took a step towards the door she felt a sharp pain shoot across her belly. She stopped, clutching at it. The women watched, impassive. Another pain griped at her, this one stronger than the last. Edyth reached for the wall to support herself but misjudged the distance and stumbled. No one moved to help her.

She closed her eyes against the cramps. It was too soon, surely. Even as she thought this, though, the babe kicked out, as if to escape, and she felt something inside her burst. Fluid gushed down her leg and Gwyneth's women glanced to their mistress. A couple moved forward but stopped dead, as if at her signal. Edyth stood panting, alone, gathering her strength. Fear was rushing through her as fast as her womb had emptied but there was no way she would give any of these cats the satisfaction of seeing it. She drew herself up and faced them.

'I will tell my husband what a great help and comfort you were to me in the birthing of his heir. Good day.'

Another pain was clawing at her but she forced herself to

walk to the door. Wrenching it open, she broke free and stumbled into the courtyard. John was at the far end rolling a barrel towards the hall but the moment he saw her he came running.

'My lady, what is it? Is it the baby?'

Edyth nodded, clenching her teeth against a new spasm.

'Can you help me to my bower? And fetch Becca and send Lewys for the midwife?'

'Of course.'

He swept a strong arm around her waist and she leaned gratefully against him. Behind her she was vaguely aware of some of Gwyneth's clowder emerging nervously from the bower and knowing they were there gave her the power she needed to keep walking away but it was hard.

'Oh God, John, it hurts.'

'I can see that, my lady, but you are strong and you are brave. Lord knows you must be to face Lady Spiteful in her own lair.'

Edyth tried to smile but another pain tore through her and it was with the greatest relief that she reached her bower and collapsed on the bed, curling herself in around the pain. She was only vaguely aware of Becca rushing in and helping her into the loose birthing gown she had not even finished sewing. The girl mopped at her brow with a damp cloth but Edyth pushed it away. What damned good was a cloth? She needed some sort of clamp to pull the thing out. She needed a miracle. She needed this to end.

But it did not. Edyth laboured on, almost delirious in the struggle. The midwife arrived with a young assistant and at some point two of Gwyneth's women – older wives with more compassion, or perhaps just a stronger sense of self-preservation – came too. Still, though, the babe did not let go its grip on her womb.

'Keep going,' they all said. 'You're doing so well. You're nearly there.'

It was all nonsense. Edyth seemed to be nowhere near there. She just wanted to drop down and sob but the endless pains gave her no respite to even do that.

'I can't do it!' she cried.

'You can,' came the determined chorus, then suddenly there was a commotion outside and a rustle of excitement ran through the women, rapidly turning to alarm as the door slammed open.

'Cariad.'

'Griffin!' Edyth threw herself at him. 'Your damned child is turning me inside out.'

'You will master it,' he said, his voice ringing round the bower, sounding somehow so much more convincing than everyone else. Edyth clung to him and the women fluttered nervously.

'Sire,' one of them dared to say, 'you should not be in here.'

'Why on earth not? My wife is giving birth to my child. It seems to me that I am the very best person to be in here.'

The women cowered back and Edyth nearly laughed, save that her body was torn by a new pain, even fiercer than any that had gone before.

'I feel it,' she cried as a great weight seemed to press between her legs. 'I feel it coming.'

At that no one challenged the king further.

'On the bed, my lady,' the midwife said but Edyth shook her head and gripped at the bedposts.

'Here. I want to do it here.'

'But—'

'Here!' Griffin roared.

Quickly the women laid sheets beneath Edyth and hovered, knees bent, like boys waiting to catch a pig's bladder.

'Push,' the midwife urged and Edyth pushed.

It hurt like the devil himself was pushing his way out but it was a relief to actually do something with the pain and Edyth fought with it, bearing down and gritting her teeth. Through the mist she heard someone call, 'the head, I have the head' and then, on a last great push, she felt the babe slide from her and her whole body grow still. She collapsed against Griffin who held her tight though she could feel him shaking like a ship in a storm.

'You're afeared,' she found the breath to tease.

'I admit it. I'd rather fight ten battles than go through that again.'

Edyth felt tears and laughter blurring in her eyes but everything cleared as the midwife lifted the cleaned baby.

''Tis a boy, my lady. 'Tis a son, a gift from God.'

'May He be praised.'

Edyth felt her husband's chest swell with pride as he took in the clear evidence of his male heir. Tenderly he dipped his big, copper-crazed head to kiss him and though the babe blinked, he did not flinch.

'Ah,' Griffin said, 'he is brave. That is good. A prince needs to be brave. Here, cariad.'

He stepped back a little and, unclasping a gleaming gold band from his upper arm, set it softly on the boy's tiny head.

'Tush now,' the midwife clucked, fingers plucking nervously at her cream skirts, 'he is but a babe, Sire.'

'Nay,' Griffin admonished, 'he is *my* babe and he is Wales' future king – is he not, Edyth?'

Edyth nodded. Pride and delight and relief were swirling inside her and she fought to find something worthy of the moment to say but for herself her baby's shiny crown was as nothing to his little eyes as they stared wonderingly up at her, as blue as his father's.

'A son,' she whispered, gathering him into her arms. 'I have a son.'

Then she burst into tears.

CHAPTER THIRTEEN

Coventry, October 1057

*E*dyth could scarcely believe she was back in England. She'd only been away two and a half years but already she felt like a stranger. She'd been sad when the news of her grandfather Earl Leofric's death had come to Rhuddlan but had seized at the chance to finally return to Edward's court for the funeral. Somehow, though, it all felt different now.

Her gowns, though sumptuous, were of Welsh fabric – soft and strong but not quite as fine to the discerning eye as those of the English ladies. Few traders dared travel as far west as Rhuddlan so the high-quality wools of Flanders and Italy or the rich silks of Byzantium rarely made it to Edyth's seamstresses. On his summer raids Griffin often brought her back beautiful jewels and fine wines but it would not occur to her warrior husband to look for fabrics and why, indeed, should it? Welsh wool was beautiful.

Even so, Edyth could not help stealing envious glances at the new fashions. Many women were wearing gowns with extravagant triangular side pieces sewn into their skirts to make them swirl elegantly around their legs as they danced and she felt the restriction of her own tighter design like a reproach. Others had gowns cut in some clever way to pull tight at the waist without the need for a girdle, making the wearer's own slim lines clear to all. Not that such a style would benefit Edyth at the moment, she reminded herself, for she was carrying Griffin's second child and her belly was swelling enough to rob her of any waist – though not enough to make it clear this bulge was more than just Welsh ale.

Sucking in her stomach, she ran her hands over the costly chains of gold looped between her jewel-studded shoulder-clasps for reassurance. She was a queen and she must carry herself as such. Even so, she felt as if all her old acquaintances had taken a step sideways, not far enough to be out of sight but definitely enough to make her stumble constantly to find her place amongst them and, disorientated, she looked around for her son. Griffin had named him Ewan – God's gift – and he had been a gift indeed, more company than she'd thought possible of a child, both in Wales and now here in the swirling English court. She'd left her lively toddler with his proud young Uncle Morcar just a moment ago and now she spotted them surrounded by the young women of Edward's court.

'Listen to him!'

'Isn't he sweet.'

'Like he's singing. He's an angel!'

Ewan flashed his admirers his cutest smile.

His father's son, Edyth thought ruefully and felt a pang of loss for her husband, for Griffin was not with her. He'd excused himself, suggesting that the man who spent his summers raiding England's borders might not be welcome at its court and pleading concern for rebellion in the south now that Gwyneth had been returned in dishonour. Edyth had accepted this, secretly believing she might find King Edward's court easier without her bluff husband at her side, but in truth she missed him. She had forgotten how tired pregnancy made her and now, with her grandfather's funeral on the morrow, she felt more vulnerable than ever. Craving her son, she rushed over and took him into her arms.

'Mam!' he cried and his admirers giggled again.

'Is that Welsh?' one asked, peering at Ewan as if he might have come down from the North Star.

'It is,' Edyth said haughtily.

'As you are now, Edyth Alfgarsdottir?'

'I am Queen of Wales, yes.'

That shut them up, for a moment at least. Edyth looked around their faces, vaguely recognising some of the girls she'd once played with at Crownwearings, but struggling to recall any names. Twelve-year-old Morcar had ducked off after a pastry tray and she was left here feeling awkward and vulnerable, especially when they so clearly knew her.

'The language sounds so strange,' another girl said, pointedly smoothing down her full skirts, 'so ancient. Earl Torr says the Celts are an old, old people.'

'That's right – long established in this land.'

'That wasn't how he put it.'

They all giggled again, delicate English tinkles that set Edyth's teeth on edge.

'From what I heard,' she said, 'Earl Torr was more than happy to spend time with the Welsh when he went on campaign there, especially the Welsh girls.'

'Lucky them. Have you seen his emblem – the sharpened spear? Well, I hear his spear is not just sharp but long!'

The others sucked in delighted breaths.

'Ooh, Sophie, careful. The Lady Judith is just there.'

Sophie! Edyth remembered her now – the Lord of Thanet's daughter. She'd been a quiet little thing when she'd last seen her but the girl had clearly grown out of that. Her friend – possibly Lady Emily of Canterbury, though she too had blossomed from a skinny ploughshare of a girl into a curvaceous young woman – pointed to Torr's wife, talking earnestly to a bishop nearby, and they all giggled madly again. Would she have been this way if she'd stayed in England, Edyth wondered, with nothing more to worry about than fashions and friendships and husbands? If so, it felt a world away. She looked desperately around for escape and finally caught a glimpse of a gown even less fashionable than hers in a meadow-sweet colour that looked enticingly fresh amongst the cloying riches.

'Svana!'

'Edyth! Lord be praised. It's so good to see you.'

'And you.'

Edyth set Ewan down and grasped her friend's hands, drinking in the sight of her after nearly three years apart.

'You are counting my wrinkles, Edyth – I am grown old in your absence.'

'Nonsense. You look the same as ever and indeed – though your letters have been a godsend to me – you are far lovelier in person than in writing.'

It was the truth. Svana did perhaps look a little older. Her hazel-gold hair carried tints of silver now and life had sketched itself in tiny lines at her temples, but her grey eyes sparkled as brightly as Edyth remembered and her slim frame was as lithe and graceful as ever. Now she bent to Ewan.

'And this must be the Prince of Wales?'

Ewan held tight onto Edyth's leg but smiled at Svana and when she held out her hand he took it as solemnly as a grown-up.

'Ewan,' Edyth said, bending down too, 'this is the Lady Svana, Mama's very best friend in the whole of England.'

'Surely not,' Svana said softly over the boy's head.

'Surely so,' Edyth countered, glancing up at the gossiping courtiers all around them. 'I'm so pleased you're here, Svana. I was beginning to feel quite . . . adrift.'

Svana laughed and leaned in.

'Fret not, Edie. Everything these women do is designed to make you feel different, unsure – wrong. They're experts at it.'

'So what's the answer?'

'Simple – talk to the men.' Svana grinned cheekily. 'Firstly, they don't judge, especially if you're as pretty as you are. Secondly, it really, really annoys the women.'

Now Edyth laughed too.

'I shall try it, though I should like to talk with you.'

'And I you but that's permitted because I'm not a woman – I'm a witch.'

'What?'

A server passed by with a tray and Svana, apparently flustered by her own words, rose swiftly and grabbed a honeyed pastry, busying herself breaking it up for a delighted Ewan. Edyth rose too, waiting pointedly, and eventually her friend met her eye again.

'That's what they say, Edie – that I've bewitched Harold.'

Edyth shook her head.

'What nonsense. I confess, Svana, I once thought you something of a faerie queen, but your charm for Harold, as far as I can see, is all human.'

'Oh no. No, they won't believe that. They are desperate for any excuse to remove him from me.' She leaned in. 'They are talking of him as the next king, Edyth.'

'King? Why?'

'Edward has no heir and his only interest now seems to be in the new abbey he is designing for Westminster. It will please God, I am sure – or, at least, *he* is sure – but it will not keep back the wolves who prowl beyond the sea. Duke William of Normandy seeks a kingdom and Harald Hardrada has never been one to rest on his own throne. He is married to a princess of Kiev, you know, and looks to make her Empress of the North.

The council fears for England's safety should anything, God preserve us, happen to the king.'

With a jolt Edyth remembered Torr's talk of such matters back before she had travelled to Wales. It had seemed foolish back then but Edward was over fifty now and the threat was less easily dismissed.

'But why, Harold?' she asked.

'Lord knows. He does not encourage it. Indeed, he spent months on the continent last winter seeking out the king's cousin. He dragged him all the way out of Hungary only to have the wretched man die within days of setting foot in Westminster.'

'Oh dear.' Edyth looked down at Ewan, licking honey from his fingers and glancing hopefully at the still-laden platters on the table. 'Does he have children?'

'Yes, three, one a boy – Edgar – but he's a mewling little thing, not like this chap.' She ruffled Ewan's red-gold locks. 'The only one of them fit for rule, if you ask me, is the middle one, Margaret, but she's a girl so no use to anyone.'

'Svana!'

'You know what I mean. She cannot rule.'

'I don't see why. Griffin says I could do anything if I set my mind to it.'

Svana smiled.

'All goes well at Rhuddlan then, Edie? You are content?'

'I am, though it seems,' she added, noticing two women pointing at her, 'that I am grown a curiosity.'

'I told you,' Svana said, 'talk to the . . .'

'Men,' they finished together.

'What men?' a deep voice demanded and the women jumped guiltily apart.

'Harold!' Delighted, Edyth hugged the Earl of Wessex but

his broad back felt stiff against her hands and, embarrassed, she pulled away. 'I'm so sorry, my lord. I forgot myself.'

'Then I am glad of it.' He pulled her in again, squeezing her so tightly her feet lifted from the ground. 'And I am glad to see you well. The way my wife talks anyone would think your father had fed you to a monster.'

'Harold!' Svana protested indignantly.

'I confess,' Edyth said quickly, 'that I thought Griffin might truly be the devil the first time I saw him, but he is not.'

'Devilish enough,' Harold spat, 'especially if you live in the Marches. There he slaughters all he comes across.'

Edyth took a step back at his sudden dark tone.

'My husband is prone to exaggeration,' Svana said swiftly but Edyth had caught the change of mood and felt dizzied by it.

She pressed her hand to her belly and the welcome flutter of life inside steadied her.

'You are with child,' Harold said, shifting subject smoothly. 'God bless you. And you have a bonny son already.'

He crouched down to talk to Ewan who went gladly to him, reaching up a podgy hand to play, wide-eyed, with his sand-blond hair,

'He's not used to such fairness on a man,' Edyth said as Harold winced at a curious tug.

'You think me fair, Edyth, Queen of Wales?'

'I think your *locks* fair.'

'Ah! Shame.'

Svana shook her head.

'Harold is used only to adulation. Every unattached woman here wants him for her husband.'

'He is *your* husband, Svana.'

'We are but handfasted.'

Her voice was light but Edyth heard the pain.

'You are the most tightly joined pair I know,' she said stoutly.

'Thank you, Edyth,' said Harold, standing again. 'At last someone that agrees with me.'

He turned to summon his bondsman, Avery, with wine and Svana clasped Edyth's arm urgently.

'Do you think I should spend more time at court, Edyth – with Harold?'

Edyth blinked.

'I'm not sure. Do you?'

'With Harold, yes, but I hate it at court.'

'Sometimes I hate it in Wales.' Svana stared at her and Edyth noticed, again, the shadows of lines on her beautiful face. 'I'm sorry. It's different. I do not have lands of my own, I—'

'No, Edyth, it is not different. You are right. I will make more effort. I will travel more and keep my husband close lest one of those cats sink their claws into him.'

'Why not marry him?'

'Love prefers to be free. If he cannot stay true without Roman bonds he is no good for me.'

'Oh Svana, the Roman bonds are not to keep Harold, but to bind up the rest of the world.'

Svana looked close to tears and Edyth had no idea what more to say so she was hugely grateful when Harold turned back with drinks and her friend visibly gathered herself.

'A toast,' Harold proposed, 'to the glorious memory of Earl Leofric. May he rest in peace.'

'Peace?' little Ewan echoed curiously and Edyth hastily passed him another pastry.

'Earl Leofric,' she said firmly and they all drank.

Coventry Cathedral was packed. Commissioned just ten years ago by the earl whose tomb would now stand at its centre, it was spacious and modern in design but never intended to house the entire court. The lords and ladies were squeezed against each other like eels in a barrel to mark the passing of the great man. Edyth stood at the front with her family, her fine Welsh crown as heavy on her head as her heart felt in her chest. She was sure everyone was staring at her.

'Nobody likes me any more,' she whispered to Edwin.

Her brother leaned down to her. He was as skinny as ever but, now fourteen, he had grown taller than her and his ever-solemn face was shadowed with the first wisps of a beard.

'You're a queen, Edie,' he said simply, 'of course nobody likes you. They're all jealous as hell – especially in that crown.'

Edyth touched her fingers to her magnificent diadem and felt Griffin's power beneath them. Thank the Lord he'd insisted she bring it; however outmoded her dress, no one would sneer at her in this.

'Griffin had it made for me.'

'He must value you very highly.' Edwin paused then added, 'We are next, you know.'

'Sorry?'

'Now that Grandfather is dead we are next. Brodie is glad of it, he is twitching for power, but I am not so sure.'

Edyth squeezed his arm.

'You need not be sure, Edwin. You are young yet and a second son. You have years to enjoy yourself and you should. You have ever been too serious. Do you have a sweetheart?'

Edwin shook his head furiously.

'No. Marc's the one who's always running around with the girls.'

Edyth wasn't surprised, for her youngest brother, though only twelve, had matured fast, growing nearly as tall as Edwin and already broader across the shoulders. A handsome boy with a mop of curly hair and a wicked twinkle in his tawny eyes, he was definitely one to enjoy himself and Edyth was glad of it; there was too much sorrow in the world. Instinctively she looked to Lady Godiva. Her grandmother held her head as high as ever but her sharp eyes were swollen at the edges and her handsome face was lined with grief. Moving closer, Edyth offered her arm. Godiva glanced down, hesitated, and then took it.

'I loved him well, Edyth.'

'And he you, Grandmother. You were lucky.'

Godiva smiled softly.

'That's exactly what he used to say and I am glad, in some ways, that he has departed a peaceful England. Storms are coming, Edyth – can you not feel them?'

Edyth thought carefully. It was certainly true that the court seemed to be turning. Earl Leofric had commanded central England through the reign of four kings and had been the last of his generation of great counsellors. With him gone, the council would be led by the younger earls – Alfgar, Harold and Torr – and uneasy rumblings behind pavilion walls suggested that only Harold was truly trusted. Earl Torr, it was said, was taxing his northern subjects to fund his southern hunting estates where, more and more frequently, he spent his time. Her own father was known by all to be volatile and she was heavily aware of barely whispered concerns about his close associations with the 'wild Welsh', of which she was now considered one.

'I have not been here,' she muttered to Godiva.

'So you will see all the more clearly now.'

'The court does feel . . . uncertain.'

'That is it exactly, Edyth, and spies will report that to the predators over the seas. It is this matter of an heir riling us all. England is not satisfied to have her present secure but must

sew up her future too. Still, it seems you have done that for
Wales. You must be proud.'

'I am.'

Edyth was grateful for Godiva's understanding. So many
others at court seemed to think of her marriage country as
nothing more than a predator on their own. She wanted to say
more but now Earl Leofric's coffin was being borne into the
cathedral and the great choir of monks was singing and she
had to content herself with squeezing her grandmother's arm
as they saw her husband to his rest.

The court lingered in Coventry, encouraged by Godiva's elaborate hospitality and Alfgar's childish enthusiasm for his new
role as Earl of Mercia, and Edyth lingered with them. November
marched in, yanking frost across the land, and it became
madness to delay, but delay she did. Every morning she woke
knowing that she should order her baggage prepared but every
morning she found reasons to stay. She missed Griffin still but
life was so familiar in the English court and her small train,
most notably young Becca and Lewys, seemed in no hurry to
leave its pleasures.

She told herself it was important Ewan became familiar with
his maternal relations but in truth most of her family commit-
ments were despatched within an hour of breaking fast and
after that she spent her time with Svana, who lingered also.
Together they took the children out riding, Ewan and Crysta
tucked safely in before their mothers and Svana's older boys
riding free and, at times, wild. They ate in quaint little inns
and bought trinkets from traders, and one ice-bright Sunday
they seized the chance to confirm Edyth as little Crysta's
godmother.

It was a simple ceremony, performed, at Svana's behest,
beneath the open skies in the frosty garden of Coventry's

Benedictine abbey. The only people there with Edyth and the kind-faced monk who offered the fur-swaddled child to God were Harold, Svana and their older children, and in the quiet of that morning Edyth felt as if she had been drawn into the family's world as magically as at the long-ago wedding but with more solidity, more reality. That same night, though, she watched a heavy sun set over the west and knew she was stealing time.

'Will you head for home soon?' she tentatively asked Svana a few days later, as they walked into the bustling Coventry market beneath grey skies.

Svana looked almost shy.

'I think I will remain in the west until Yuletide,' she admitted. 'It seems foolish to trek the children home only to turn back for Gloucester within a week or two.'

Edyth clasped her friend's hands.

'That's wonderful, Svana. I'm sure Harold will be delighted to have you with him for so long.'

'If I stay sweet-tempered.'

'Oh Svana, you are always sweet-tempered.'

'Not recently. I think I am with child again, Edie.'

Edyth flung her arms around her friend.

'You too? That's wonderful.'

Svana hugged her back.

'It is, though I do not seem to be carrying as well as you, my sweet. I have been sick as a dog this morning and feel ridiculously dizzy at times. That, mind you, may be from the spinning conversations in the bower. Do you know I heard them saying yesterday that you spend your time in Wales in bacchanalian orgies?'

'If only that were true. Perhaps I should ask a few to visit – just to see them try and wriggle out of the invitation.' She swallowed. 'I should really travel back, you know.'

Svana bent to pluck a brave winter anemone from the ground, playing with its delicate petals as a child might.

'Must you?' she asked. 'Could you not stay on for Christ's mass? Ewan and Crysta are so sweet together.'

Edyth took the mutilated flower from her friend.

'You know I cannot. Griffin would be angry. Lord knows, he is probably already angry.'

'Angry?' Svana looked up sharply.

'Not like that, Svana. He is not a violent man, not in his own home anyway.'

'But out of it he is vicious,' Svana countered. 'Truly, Edyth, you may not see it but Harold does. He says the people of the Marches are terrified of the Red Devil and he must ride to Hereford soon to inspect their new defences before your husband starts terrorising them again. He worries you are blind to Griffin's murderous ways.'

Edyth drew herself up.

'I thought it was just the gossips who spoke of me so.'

'Oh Edyth, please, I do not mean it cruelly.' Svana grabbed Edyth's hands urgently in her own. 'I am just afraid for you. Griffin's attacks on England grow more impudent every year. Soon he will have to be subdued.'

'Subdued?!' Edyth asked sharply.

'That's what Harold says.'

'Is it now?'

'Don't be angry, Edie.'

'I am trying not to be.' Edyth looked at her dearest friend, the woman whose letters had sustained her through several dark Welsh winters, and felt suddenly lost. 'What would you have me do? Hide with my father? How would that help? And what of Ewan? Wales is his birthright; I cannot rob him of that.'

'I'm sure he could be an earl or, or . . .'

'An earl?' Edyth dropped the little flower and stamped on it. 'An English earl is better than a Welsh king, is that it?'

'Not better, Edyth, just – safer.'

Edyth tossed her head.

'Ever, Svana, you worry about what is safe. What if I don't want to be safe? What if I want to *live*? What if I love my husband? What if I love his country? Have you considered that or are you, like all the rest, too wrapped up in the unquestionable wonders of England?' Svana sank back against a tree, suddenly looking like the fragile, otherworldly sprite Edyth had once considered her, and she felt instant remorse. 'Oh Svana, I'm sorry. The babe – you are not well. Can I . . . ?'

But Svana brushed her proffered arm aside.

'Nay, Edyth, do not apologise to me. It should be the other way. My comments were ignorant, foolish – cruel even. You are right, I do prize safety, perhaps too highly. I know Harold thinks so. I irritate him by coveting peace and security and quiet. I am just a backwater girl at heart, Edie. Harold's father knew it but I thought I could prove him wrong. I thought I could be enough.'

'You *are* enough. Harold needs you. He could not be half as daring or strong as he is without the peace you offer him *and* the security *and* the quiet.'

She watched Svana anxiously and, to her great relief, saw a small smile steal onto her friend's lips.

'You are grown very wise, Edyth Alfgarsdottir,' she said, 'and I very foolish. I blame the babe, making me so sentimental that I dispense stupid advice to people who, thankfully, know better than to listen.'

Edyth kissed her but Svana felt frail in her arms and she thought instinctively of Edwin's words: '*We are next.*' Was she ready for that? Was anyone ever ready? Better, surely, just to make the most of now?

'Come to Hereford,' she urged. 'If Harold has to ride out I can go that far in his train and if you come you can stay with us for longer. Oh, say you will, Svana. It is very beautiful and on clear days you can see all the way to Wales.'

'Your Wales?'

'My Wales, yes.'

Svana nodded slowly.

'I would like that, Edyth. I would like that very much.'

'Then 'tis settled. Come.' Edyth held out her arm. 'There is shopping to be done. I need presents to take home to my husband.'

Svana nodded and seized her arm, pulling herself to the elegant height Edyth knew so well.

'And victuals for our journey. 'Tis a long way to Wales.'

'Nay, Svana,' Edyth corrected softly. ''Tis not so far.'

CHAPTER FOURTEEN

Hereford, November 1057

Harold looked at the great stone wall shoring up the western face of Hereford and smiled in satisfaction.

'See, Avery,' he said, turning to his recently promoted squire. 'Do the new reinforcements not look fine?'

Avery wrinkled up his nose.

'They are stone.'

'Yes, Avery, they are stone. It was Earl Ralf's idea.'

'Earl Ralf is a Norman.'

'It is not necessarily a bad thing.'

'His cavalry were slaughtered when the Red Devil attacked.'

'Only because he didn't use them wisely. Cavalry can be very effective – as can stone.'

'If you ask me,' Avery snorted, 'cavalry are about as much use as the mole on my shoulder.'

Now, though, someone else rode up and Harold turned to see Edyth throwing back the fur-trimmed hood of her great riding cloak and looking eagerly around.

'So, this is Hereford.'

'It is. Avery and I were just admiring the reinforcements.'

'Stone,' Edyth said. Avery smirked but the young woman

150

hadn't finished. 'That seems a good idea. I sometimes wonder why we don't use it more.'

Now it was Harold who smirked, before turning uncertainly back to Edyth. Was she teasing? He usually found people easy to read but Edyth, or at least this new, grown-up Edyth, didn't seem to think as others did and he was still puzzling her out.

'Do you really wonder about such things?'

'Why not? I may not wield a sword, Harold, but I'm as much a victim of its path as you – maybe more.'

'You sound like Svana, Edyth,' he told her, glancing back to where his pregnant wife was riding in the wagon with Elaine and the children. 'She thinks men should not fight.'

'She is right but that will not stop you so we must make the best of it. A woman cannot ride out and fight so a town's defences are very much her concern. Perhaps we should have something like this at Rhuddlan, though not many would attack that far west.'

'Griffin thinks himself unassailable?'

'Of course not. He's not stupid, you know. There are many enemies on both land and sea and Rhuddlan is very well defended against them all. You just asked me about stone.'

Her eyes were blazing and Harold put up his hands in mock surrender.

'I apologise, my lady queen.'

She shook her head ruefully.

'Good and don't call me that.'

'It is your title.'

'As Earl of Wessex is yours but I do not use that mouthful every time I address you. Surely you are my friend?'

'I hope so.'

'Then call me by my name.'

'You do not like being royal?'

151

She tossed her head, her honey-blonde plaits lifting in the wind.

'You wilfully misunderstand me, Harold. I am more than happy to be queen but it does not define me. Come now, will you show me this stony city of yours or will we stand outside all night like besiegers?'

She kicked up her beautiful horse – a fine dark mare she called something mystically Welsh – and made for the gates, cloak streaming out behind her.

'She's a fiery one,' Avery muttered.

Harold thought of her tumbling out of the tree into his arms so many years back now and smiled.

'Always has been,' he said and set his own mount cantering after.

There was a grand feast that night and all the local dignitaries seized the chance to dine at their lord's expense. The land hereabouts was fertile but life was tough, for Griffin's brigands were forever skirmishing at their doors. Edyth, Harold feared – or maybe hoped – knew little of her kingly husband's darker orders. She thought 'Red Devil' nothing more than a glamorous nickname, a compliment perhaps, but the people of Hereford knew the truth. Even with the new defences, they had to be very cautious with their supplies, forever shoring up 'in case', and tonight was a rare relaxation for them all.

As the night wound to a close, Harold looked around at his people sprawled out on pallets at the edges of the great hall. Many of the lords and ladies had retired to their homes in the city, bellies full and heads swimming with their lord's ale, but others had chosen to sleep here. Some lay alone, others with their women in their arms and others yet had delved beneath the blankets for something more energetic than sleep.

Harold felt his loins stir and thought longingly of his wife.

He was delighted Svana had ridden west with him but concern for her health gnawed at his enjoyment of her company. She had been grey with fatigue before the meats had even been cleared and he had called the ever-solicitous Elaine to help her to bed but now, as he looked at the humps of couples, his arms ached to hold her. He should go to bed. He *would* go to bed, but first he wanted to try and find out more about the elusive devil king, and Edyth, despite her own lightly swelling belly, was still at his side.

'Will you take a last drink with me, Edyth?'

'I should retire,' she said, 'I have a big journey on the morrow.'

Yet she held out her goblet and Harold beckoned Avery. His squire peeled himself off the wall to pour and Harold shook his head fondly at him.

'Leave the jug, Avery, and be off to bed.'

'Oh no, my lord, I wouldn't dream of abandoning you to serve yourself.'

'It's no matter. You were up very early arranging our travel.'

Still his squire shook his head but then Edyth spoke up.

'Truly, the earl likes serving – he has done it for me before.' Avery coloured. He looked from Edyth to Harold and back again and then, bowing low, backed hastily away. 'Oh dear,' Edyth laughed, 'I fear he thinks I meant something earthier than wine.'

'Some people have such filthy minds.'

She looked at him sharply.

'Do you speak of me?'

'I wouldn't dream of it.'

Edyth smacked at his hand and he laughed. The young men at the fire looked up and then quickly away again. Now they both laughed.

'Bedding you,' Harold said, 'would be like bedding one of my sisters.'

'Oh.'

Edyth's hand fluttered to her necklace and Harold was suddenly aware of the curve of the fine gold chains over her breasts.

'Perhaps not quite like one of my sisters,' he stuttered, his tongue curiously thick as if the air had somehow clogged.

She looked up at him, her eyes dark, but then seemed to shake herself a little.

'I should like to think of myself as your sister.'

He snatched at this.

'Yes.'

'Svana's too.'

'Of course. You are very dear to her.' Still the air seemed tight and hard to breathe and Harold cast desperately round for a way to ease it.

'You already have several sisters,' Edyth offered.

'I do,' he agreed hastily. 'Hannah and Emma are much younger than me but Aldyth and I used to play together all the time when we were children.'

'Queen Aldyth?'

'As she became, yes, thanks to my father's endless petitioning, though it wasn't a happy union at first. King Edward resented my father's power and for the first few years he refused to consummate the marriage.'

'That's why they have no heir?'

Heir! The word tore through Harold; it was all he ever heard these days and he was sick of it. He sloshed wine into his cup.

'At first, yes, but later they tried. They try still but to no avail.' Harold drank deep. 'It is eating my poor sister up inside, Edyth. She feels she has failed Edward, failed England. It is why she hunts so desperately for a substitute.'

'Why you had to travel to Hungary?'

'Yes, godforsaken place. Six months I was gone from England

and for what? To drag some far-flung prince all the way to England just to have him die on me.'

'Was he . . . murdered?'

'No. No foul play, Edyth, just a weak stomach – a weak heart if you ask me and his son looks to be little better.'

He looked across the hall to the fire flickering in the centre of the last group of men. One of them had thrown on fresh wood and it was sending flames dancing up into the air. Harold watched, mesmerised, until Edyth's voice said softly:

'Those sparks remind me of your wedding day. Remember how we danced around the fire? It threw up sparks too and I chased them as if they were fairies.'

'You did?' He glanced at her. Her eyes were glowing with the memory and he let himself drop into them. 'It was rather magical.'

'I thought Svana the faerie queen herself.'

'Some still do.'

'You are lucky to have her – and she you.'

'I'm not so sure about the latter.' Harold looked back at the fire, trying to grasp the man he'd been all those years back, though it was as hard as catching the sparks before they died. 'She hates my "politicking" and yet, somehow, I do it more and more.'

'You are fearful, Harold?' Edyth's voice crept around him so he was barely sure it was even her speaking. 'You are fearful they want you as king?'

Harold sucked in his breath. He couldn't look at her, couldn't let the words connect.

'I am not royal, Edyth.'

'But you are strong. Griffin has birthright over only a quarter of Wales but he rules it all.'

'That's his choice.'

'You choose not to rule England?'

'Yes!' It came out as a bellow and the men at the fire jumped. 'Yes,' he repeated, lower, 'I choose not. My father would despise me for it but I am not my father and I have no desire to rule.'

'Then, Harold, you must withdraw from court a little. Spend more time at Nazeing or on your own lands in the south, for if you do not they will rely on you more and more.'

'They?' Harold whispered.

'Your sister the queen, King Edward, the council – England. I've been away so can consider the situation with the clarity of a stranger's eye and I'm telling you, Harold, that they all look to you to lead. The king is caught up with plans for his new abbey at Westminster, the queen with her nursery of borrowed babes. My father is . . . unreliable and Earl Torr is busy in the north.'

'Ha!'

'And about his own pleasure. You are the only one truly serving England and England will notice.'

Harold shook his head, trying to clear it. Edyth's fingers hovered at her chains once more, sending a strange shiver through him as if it were his own skin they caressed. What did she know? he asked himself crossly. She was but a woman, and yet no one else had dared to challenge him so closely on this matter, not even Svana, and now the subject had been released into the air he longed to grab at it.

'How do I say no?'

'That I can't help you with, Harold,' she said ruefully. 'I fear I am no good at it myself.'

'Edyth Alfgarsdottir, you have come a long way since you fell out of a tree into my arms.'

She flushed.

'Not so very far. I still fall way too often for . . .'

'A queen?'

'I suppose so.'

'Though that does not define you?'

She looked at him curiously and he felt, briefly, as exposed as if he were stood before a ruling council. So what if he was curious about the nature of kingship? It was an important philosophical subject.

'Friends define you,' Edyth said softly. 'Friends and loved ones; people, not titles.'

With that she rose and kissed his cheek before sweeping from the hall. The men at the fire looked up as she passed. Harold saw admiration in their eyes and knew it to be mirrored in his own. Fleetingly the thought of big, lusty Griffin claiming this wild beauty tore at his flesh but he shook such foolishness away and rose to seek his own bed and his dear wife.

CHAPTER FIFTEEN

Rhuddlan, March 1058

'*L*ord Alfgar is come!'

Edyth stared at her maid.

'Lord Alfgar? My father? You must be mistaken, Becca.'

'No, truly, my lady. Lewys has just told me. Look.'

She ran to the window and, reluctantly, Edyth pulled her babe from the teat and crossed to join her. Her second son, Morgan, had been born three weeks ago and, though greeted as exuberantly as his older brother by a proud Griffin, he was proving a far more demanding little prince for his mother. Now his indignant wailing rang out around the whole compound and the new arrivals at Rhuddlan's gate looked upwards.

'It *is* my father! Edwin too. Lord help us, what's he done now?'

'Perhaps he comes to see his new grandchild,' Becca said, taking the still-protesting baby from her mistress.

'I only wish that were so, Becca,' Edyth said grimly, 'but I suspect this visit is not of my father's choosing, whatever words he may gloss it with. I must go down.'

She hastily fastened her dress, wincing as the fabric grazed her still-full breasts. Morgan was a big baby and fed as fiercely as he had bruised his way out of her. Becca was urging her to take a wet nurse and, although she'd chosen to feed Ewan herself, Edyth was considering it for this hungry boy. There was too much for a queen to manage to be stuck in a feeding chair all day and, besides, she needed to return to Griffin's side. For her husband had not lain in an empty bed whilst she had ridden to England and on her return to Wales she had faced lashing rain, a sniggering court and an exuberantly loving husband.

'I missed you, wife,' he'd said, clutching her to him the moment they'd been alone. 'No one else is quite the same.'

'Indeed?' she'd questioned, looking back out of the bower door to where the sultry Lady Alwen had stood alone, her soaked dress clinging to her obvious curves. 'Why does Alwen stare at you so?'

He'd tossed his great mane of hair.

'Why not? Am I not worth staring at? Come, cariad, she is nothing. Just a body. You, you are—'

'You have been bedding her?'

'You weren't here. I am a man, Edyth. I have needs.'

'As do I. You know what I am like when I am with child but I haven't leaped into bed with the nearest wanton.'

'Are you sure?' Griffin had gripped suddenly at her shift. 'You took your time returning to me. Maybe you were getting your share of Englishmen whilst you were home. Some ripe young southerner perhaps, or some Marcher lord looking to get one up on me.'

'Griffin, no.'

Edyth had reached out for him, dismayed, but he had grabbed at her wrist, pulling her fiercely towards him.

'It's not that Harold, is it? The messengers said he'd accompanied you to Hereford. Why was that, Edyth? Couldn't have enough of you, could he . . . ?'

'Griffin, stop!' she'd cried desperately. 'This is madness. Earl Harold was going to Hereford anyway, the Lady Svana with him. It was she who kept me company. I am your wife, Griffin. I am carrying your child. I would never lie with another man – not now and not ever.'

He'd yanked her against him, kissing her fiercely.

'Good. You are mine and mine alone.'

'Not, it seems, alone.' It had been out before she could stop it and Griffin's eyes had turned a stormy grey. 'I'm sorry,' she'd stuttered, 'I'm sorry, Griffin. I'm just . . . just jealous.'

'Jealous?' Griffin had stared at her, perplexed. His voice had softened. 'Why are you jealous, cariad?'

'You might prefer her.'

'Oh, goodness me, Edyth, why on earth would I do that?'

'Look at me, all . . .' She'd gestured to her belly.

'All ripe and gorgeous with my bairn? You are my wife, cariad, my queen. Nothing is more important than that. You are my bread of heaven and you mustn't mind if I have a nibble at the occasional rough cracker for variety.'

'Rough cracker?' Edyth had spluttered, dismay turning to incredulous amusement. 'Only you could call a girl like Alwen a rough cracker.'

'And only you could object to her paltry place in my life. Now, promise me – no more jealousy.'

'No more jealousy,' she'd agreed, chin high.

It had been a lie but one she had held to. A tiny, guilty part of her had recalled her tense late-night exchange with Harold in Hereford and over the long, dark months of winter she had charged herself to love Griffin with renewed commitment, even ferocity. He had responded lustily and now, with a second son safely delivered and spring sunshine creeping back across even these westerly lands, he had eyes only for her. She just hoped her fiery father wasn't going to ruin her new-found peace.

Taking the still-wailing Morgan back, she made for the stairs, moving as fast as her aching body allowed, and out into the compound. Griffin was striding from his great hall and they exchanged glances as they came together to greet their guest.

'King Griffin. Sire!' Alfgar bowed low before them. 'Well met, man, well met. Pleasure to see you looking so hale, my daughter too. And who is this bonny lad? Another heir for Wales, I see. She's done well, has she not, my Edyth?'

'Very well,' Griffin said smoothly as Morgan, startled by his loud grandfather, grew silent at last. 'I treasure her.'

'As you should; she is an angel.'

The English earl's voice was strident, his cheer clearly forced, and as Griffin led him to the hall, Edyth turned gratefully to Edwin. Her brother looked gaunt and hunched, keeping a much lower profile than the blustering earl.

'What's Father done this time?' she hissed.

Edwin shrugged his slim shoulders.

'I'm not sure. It was in a closed council and he won't speak of it. It's something to do with Lane Godwinson getting an earldom. Father could just about accept Lord Garth being granted East Anglia when he relinquished it to rule Mercia, but now Lord Lane has taken command of Kent and he's convinced it's some sort of conspiracy.'

'And is it?'

Edwin rubbed a hand across his thickening beard.

'Partiality perhaps but to Father that is much the same. With Brodie about to turn twenty-one he wants a title for him and he's prepared to fight for it as hard – and as rough – as he used to fight for his own.'

They both winced at the memory of the horrific council of 1055.

'Will he never learn?' Edyth moaned.

'I don't know, sister, but I think they put him up to it.'

'Who? Who put him up to it, Edwin?'

'The Godwinsons. I overheard Earl Torr laughing to some girl about Father's temper and I swear he riled him in council. It's not hard.'

'No, but why would they do that?'

'Why d'you think? Mercia is the only earldom not controlled by their family. We are the only ones who can stop them taking over the whole of England.'

'They won't do that.'

'Who says?'

'Harold.' Edwin looked curiously at her and Edyth felt herself blush. 'He told me himself on the ride to Hereford after Father's investiture. He seemed very sincere, Edwin.'

'He is good at that.'

'No, he – ' Edyth stopped herself. 'They are stupid to rile Father. Now he will just take Griffin and attack.'

'Perhaps they want that too.'

Edyth stared at Edwin in horror as they moved into the hall.

'Why would they?'

'Justification.'

Edyth did not ask more; she understood all too well. King Edward was looking for a reason to stamp on Griffin and if his armies took her irascible, forceful father at the same time then even Harold would not mourn the loss. *Even Harold!* She mocked her own partiality; ever she remained naive.

'I love this country now,' she said softly to Edwin.

'I see that, sister, and I cannot blame you. I'd forgotten how beautiful it is. I would like to ride on the beaches with you before we leave.'

'I'd enjoy that very much, Edwin.'

'And I'd like to see the mountains. Have you been into the mountains?'

Edyth shook her head, her eyes still fixed on the men. Several times Griffin had tried to persuade her to take a trip out to see the great Eryri but she had resisted the pull of the dark peaks.

'Not fearful are you, Edyth?' Edwin probed.

'Not of the mountains, no, but maybe of Father. What is he doing now?'

Alfgar was pacing around the king, talking hard and gesticulating wildly.

'Plotting,' Edwin said wearily and, watching, Edyth knew her brother was right.

She clutched her baby tight against her chest, fearing her peace was, indeed, at an end with her volatile father's arrival in Rhuddlan. And then, barely a week later, it was shattered completely.

'*Llychlynwyr*!' The cry went up from the guard tower, shrill and urgent. '*Llychlynwyr*! Vikings!'

In the compound, the men raised their heads from combat practice and up in the bower the women rushed to the window opening on the seaward side.

'It *is*,' Becca confirmed in a horrified whisper. 'It is Vikings.'

'God help us, they will rape us all!' Alwen screamed, looking, Edyth thought cattily, as if she might welcome this. Griffin had ignored the Welsh woman since Morgan's birth and sultry had turned to sulky as she fell from favour.

'Why us?' another wailed. 'Why Wales?'

'Why not,' Becca shot back, though she was shaking.

'We must arm ourselves,' Edyth said. 'We must barricade the door and find what we can to defend ourselves. The king and his men will fight to keep them from the compound but we should be prepared.'

She grabbed the poker from beside the brazier and brandished it in a show of bravery. The other women looked around but there was little more in the room save needles – sharp, yes, but hopelessly short. Edyth's heart pounded. Morgan was squirming in her arms and Ewan had buried himself in her skirts. What would happen to her little princes if Vikings overcame the men? Edyth remembered Griffin's words that magical day on the beach so long ago: '*I could be king for another twenty years, Edyth, or for just a few more hours.*' Had those last hours come? And with her father and Edwin here too. Fleetingly Edyth thought of her mother and prayed Meghan would not lose them all.

Her women were cowering either side of the big window opening, risking timid peeks out, like mice from a hole, but if the Vikings were truly coming there would be no hiding. Edyth had to see what was happening. She strode back to the window and stood dead centre, focusing on the sea, some half a mile from the palace but clear to the eye on this bright morning.

The Vikings were sailing their sleek longboats between Griffin's tethered fleet. There were three vessels, two of average size, maybe fifty men, but the third was a vast ship, boasting a great dragon's head at its prow, mouth carved wide to spew scarlet flames towards the shore. All three sailed on towards the beach, out of view, and within all too short a time soldiers began to appear up the cliff path, bright shields flashing in the spring sun.

Directly below the window their own Welshmen were hastily assembling before the small back gates, pulling on helmets and buckling swordbelts. They were a formidable group but the lines of Vikings on the cliff seemed, from this distance, to swell relentlessly. Then suddenly four trumpeters rang out a volley of triumphant notes and a huge figure rose almost magically over the line of the cliff. Edyth sucked in her breath. It couldn't be – could it? Becca looked at her and she saw the same horrific possibility in her maid's eyes.

'Harald Hardrada,' Edyth breathed.

'I have only heard tales,' Becca said, 'but I fear it is him. Lewys says the men speak of him round campfires like a monster of the night. They say he is as tall as a mountain and as white as snow. They say he has legs like oaks and can wield a sword bigger than any other man's. They say he has eyes like a storm and a scar down one side of his face from his eye to his lips as if God – or the devil – had drawn a line between them. They say—'

'They say too much, Becca. Hush, you are frightening everyone.'

'*I* am frightening them? 'Tis not *I* on the clifftop brandishing a blade.'

Edyth waved her to be quiet and leaned out over the wooden sill to confirm what she thought she had seen. She smiled.

'He's not brandishing a blade, Becca,' she said, turning, 'but a flag. He is waving a white flag.'

The women crushed into the window opening in a clamour of joy and relief and even, Edyth noted with amusement, with murmurs about changing into better gowns to receive the 'honoured guests'. For the moment, though, they were all glued to their vantage point as the guardsmen rushed to crank open the slim back gates and the Viking horde pounded through. The white flag was being waved high and the Northmen had their swords sheathed and their huge shields strung across their backs, but still they were a sight to chill the blood.

Swathed in large cloaks and strung with furs against the sea chill, they seemed even stockier than nature had created them. They wore their hair and beards longer than the boldest Saxons and many of them were so blond it was as if the sun had bleached the colour from their locks. On their heads they wore plain steel helmets with long nose-pieces that cast their eyes into unfathomable shadows and as they lined up in sharp battle order across the compound, Edyth longed to be able to find a sturdy chest and hide within it. She was queen, though, and she must go down and receive these . . . these soldiers. Swallowing back the bitter bile that had risen in her throat, she thrust Morgan at his nurse and sought out her own maid.

'My purple gown, Becca – pray God it fits – and my crown. And fast.'

The great party were shown into the hall where Griffin had hastily set up his and Edyth's thrones to receive them. Welsh courtiers clustered along the walls, chattering and bowing and trying not to look nervous and Earl Alfgar fretted at Edyth's shoulder.

'Welcome, welcome.' Griffin spoke in rough, forceful English as he rose to shake his guest's hand.

Edyth stood at his side and tried not to stare but it was hard. King Harald of Norway, long known as Hardrada, or Ruthless, was even taller than Griffin and his white-blond hair was a startling contrast to her husband's coppery locks. He did, indeed, have a scar on his cheek, though faint and not as long as legend would have it, but it was his eyes that held you. *Eyes like a storm*, Becca had whispered, and they did seem to swirl in flinty flecks of grey and yellow towards gaping pupils that pulled you towards him if you looked too long. He moved fluidly for one so large, like a wolf in a night-time forest, and his hands, though calloused from years of sword-grip, were surprisingly slender.

'My wife, Sire – Queen Edyth of Wales.'

Edyth stepped forward and held out her hand. Her knees trembled to curtsey to this great man but she kept her back rigid and her head high so that her crown glowed in the hastily sparked rush lights around the walls. Hardrada kissed her hand gently.

'It is an honour to meet you, my lady. I thank you for your gracious hospitality.'

His voice was cultured, his accent soft and teasing – not just a warrior then, but a courtier.

'It is our pleasure. You have travelled far?'

'Indeed. I have been overseeing some business around the Irish seas and heard great tales of your Red Devil. As we needed a safe harbour on our return to Norway, I thought I would come to see him for myself.'

A smile slid across his face, pulled disarmingly crooked by the scar. He was playing with her – testing her. She knew the game well.

'You won't be disappointed, Sire. Wales is a jewel.'

'Her queen certainly is, though not, I think, Welsh?'

'Welsh now.'

'But not by birth. How goes it in England?'

'You should ask my father,' she said, indicating Alfgar, bobbing eagerly in the background.

'Oh, I will,' King Harald agreed, barely glancing at him, 'but for now I ask you.'

Edyth swallowed.

'I have scarcely been there these last four years, Sire. I am content to dwell at Rhuddlan.'

'And you have exchanged *no* news?'

Despite herself Edyth flushed. Svana's latest letter had arrived but a few days back.

'I have correspondence, Sire, yes, but it is mere women's trifles – tales of gowns and children.'

She smiled sweetly at him and he laughed.

'You do not seem to me, Edyth Alfgarsdottir, to be a woman much preoccupied by such things.'

'You do not like my gown?'

167

He let his rich eyes run slowly over her, lingering at the curve of her milk-ripe breasts.

'I like your gown very much. Griffin is a lucky man.'

'I am.' Griffin seized a chance to break in. 'My wife has but recently given birth to our second little prince.'

'Congratulations!' Hardrada clapped Griffin on the back. 'My first-born son is with me, learning how to be a warrior. Magnus!'

He clicked his fingers and, to Edyth's surprise, a slight, almost fragile-looking boy moved up to his father's side.

'You Norwegians learn early,' Griffin said with a half-laugh. Hardrada frowned.

'Magnus is older than he looks. He was born early.' He peered down at his son as if he were a foal at market. 'He will catch up and he is brave enough.'

'I have killed a man,' Magnus informed them proudly and even Griffin had no ready answer for such an assertion.

He glanced awkwardly at Edyth who forced herself to step forward.

'You must be very proud, Sire,' she said smoothly, 'and you have other children too, do you not?'

Hardrada's eyes caught on Edyth's and he smiled lazily.

'I do. I have two sons and two daughters and, indeed, two wives.'

'Two wives?'

'Yes – why not? Elizaveta, my beautiful Slav princess, is my Roman wife, and Tora Thorbergsdatter is my handfast woman – though I count them equal.'

'And do *they*?' Edyth asked.

'If they know what's good for them, yes.'

Edyth felt herself shiver at the rapid shift in his voice and even Griffin looked taken aback.

'Don't get any ideas,' she said crisply to her husband.

'Just like her mother,' Alfgar put in, rolling his eyes and Hardrada, thank the Lord, laughed.

'I think, my friend,' he said to his host, as the gong sounded to call them to table, 'that you have two wives in one here. I'm sure she is enough for any man.'

His eyes bored into her and Edyth felt herself pinned down beneath his appraisal. She glanced uneasily to her father. He had told her a little of Hardrada's history as commander of the much-feared Varangian guard when she was a child and, like Becca's whispered tales, it had taken on a quality of legend so it felt unreal to be stood before the great man. She forced herself to stay calm as she took her throne and he slid his long frame into the specially placed chair between herself and Griffin.

The servers came forward with their first course – fresh fish with a rich garlic sauce and hunks of soft white bread. They could not usually afford to discard the coarser grains but Edyth had ordered this to be baked specially for the fearsome guests and she was glad of it as Hardrada took a bite and nodded approvingly.

'You say you are returning to Norway, Sire?' she asked politely.

'That was my intention,' he agreed. 'If nothing more interesting presents itself.'

'Oh, I'm sure there is little of interest here for a man such as yourself,' she said quickly. 'Unless you are skilled at birthing lambs?'

His lip curled.

'I think that may be a skill I lack, my lady. My talents are not so much in the bringing of life.'

Edyth drank deeply of the costly Rhenish wine Griffin had brought back from his raids last summer, casting for some way out of this uneasy conversation, but now her father was leaning forward from her other side.

'Your reputation as a warrior precedes you, Sire.'

'I thank you, Earl Alfgar.'

Alfgar coughed.

'Sadly, Sire, I am not an earl at the present time. The fools in the English council are playing with me for their own gain.'

'Really?' Interest sparked in the swirling eyes and for the first time since he'd strode onto their shores Hardrada truly looked at the English exile. 'You seek, then, to make them see sense?'

'I do, Sire. And I seek partners in that mission.'

Hardrada laughed, low and rasping.

'I am no man's partner, *Lord* Alfgar.'

'Of course not, Sire,' Alfgar stuttered, pushing away the calming hand Edyth tried to place on his thick thigh. 'Of course not. What I meant to say was that I seek a leader.'

'A leader. Interesting. Is that not interesting, King Griffin?' He swivelled suddenly to his host. 'Lord Alfgar seeks a leader to mount an attack on the English.'

Griffin instinctively touched his crown. He looked to Edyth and she knew that he was wondering how to tell the great Norwegian that when it came to attacking the English *he* was the leader. He did not find the words in time.

'I was planning on heading home,' Hardrada said, 'but with such a tantalising alternative it would seem a shame to take to the seas too soon.' He glanced around his men who were drinking deep of Griffin's ale. 'A war with the English,' he went on, as if it was somewhere you might ride out to for the day, 'why not?!'

There was nothing Edyth could do to stop them. The three men sailed just a few days later, the Welsh ships riding the waves proudly between the slightly larger Viking craft as they headed for the Mersey river – 'the back gate to England' as Hardrada gleefully called it. They were all in high spirits on their departure but Griffin's men returned alone three months later, muddied and bloodied and crawling with lice and bounty.

'Good Lord, husband,' Edyth greeted him, hustling the boys behind her, 'you look as if you have travelled to hell and back.'

'Mayhap we have,' was all she got in return and, scared by his dark mood, she turned her attentions to bathing, combing and feeding him and his troops.

It was a long job and one carried out for men who had none of the usual exuberance of a returning warband. More stared into their ale than drank it and when the spoils, as was customary, were cast out across the tables, only the poorest soldiers moved to take their share. Edyth stared at the bounty in horror, sickened at the sight of so many domestic tools and trinkets. These were not treasures taken from dead enemies on a battlefield but from innocent people with the misfortune to live in the path of a rampaging army.

'Hardrada is well named,' was all Griffin would say when she quizzed him in the privacy of their bedchamber later. 'He is ruthless indeed.'

Seeing her devil of a husband so cowed scared Edyth more than anything.

'At least he has gone,' she offered, gesturing to the blank horizon over which the great Viking had sailed his dragon boats.

'For now,' was all Griffin would say, 'but I do not think he is a man, Edyth, who is ever truly gone. My only consolation is that he liked the look of England more than Wales, though he left precious little of it behind to return for.'

'And my father?'

'Earl Alfgar is back in Mercia, your brother with him. He

made terms within weeks. Your father talks a good fight, Edyth, but in truth he has little stomach for it these days, unlike the King of Norway. He only left when he feared his haul was growing great enough to sink his precious dragon boats.'

He stared vacantly at the chamber wall as if seeing through to some sort of nightmare beyond and Edyth dared ask no more.

'Come to bed?' she suggested softly and, like a lamb seeking protection from a fierce wind, he came, but for once he was in no mood for sport.

'I fear I have made an error, cariad,' he whispered into the darkness. 'I fear, for once, I have fought too far. I have driven the English too far. They believe it was I who led the Vikings onto them and they will want revenge. We must look to our defences.'

Edyth kissed him softly.

'We will, Griffin. We will make it a priority for the spring but the snows will soon be upon us and they bring a safety of their own. You must rest.'

'Rest,' Griffin echoed, half-asleep, but his voice was strained and even in his slumbers he cried out against the possibility.

CHAPTER SIXTEEN

Nazeing, September 1062

'You are not to write to her.'

Svana looked up from the vellum as Harold strode into the kitchen at Nazeing, shaking wet leaves from his boots.

'Don't be ridiculous, Harold. I must. She will be grieving.'

Harold looked down and Svana went to him, keen to press her point. News had come to the court that Edyth's older brother, Brodie, had died at Rheims whilst returning from a pilgrimage to Rome and she was worried at how her friend would take the sad tidings.

'She is all alone out there, Harry.'

'Not all alone,' Harold said gruffly. 'She has Griffin.'

'But he is not a woman.'

'Indeed he is not, nor a man either. He is a beast, Svana. His raiding was worse than ever this summer and King Edward is furious. I swear he's still smarting from the Viking incursions – they remind him of the raiding on King Ethelred when he was a boy – and with these further attacks he's ordered all communication with Wales halted. How would it look, then, if it was I who defied him?'

'It is not you,' Svana pointed out, 'but I, and I cannot see how a few words of comfort to a friend might endanger the country.'

'It's not a jest, Svana.'

'Indeed it is not. I imagine Edyth is lonely enough without us abandoning her too.'

Harold groaned.

'We are not abandoning her, my sweet. Please try and see. I am truly sorry for the loss of her brother but the situation with Wales is serious. Edward is out for blood and Torr is encouraging him. It's taken almost four years to re-establish the Northumbrian villages that were wiped out to satisfy Hardrada's gold lust and the people aren't happy. Torr has been taxing them at a crazy rate – far more than it costs to rebuild a few cottages – and Edyth's damned husband makes a handy scapegoat. If anyone has deprived her of your comfort it is him.'

Svana went to the fire, stirring away her anger in the oatmeal pot. Once again, it seemed, it was the men who acted and the women who suffered. She heard Harold sigh and felt his arms creep around her waist.

'I'm sorry, Svana. I know it hurts you but Edward wants Griffin defeated. *Everyone* wants Griffin defeated.'

'Everyone?'

'Well, maybe not Alfgar, but he's taken to his bed. Lady Meghan says he's sick with grief.'

'I have no doubt he is.'

Harold inclined his head.

'Perhaps, Svana, but I think he's avoiding military involvement against Wales too. Stupid fool didn't know what he'd taken on riding out with the Vikings but that's Alfgar for you. It's Griffin who's the real problem here.'

'And, as usual, it's you who has to sort that out?' Harold's arms tightened around Svana's waist and she bit down on her usual protests and turned in his arms to look up at him. 'Torr isn't usually one to put himself out for his people,' she remarked mildly.

'That's true enough but he's fearful of unrest and when Torr's fearful he lashes out. He's hot for Griffin's blood and, besides . . .' he rolled his eyes, ' . . . some of the best hunting is in the Marches and he wants it for himself.'

'You don't like him much, do you?'

'Not much. He's a taker. Always has been. He thinks he's owed an easy life and I don't like that, no. Why should I?'

'No reason at all.' Svana reached round and dug her fingers into the knotted muscles around Harold's shoulders; they were tight with tension. 'And I agree, if he had even half your sense of duty he would be a better man.'

'And if I had half his sense of fun you would be a happier wife.'

'No!' She pressed her lips to his neck, nuzzling in against him. 'I don't like Torr's sense of "fun", Harry, and I love you just as you are. You're ten times the husband he is.'

'Even when I'm not here?'

'Even then, though I would rather you did not ride to Wales.'

'It will not be yet, my love, not unless things change. The days are drawing in and Yuletide will soon be upon us. That is no time to make war.'

'For once,' she said, kissing him, 'we are in agreement.'

He kissed her back, lightly at first and then harder.

'Let me send my letter,' she whispered, pressing against him. 'Just this once.'

He groaned.

'Just this once, then,' he agreed huskily, 'and, Svana, I promise you – whatever has to happen to Griffin, I will see Edyth safe. No one will hurt her or her children – no one.'

'Griffin might.'

'No. He loves her, Svana, as I love you. Actually no, no one could love anyone as much as I love you, but somewhere close.'

Svana shook her head, though her mood was softening now she had his approval for her letter.

'You are sweet-talking me,' she accused him with a smile.

'Is that not allowed?' he asked, dipping his lips to her neck. 'You are, after all, very sweet.'

'I'm too old to be sweet,' she objected but now he was smiling too.

'So what are you now that you are so "old" then – bitter?' He squeezed her waist, making her squirm deliciously. 'Twisted?' His hand crept up and tickled beneath her arm until she was helpless. 'Crooked?'

'Harold, stop! Do not tickle me, I beg you.'

'You beg me? Very well then, but only if you let me tickle you somewhere nicer later?' Svana flushed. 'See – not so old now, wife.'

'Not so old now,' she agreed, looking up into his amber-ringed eyes. 'I do love you, Harry.'

'And I you. I cannot stop King Edward ordering war, my sweet, but I can, and I will, bring Edyth safely back if it is the last thing I do.'

CHAPTER SEVENTEEN

Rhuddlan, Yuletide 1062

Edyth looked out across the Yuletide court, trying to absorb the festive merriment. Rhuddlan sparkled with life and colour and her big, bold, resilient husband sparkled with it. He had long since cast off his Viking troubles and was revelling in all he had and Edyth admired him greatly for it. The southern lords had kept their usual distance but all the great and the good of northern Wales had been here for the last two weeks to pay homage to their king and queen and to drink their cellars dry.

Now it was Twelfth Night and they were celebrating the end of the nativity period with a wedding. Becca had finally taken Lewys, newly Lord of Bethseda, as her husband and the court was making the most of the last chance to feast before austerity bit once more. The Yule decorations were still just about in place and the hall was rich with greenery. In Celtic Wales they did not bring in a tree like the English, for trees, Griffin had assured Edyth earnestly on her first year here, held ancient spirits and uprooting them would bring bad luck for the coming year. Ivy, however, apparently sucked the spirits from the trees, so prising it away from the bark earned favour and great swathes of it were always hung triumphantly around the hall.

Edyth had found the creeper unnerving at first, especially when it put out its tiny feelers into the very walls, but Griffin had insisted it represented victory and as that was his favourite thing she'd tried to make the best of it. She had ordered the little leaves daubed with limewash to mimic snow and collected fine gold dust from the king's jewellers to sprinkle into the paint so that it shimmered like magic in the rush lights. Griffin had been delighted the first time he'd seen it.

'You're so clever, cariad,' he'd said, kissing her and on Christmas night he'd taken one of the vines to bed with them to wrap it around her naked form.

'What if it sucks the spirit from me?' Edyth had objected but Griffin had just laughed.

'Nothing could suck the spirit from you, my beautiful girl.'

That had certainly felt true then and she tried to believe it now, though at times this Christ's mass she had felt sadder than she had dared show. Even tonight, with Becca looking radiant, her little princes running around, wide-eyed with excitement, and a sickness churning in her belly that suggested another babe might be on the way, she felt choked.

It had been several weeks now since she had eagerly opened a letter from her mother to find the terrible news of Brodie's death, but still the thought of it froze her blood. She had barely seen her brother since he had ridden off to his first battle with Griffin and knew little of him as a man but his sudden absence had sucked a hole in her world. Her mother's tidings had been taut with heart-wrenching sadness and she had turned gratefully to her second missive, stamped with a familiar laden-vine seal.

My dearest friend,
My heart goes out to you at this sorrowful time and I pray
you can find some comfort in your grief. You should know

that the whole court is in mourning and Harold has ordered prayers said in every church and abbey across England to commend your brother's soul to God.

For myself, my thoughts are all for you. I am not, as you know, one for conventional worship but I have sought God in the trees and in the everyday miracles of continued life and I have asked him to watch over you. I know he will, for you, Edyth, are worth more watching than most.

I pray this letter reaches you across the harsh border that separates us and know that by the time – pray God – it does so, winter will have laid its hand across the land. I fear you will not be able to travel, but perhaps you could ask your husband for a trip to Coventry when the sun returns? Your father suffers sorely and you could be of great comfort to him.

Perhaps, too, you could advocate peace with Mercia at this sad time? Your father has been ever stout in King Griffin's defence and perhaps now the king could honour his grief by honouring his boundaries? It would, my dear, dear friend, be timely. Very timely. In the wake of this sore loss we need, I am sure you will agree, a woman's year of peace to cushion our hearts.

I will write again very soon. With much fond love,
Svana

Edyth had been touched by her friend's concern but it had spiked her grief with fear. A woman's year? A timely peace? It had been a warning, carefully worded to enter her heart unnoticed by prying eyes. She had done little with it during the feasting but maybe, with the New Year, it was time to make plans. She leaned over to Griffin who was indulgently watching some of the youngsters of the court dance to the minstrels.

'I think the English plan to attack soon, Griffin,' she said. 'I think they have had enough of you niggling at their border.'

'Niggling? *Niggling*, Edyth?'

'You understand me well enough.'

'Yes.' He turned to her. 'Yes, I do. You think we should beat them to it? Mount a proper attack. Take Hereford maybe?'

'No!' Edyth grabbed at his hand. 'No, Griffin, I did not mean that. Why not just be content with the kingdom we have?'

'Edyth . . .'

'Wales is a fine country, Griffin, and you have achieved so much here. Do you not want peace?'

'Of course I do but can't you see – that is what I am giving us. Whilst we fight the English we do not fight amongst ourselves.'

'And when the English attack?'

'We will be ready for them. Tonight is the end of the Yuletide feasting; tomorrow we can turn our thoughts to more austere matters. Niggling indeed! Come, cariad, grief is addling your brain. Drink, be merry.'

He poured her fresh wine and she obediently took a deep drink. It was rich and spicy and warmed her stomach if not her heart. Griffin drew her in against him. One of Lewys' fellow soldiers was singing a wedding ditty, ripe and lusty, and her husband's hand slid down to her thigh.

'I hope your maid is as eager into her marriage bed as you were, cariad,' he murmured in her ear.

'I was so young, Griffin.'

He squinted at her.

'You are hardly ancient, Edyth.'

'I have felt it of late.'

He sighed and withdrew his hand, caressing her face instead.

'I know and I am sorry for it.'

'I am told my father is greatly grieved at my brother's death.'

'I am sure that is so. Imagine if it was Ewan, or little Morgan; I'd tear the heavens apart!'

'Why does it always have to be about fighting, Griffin?'

'Why does it not, cariad? I'm sure Earl Alfgar wants to cut down everything in sight right now. We must do all we can to help him. Maybe, come the spring, we can persuade him to bring your family to visit us?'

Edyth's heart leaped.

'Truly? I would like that very much, Griffin.'

'And so, I hope, might they. Their memories of Wales are not, I trust, unhappy ones. You know, cariad, I bless Earl Alfgar every day for bringing you to me. Young Lewys will be lucky indeed if he has as much joy of his wife as I have of mine.'

Touched, she kissed him and he pulled her so tight against him that the whole hall whooped encouragement. Smiling more broadly now, she fought to free herself.

'Unhand me, husband – I wish to propose a toast.'

She rose, rattling her eating knife against her silver drinking cup, and everyone turned her way. The myriad faces were blurred by the smoke from the fire and the steam from the mead and the swirling light from the brave little rush lamps shining from the greenery on the walls but Edyth knew them all anyway. Her people.

'Let us drink,' she said, the Welsh tripping off her tongue like a native. Everyone cheered but she held up a hand to silence them. 'Let us drink to the memory of my brother, Lord Brodie.'

The assembled crowd roared approval and Edyth felt their approbation like a balm to her grief.

'And let us drink also to my husband,' she went on. 'Griffin, King of all Wales. May he rule us in honour for many years to come!'

Now the cheer rang around the hall once, twice, three times. Edyth turned proudly to kiss Griffin but he was pale and his blue eyes were staring unseeing between the ranks of lusty men.

'Griffin?'

'Hush.' He leaped up. 'Hush!'

The lords and ladies silenced instantly. Even the children, at the far end with their maids, stilled, and between them all crept a cry, muffled by the howling wind and snow, but clear as the finest bell: 'Attack! Attack!'

People leaped to their feet, scattering goblets and platters and clattering into each other in their panic. Lewys clutched his bride to him in the centre of the room as all around men snatched shields from the walls and women ran for their children. Chaos ruled.

'Stand still!' Griffin bellowed from his throne. His men froze, though women still skittered to the nursery table. 'Stand still! Do you want to get yourselves killed?' A woman whimpered. Eyes flickered fearfully around the hall. 'Women and children to the back – behind the tables. Men, to arms – three-line formation before the doors. Now.'

Griffin turned to Edyth as everyone swept into action.

'You will manage the women?'

'Yes. Who can it be, Griffin?'

'Prince Huw perhaps? Gwyneth will have been spitting away at him and this is just his sort of sneaky tactic.'

'But it's Yuletide.'

'Not any more, cariad. Don't worry: Rhuddlan is strong and her men even more so. We will see them off. Now – the women!'

It seemed an impossible task, like two tides surging against one another as the groups sought opposite ends of the hall, but at last it was accomplished. Edyth pulled a shaking Becca behind a table as Griffin, flanked by his finest guard, threw open the great doors and the revellers looked out across the compound. There was a stunned silence. Beyond Rhuddlan's huge gates flames seemed to be running down the dark hill. Hundreds of beacons of death were spilling out of the darkness towards them and they seemed to be roaring, a relentless, guttural cry: 'Ut! Ut! Ut!'

'The English!'

Recognition rippled around the hall as men stood, swords bared uselessly against the encroaching flames. Already the first torches were being thrown, whirling through the night sky like flying stars and flaring up in the watchtowers. One caught the thatch topping the left guard tower and it burst into light as men leaped from the window. The court would not be safe for long. If the vast palisade fencing caught, the fire would consume them and with no warning of the attack it was already too late for Griffin's army to march out and cut it off.

Griffin looked down the hall at Edyth, his eyes narrow.

'You knew about this?' he bellowed over the cowering people.

Edyth leaped to her feet.

'No! No, Griffin, I knew nothing.'

'You said they were going to attack.'

'Only because Svana said there were mutterings at court. No more, truly. I have never known men attack in mid-winter.'

'Well, you know it now. We all know it now.'

He squared his great body and as she gazed at it silhouetted against the advancing flames, Edyth thought she had never seen him look more kingly and ached with sorrow that he might think her anything to do with this horror. She remembered what he had told her once – *it's amazing how alive you feel in proximity to your own death* – and realised that he was ever ready for a day like this.

'The bastards have sprung us,' he spat. 'They have broken the Christ child's holy feast and defiled the sanctity of the marriage ceremony. They have brought the devil to our doors.

We have only one choice now – to the boats! And in silence or we will all be cut down.'

'You heard your king,' Edyth said loudly. Every fibre of her being longed to beat her way between the crowd and clutch her children to her but she was queen – she had to lead. 'We must move quickly and quietly and we will be safe.'

'What if they wait on the beach?'

'They will not,' Griffin promised. 'It is too dark to see and they do not know the land. We must thank God for the lack of snow to lighten their way. They can only attack the palace because it is lit up like . . . like Christ's mass. Besides, what choice do we have? Go!'

The women huddled together and scuttled towards the doors where Griffin's men waited to close ranks around them, their shields and swords a tough skin to protect the soft centre of their loved ones. Edyth stepped out into the compound and watched as they were hustled along the shadows of the great hall towards the tiny back exit. She thought of how many times she had slipped out of that secret pleasure-gate on Môrgwynt; now it could save their lives.

Prince Bleddyn had pulled the gate softly open and stood at one side with his brother, Prince Rhys, at the other. Their broad figures imposed quiet and order on the terrified group as they crept out into the dark. So far there was no noise from beyond the wall to indicate that the invading English had spotted the exit of some hundred of North Wales' greatest nobles. Edyth could see torches moving along the hillside, though, and knew it was only a matter of time before they were surrounded and the long, rough track to the snarling sea became a route not to escape, but to death.

She looked to Griffin. He had moved into the centre of the courtyard, facing away from his departing people and towards the flaming entrance of his royal palace. Swallowing back her fear, she moved to his side.

'What are you doing, my lord?'

'My people need time to retreat. Whilst the English think we are cowering inside they will have it. You go.'

'No. I am queen. I stay with you.'

He said nothing but his hand reached out and grasped hers, then he squared his shoulders.

'Who are you that would violate the Yuletide feast?' he called, his voice strong on the crackling night air.

'Men on God's work,' came an all-too-familiar voice over the gates. Edyth caught her breath. 'Surrender, Griffin. Surrender now and you will not be harmed.'

'I am King of all Wales,' Griffin growled. 'I will not surrender to you, Harold Godwinson.'

'You must or we will burn your palace to the ground.'

'You will never burn my spirit!'

'We do not seek to. Simply to tame it.'

'You cannot tame a dragon.'

'You will be consumed by your own flames.'

'Never!'

'Then send me your queen.'

Griffin froze. His eyes locked onto Edyth's – a question – but she did not even hesitate before flinging her response out to the night.

'I stay with my lord.'

'Edyth!' For a second Harold's voice flickered – the man, not the soldier – but then he drew it back. 'I have news. Sad news. Your father is dead. Do you hear that, Griffin? Earl Alfgar, your ally, is dead. There is no one to protect you now.'

Edyth felt pain wrench at her knees and she buckled. Griffin pulled her tight against him.

'He lies,' he hissed.

'Why would he?'

'It is a tactic as underhand as attacking at night, on one of Christ's own feast days.'

'It is and yet it is true. I know it.'

'All the more reason, then, to keep you safe. Come, cariad, our little princes await us in the boats. Let the English bastard have today.'

Edyth looked around her. The left watchtower was a pillar of flame, the fire was licking along the top of the palisade and there were more torches on the hillside, moving close to the seaward side of the palace. The others were gone, down through the long, frosted grass to the safety of the boats less than a mile to the north but her own legs felt too weak to follow.

'It will be a hollow victory,' Griffin urged, 'and we will live to fight again.'

'I am weary of fighting, Griffin.'

'Then you are not the queen I thought you were.'

His eyes, as they found hers, glinted as sharp as steel in the moonlight. Edyth looked deep into them and saw, again, the girl who this great man had crowned.

'I am that queen,' she said. 'I am.'

A great crack resounded behind them as the huge front gate split apart from the flaming watchtower. Swords and axes appeared in the gap, hacking mercilessly at the charring wood. There was a sharp clang as the metal bolt fell to the ground and the gap widened.

'Quick,' Griffin gasped and yanked Edyth out of the back gate. He paused to pull it shut behind them and Edyth had time to look down the yawning darkness of the hillside.

'Where is the path?' she gasped. 'I cannot see the path.'

'Trust me,' Griffin said, clasping her hand again. 'I know it as well as the patterns on my sword handle. Come.'

To their left English torches were flaring dangerously close and behind them roars of fury told them the enemy had already discovered they were gone.

'Trust me,' Griffin said again, and then plunged into the night at speed.

Together they ran, their feet flying over the frozen ground, their royal cloaks streaming behind them like raven's wings. The path twisted and turned but Griffin pulled Edyth securely down its centre, not pausing even when they heard the back gate flung wide and the English soldiers pounding after them. The fierce rustle and scrape of the long grass told them that their pursuers were not as adept at finding their way down the rough hillside as they and they hit the beach unhindered. Four of Griffin's boats were already way out at sea. The fifth hovered uncertainly in the shallows, the oars straining to grasp at the waves and pull them out to the safety of the dark waters.

Griffin swept Edyth into his arms and waded waist-deep into the freezing shallows. She felt the icy water snap at her toes where they dangled and did not know how her husband could bear it. His teeth were gritted and she could feel him shaking against her, but he did not falter until, at last, they were at the boat. Griffin lifted her onto the deck before he was hoisted onto the boat by Bleddyn and Rhys. Instantly the captain gave the order and the oars bit into the water and jerked the big boat away from the shore just as the first English soldiers poured onto the sand.

That night Rhuddlan burned to the ground. The refugees felt the heat of it even from far out at sea and sat, clutched together, watching their precious palace consume itself.

'All that labouring,' Edyth groaned. 'My tapestries, my hangings – it's such a reckless waste.'

Griffin pulled her fiercely to him. The nursery maids had restored the princes to them and now Morgan slept in the curve between their bodies and Ewan sat, fiercely upright, on his father's broad knee, staring in horror at the beacon of fear his home had become. Edyth watched the flames fire in his solemn little eyes and thought suddenly of Edwin. If her father was truly dead he would be Earl of Mercia now and terrified by it. '*We are next*,' he'd told her at their grandfather's funeral and it seemed that next was now here, gripping at her skin as surely as the bitter sea winds.

'It is but a palace,' Griffin said roughly. 'Mere planks and stitches. If that bastard Harold thinks he's destroyed my kingship tonight he's more of a fool than I thought. Here is my rule – here with these people and here in my crown and above all here . . .' He thumped his breast. 'In my heart.'

A ragged cheer went up from their boat and those in the others either side looked hopefully across but soon dipped their heads again. Their concern tonight was not for the future of Wales but for staying alive. There were sealskin sleeping sacks on board but not enough for all and already party gowns and tunics were soaked by spray from the grumbling sea. Edyth looked around for Becca and Lewys and saw them huddled in the prow of the second boat. This was hardly, she thought sadly, the sort of wedding night they would have imagined.

'Where will we go?' she asked Griffin.

'Where the sails take us.'

He gestured up to the great waxed linen sheets bulging in the wind as if they, at least, were glad to be free of the land.

'But—'

'To Ireland, cariad, just for a time. King Diarmid is always willing to offer aid against the English, especially for those who can pay.' He indicated the great locked chest his men had hefted from the hall. 'He will succour us for a few weeks until Harold stops raping my home and then we will return.'

Edyth turned her eyes back to the receding shore. Rhuddlan

blazed more ferociously than ever and they could see the English forces, dark demons against the light, dancing in fury at losing their quarry. Griffin smiled grimly but Edyth had caught another sound on the bitter wind – a whinnying and stamping of hooves on wood.

'Môrgwynt!' she cried, pained.

Griffin's hand closed over her knee.

'Môrgwynt will be safe. Even the bastard English don't destroy good horses and she is one of the best.'

'But she is *my* horse.'

'Not any more.'

His words sat cold upon her, grief upon grief.

'My father is dead.'

The fact dug into her bruised heart like a jagged flint.

'I am sorry for that, cariad, truly. He was a good man. A little impetuous at times but I liked that.'

Edyth nodded but did not dare speak. She watched Harold's men running around in a hell of their own creating, trying to hook herself into this present crisis, but all she could see in the leaping flames were pictures of her father – throwing her in the air as a little girl, taking her up before him on his horse, sitting her on his lap at dinner.

'My best girl,' he used to whisper as she drifted to sleep, lulled by the adults' dull conversations. 'My angel.' And now he was the angel.

Despite her grief Edyth smiled at the image. Her father had been many things but never an angel. He had loved as fiercely as he had lived. He'd made mistakes, yes, but mistakes caused not by foolishness but by passion.

'You made him very proud,' Griffin whispered in her ear and Edyth pictured Alfgar's face when he'd first seen her wearing her beautiful crown and knew it was true. She bit back tears.

'He'd be furious if he saw this,' she said now.

'Furious,' Griffin agreed. 'Earl Harold has tarnished his memory with this barbarism.'

A fresh pain cut through Edyth; what Griffin said was true. She hated that her beloved father was dead, hated that her maid's wedding was spoiled, that her palace was burned and her people in danger. Above all, though, she hated that it was Harold who had done this to her; she'd thought him a better man than that.

CHAPTER EIGHTEEN

Deheubarth, May 1063

'You may hate me all you like – it has ever been thus – but one thing you should know: you need me. *Wales* needs me.'

The crowd muttered violently. It was only a few months since they had fled Wales but Griffin had let nothing stand in the way of reclaiming his country, not even its bitter internal rivalries. Way back when he had first shown Edyth his ships he had told her firmly that they were not so much for escape as to 'regroup and mount a renewed assault' and that was exactly what he was trying to do now. The Welsh, however, were not leaping to his side.

Today they were in the beautiful seaside moot-point at St David's and Edyth's heart was scudding with fear as she faced Deheubarth's greatest nobles. She'd been pleased, fool that she was, when Griffin had told her they would tour his kingdom. He'd warned her time and again how it would be in the south but still it had been a shock. She'd been spat at, jostled and, just a short time back, coated in flour. The coarse grains clung to her hair yet. She could feel them prickling her scalp beneath her hastily changed headdress but she was not going to scratch at them. That would belittle the crown on her head – the crown with the four rubies to represent the four quarters of Griffin's kingdom. She'd always been so proud of carrying his father's dream on her brow but it was only now, eight years after he'd first placed it on her head, that she was realising how much of a dream it still was.

The southern territories acknowledged Griffin's rule begrudgingly. He had told her as much time and again but now she was truly seeing it for herself. In Glamorgan they had been met with icy politeness. The burghers of the city of Cardiff had been cautiously welcoming but the old lords, led by the nephews of the king Griffin had assassinated, had refused to sit with them. Even the people in the street had stood in stony silence as they'd ridden through and it had been even worse in Deheubarth. Now they stood before an assembly of the rich and disdainful elite of this fertile southern territory, led by the snooty-nosed Lady Gwyneth and her slimy nephew, Lord Huw, and their hatred was palpable.

Edyth was weary. She had been long in the saddle and missed Môrgwynt sorely. On their return to Wales she had hunted the ruins of Rhuddlan for her precious mare but, though many of the other royal horses had been found, there had been no sign of hers and she had been forced to ride out on a new mount. She had slept in a different bed every night, and that but little with guards at all four posts and Griffin jumping for his sword at the slightest sound. She felt as if she had not rested properly since before Harold had brought his flames down the hillside to Rhuddlan and could see little chance to do so ahead. She was, indeed, with child again and the babe grew large within her but she was afraid for it. She had thought the people would be pleased to see evidence of another heir for Wales but instead they had booed.

'Do your children not offer them security?' she'd asked Griffin.

'They do not want security, Edyth. They prefer uncertainty
– it is easier to drive a knife into.'

Edyth had thought of England, so desperate for a valid heir
that they had sent Harold all the way into Hungary to dig one
up, and marvelled at the contrast. She and Griffin were offering Wales all the security England craved but they were being
hounded away like outlaws and she was so, so tired.

King Diarmid of Dublin had, as Griffin had anticipated, been
most welcoming, especially when he'd set eyes on Griffin's
casket of jewels. The refugees had been richly clothed and fed
but Diarmid's court had made Griffin's look tame. They'd
dunked wooden bowls into great pots on the fire to fish out
their food and mopped up the mess with coarse dry bread.
They'd drunk a rich dark ale in vast quantities, washing away
the bitter taste with a golden fire water.

Edyth had tried it but once and had felt as if her very innards
were being burned out. She'd coughed till her chest nigh on
burst and King Diarmid had laughed so much he had fallen
off his bench, revealing to all exactly what he did – or rather,
did not – wear beneath the strange woollen tunics they
favoured, and causing even more laughter. Edyth had had to
work very hard not to purse her lips like her mother and had
been hugely grateful when Griffin had declared it was time to
sail for home. Home, though, had been a pile of ashes blowing
about in the last of the winter winds.

'We will rebuild,' Griffin had declared stoutly. 'Rhuddlan
will be bigger and better than before with stone defences and
double ditches. No one will ever surprise me again.'

He'd been so determined, so strong. The new hall had gone
up faster than any could have imagined possible and the royal
bower had followed just as fast. For a few weeks Edyth had
caught sight of some cherished form of normality but then
spies had reported murmurings in the south – rumours that

Griffin was weak and ripe for the taking – and he had not been able to bear it.

'There's no way I'm sitting here waiting to be sprung again. They needn't plot to come to me; I shall go to them.'

And so here they were, the royal family of Wales, with Griffin in full armour wherever he went and the boys, to their delight, kitted out in miniature versions and even Edyth with a cleverly worked chain-mail tunic beneath her gown. It lay heavy on her shoulders and even heavier on her now-bulging belly. It clinked when she moved but she was grateful for it all the same. So far the flour was the worst thing to have hit her but it was impossible not to fear a more damaging missile.

'The English are coming,' Griffin was saying to the gathered nobles of Deheubarth. 'King Edward wants Wales and if you think I am a poor excuse for a king, wait until you see him.'

'If he's so puny, he will never defeat us,' Huw challenged.

'True, but know this, Edward does not really rule in England. Earl Harold does and Earl Harold might well defeat us if we do not stand together. They say he has the greatest army in Christendom and the riches to pay for it, even to march as far as Deheubarth. You are not immune out here, you know. Harold destroyed Rhuddlan. There is no target in the north now and he will have his sights set on Cardiff and Swansea and, yes, St David's.' Griffin swept an arm around the beautiful city in which they now stood. 'Our only chance is to stand against him together.'

The nobles murmured amongst themselves, turning their backs on Griffin, who stood rigid, staring ahead. Edyth could not tell what he was thinking, but her own thoughts were in a whirl. Did *she* stand against Harold? She remembered him walking her into Westminster all those years back. Despite finding her falling out of a damned tree, he'd shown her great respect and she held him deep in her heart for that, so how had they ended up on the opposite sides of such a bitter struggle?

Prince Huw squared up to Griffin.

'We do stand against the English. We will always stand against the English.'

'So you are with me?'

Huw shifted his feet.

'We are with you – for now.'

Griffin held out a hand.

'For now, my prince, will suffice. We must make plans.'

Huw shook his head.

'The plan is simple, Griffin. If the English come to Deheubarth we will defeat them. If they come to Gwynedd, you will defeat them.'

'It's not enough.' Edyth heard Griffin's ready temper flare and tensed. 'Can you not see, man – if the English come they will bring great numbers of infantry, highly trained.'

'*We* are highly trained.'

'This will not be skirmishing, Huw, this will be war.'

'Yes, but on our terrain. We will trap them like mice in a barn.'

The crowd roared approval. Griffin glanced back to Edyth and she saw frustration in his blue eyes and something else too – despair?

'You may trap some,' he tried again, 'but they will keep coming. They mean to annihilate us.'

Huw, however, just smiled.

'Nay, my lord king, they mean only to annihilate *you*.'

Huw was right. Edyth and Griffin were barely back in their newly built hall at Rhuddlan before news came that the great earl had sailed his ships into Cardiff and that the city had surrendered almost before he'd set foot on the beach. From there he marched his army through Glamorgan and on into Deheubarth, making straight for Rhuddlan. Griffin's spies brought daily news, offering it to the floor at their lord's feet, afraid of its terrible power, and all said the same – the brave Welshmen were parting before Harold like the waves before Moses.

'He is putting up stones,' one lad told Griffin. 'Stones inscribed in Latin – *Hic Fuit Victor Haroldus* – and wooden crosses. He is leaving camps around each one to ensure no resistance gathers once he is passed.'

'How can the Welsh do this?' Edyth hissed in the royal bower one night. There was precious little sleeping room in the broken compound and even here their only privacy came from the curtains of their bed, beyond which Griffin's guards slept on pallets. 'Have they no pride? Do they want to be ruled by the English?'

Griffin kissed her quiet.

'They do not want to be ruled at all, cariad.'

'Well, they should and by you.'

'Your good opinion means more to me, Edyth, than you will ever know but I have never expected it from these bastards. Wales is not ready for a single king.'

'So why welcome King Edward?'

'They do not, they welcome . . .'

'Earl Harold, I know, but he fights for Edward. He is not a god, Griffin, just a soldier, like you.'

'Not like me, Edyth, no. Earl Harold has no foolish dreams to drive him. He is a pragmatist – a winner of battles, not a forger of nations. He does a job and, sadly, he does it well. If he wins, Edyth, he will split Wales up again so that we will spend all our time fighting each other and leave England well alone. And it will work.'

'*If* he wins.'

'Which he will not. I will muster the men of the north and we will ride to battle. He will not ride past Caernarfon alive.'

The words chilled Edyth's blood and as Griffin turned Rhuddlan into a battle camp her fear grew. Princes Bleddyn and Rhys marched in with a thousand grim-faced soldiers and news came that more were waiting to join them at Conwy and Bangor. The mood was ferocious against the man who dared to bring the English around Welsh shores and, fearing for Harold's life, Edyth began a tearful letter to Svana.

Even as she was searching for the words to express her sorrow, however, two messengers skittered into the tent-strewn compound, eyes wild and hands shaking as they leaped down from their lathered horses. Gratefully abandoning her letter, she ran from the bower to join Griffin and his brothers in his hall. The Welsh king looked imposing in his war gear with his copper hair flowing from beneath his royal helmet, but he was unusually pale. She rushed to him.

'Griffin? What has happened?'

He gestured to the messengers, both on their knees.

'These men come from my mother in Powys. She is under siege.'

'Siege? But Harold is surely in the west?'

'He is, my lady,' Prince Bleddyn confirmed, 'but our mother is under attack all the same.'

'By whom? Who has invaded?' She turned to Griffin. 'Is it Hardrada?'

'No!' Griffin laughed bitterly. 'No, not Hardrada, Edyth, though he may be at the root of it. It is Earl Torr. He and Harold are working together to trap us from both sides.'

'Torr and Harold? Together?'

'That surprises you?'

'Harold hates Torr.'

'Not as much, wife, as he hates *me*. I knew I should not have taken the Viking into England.' For the briefest moment he looked lost but then his eyes hardened, the aquamarine run through with flint. 'No matter. We will ride east to see off Earl Torr and then we will turn west and kill Harold. No one fights the Welsh in their own land and goes home to tell the tale.'

He kissed her, hard and fast, then strode out to summon his captains. Within but a few hours, the entire camp of soldiers had marched out and the women were left to pace the half-buildings of Rhuddlan. Edyth felt as if she had been plunged, warm from her bed, into ice water but now was no time for shivering.

'Griffin always wins,' she said stoutly to Becca as they closed the curtains on the boys' bed, tucked, for now, into the oppos-ite corner of the bower from her own. 'No one defeats him.'

'Not even Earl Harold?'

'He's not battling Earl Harold.'

'Not yet.'

Edyth dismissed this with a scornful wave.

'This first battle should not trouble our troops too greatly; Griffin will not let a self-seeking, jumped-up idiot like Earl Torr defeat him. He'll be back before Harold gets anywhere near Caernarfon.'

She could not, however, stop herself opening the curtains to check on her boys, as if they might already be under threat and, sure enough, Harold moved with the speed of a hunting hawk. Within two days messengers rode in to say that he had reached the city. Edyth received them on her throne with just her sparse guard and her maid for company.

'What do we do if he brings his army here?' Becca dared to ask as the messengers were shown to the rough camp kitchens for food.

Edyth looked down at her belly, so full now she feared she

might give birth at any moment, and then to her maid's, also sweetly curved.

'We can hardly fight, Becca. We would have to surrender but Griffin will be here. He will not abandon us, I know it.'

She banged the arm of her husband's vacant throne in defiant affirmation and sure enough, as the sun began to set, one of the young guards left on watch shouted out that the troops were sighted. Edyth was out of the hall and up the steps of the half-built watchtower within moments, Becca hot on her heels. As they reached the top they saw men coming over the hillside beneath the great dragon standard.

'They return victorious!' Edyth called down to the other women, amassing in the compound below.

They cheered but Becca was tugging urgently at her sleeve.

'What is it, Becca?' she demanded.

'My lady, look, please. Does that seem like a victorious army?'

Edyth turned back to the horizon and she had to admit that although the men marched in formation of a sort, their shoulders were low and their steps slow.

'It looks like a tired one, that is all.'

'And a small one.'

The troops were all over the smudge of the horizon now and it was clear that there was scarcely a quarter of those who had marched out this morning. Becca's hands went to her mouth.

'Lewys,' she choked and then she was gone, clattering down the wooden steps and heading through the gap where the gates would one day, God willing, be hung again.

The other women ran after her and suddenly the night was filled with names sent hopefully out towards the bedraggled troops like fishing rods into a dark ocean. It was horrifically clear that too many would hook no prize and Edyth felt despair close in on her. How had this happened? How had the first

King of all Wales been defeated? She could see Griffin riding at the head of his men, seemingly whole, but Harold was coming and how was he going to fight again now?

Slowly Edyth went down the steps. She fetched the boys from their makeshift nursery and stood with one either side of her at the base of the tower, a miniature guard of honour to welcome her husband home. 'My lord.'

He slid from his horse and his feet buckled. Edyth jumped forward to steady him and nearly collapsed under his weight. 'Griffin, you are hurt?'

'No, just weary.'

She looked more closely and saw bruising beneath the skin of his cheek and a jagged scar below his ear. She saw dirt ingrained in his glorious burnished hair and exhaustion clouding across his blue eyes.

'You must rest.'

'Rest?!' He laughed bitterly. 'There is only one way, now, that I will rest, cariad, and that is in the soil.'

'Griffin, do not speak so. What has happened today? Were you defeated?'

'No, not defeated but not victorious either. They withdrew when the light turned. Earl Torr, it would seem, did not want to chance his men in the darkness and he had no need. We are decimated, Edyth.'

He pushed shaking fingers through his matted hair and glanced back to his men who were limping towards the hall, supported by their women, whilst those who had found only cold air comforted each other behind. Edyth looked frantically round for Becca and saw her nestled up against a limping Lewys.

'Praise God,' she murmured.

At her side Griffin laughed bitterly.

'I see nothing of God in this, Edyth. Any news of Earl Harold?'

'A messenger rode in earlier,' she admitted nervously. 'Harold has been sighted at Caernarfon.'

'He is upon us then. Has he many men?'

'The messenger said two thousand.'

'A thousand more than was reported at Cardiff. It seems he has new recruits.'

Edyth looked at the floor. She knew what that meant. This far from English shores there was only one way Harold's ranks had swelled – the southern Welshmen had turned traitor.

'What can we do?'

'We cannot fight, not yet.'

Griffin turned his eyes south. The sun was all but gone now and the only thing Edyth could make out was the ripped-up edge of the Eryri.

'So . . . ?' she whispered.

'So we do what we must – we go to the mountains.'

CHAPTER NINETEEN

*T*he men could go no further that night. Griffin let them eat and rest in the great hall whilst the women flew around tending wounds and packing food and tents into saddlebags. John and his lads strapped the provisions to stout ponies and the moment the sun showed its face, those of the rough and weary party who were able moved out of Rhuddlan and headed south-west towards the great Eryri.

Edyth walked at the front with Griffin, leading a stocky mountain pony with their two little princes on its humble back. Their crowns were packed away beneath oatcakes and dried meat and other such vital supplies and they trod as equals with the fifty or so men, women and children seeking refuge on the mountainside. There would be a hard day's walk before they even reached the forest that swarmed all over the peaks and although they loomed, dark and foreboding, Edyth longed to reach them for they were very exposed on the open road.

'I don't like it, Mama,' Morgan whispered.

Now five years old, he had his father's physique and wild copper hair and usually bruised his way through life, but today he was cowering back.

'There is nothing to be afraid of, Morgan,' Edyth assured

him. 'The mountains are our friends. No one will dare follow us in there.'

'Why? Why will they not dare, Mama?'

'Why? Because, because they do not know it as we do, Morgan. What is safety for us is danger for them.'

'But why?'

'I know not!' Edyth regretted her sharpness instantly. 'I know not, Morgan,' she repeated more calmly. 'I have never been there but your father says so and I trust him, as should you.'

'I do,' Morgan agreed stoutly, though his lip wobbled.

'We will grow strong again in the mountains,' Ewan told him. 'And then we will go back and attack.'

'Are the mountains magic?' Morgan asked.

'Yes,' Ewan agreed firmly and, grateful for her sturdy six-year-old's confidence, she did not have the heart to contradict him.

They reached the safety of the forest at nightfall and pressed on in the dark for some time before Griffin would let them rest. The next day they began to climb, tracing a way up one of the numerous streams that tumbled carelessly downwards. The water was so very clear and sweet that Edyth began to feel better – surely such purity could not come from an evil source?

The sun was bright and birds sang from the trees and she felt the whole party start to relax. Rabbits and squirrels scuttled across the path before them and, if Edyth squinted into the light, the scratched armour of the men nearly shone and the saddlebags might be bulging with feastings and the children could be jumping with excitement, not fright. She could not, however, squint for long and she soon sank into a dull, grinding silence with the others.

The light clung on longer than their spirits and slowly they came to stop in a clearing and found the sky still blue above.

The hillsides curved gently up and away and before them was a vast lake, not so very wide but stretching out between two peaks as far as the eye could see.

'Lake Colwyd,' Griffin announced proudly, 'named after a great Welsh warrior who fought with the legendary chieftain Arthur. We will make camp here but no fires. We are not yet far enough away.'

'We will never be far enough away.'

'Who said that?' Griffin demanded.

A soldier came forward, a rugged man, long one of Griffin's prized warrior-band, though now he looked at the ground like a boy caught in mischief. As his wife tugged fearfully on his arm, he dared to lift his head and speak out.

'I am your loyal subject, Sire, but I see no purpose in this flight. Are we to live like wild animals the rest of our days?'

'At least we will *have* days.'

'We could surrender.'

A shudder passed through the bedraggled group.

'We cannot surrender.'

'Not to the English.'

'They will kill us all.'

Griffin waved around.

'My loyal subjects speak true – the English will hound us to our deaths. You are right to voice your fears, soldier, but those fears are misplaced. Now – our camp.'

The soldier looked to the ground again then backed off, taking his wife with him, and everyone went to work. Although there was space aplenty on the softly sloping banks of the great lake, Griffin insisted they camp in the shelter of the pines so the tents ended up spread out for some distance. A light rain had started to fall and though it barely penetrated the trees it was mumbled as an excuse to retire to bed. There would be no shared meal tonight, no singing around the fire, just a string of dark shapes joined by little more than hatred for the English. For Edyth, squished in with Griffin, Becca, Lewys, the boys and her own swollen belly, it was an uncomfortable feeling.

'*I must kill him*,' Griffin had said and Edyth could see that was his only chance now – a surprise attack, an ambush. She should support him in it but, God knew, in her heart she did not want Harold dead and as the night crept on she felt that hideous knowledge like a pain all through the centre of her being.

A long, frightening week ground past, alleviated only by almost absurdly warm weather. The refugees traced their way through the Gyderau mountains, moving from lake to lake, heading for the furthest range, the Moelwynion. At first Griffin pointed out peaks and lakes to Edyth, sharing a little of the stories that seemed to surround them all, but as the days wore on he stopped, as if even he recognised now that this flight was not part of a great warrior tradition but something far more basic.

Soon, though, the journeying would be over. Tomorrow they would reach the slopes of Moel yr Ogof where Griffin said there was a deep cave that could shelter them in safety. The promise of rest had heartened the weary travellers and they'd picked up pace this morning but now they were skirting around the edge of the tiny valley hamlet of Beddgelert, unwilling to be seen by even a handful of peasants, and the way was tight and overgrown.

Edyth had been persuaded onto the pony with Morgan, and little Ewan was walking stoutly ahead, like a midday shadow of his big father. Edyth was just watching his brave progress with pride when she felt a sharp spasm. She put a hand to her belly and closed her eyes – surely not? Barely a moment later, however, another pain tore through her and she had to clench her teeth against it.

'No,' she whispered down to the babe. 'Not now, please – one more day.'

'Mama?' Morgan asked, looking back at her. 'Are you well?'

'Quite well,' she sang but already a new pain was jabbing at her, and the pony, sensing it, skittered sideways.

'There now,' Edyth soothed, 'steady now, keep going.'

She was talking as much to herself as to the beast. She curled her hands into its wiry mane and tried to focus on the rocky path immediately ahead.

'*Just a little longer,*' she willed her baby, '*then we will be at camp and you can come in safety.*'

The word 'safety' echoed hollow inside her and then, as if from afar, came a voice, low and certain: '*You are safe now.*' Harold! What was he doing in her head? Another pain shot through her, so sharp this time that she jumped and Morgan was nearly knocked from the saddle. His squeals alerted everyone.

'Morgan,' Griffin snapped. 'This is no time for fooling around.'

'It was not his fault,' Edyth managed before her body jerked again and Becca, quicker than the king, spotted her face and ran over.

'The babe?'

Edyth could only nod.

'Christ preserve us,' someone said, 'not now.'

They all looked nervously around. The smoke from the hamlet fires could be seen rising out of the trees and ahead of them was an open plain. If any scouts made it this far they would be rewarded with an easy arrow-sight.

'I can go on,' Edyth insisted as the pain passed. 'It will not come for hours. Ride – please.'

'But my lady . . .'

'What choice do we have?'

Griffin strode over.

'Ride with me, cariad. I will look after you.'

He took Morgan down from the pony and Lewys lifted the little prince onto his broad shoulders instead. Morgan was delighted with the swap, the poor pony perhaps less so, but it bore its load bravely and the party moved on once more.

'Can you do it, Edyth, truly?' Griffin whispered in her ear.

She leaned back against his chest, hoping to suck strength from it.

'The pain is no worse on horseback than off it. I may squirm a little though.'

He laughed softly.

'It is your squirming that has brought us to this, cariad.'

'You squirm too,' she protested and then pushed against him as another pain came.

It was a hazy day for Edyth. They climbed sharply out of the valley and up into the Moelwynion. The mountain peaks seemed to lean in around her and the sun to stroke her brow. The crazy world of tumbling streams and jagged rocks swam in and out of her vision as she fought the mounting spasms, rocking against Griffin whose arms held her tightly on the poor pony as they plodded ever upwards, the forest growing denser as they climbed.

'Not far now,' Griffin promised. 'We will be there by night-fall. It will be sheltered, dry, warm. We will be able to make you a bed and . . .'

Edyth, however, could no longer stop herself crying out. She all but climbed up her husband and Becca pulled alongside.

'We must stop, Sire. The babe is surely coming.'

'It's not safe yet,' one of the soldiers said but Becca turned on them, hands on hips, eyes sparking.

'Then you go on and find your "safety" if you will. I shall stay here with your queen.'

The men looked down, shamefaced, and Griffin stroked Edyth's hair from her face.

'Can you go any further, cariad?'

'Of course I . . . aaah!'

This pain was the worst. It shuddered through her, stabbing downwards as if breaking the baby free. Waters gushed down her leg and the pony reared in fright. It was only Griffin's quick reactions that kept them both from tumbling to the ground but as soon as he had settled the beast, he leaped off, bringing her tenderly down with him.

'We stay here tonight. We have heard and seen nothing all day and the royal child has spoken out. John, we need a tent and fast. Can someone find water and blankets? Any women with midwifery skills, we need you. This prince or princess will learn to be a fighter from its very first moments and I trust you all to help bring it into this world we are striving to hold in our hearts.'

It was a noble speech and Edyth longed to respond but her body had other ideas. She clutched at a tree trunk as Becca, mercifully, rushed to her aid and it was left to Lewys to say:

'I think, Sire, it may be too late for that.'

Edyth clenched the bark, forcing her nails deep into its rough softness as she bore down with all her strength. This was no royal bedchamber with soft sheets and warm water and clucking midwives, but it mattered not – for this moment was all contained within her pulsing body and she obeyed its instincts.

'That's it,' she heard Becca cry. 'That's it, my lady – one more push.'

Edyth gritted her teeth and bent her knees as Becca lifted her skirts. The tense hush of the little band of woodland courtiers sealed her in as Griffin gained her side. It was not dignified but what use was dignity anyway? All she wanted was her babe safely in her arms and she pushed with the wrenching pains, down into the mossy earth of the Eryri's wild slopes until she felt the blissful release of birth.

'I have it!' Becca cried.

Edyth collapsed against Griffin as a plaintive cry rippled between the pines and her maid, like some sort of sorceress, lifted a tiny, pink baby from under her sodden skirts.

''Tis a girl,' she cried, 'a baby Princess of Wales!'

Edyth felt a light, giddy happiness rise within her weary body. Slowly she turned and reached for the child and Griffin's arms tightened around them both as the courtiers stepped respectfully back. Sucking in deep, clear breaths, she looked down in wonder into the sky-blue eyes of her daughter, gazing at her as if it was perfectly normal to be born beneath the trees on the very top of the world.

Edyth was in bed at last. The tent was rough and the bedding damp but Griffin was warm at her side and the babe was suckling contentedly and for now it felt as rich as any palace in the land.

'It is a good sign, cariad,' Griffin whispered, stroking her hair back from her face. 'God has granted us the blessing of this beautiful daughter and he will watch over us all for her sake.'

'I hope so, Griffin.'

He drew her closer.

'I have not been the best of husbands, Edyth, but I do cherish you, and the boys, and now this little princess. I wish—'

'Wish not, Griffin. We will find a way forward; we always do.'

She was struggling to keep her eyes open and he kissed her softly.

'You need to sleep, cariad. Here, let me take the babe.'

Gratefully Edyth passed the now sleeping child to her

husband and watched as he cuddled her tenderly onto his broad chest. She was safe with him and Edyth felt herself drift blissfully towards sleep, but just then a sharp call from outside jerked her rudely awake.

'Who goes there?'

There was a rustle of undergrowth being parted and a squeak as someone was hauled forth.

'Beg pardon, my lord,' came a shaky voice. 'I mean no harm. I come from Beddgelert. I was hunting. I heard noises. Are you . . . the king?'

Edyth glanced at Griffin, who had raised himself slightly, the baby still beneath his chin.

'Of course not, lad,' Lewys said roughly outside. 'What would the king be doing in the mountains?'

'We heard tell he had fled from Earl Harold.'

'Not with us he hasn't. We're villagers, fleeing the English bastards.'

Edyth could hear the whole camp holding their breath. It was dark and they were dirtied and torn from their travels but a single look at the quality of Lewys's travelling cloak would tell anyone with half a mind that they were no mere villagers. The boy, however, simply said:

'Why?'

'Why?' Lewys echoed.

'Yes, why? They say Earl Harold is treating the Welsh graciously. He has no truck with common folk. He just wants the king – the queen too, or so they say.'

Edyth felt Griffin's arms clench around her and had to bite at her lip to stop herself crying out.

'What is that man to you?' he hissed.

'Nothing, Griffin.'

'So why, then, does he hunt me down? Is this whole war over *you*, wife?'

'No! Griffin, I have ever been true to you. I swear it. Please – I have just borne your child.'

At this the babe awoke and wailed. Edyth snatched her back from Griffin and clasped her to the breast but she could sense the tension rising beyond the tent flaps.

'Griffin,' she urged in a whisper, 'this is not the time to argue. Please.'

He nodded tersely and rose.

'The boy has to go.'

'Go?'

Griffin, however, was up and ducking out of the tent and, weary as she was, Edyth scrambled to her feet to follow. She stepped out just in time to see her husband stride across to the fire and, like a lightning flash, drive his sword up and through the boy before he could even lift an arm to defend himself. His thin body thudded to the ground amongst the branches and moss and Edyth stared at it. The camp seemed to visibly shiver as men poured out of tents, circling the corpse.

'You should not have done that,' Lewys said quietly.

'You question me – your king?'

'Out here there are no kings.'

Edyth saw the men shift in the big guard's direction then Becca flashed past her and ran to his side.

'He's right,' another man said. 'We are all exiles, running like cowards.'

Griffin bristled and planted his big feet more firmly in the ground. Edyth stroked her hand fiercely up and down the baby's back. She wanted to intervene, *had* to intervene, but she was so tired.

'I am your king and while there is breath in me I will remain your king.'

'Is that so?' The words were low, menacing.

'Please,' Edyth started but no one paid her any attention.

'The boy had done no harm,' Lewys went on.

'He would have alerted the hamlet,' Griffin shot back. 'Someone might have spotted a chance for gain and run to the bastard English who seek to take everything from us.'

'Including our decency?' Lewys growled.

'How dare you?!'

Griffin lifted his sword again and Becca screamed and leaped forward. Griffin saw her move just in time but could not curb his weapon. He twisted it so that it was the flat, not the blade, that caught her but still the force of it cracked across her slender shoulders and sent her reeling. In a flash Lewys's own sword was up.

'No!' Edyth cried.

Lewys was still holding Becca with one arm. He glanced at her and Griffin took his chance. His sword lifted again, visibly quivering with rage, but as he moved to strike he cried out in agony and dropped his weapon as if God himself had struck it from his hand.

'Griffin!'

He turned, slowly, and Edyth saw horror swirling his blue eyes like a grasping undercurrent tugging at the sea. A sword protruded from the soft spot beneath his arm, too deep in to doubt its deadly path. Behind him a soldier stood, hands to his mouth as if in disbelief at his own action, but already his fellows were enclosing him, shielding him. Everyone watched as Griffin put up a hand towards Edyth. She ran forward but he crumpled to the ground before their fingers could meet. Edyth flung herself down and clutched his dear head in her free arm. He looked up at her, drew in a ragged breath, and spoke one final word: 'cariad'. Then he was gone.

No one spoke. No one moved. From somewhere, as if miles up on the top of the Eryri, Edyth heard her baby crying and the sound echoed around her heart. Griffin had come so far, fought so hard – for *this*? She remembered him on the beach the day he had asked her to help him keep his kingdom, so determined and yet so vulnerable underneath. Only she had ever truly seen his fears; everyone else had been offered the fierce warrior and the riotous courtier – the face of kingship, not the heart.

All his life Griffin had truly striven to rule Wales as he felt she should be ruled and all his life Wales had resisted him. Now she had hounded him to an ignoble death in her own heartlands and for a moment Edyth hated the country she had shared with her brave husband for nigh on eight years. Yet, he had known it would come. '*I could be king for another twenty years, Edyth,*' he had told her, '*or for just a few more hours. It is best, I find, to make the most of all this wonderful life offers.*'

Well, he had done that and she had been lucky to do it with him, if for all too short a time. Drawing her sorrow around herself like a cloak, Edyth buried her face in her husband's fading copper curls and wept. Still no one else dared do anything until, from across the fire, someone said: 'God bless the king.' It was a soft, clear voice and it drew Edyth's head upwards. 'God bless the king,' Becca said again. She was on her feet, her hand clutching tight at her injured arm but her head high. Slowly others joined her: 'God bless the king.'

Moved, Edyth sat back and, clutching her fatherless babe in one arm, she pressed the other hand to her heart as if she might physically hold it together. How could she hate Wales when it had given her so much? How could she hate these people when they had stood side by side with her and Griffin through all their troubles – and stood still? No one dared look at each other. No one spoke of blame and no one ever would. Griffin's world had been shrinking for too long and this night it had sunk right in on itself. He had died by the sword and in this particular battle it was not their place to question whose.

Edyth joined the chant, a whisper at first and then a proud, fierce cry. They would be heard now. They would be heard by the people of Beddgelert. They would be heard by Harold's scouts. They would be heard by Harold himself but it no longer mattered. Nothing mattered. The first King of all Wales lay dead in the dirt, halfway up his beloved mountain – halfway up to heaven. Tomorrow the men would deliver him to Harold as a prize of war but tonight, beneath the stars, in a space out of time, they would sing him to his rest.

CHAPTER TWENTY

Rhuddlan, August 1063

arold knew he should feel triumphant. Certainly
he had arranged everything to look that way.
He had ordered Avery to have Griffin's throne
brought out of his great hall and set on a hastily erected dais
in the centre of the royal compound, still marked out by the
charred fencing his own men had burned to the ground at the
start of this portentous year for Wales. He was sat upon it in
his full regalia as Earl of Wessex awaiting the humble entrance
of his captives so he definitely should feel triumphant. Why,
then, was his stomach churning as if he had drunk a whole
damned barrel of Welsh ale?

Edyth's throne was at his side and he swore he could see
the shadow of her fingers in the soft wood of the beautifully
carved armrests. When they'd brought it out he'd seen one of
her honey-blonde hairs caught on an edge, drifting on the crisp
air like a spirit, but it was there no more and now Earl Torr
lounged on the throne, one booted foot over an armrest, his
slim leg dangling nonchalantly as if he were in a poor man's
tavern not a royal court.

'Sit up!' Harold urged him under his breath. 'Show some
respect.'

Torr's amber eyes narrowed.

'For whom? The treacherous runaways who slew their own king in their blessed mountains?'

'Torr, enough! We should be gracious in victory.'

'I do not see why.'

Harold turned away from his brother. Fighting with him had been a trial and winning with him was worse. Torr had taken Rhuddlan first, flying his glittering 'sharpened spear' emblem high from its single tower before letting his troops loose on its meagre supplies. Harold had arrived to find soldiers asleep all around the compound and Torr himself sprawled out across the king's bed with three helpless young women. His instant imposition of discipline had been met with begrudging shame from the men and gloating petulance from their leader.

'Don't be so dull, Harold,' Torr had moaned. 'What's the point fighting if you can't enjoy the spoils?'

He'd pouted even more when Harold had sent his three 'spoils' away.

'They enjoyed it,' he'd insisted.

'You mean you paid them.'

'So? I've been in this godforsaken country for weeks without female company. A little pleasure is surely the least I deserve?'

'It's always pleasure with you, isn't it?' Harold had snapped. 'What if the Welsh had come?'

Torr had just grinned lasciviously.

'Oh, they did, Harry – well, three of them at least!'

Harold had forced himself to walk away and had avoided Torr as much as possible in the long days since. Garth had ridden through Wales with him but had returned to England to report the victory to King Edward the moment it had been secured and he missed his easy company. He had not even been able to seek refuge with God, as Griffin's chapel had burned with the rest of the compound. He itched to return home but now, at last, the hostages were to be brought before them and they could make peace and turn east.

He lifted his head. Trumpets were sounding on the breeze – the surrender party approached. He slapped Torr's leg down and rose, pushing himself out of Griffin's throne. He'd ranged all the men in full armour to greet the prisoners but it was a poor sight that met their eyes. Griffin's soldiers shuffled into the bleak compound, heads low, bearing a platter of gold. A gruesome object rolled upon it and Harold knew before it drew close enough to see that it must be Griffin's head – proof that he was dead. It would be his duty to accept it and he braced his spine in readiness even as his eyes sought the queen. He'd expected to see her at their head, high on a horse with her crown proudly on her head, but no such figure led the group of prisoners. His heart skipped. Reports had said she was frail. Had she not made it? The men dropped to their knees before him. Harold stepped to the edge of the dais to take the platter, but all the time his eyes searched and then he saw her.

She was in the lead cart with the other women. She had clearly been prostrate but now she roused herself and sat up tall, her back as rigid as his own. Her two boys sat tight to her side, little eyes flashing horrified defiance, and in her arms was a tiny swaddled bundle. Harold noticed all this as his hands met the platter and he almost missed his grip. His fingers tightened just in time and he raised Griffin's head aloft to a great roar from his troops, but his own mind was racing. She must have given birth in the wild, like the poorest commoner. She must be very weak. She might take childbed fever. She might die before he transported her over Offa's Dyke and what, then, would Svana say? His great victory would count for naught in her eyes.

There was an oak table just behind his throne, set with wine, and he pushed the jug aside to put Griffin's head down. It rolled precariously and only the matted, bloody mass of rusty hair held it from tumbling to the ground at the soldiers' feet. Torr laughed.

'See,' he cried out, 'what happens to the enemies of King Edward!'

The soldiers roared and for once Harold was grateful to his careless brother for supplying the ceremony that stuck in his own throat. He held up his hands.

'We accept this token of Wales's surrender and we will honour King Griffin with burial here, at his palace of Rhuddlan. Then we will seek terms with those who submit to our rule. But first, all prisoners must bow and swear loyalty to King Edward of England as their ultimate overlord.'

'King Edward, King Edward!' the English troops shouted out and the sound seemed to crack against the new walls of Rhuddlan's great hall.

Edyth stood. She passed the baby to a pale-faced woman behind her and held out a hand to be helped from the cart. Avery rushed forward to hand her down with all honour, then lifted her two little princes to the ground. Holding them each by the hand, Edyth traced her way through the slim ranks of men until she was before Harold. She walked awkwardly, as if it hurt her greatly, and he longed to spare her the pain, but he knew it had to be done and admired her beyond words for doing it. She dropped to her knees and bowed her head but her voice was firm and rich and carried on the sea breeze all around the hushed compound.

'As Queen of Wales, I and my sons, the princes, submit to you, Earl Harold, as honourable representative of King Edward. May God bless and keep him and those who serve under him.'

Harold stepped forward and offered his hand. Edyth took it and he grasped her fingers tight, trying in that one touch to convey all he wanted to say: that he would see her honoured,

respected, safe; that he would see her home as he had promised
Svana he would do. Her fingers, at least, were cool in his and
her face, when she turned it up to him, was pale but strong.

'We accept your submission, my lady, and take you and your
sons into our safe keeping.'

'And my daughter.'

'And your daughter.' Harold ordered the tiny creature
brought forward, then took her into his own arms and looked
down into fierce blue eyes. 'What have you named her?'

'Nesta. It means pure, for she was born into strife but brings
none of her own.'

Harold bowed his head.

'Nesta. She will be safe with us as, together, we work to bring
peace.'

'Peace,' he heard Edyth mutter, a sigh almost, and he tightened his fingers around the babe as cheers rang out all around.

Then Torr stepped forward, his wolf's eyes flashing.

'You can submit to me any time, Edyth Alfgarsdottir.'

Harold's hand twitched to strike his brother but Edyth
simply turned her face to Torr and quietly, almost genteelly,
spat at his feet and walked away.

'The little vixen, I'll have her!'

'You will not,' Harold said to his furious brother. 'She is
Queen of Wales yet and an earl's daughter besides and she is
not to be treated like your poor strumpets.'

'Oh for Christ's sake, Harold – she's a prisoner. She's ours
to do with as we wish.'

'And I wish to deliver her, whole, to her brother Edwin, Earl
of Mercia, our ally – our *much-needed* ally.'

Torr just snorted.

'You know what I think, Harold? I think you want her for
yourself.'

'I do not.'

'You've always been possessive of her, ever since that time in the woods. Are you jealous, Harold? She was watching me that day, you know, and she liked what she saw too. I wager she'd give herself to me willingly. I wager she'd love it.'

Harold's hand shot out, too fast for Torr to avoid it. He grabbed the rich fabric of his brother's tunic and twisted it tight, yanking him towards him.

'Your spear is ever too sharp, brother. She is fresh out of childbed and that a bed of twigs and fear. If you so much as touch her, I swear on Christ's blood, I'll kill you.'

Torr just raised one eyebrow. Harold reluctantly released his hold and his brother stepped back, brushing himself down with a snide smile.

'Definitely jealous,' he said and sauntered away to his place at the table.

Harold slammed his fist hard into the wall. Blood oozed from his knuckles but he welcomed it. Sometimes he thought he really would kill Torr. He had to conclude this peace and fast, for it would do the troops no good to see their leaders divided. Taking a deep breath, he turned and approached the table. He'd make this sharp and fast.

It wasn't hard. The northern Welshmen caved to his every demand as their southern counterparts had done before them, dissolving into defensive local groups like wild animals seeking the safety of their own packs. Having left Glamorgan under Prince Caradog's command, and Deheubarth to the arrogant but safely inward-looking Prince Huw, Harold divided the north between a cowed Prince Bleddyn and his younger brother, Rhys. He also took the obligatory chance to enrich himself and Torr with the great parcels of borderland won by Griffin's relentless skirmishing, leaving only one town – Billingsley – in its former hands. Perhaps one day Edyth would offer it as a dowry to the little girl born amongst all this horror. He hoped he'd be around to see that but the years ahead were shrouded in mist and he feared parting it to even try and do so.

The night they were due to leave he went to visit Edyth. Despite Torr's taunting he had insisted on her being given the privacy of the bower, telling all that King Edward had expressly asked that she be returned to his court in safety. She had accepted gratefully and retired with her children and her pregnant maid, who also appeared to be injured though none would tell him how. He had ensured she was well guarded and fed but now, after three days in the half-built palace, the troops were growing restless and costly and they had to leave for England. He knocked at the door and the maid admitted him, eyes downcast.

'My mistress is feeding her daughter,' she told him in broken English, 'but I will fetch her.'

'No. No, I can wait. Let the babe have its supper.'

The girl almost smiled. Her arm was in a sling but she tended him attentively. He accepted wine and tried not to look at the drawn curtain of the big bed, behind which he could just make out Edyth's silhouette as she nursed.

'Will you come to England with us?' he asked the maid to cover the sound of the suckling child.

'Me?' She turned big brown eyes on him, too surprised to avoid his gaze. 'No. I speak not good English. My lady has taught me a little, but . . .'

'She speaks to you in Welsh?'

'Of course. This is Wales.'

Harold thought of Edyth, delivered here by her father aged fourteen, and tried to imagine how it must have been for her.

'It is.'

'She has had letters from England, from the Lady Svana.

They have been her . . .' She fought to recall the word. 'Her lifeline.'

Harold smiled.

'The Lady Svana is my wife.'

'I know, my lord. My lady queen has spoken often of it.'

Harold was curious to know more but the girl had looked shyly away, her hand curved protectively over her belly.

'You are with child?'

'I am. My husband is one of the king's . . . I mean . . .'

'Your husband is a guard,' Harold suggested gently.

'Yes. A Welsh guard and we belong here. In Wales.'

'And the Lady Edyth? Where does the Lady Edyth belong?'

She shrugged.

'Lady Edyth belongs wherever she chooses.'

'Lady Edyth,' said the lady herself, emerging, 'does not like to "belong" at all. Good evening, my lord. Does this mean we must depart?'

'If you are well enough?'

Edyth looked straight at him.

'I am.' She glanced at her maid. 'I will leave good friends, for which I am sorry, but it must be so and at least I will have my children.'

'Of course. Their uncle, the Earl of Mercia, will welcome them, I'm sure.'

'You are too kind, my lord.'

She was so formal with him and he was surprised at how much it hurt.

'I have brought you something for the journey home.'

'You have?'

Still, her voice was dull, distant. Harold cleared this throat.

'I thought you might like your own beautiful mare to carry you.'

'Môrgwynt?' Her head shot up and Harold was delighted

to see a spark of life in her eyes at last; it had been worth saving the animal from the fire. 'Oh, Harold, thank you!'

She took a step forward as if she would hug him, but recollected herself at the last moment and held back. Even so, Harold felt he had melted just a little of her ice and was glad of it. This speck of warmth, at last, was like a trace of the old Edyth, a seed that could grow and maybe even blossom again. The maid had described Svana as Edyth's lifeline and now he vowed to himself to make sure he carried this poor, deposed Welsh queen safely home to her care.

'You are ready to ride for England then?' he asked.

Edyth set her chin up.

'Yes, my lord, I am ready to ride for England.'

PART THREE

CHAPTER TWENTY-ONE

Westminster, October 1063

*E*dyth could hardly believe how Westminster had been transformed in the eight years since she had last been there. Thorney Island had been flattened and mounds of earth brought in to rid it of the marshy softness that had long caught at unwary shoes. The old abbey church had been torn down and King Edward's grand new one was rising from the ground in layer upon layer of glowing Reigate stone. Already the pillars that would support the nave were heading for the sky as if urging the rest of the walls upwards towards God.

Edward had called the court together at first light to bless the footings and they were all stood in the crisp autumn air, shivering in their finest clothes and trying not to yawn as Archbishop Stigand of Canterbury sprinkled holy water and chanted a benediction. Edyth knew her eyes should be cast down in devotion but she could not tear them away from the masons and craftsmen all around. For it wasn't just the abbey; all of London was expanding.

Beyond the rivers surrounding Westminster, houses were springing up everywhere so that, from where Edyth stood, she could barely glimpse grass at all. Much woodland had been cut down and the village of Chelsea to her west seemed to be creeping up to the very edges of the Tyburn. Even on the far side of the great Thames people were building homes, pushing out across the Southwark meadowlands like eager pilgrims. There were also more and more merchants operating along the beaten-down streets, selling foodstuffs and textiles and fancy goods brought in on the ships that lined the banks of the Thames. It was like a permanent market and Edyth marvelled at it.

She had known herself to be stepping back in time in Wales but had not realised how far England had been leaping forward. Years of peace had given the country time to grow and prosper and she found herself wondering what Griffin would have made of all this. She thought of him every day. She missed his bulk at her side, his incautious enthusiasm, even his temper. She missed his pride in the children and his fiery dancing and his attentions in bed. She hated that little Nesta, thriving oblivi- ously, would never know her father and cherished the fact that his last hours on earth, however confused, had been given to bringing her into it.

His death haunted her. She went over and over it in her mind and longed to have Becca to talk to, though her maid's part in the tragedy had been, perhaps, too raw to allow that. Such a silly argument, such a simple flare of Griffin's ever-ready temper, and he'd gone. Yet, had it not been that, it would have been something else. Looking back now, his death seemed a hideous inevitability. From the moment Harold had brought fire to Rhuddlan they'd been running and they'd been bound to trip at some point. Or he had. She, it seemed, had been caught in Earl Harold's competent arms again and was safely back in Westminster, almost as if her life in Wales had never been.

'We are both widows now, my dear.'

Edyth turned to see her grandmother at her side. Lady

Godiva looked as composed and elegant as ever but her voice was quieter and her eyes not so sharp. Edyth nodded.

'I was just thinking of him – Griffin.'

'You will do that for a long time to come but you are young. You will marry again.'

'I might not.'

Godiva inclined her head.

'You might not. It is your choice.'

'You think so, Grandmother, truly?'

'That depends on you. In law you are beholden to no one.'

'But I have my children to protect and everyone says I can do that best with a husband.'

Instinctively her hands went out for Ewan and Morgan but the boys were with their baby sister in the royal nursery and she met only thin air.

'They are thriving?' Godiva asked.

'They are. My Princes of Wales are turning themselves into little English lords so fast it makes me giddy.'

She had been worried for them with their sparse English and Welsh manners, but both boys were tall for their age and possessed the natural confidence of their royal upbringing and they seemed to have been treated less as foreigners than mystical heroes. They had slotted straight in with the other children and already they were shedding the lilt from their tongues like an adder its skin.

'Children recover fast.'

It was true, and if Ewan still cried out for Papa in the night and Morgan still wandered the fields looking for the sea it would pass. By the time they were men they would probably remember Wales only as a fleeting trace in their minds, like a dream of the country they'd been born to rule. Edyth shook herself.

'We cannot, I suppose, dwell on the past.'

'No, my dear, we cannot, but we can treasure it still.'

Edyth smiled her thanks. Godiva, as so often, understood what others did not – that her time in Wales had not been some interlude best put behind her, but a part of her life. Even so, she had to go forward, as Westminster went forward.

The blessing was over and the court was milling round in the autumn sun. Edyth saw Archbishop Eldred talking earnestly to a gang of young lords, borrowing a sword from one of them to point to some key architectural feature. She saw Lord Garth – now Earl Garth of East Anglia – bowing low before a blushing young lady and Earl Torr watching him darkly with his wife Judith, for once, on his arm. She saw her own mother, sadly shrunken without Alfgar at her side, and young Morcar scooping her protectively up to talk to a nearby group of lords and ladies. Edyth smiled and moved to join them but at that moment the king himself stepped up at her side.

'Welcome home to England, my lady. I trust you have been made comfortable.'

'Very, thank you, Sire.'

Edyth swept into a curtsey but the king raised her immediately and offered her his arm. Godiva nudged her subtly forward and she took it, glancing in amusement at the furious courtiers forced to make way for her either side.

'What do you make of my abbey?' Edward asked.

'It's beautiful, Sire, truly. I have never seen anything so magnificent; it honours God greatly.'

'I am glad you think so. It's based on the abbey at Jumièges – a magnificent church, though I flatter myself I've added a few improvements.'

'We must progress, Sire.'

'We must, my lady!' Edward beamed at her. Now fifty-eight years old, his tall frame was stooped and his thin figure gaunt but he held her arm strongly and his pale eyes still burned with life. 'Stone is the future, you know.'

'I believe you are right.'

Edyth thought of Harold's stone defences at Hereford and of Griffin's refusal to have the same at Rhuddlan. If he'd built in stone, Harold would not have been able to burn the palace and they would not have had to flee to the boats and . . .

'What do you think?'

The King of England was looking intently at her and Edyth realised, mortified, that she had let her attention wander.

'I'm so sorry, Sire, I did not hear you right.'

'Bless you, my lady, you have been through much.'

'I'm sorry,' Edyth stuttered again. 'And I'm sorry my husband made war on you.'

'It was not your fault, Lady Edyth. Queens have a lot to put up with – ask my wife.'

He gestured to Queen Aldyth who had come up at his side.

'It is good to have you home, my lady.'

Edyth felt her eyes welling up with tears and had to glance to the skies to force them back. One drop of kindness from the elegant king and queen and she was melting away!

'You are very gracious,' she muttered but now, thankfully, they had reached a great slate showing the mason's plans for the abbey church and she was able to focus her attention on the intricacies of stone carving and architrave design.

'Magnificent,' she said again.

'Yes,' the king agreed, 'and it should last many years, centuries even. It is my legacy to England.'

'But who will carry that legacy?'

Queen Aldyth's words were soft, like a whisper on the breeze. Edyth turned to her, puzzled, and a courtier seized the chance to step up to the king. Queen Aldyth smiled sadly at her.

'You have children.'

'Yes. Three.'

'You are blessed.'

'I am.' Edyth saw her pain and longed to ease it. 'You are very slight, my lady,' she offered. 'Perhaps God did not wish to risk losing you in childbirth?'

The queen looked startled but then she smiled.

'What a lovely thought, Lady Edyth, thank you – though I find it hard to believe I am so precious. Queens are meant to have children, you know. It is our duty.'

'One of our duties – I mean *your* duties.'

'You are a queen too, Edyth, and I'll warrant a good one.' Aldyth drew her aside from the crowd. 'I am glad you are back, truly. Your father was a great loss to the country, as I'm sure he was to you.' Edyth inclined her head, desperately hoping she wasn't going to cry again. 'He was a . . . lively man but an experienced earl. Your brother is doing very well but he is young, God bless him, and was not raised to rule. I am sure you will be a great support to him in keeping Mercia strong for the king.'

'I will do all I can to help, my lady.'

'And you will marry again.'

Unlike Godiva, the queen made it a statement not a question.

'Maybe, in time.'

'You have land?'

'A little.' Much of Edyth's dowry lands had been in Wales so they were now lost to her. She had some in the Marches but it did not amount to a great living. 'I have Billingsley,' she remembered aloud. 'It was gifted to me by Earl Harold in 1055.'

'Of course. My brother takes a keen interest in you, Lady Edyth.'

'He has been very good to me. His wife too.'

232

'Lady Svana, yes.' The queen stroked her hand across Edyth's arm. 'She is not, though, you know, truly his wife.'

Edyth jerked back, then remembered herself and had no idea how to retract the slight. Confused, she curtseyed, her cheeks flaming scarlet, but the queen simply took her arm again and walked her still further from the crowd. Edyth looked frantically around. Svana was here. She had spent a wonderful evening with her just yesterday but she was always awkward around churches, even half-built ones, and had avoided this morning's blessing. Edyth cursed her friend lightly under her breath. She should be at Harold's side stopping such talk, for if it was coming from the Queen of England herself it was surely dangerous.

'I have never seen a couple more closely joined,' Edyth said stiffly.

'"Tis true,' Aldyth agreed easily. 'My brother loves Svana dearly, as do I, but she is still not his wife in the eyes of the church.'

'But in the eyes of God she is.'

The queen smiled tightly.

'Your loyalty does you credit, my lady, but ask yourself this – can Lady Svana be queen?' Edyth looked around, horrified, and Aldyth sighed. 'You do not approve of my loose tongue.'

'No, my lady, of course not, I . . .'

'Peace, Edyth. You are right, but I cannot help but worry. I have not provided an heir for England. It means we have no foundations.' She gestured to the deep-set stones all around them. 'And without foundations this beautiful country my husband has worked so hard to build could crumble away. We had a letter last week from Duke William of Normandy.' Edyth blinked; the conversation was shifting too fast for her post-birth mind. 'He wrote to tell us personally of his conquest of Maine, a province he believed he was promised the inheritance of.'

'As he believes he was promised England?'

The queen nodded urgently.

'You see, you understand exactly. Not only that but he wrote that the Duke of Maine had been taken ill – something he ate at the victory feast, or so William claims. He is dead, Lady Edyth. He will not challenge William's right to his land again. Do you understand *that*?'

'Too well, my lady.'

'The duke will stop at nothing to secure what he believes he is owed, bastard-born though he is. His connection is tenuous, you know, and in the maternal line too – Queen Emma, our dear Edward's mother, was his great-aunt – but he swears that Edward promised him the throne in 1051.'

'And did he?'

'I was not there but I'm told it was spoken of, yes. Nothing was sworn, though. Edward owes a debt of gratitude to the Normans for sheltering him when his father was in exile from the invading Vikings and it is a debt he still intends to repay, but not with the throne. William, however, is not a man to settle for second best.

'He writes that he has had his son – his first, Edyth, of three – invested as his heir. He writes that Robert is proving an able leader of men and with his formidable mother, the Lady Matilda, would make an excellent deputy should William ever need to go to war again. He writes that he hopes, though, that all his other dues – meaning England – will come to him without the need for violence.' Edyth stared at the queen, the rest of the buzzing, fawning court fading into ineffectual insects in the face of her words. 'He is very clear, is he not?'

'He is.'

'So the king and I need to be very clear too and we are. In our minds there is only one future king for England and it seems to me, Lady Edyth, that there is only one queen too.'

She fixed Edyth in her ice-clear eyes for a moment then spun away. 'Ah, is that your dear brother? He looks quite lost in Edward's architectural discourse. Shall we rescue him? Earl Edwin, good day. How pleased you must be to have your sister with you once more.'

Edwin bowed low and agreed that of course he was delighted and Edyth was drawn back into the smooth conversations of English court life, but underneath her head was spinning. The queen could not mean her to marry Harold? To betray her best friend and he his wife? Her understanding of court subtleties was rusty, that was all – she must have misunderstood. She *must* have. Her blood pulsed ridiculously, setting her head throbbing. As soon as she politely could she excused herself and, desperate for distraction, sought out her fun-loving younger brother. Morcar was juggling stones for a crowd of simpering young ladies but abandoned his sport as she drew close.

'You look troubled, sister.'

'Just disorientated, Marc. I'm not used to court life any more. I will be glad to return to Mercia for some peace.'

'You will?' He grimaced. 'It's a bit *too* peaceful up there for my liking.'

'You are bored?'

He glanced guiltily around but the gong had sounded and the people of the court were heading eagerly across to the great hall to break their fast so no one was paying them any attention.

'In truth, Edyth, I am. I help Edwin where I can but he is reluctant to let others in. It's fair – he must take command of his earldom – but it leaves me loose.'

'Too loose by the looks of it.'

Edyth indicated the young ladies, following close by, and her handsome brother grinned.

'Can I help it if women want me? Anyway, you weren't so slow off the mark yourself. As I recall, Griffin stood no chance.'

Edyth blushed.

'Was I really that bad?'

'Not bad, sister – determined.'

Edyth scuffed at the edge of a flagstone with her foot. It was true. Even at fourteen she had been hot with curiosity and keen to make a conquest and she'd succeeded.

'Imagine,' she said to Morcar, 'if Father had been granted Northumbria instead of Earl Torr.'

Morcar grunted. 'The Northumbrians would have been glad of it. Word is they hate him. His taxes are higher than any and he spends most of them building hunting lodges in Wiltshire and the Marches. Needless to say, the Northumbrians resent that.'

'How do you know?'

Morcar shrugged.

'I've been hunting with a few of the local lords – there's good game up there, you know, whatever Earl Torr thinks. I speak with them.'

Edyth glanced anxiously around.

'Be careful, Marc.'

'I am but they need me and it's good to be needed. Besides, I told you, I have loads of time on my hands. What else am I meant to do?'

'I don't know, just don't go getting into trouble.'

'I'm not Father, Edyth.'

His whole body had gone rigid and she felt instant remorse.

'I know, Marc, I know. I'm sorry. I'm tired.'

She thought longingly of Coventry. There she would be safe from the calculating court. There she would be free of royal expectations and could nurse her still-raw wounds and calm her hot blood.

'Edyth!' Svana materialised between the crowds as if she had been there all along. 'How was the blessing?'

Edyth smiled at Svana's approach. Her friend looked as fresh as ever in a pale yellow gown, embroidered – no doubt by the talented Elaine – with delicate flowers in a deeper shade.

'Formal,' she told her simply. 'You'd have hated it.'

'You know me too well.'

'And understand you better all the time. I was just telling Morcar how good it will be to escape the court and go home.'

'Home?'

'Coventry. I am in my brother's keeping now, it seems, if I am not still prisoner.'

'Edyth! Of course you are not. Harold would never imprison you and you must go where you see fit – though Coventry is not the only peaceful place in England.'

Edyth peered at her, then releasing Morcar to the ladies with a smile, drew her closer.

'You sound, my dear friend, as if you have another idea.'

'Not at all, though I *was* thinking that you could, perhaps, visit me at Nazeing after Yule, as was once planned so very long ago. Crysta is nearly eight now and should see more of her godmother and it would be so lovely to have you to stay.'

Edyth pictured Nazeing as she had seen it last on the long-ago day of Svana and Harold's wedding, all meadow grasses and fire sparks and magic. She longed to return and yet . . . The royal couple were taking their places at table and as Queen Aldyth settled herself, her eyes found Edyth and she seemed to almost pat the arms of the beautiful carved throne as if inviting her to take inheritance of it. Edyth recoiled.

'Will Harold be there?'

Svana shook her head and something about the way her elegant shoulders drooped pulled Edyth's eyes from the queen's piercing stare.

'Svana? What is wrong?'

Svana looked to the thatch as if gathering herself then finally she said: 'King Edward has asked Harold to sail for Normandy in the spring.'

'Normandy? Why?'

'To try and form a new treaty with Duke William.'

Queen Aldyth's words sprang instantly to Edyth's mind. If she was to be believed, William poisoned dukes on their own land so surely it was madness to ride into the heart of his court? And yet she had learned to her own cost that Harold was not a man to sit and wait for his enemies to come to him. The thought tore at her heart and she grabbed Svana's hands.

'No, Svana. You must stop him. He must refuse.'

'Refuse the king? He would not know how.'

Svana sounded bitter and for once Edyth understood why. Her poor friend just wanted her husband at home but women, Edyth was learning, had little power to secure even such seemingly small demands. They could, however, look after each other and maybe, whatever others plotted, God had sent her back to England to assist Svana in these turbulent times?

CHAPTER TWENTY-TWO

Nazeing, May 1064

Svana watched her girls helping little Nesta to feed a rejected lamb and sought for the usual rush of joy in her heart but it did not come. She felt furious with herself and then furious all over again for being furious. She was turning into the witch people had once claimed she was, only less a magical enchantress than an old crone.

'Isn't it lovely?' Edyth said. 'A miracle really.' She looked knowingly up at Svana.

'Is that something I said?'

'Yes – well, wrote. It was a letter back when I was first in Wales. You'd helped birth three winter lambs and you said that no matter how many times you saw new life come into the world it felt like a miracle.'

The memory seemed to spin in front of Svana's eyes, unsettling her, and she fumbled for the stall rail to steady herself. Edyth leaped up.

'Svana, you look strange. Are you unwell?'

'It's this pregnancy, that's all.'

Svana waved away her friend's concern and moved to the barn door, pressing a hand to her belly. She'd been delighted when she'd first realised she was carrying Harold's sixth child

– a piece of him inside her whilst he was over the narrow sea – but it didn't feel so good now. It was not just the nausea this time but cramps too. She'd even bled, though not enough to worry anyone else with.

'It seems to be harder every time,' she admitted.

'It will.' Edyth left the girls and joined her. 'You are older now.'

'Old.'

'Old*er*. If you were old you would not be able to conceive at all.'

Svana smiled ruefully.

'I sometimes think that would be a blessing.' She saw the shock in Edyth's pretty face and felt awful. 'I don't mean that, truly. Carrying Harold's child will always be a blessing. I just wish him home, that's all.'

She closed her eyes against the sorrow that seemed to sting at her wherever she went. Harold had sailed for Normandy as soon as the worst of the winter winds had died away but the first news she'd heard had been that his ship had foundered on a wrecking tide at Ponthieu. He had written, thank the Lord, from safety at Rheims but that safety had come at a sore price. It was the Duke of Normandy himself who had ridden to release him from the avaricious Duke of Ponthieu, leaving Harold in dangerous debt. The next she'd heard, he'd been commissioned to help invade Brittany and she had known then that he would be a long time away from home.

Spring was normally her favourite time of year but for once it had dragged terribly. She might not have survived the fearful waiting for his return without Edyth at her side but finally, last week, messengers had arrived to say Harold would be setting sail for his manor of Bosham at the start of June. Svana had greeted the news with joy – had feasted all her people in the meadowlands to celebrate – but somehow this last week had felt longer than all those that had gone before. Now she looked out across the rich colours of the sweet Maytime sunset and wished she could enjoy it as it deserved instead of counting it fearfully away.

'I remember your wedding so vividly,' Edyth was saying, looking out across the soft meadowlands where the boys were playing a noisy game of tag. 'Here, on the most beautiful day, with everyone dancing and singing. It was all so magical, so perfect.'

Svana drew in a breath and considered the waving grasses as if some shadow of that wonderful night might still be imprinted across them.

'It was,' she agreed softly. 'Back then it truly was,' but the magic, if such it had been, was gone now and she could no longer keep Harold in the faerie-circle of her Nazeing estate.

'*He will be king*,' the ladies of the court would whisper in her ear. '*Who else? Who else can it be? And then . . .*' They'd look at her, eyes sly, and even nod to Queen Aldyth as if they could remove her crown and her jewels and her furs and personally drape them onto Svana.

'*And then Duke William will attack*,' Svana would say and they'd recoil, not at the idea of invasion but at her refusal to play the dream. It drove her insane. Couldn't they see that queenship wasn't something you put on like your mother's gowns? Couldn't they see that a royal crown had thorns inside? Why would she choose that? Yet how could she not?

'It's very peaceful here, isn't it?' she said, gesturing fiercely to the rolling horizon.

'Beautiful.'

'Beautiful – yes. I am lucky.'

'Svana? What's wrong?' Edyth asked. 'Tell me, please. Do you not like it here any more?'

'Oh yes. I love it. I would gladly remain here always, coward that I am.'

'Coward?'

'That's what Godwin called me last winter. He was angry because I would not let him sail for Normandy with his father. He believes he is full grown and mayhap he is right, Edyth – he will soon turn sixteen after all – but the world is such a bitter place, even for a man.'

'Is he angry still?'

'Not so much. He is a good son and he loves it here as much as I, but he still suspects me of cowardice and does not wish to be tainted with the same.'

'What's cowardly about loving your own homeland, Svana?'

'I suppose that depends how wide you should consider your homeland to be and what is expected of you.' She swallowed. 'I do not wish to be queen, Edie.'

She looked at the younger woman and saw her flush in vivid lines of scarlet, almost like wounds across her cheeks.

'It was never what you intended,' Edyth said carefully.

'Nor Harold either but he is not so selfish as I.'

'It is not selfish to want your husband at your side.'

'Nor for him to want his wife at his, wherever he may have to ride.'

'No.' Edyth picked awkwardly at a meadow grass, scattering the seeds to the wind, then her eyes lit up. 'You should ride to Bosham, Svana. You could be there to meet Harold when he returns over the narrow sea. He must be very lonely; think how he might need you.'

For a fleeting moment Svana felt like crying out that she did not want to be needed, that it was too much to bear, but she knew how pathetic that was, how weak, and she did not want to be weak. She looked from the boys, throwing an old pig's bladder between them, to the girls, busily tying a hair ribbon around a lamb's neck, and then back to her friend. She could not hide here forever and she could not leave Harold to face the world alone.

'I will go,' she said fiercely but already her very body seemed to jerk against the idea.

That night Svana lay awake, trying to dream of standing on Harold's beach to welcome him home. She tried to picture the pleasure on his face and the feel of his arms around her, but her back ached and her head was pounding. She needed sleep if she were to make the journey south but her damned body felt so insistently awake. It was not the babe for she had not felt it turn all day, but more the womb itself, as if it was giving out heat. And pain.

She heard the cry as if it came from somewhere else – a ewe in the barn perhaps – but there was no doubting the next vicious stab. This was her own pain and she could not silence it.

'Mama?'

Through a red haze she saw Hannah and Crysta at the foot of her bed but when she tried to rise to go to them it felt as if someone was sticking a sword into her. She put out a hand but they hung back, frightened, and then, thank the Lord, Edyth swept in.

'Fret not, girls,' she heard her say. 'You run and fetch Elaine and I'll watch Mama. Quick now!'

Crysta ran for the door, dragging her little sister after her, and Svana only had time to give thanks that they were safely away before the pain doubled her in on herself. She looked wildly up at Edyth.

'Am I losing it?'

Edyth clasped her hands.

'I know not yet. May I look?'

Svana nodded and forced herself to sit up as Edyth pulled back the sheets. Blood stained the mattress, spreading out from beneath her in a scarlet flood that seemed to pull her whole world inwards.

'I *am* losing it!'

'It seems so.' Edyth's voice was calm. 'I'm sorry, Svana, but we must care for you now. There's no way we are losing you too.'

Svana stared deep into the scarlet stain. Was that her life-blood soaking away? Was God taking her for obstructing Harold's duty to his country? Suddenly it all seemed horribly clear.

'My death would solve a lot of problems,' she said bitterly but Edyth grabbed her shoulders, holding her tight and forcing her to look into her face.

'It would solve nothing. Nothing! You are not to speak like that. Crysta and Hannah need you. The boys need you. Harold needs you. Lord have mercy, Svana, *I* need you. Fight for me at least – promise?'

Svana wanted to promise but a new pain shot through her and she could only cry out against it.

'There now,' said a voice – Elaine. 'This won't do. Come, Svana, my love, rise. It has to come out. All of it, the afterbirth too. If any lingers in your womb it will turn to poison. Can you rise? Good. Very good. Now, sit here.'

Svana looked down. At her feet was a pail, its edges padded with soft linen but its gaping hole dark as the mouth of hell itself. She shuddered but her knees were giving way as a new pain came and she had no choice but to allow herself to be sat upon it.

'You will need to push, my love,' Elaine said. 'You know how to do that, don't you?'

Svana set her teeth. She did not want to be here. She did

not want to do this, to expel Harold's dear child into a filthy pail. This was no miracle of life. This was pain and loss and fear and blood – this was a woman's battlefield.

'Fight, Svana,' Edyth urged at her side. 'Please fight.'

Svana's whole body tensed, as if squeezing itself downwards. She longed to resist but the force was too great and with a roar of anguish she pushed with it. She heard a sickening rush of fluid and rocked against the horror of it all. Only Edyth's hand on her back steadied her, rubbing so fast she felt the heat of it burn her skin.

'And again, my love,' came Elaine's voice, soft and soothing.

Edyth's hand ceased its motion but Svana felt it against her still, strong and tight, and pushed back against it as, with another sickening gulp and flop, her poor womb emptied itself into the pail.

'There,' Elaine said. 'There, 'tis done. 'Tis over.'

'Over,' Svana repeated, more a wail than a word, and then she collapsed.

She wanted Harold. She wanted his strong arms around her and his soft voice in her ear and the blissful security of his body against her own. She thought of him splashing back onto England's shores without anyone there to draw him safely onto land and more pains shuddered through her. She reached out and grabbed for Edyth's arm.

'You must go, Edie.'

'Go?'

'To Bosham.'

'What? No. No, Svana, I will stay here. I will stay here with you.'

'No.' This sorry night Svana seemed to have lost control of so much, but there was one thing she knew for sure. 'You must go to meet Harold. I do not want him landing alone. I do not want him hearing of this alone. He is not good alone.' She forced herself up, desperate now. 'Please Edyth, go to Harold for me, as I fought here for you.'

It seemed to take forever for the reply to come but when it did she felt it lift a great weight off her shoulders.

'I will go, Svana. For you I will go.'

And on that blissful promise Svana surrendered herself to leaden sleep at last.

CHAPTER TWENTY-THREE

Bosham, June 1064

The winds teased at Harold's ship like a cat with a helpless prey, sending it lurching crookedly across the water. Edyth stood on the beachhead and held her breath, the tension winding inside her like wool round a spindle. The sea, churned up by a summer storm, seemed reluctant to finally hand the earl back to English shores and she crossed her fingers behind her back, willing him onwards.

Steadily the ship grew until she could make out the pulsing figures of the oarsmen battling to direct the craft to the safety of the beach. She watched, fascinated, as the sails were dropped and the wooden hull scythed through the sand, oars high in the air like insect legs. Once the prow had cleared the greedy edges of the waves, men leaped out to heave the boat to safety above the waterline and the spray from the sodden ropes splashed against her in a shock of cold. She flinched back but then a dark figure jumped down before her.

'Harold!'

She ran forward and clasped him. His arms went around her and she felt his fingers dig into her back as if tethering himself to her.

'Edyth, thank God. It's so good to see a friendly face.' He

pulled back and scrutinised her. 'Are you well? Is . . . Svana well?'

'Quite well, Harold.' He did not believe her; she owed him the truth. 'She lost a babe.'

'A babe? I had no idea she . . .'

'She only found out a little time before, though it was big enough to give her some trouble coming out.'

Edyth squeezed her eyes shut against the blood and the fear and terrible hopeless plop of a life dropped away into a pail.

'And Svana . . . ?'

'Is well, truly, Harold. A little sad but cared for by Elaine. She took no fever and she is hale, the rest of your family too. They are eager to see you.'

'And I them. It has been a dark time, Edyth.'

A shadow sat itself on his face.

'Come,' she said, taking his arm. 'We have fires lit and wine warming. There is hot stew and fresh bread for all.'

'You are a good steward, my lady.'

'Nay – you must thank Joseph for that. I am merely here to carry Svana's love.'

'And a little of your own?'

'Of course.' She looked aside. 'You are like a brother to me, Harold. Now, come!'

Later, as the men thawed around the fire, food settling in their stomachs and wine coursing through their veins, Edyth saw them visibly unfold. Their shoulders relaxed, their backs unbent, their legs stretched out and even, slowly, smiles broke out on their lips as colour seeped back into them. As the evening rolled on only one man remained tight and hunched and Edyth hated to see it.

'It has been hard?' she hazarded.

'Hard?' Harold rolled the word around his mouth, testing

it, then frowned, finding it wanting. 'Nay, Edyth, it has been hell itself.'

'The duke was not, then, welcoming?'

'Oh no – no the duke was *very* welcoming. He is like melted butter, impossible to grasp and leaving you slicked with his residue. I feel I will never be clean again.'

'I could order you a bath . . . ?'

'No, Edyth, thank you. This dirt is inside me.'

'He treated you cruelly?'

'Nay, he treated me like a king. He fed me royally and accommodated me royally and his wife, the Duchess Matilda, offered me every courtesy. They rode me out at their side and showed me their dukedom all the way to the borders and, indeed, beyond. Matilda's father is regent of France, you know, along with the boy-king's mother, Anne of Kiev – sister to Hardrada's queen. Forces are gathering all around us, Edyth, wicked forces, and William is the wickedest of them all.'

'You did not like him?'

Harold sighed.

'I wish it were that simple,' he admitted. 'He is a fascinating man, Edyth – driven and focused and so very astute on the battlefield. We had much in common; mayhap that is why I was fooled into believing all was well between us. I rode with him into Brittany as a fellow commander and he praised my battle skills as I praised his. I thought we worked well together but it seems he was just playing me against his enemies and then, right at the end, he tricked me.'

His voice rasped into his cup and he sucked down wine, as if trying to drown the sound.

'Tricked you?'

'On the very last night, as if he'd been saving it up for me the whole time, as I'm sure he was. He is a patient man, Edyth – a cold, determined, dangerously patient man. He knows how to stalk a prey and he knows how to finish it off when the time comes.'

Harold drank again and Avery moved forward to refill his cup. The young squire had filled out into a strong soldier over the last year and something about him reminded Edyth of Lewys. She felt a pang of sorrow. She had sought news of her dear friends, of the birth of their child, but the borders to Wales had locked down and she had been unable to find out anything. It was almost as if they had never existed. She looked again at Harold's steward and saw dark rings of tiredness around his young eyes.

'Go to bed, Avery,' Harold said.

'But my lord . . .'

'Truly, lad. You have served me well these last months and you deserve your rest. I will retire shortly.'

Avery looked from Harold to Edyth and then bowed low and backed away. Many of the men were setting their pallets now, worn out from their rough trip, and it was as if the whole world was going to sleep around them. Edyth longed to know what had happened but feared hurting Harold further by dragging the facts from him. She waited, watching quietly, and eventually he looked up again.

'He made me swear, Edyth.'

'Swear what?'

'Swear loyalty – swear to support his claim to the throne, swear him in as King of England.' His voice cracked and he pounded his fist into the table. 'Does God hold a man to such a vow, Edyth? A vow made under duress and against the deepest reaches of his heart?'

Edyth took a deep breath; never had words felt more crucial.

'I do not believe so, Harold. Men see actions, God sees intentions.'

He looked at her and his eyes cleared, but within moments the shadows crept back.

'Yet I am sworn, Edyth.'

'How?'

'How?! I hardly dare recount it.'

'I'm sorry. You do not have to. I am too curious – it has ever been thus.'

A smile ghosted across his lips.

'It has, Edyth, and that is good. There is much to learn of this world, more than I, fool that I am, ever truly realised. I will tell you. Nay, I must tell you for the fact of it is scratching away inside me like a trapped beast.'

He drew a breath and Edyth leaned in. She blocked out the clattering of the platters as the servants cleared the last of the food and the slam of wood on wood as they took down the trestle tables to make way for the pallet beds. She blocked out Joseph dismissing the men to bed and the snores of the sleepers and even the occasional whimper that told of haunted dreams brought home like stowaways from Normandy. She blocked it all and filled her ears with Harold's words as he tore them from himself and laid them before her.

'It was meant to be a feast. Nothing more. It was Duchess Matilda's idea, or so she presented it. She was so friendly to me, Edyth, so solicitous but she, it seems, was playing me as much as her precious husband. We'd agreed terms, you see. Way back when William first welcomed me to Rheims we'd agreed terms. I'd told him, as King Edward had instructed me, that he now wished to nominate an English heir but that he recognised William as his maternal cousin and would like to honour that link with an alliance. I'd offered him the lordship of all Cornwall in honour of such a treaty and he'd accepted. We'd shaken hands, Edyth.'

'You'd sworn an oath?'

'No. No, we had not, for news had come in the very next day of unrest in Brittany and we'd ridden forth together, but we'd shaken hands. I'd even offered my dear sister Emma as wife for one of his Norman lords. We'd *agreed*, Edyth. Pah! It seems Duke William cares little of honour. He is a bastard indeed.'

'What happened at the feast?'

'Oh, the usual, lots of fine food and wine – the Normans are very precious about their "cuisine" – and then William announced we were to declare friendship before all. I was expecting that, we were due to swear an oath, but he changed it. He stood before them all, out in the open for public witness, and he laid the words of the oath on a beautiful box and when I looked at them, when I . . .' Harold sucked in his breath. 'They said I swore to uphold William's claim to the throne of England on the death of his cousin King Edward and when I looked up to protest there were Norman swords at my throat. I had no choice, Edyth, not if I wanted to live.'

'Oh, Harold.' Edyth placed her hands over his. 'Such an oath is not binding.'

'Ah, but Edyth, I haven't told you the worst of it yet. I thought that too. I spoke the words with my own men looking on in horror and the duke circling me like a beast of prey and I meant not one word and he knew that. But then, when I had finished, he opened the box and inside, Edyth, inside were all of Normandy's finest relics: the bones of St Rémy, St Philibert, St Barbara, St Eternus, even St Maximus. I swore on all their sanctified remains, Edyth – how can that be gainsaid?'

'You did not know.'

'No, but I know now and it sits like a lodestone on my heart.'

'It was a trick, Harold, nothing more. You cannot let it bind you. Only a coward would make you proceed so.'

'A coward?' Harold almost laughed. 'He would not like that,

Edyth, but I think you are right. Duke William *is* a coward, but a ruthless one and he wants England for himself.' Edyth felt his fingers counting through her own as if they were tally sticks offering magical numbers. 'One thing and one thing only has this ill-fated trip told me – that Normans cannot be allowed to rule England.'

'Then, Harold, it must be you.'

'The Hungarian, Prince Edgar . . .'

'Perhaps, if the king lives many years yet.' There was a pause. 'But if he does not, then it must be you.'

'The people won't want it.'

'They will. They love you. Wessex loves you as its own. We will bring Mercia and Torr Northumbria.'

'Ah. Torr. The Northumbrians do not much like him, you know.'

'I know. Morcar told me.'

'So why should they not extend that dislike to his brother? They hate Torr for exploiting their land for his own gain and is that not what I, too, would be doing if I took the throne?'

'Do you see it as gain, Harold?'

'No, but they will. Royalty glitters from afar; it is only when you are close that you see the shine is not gold but steel. If the people of the north do not want a southern king they will find themselves a new one. They have done it before – how do you think King Cnut conquered England?'

Edyth stared at him.

'Hardrada,' she breathed.

'Hardrada, yes. Many Northumbrians still feel they have more in common with Norway than England. York might welcome him in and then we would be doomed.'

Edyth remembered the stormy eyes of the great warrior boring into her at Rhuddlan and knew Harold was right.

'Torr must be made to rule more fairly then. You must talk to him, Harold, make him see how important this is to England.'

Harold snorted.

'My brother is more interested in what is important to himself.'

'Perhaps I could talk to him?'

'No!' Harold grabbed her hands once more. 'No, Edyth, you must not go near him. He would—'

'Spear me?' Harold shuddered at these words and Edyth only just stopped herself from laughing. 'I am not a girl any more, Harold. You do not need to protect me, my innocence is all gone.'

'Not *all*, Edyth. We are more innocent than we think. I was innocent enough to believe William was dealing honourably with me. There is more darkness in the world than we can know, than we *should* know, especially some of us.'

'Svana,' Edyth breathed.

'Svana sees all the good in God's creation,' Harold agreed, his eyes softening. 'She has created her own world at Nazeing and, Edyth, it is a beautiful place. It has its problems, what farm does not, but it has no divisions, no politics, no damned fighting. In that sense, it is perfect but it is also unreal. Svana wants the rest of the world to be the same and she is right to do so but . . .'

'But it cannot be, not until the rest of the world is as pure of heart as she.'

'You see that, Edyth.'

'How can I not when I grew up in my father's household? He lived and breathed politics.'

'As did mine, Edyth, as did mine. We are the same sort of creatures, you and I, driven by our duty to a wider family than our own. Sometimes I wish I was not made so and I could retire to Nazeing and live the life of a country squire but to do that I would have to surrender my earldom and my whole being rebels against such an act. My father won Wessex, Edyth, and I am proud to hold it for him, as I am proud to be part of the great council of England.'

He sounded so bitter, so confused. Edyth put out a hand.

'There is nothing wrong with pride, Harold. Or with duty.'

'But duty to whom, Edyth? I feel every bit as protective of my country as I do of my children, perhaps more so, and I worry that is wrong of me. Svana certainly believes so and I love her for it, but I cannot escape my own conscience. I do not want to be King of England, Edyth, but if in the end England wants me I will be unable to say no. All I ask is that I do not have to bear the burden alone.'

'You will have Svana.'

'As I have her here now?'

'That's not fair. She has been unwell. Travelling would have endangered her.'

'Travelling always endangers her. She cannot truly breathe court air, not for long, not as you can, Edyth.'

'Harold, don't.'

'You have been a queen once; you could do it again.'

'Not like this . . .'

'Marry me.'

'No! No, Harold, do not speak of this. Not you.'

'Others have spoken of it?'

'Too many but they do not know. They think only of politics, not of love.'

'And this would be a *political* match.'

'Not a love one?'

'I care for you deeply, Edyth, you know that.'

'As a friend.'

'Yes, but . . .'

'You mean we would . . . pretend? A platonic alliance only?'

Something deep inside her kicked furiously as he considered this, but then he shook his head.

'No. No, not that, Edyth. My sister had such a marriage at first and it nigh on killed her. A wife must be a wife.'

Edyth looked up at him. His face was close to hers, his breath warm on her cheek, his eyes swirling with undefinable emotion.

'But Svana . . .' she whimpered.

He stoppered the word with his lips. They covered hers fiercely, demandingly. All the air seemed to suck out of the room. Edyth's head spun and her body flared and pulled towards him like a boat on the tide. A glorious madness seemed to rush in and she clutched at him to hold on but as her fingers caught behind his neck they snagged on sanity and she yanked back.

'No,' she said, then louder, '*no!*' Then she turned and ran, out into the night and across the compound, to burrow into her own bed, already knowing that she would never be able to sink deep enough into the soft feathers to escape whatever had just happened.

Edyth kept to her room the next morning, praying that Harold would leave to report to the king at Westminster without her having to see him again. She was horrified at his kiss and still more so at how eagerly she had leaped to meet it. What had he said of innocence last night? How was it possible to be so very innocent even of your own desires? Not that she desired him. No. It had just been the lateness of the hour and the richness of the wine and the emotion of seeing him so battered by the bastard duke. Even so, she had no wish to expose herself to the whims of her widowed body again and she crept around her chamber waiting for the sound of troops mustering to ride out.

It never came. Instead, as the sun reached its apex sending the confined room into shadow, there was a knock at the door. Edyth stared at it in horror.

'Edyth?' His voice was gentle, nervous. She looked to the ceiling. 'Edyth, it is I – Harold. Can I enter? Please?'

'Better not.'

'Nay, Edyth, we cannot leave it like this. It was but a kiss.'

But a kiss? Nay, it had been a touchpaper to needs and wants she had buried when Griffin had been cut down before her in the Welsh Eryri. If that's how he saw it, though, maybe she could do so too.

'You were tired,' she suggested.

'Tired and lonely and confused. Nay, not confused, but . . . foolish. Edyth, please can I come in?'

Slowly she lifted the latch and the great Earl of Wessex sidled inside.

'Svana,' she said and this time he did not stop her but hung his head. 'You love her?'

'Of course I do, more than life itself. Why do you think I don't want to make her queen?'

Edyth frowned and he grabbed her arms, pinning them to her sides. Her body sang at his touch and she fought it, disgusted with herself.

'Being queen would destroy Svana, Edyth. She needs to be free, not shackled by the demands of a petulant country. She cannot stand even being at court, you know that – how much more, then, would she hate ruling it?'

Edyth looked down at his big hands wrapped around her arms and tried to focus on what he was saying. It was true, so very, very true.

'Then you will have to reign without a queen.'

He shook his head.

'I am not strong enough to do that, Edyth. Maybe I am not strong enough to reign at all.'

'Nay, Harold – you are.' She looked urgently up at him and suddenly their faces were close again and madness was closing in fast. 'Let me go.'

He stepped back as if stung and Edyth saw his chest heaving as she knew her own was doing. 'This has to stop, Harold. Go to Edward, give your report, muster forces if you wish, but there is no cause for panic, no cause to rush into anything . . . foolish.'

'Edyth . . . Please. Edward is hale yet. So much could change. We cannot know what the future will bring; we can only proceed with our best intentions.'

'God sees intentions.'

Edyth heard her own words like a terrible accusation. God would, indeed, know exactly where she would have intended last night's crazy kiss to go. Harold spoke true. Being queen would destroy Svana and if Edyth could take her place just to save her friend, or even just to aid Harold, then it might be possible but this dark night had awakened dangerous feelings inside her, feelings that would mean she would not be saving her dearest friend but betraying her. The truth was that she could only have married Harold if she cared less for him, much, much less.

'Good day, Harold,' she said stiffly. 'God speed you to Westminster.'

'You will not ride with us?'

'I must return to Coventry. My family will need me – as yours need you.'

Harold sighed.

'I meant you no dishonour, Edyth.'

'Which is why we must now part and say no more of marriage. You *will* say no more of it, Harold?'

Harold, however, simply bowed low and backed from the room. At the door he paused and Edyth had to reach for the bedpost to stop herself running to him.

'God bless you, Edyth Alfgarsdottir,' he murmured and then, at last, he was gone.

CHAPTER TWENTY-FOUR

Coventry, October 1065

My dearest Edyth,

I hope this letter finds you well and safe at Coventry, though I begin to fear that the very safety you know I have long cherished is becoming an illusion. Harold has been in attendance on the king for longer than ever before. Edward has been very sick, Edyth. For a time the court feared for his life but, God be praised, he has recovered and Harold has taken him to Torr's beautiful new hunting lodge in Wiltshire to restore his vitality. I only pray it works for I dream in shadows of crowns and fear the demands of the king's death more and more with every day that passes.

They are calling Harold the sub-regulus, Edyth, and in truth, with Edward ever at his precious abbey, he controls all the daily business of government. There is no one else to do so. The young Hungarian prince. Edgar, remains as mewling a creature as he was the day his father died, though he has my pity. He is as much a victim of this country's hunger for an heir as Harold but he, at least, has his youth to protect him and he clings to it. Harold says he makes little effort with his military training and eats like a girl. There is no

*chance of him leading an army any time soon and one will
be needed if King Edward is called back to God.*

*There is one Englishman who would take the throne will-
ingly, indeed with joy, but Harold fears his rule more, perhaps,
than that of Duke William or even the Viking, Hardrada.
Earl Torr is ever hungry for advancement and despises his
own earldom. He is there so rarely that the younger northern
lords barely recognise him when they come to court and when
he does return it is only to tax and to punish. He does not
deserve the title he so looks down on. Please warn your brother
to be wary of his neighbour in the north, for trouble in
Northumbria might visit itself on Mercia too.*

*I long to see you, Edyth. I missed you so much at the
Whitsun Crownwearing and Christ's mass seems such a long
time away. I know I have ever been too fearful and I know
you laugh at me for it, but the world is spinning and it will
throw us away from each other if we do not guard against it.
I pray yet for our woman's year but fear 1066 will not be it.
Do come and visit. There are things we should talk about
but a scratchy piece of vellum is no way to do so.*

Take care, my dear friend, and look to your borders.

All my love,

Svana

Edyth folded the letter carefully and laid it on her lap. It was
a beautiful autumn day and the leaves were dancing around
the elegant compound at Coventry but Svana's words chilled
her like the sharpest winter wind.

'Come now, boys, harder. Parry and thrust and, ow! Excellent,
Ewan, excellent!'

She looked up. Morcar was clutching his thigh dramatically
where his eldest nephew, now a cornstalk of a nine-year-old,
had just inflicted a killer blow with his wooden training sword.

Morgan, not to be outdone, was charging wildly at his Uncle Edwin.

'Go on, Morgan,' Ewan encouraged, 'pretend he's a Norman – slaughter him!'

Edyth shivered and ran her fingers over Svana's letter. It was true that her friend had ever been cautious of risk but more and more Edyth felt she was the one in the right. Watching her precious boys training in the safety of the compound at Coventry was all very well but if the Normans truly were to invade they would all need their shields.

As the falconer came to claim the boys for their next lesson, Morcar joined her, still ruefully rubbing his thigh.

'Your sons are tough fighters.'

'As was their father, God bless him.'

'You miss him still?'

'I miss him. I miss my life as queen. Above all else, I miss knowing who my enemies are.'

'You seem melancholy, sister.' He looked at the vellum in her lap. 'Who has poisoned your spirits?'

Edyth sighed.

''Tis Svana. She frets for Harold as the king sickens and for us too.' She grabbed Morcar's arm. 'She says there is trouble in Northumbria, Marc, and that we should look to our borders. I should talk to Edwin.'

She made to rise but he stopped her.

'Edwin knows.'

Something in his bearing, a sudden uncharacteristic solemnity, caught at Edyth's breath.

'What do you mean, Marc? Has something happened?'

Morcar shifted and beckoned Edwin over.

'There is trouble in Northumbria,' he admitted. 'Earl Torr demanded a huge tax this harvest time and many voices are being raised against him, especially in York. It could be dangerous.'

'Hardrada?'

'It's a possibility,' Edwin agreed, joining them, 'but I think the troubles are more local at the moment.'

'What do you mean?' Edyth looked from one brother to the other. 'Why won't you tell me?'

'You need not be troubled, Edyth,' Edwin said. 'You have your children.'

'And that stops me understanding the wider world, does it? Stops me having an interest in the England they will grow up in?' The two men looked awkwardly at each other and Edyth stamped in frustration. 'I've been a queen, Edwin. I've run a country. I've stood up and spoken to hostile crowds. I don't need to be sheltered.'

'I think she deserves to know,' Morcar said. 'It will be inescapable soon.'

'What will?' Edyth roared but both brothers had turned away, fixing on the watchtower where the guards were having a furious conversation with someone beyond.

'Perhaps, indeed,' Edwin said quietly, 'it is inescapable already.'

He strode across the compound and took the watchtower steps two at a time, appearing in the window opening above them.

'Let them in,' he commanded the guards, then to the men beyond: 'Welcome in peace.'

'Marc,' Edyth said sharply, as they hurried across, 'what's going on?'

The gates were opening and three men – lords, judging by their fine cloaks – were riding in, flanked by guards. As they saw Morcar they dismounted and dropped to their knees before him.

'Lord Morcar, we come with news. Rebels have taken York and driven the errant earl's men away. They have taken the treasury and declared Earl Torr outlaw for crimes against his people. We come to beseech you to stand as Earl of Northumbria in his place and to offer our arms in support of your claim.'

Edyth could hardly believe it. The people of the north had cast out their own ruler and wanted Morcar in his place? She looked to her brother, standing tall and handsome before the men as if such supplication was nothing more than his due, and realised this was no surprise to him. Svana had been right to warn her but her letter had come too late for Edyth to do anything about it.

'Morcar, it's dangerous,' she choked out. 'To stand against an earl is to stand against the king.'

'Not the king,' Morcar said calmly. 'I am loyal to King Edward. We are all loyal to King Edward. We simply want our voice heard.'

We? Our? Morcar spoke with assurance and certainty and it was clear that he had been their leader, albeit from afar, for a long time before this moment. The men were not beseeching his support but confirming it.

'I accept,' Morcar said now and raised the three lords. 'Come, you need refreshment and I need news. There is not a moment to waste.'

Edyth dared not sit with the men at table though she hovered with her mother and grandmother, overseeing their service and listening intently to all they had to say. The rebels were many and their numbers growing all the time. Messengers had ridden not just through Northumbria but Mercia too, and all over the north villagers were mustering against Earl Torr.

'Torr will be furious,' Edyth whispered to Godiva.

'He should have thought of that sooner,' was her tart reply.

'Quite right,' Meghan agreed. 'An earl owes a duty of care to his people. Alfgar always said so, God bless him. That wretched Godwinson has neglected his duty and now he pays the price. Morcar will make a wonderful earl.'

'But Torr will not take it lying down. He will fight.'

'With what army? His men stand against him.'

'The king will call out the fyrd.'

'And set Englishman against Englishman? Now, with him so weak and his precious abbey due for consecration and his mortal soul wavering in the balance? Do you truly think so, Edyth?'

Edyth looked down. The fyrd – troops of men provided by the petty lords and villages as their dues to the king – could be summoned at any time but Meghan was right that only a madman would call them to civil conflict. So what now? Svana had said Harold was with Torr in Wiltshire. He would have to face the news at his brother's side. What would he do? What *could* he do? And what could *she* do to ease the way for them all?

She thought of Griffin and his life of fighting rebellions. Factions had torn Wales apart making it so, so easy for her husband's hard-won country to be taken by a foreign enemy. That could not be allowed to happen to England and she had an idea how to ensure it did not. Slipping away from the men she headed for the stables. It was time Môrgwynt had a decent ride out; it would not hurt her either. Svana might crave safety but Edyth, Lord help her, tired of it far too easily for her own good.

CHAPTER TWENTY-FIVE

Wiltshire, October 1065

*H*arold was up at dawn, striding across the compound of Torr's luxurious new hunting lodge at Britford. The minstrels had played late last night in the elegant great hall – later than either King Edward or Harold had been able to stand – and he feared his brother would be slow out of bed. He strode restlessly into the hawkhouse. The weather was perfect for hawking, crisp and fresh with a light breeze to tempt the birds to wing, and if he had to be stuck here with Torr then he planned to make the most of it.

Harold moved to his own hawk, Artemis, chucking softly under his tongue to rouse her. A few more days here and he would ask leave of the king to ride to Nazeing. Edward was enjoying his hunting and was in far better health now so there was time before the Yuletide court for him to return to Svana. He needed to arrange Godwin's education. Joseph had seen him well trained but the boy would turn eighteen soon and should join a full military household. Perhaps he should see Edmund placed too? He had been far too soft with them and it would do them no good when they came out into the world beyond their mother's rich pastures. He grimaced and reached for Artemis's hood but a clatter of hooves in the yard beyond made him pause.

'Who can this be?' he asked the bird but, still hooded, she did not even turn her head. 'Just a moment more,' Harold promised her and went to the door of the hawkhouse.

Two messengers were dismounting and talking urgently to the guards.

'Can I help you?'

They turned and scuttled over, dropping into low, nervous bows before him.

'We bring news, my lord – grave news.'

Harold's mind raced. King Edward was here so it could not be him.

'Invaders?'

'Oh no, my lord.' The messengers looked briefly relieved, then drew themselves together. 'Rebellion.'

'Rebellion?! Here, in England?'

'Yes, my lord, in the north. The rebels have taken York and claim the earldom of Northumbria for their own man.'

Harold glanced to the window of Torr's bower but the shutters were firmly bolted and he was doubtless not alone within.

'Tell me more,' he said uneasily.

'They are a strong force, my lord, and well organised. They have ejected Earl Torr's guard and seized the treasury. They are marching south, collecting men everywhere they go – Lincoln, Nottingham, Leicester. They are heading, even now, for Oxford.'

'So close?'

'They have declared Earl Torr outlaw and have taken, in his place, Lord Morcar of Mercia.'

'Marc? Good God, he's but a lad.'

'A very popular lad, my lord, beg your pardon.'

The messenger dipped his head, horrified at his own daring,

but Harold patted his shoulder. He needed frank opinions right now.

'How many follow him?'

'It looks like about five thousand and they say there are Welshmen marching too – top soldiers, my lord, not just peasants with pitchforks.'

'Welshmen?'

Harold closed his eyes; there was only one person who could raise Welshmen. How dared she? He'd thought she was his friend, thought she was on his side, thought she cared. '*We will bring Mercia*,' she had promised him back in Bosham when he had been fool enough to ask her to marry him. Well, she had brought Mercia indeed but in anger and in opposition. Was she laughing at his gullibility now as she marched her dead husband's troops on his family? Sickened, Harold looked again to his brother's bower. What had his loose living brought upon them? Their conversation from the previous evening echoed through his mind.

'God, Harold, you've become such a bore,' Torr had accused him when he'd risen to retire not long after the king. 'You should make the most of the riches around you.'

'Perhaps, but such excess is wrong, Torr. An earl should rule wisely, not greedily.'

'Like you, brother? You are not greedy? At least I'm only after women – you're the one wanting a crown.'

'That's not true,' Harold had replied, stung. 'The king orders me to serve.'

'Only because you are forever there to order. Besides, it's easy for you, isn't it? Edward likes it in Wessex; you don't catch him riding to hunt in Northumbria.'

'Maybe,' Harold had shot back, 'if you built a palace like this one he would. Garth or Lane are seldom out of their earldoms and they are far less experienced than you. You neglect your people, Torr, and it's wrong.'

'Wrong? You're obsessed with wrong. Live a little, Harold.' He'd clicked his fingers for wine. 'Come, brother, let's not argue. The king has gone to bed and we can have some fun at last.'

'Torr!'

'What? Oh come on, Harold, don't say you were enjoying the old dote's company?'

'Ssh,' Harold had hissed. 'Show some respect – he's the king.'

'He is and an old dote too. We barely caught anything today with him riding so slowly.'

'He's been unwell.'

'So let him snooze on his throne and we'll all be better off.'

'Torr, please – this is treason.'

'Hardly! Come on, Harry, I've done my duty. I've ridden at the king's pace all day and talked abbeys all evening. Now I think I deserve some fun.'

'You always think that.'

'And I am always right. You deserve it too, Harold, you just don't know how to find it.'

Harold groaned at the memory now. Torr, it seemed, had finally lived too much and for once Harold hoped he'd enjoyed his night of lechery for it seemed that this crisp dawn had brought an end to all his careless fun.

The rebels gathered on the hillside just beyond Torr's hunting compound later that morning, orderly and controlled – not a rabble but a sharp and worryingly intelligent force. King Edward wandered out of his chamber and regarded them curiously over the fencing, much as he might look into the royal nursery. Harold rushed to escort him to his throne, which had been lifted onto the centre of a hastily erected dais to receive the rebel delegation.

'Waste of a beautiful morning,' Edward muttered as Harold handed him up.

'This is serious, Sire,' Harold warned but Edward just grunted and ran a careless finger along the sparkling length of his sceptre, a beautiful, jewel-encrusted rod symbolising his right to pass judgement on his subjects.

'We cannot afford civil war,' Harold pressed. 'You are hailed all over Europe for your peaceful rule and with your abbey due for consecration we must surely keep that peace.'

'With me being so unwell, you mean. Everyone is waiting for me to die, Harold.'

'Everyone is wishing you health, Sire. The longer you reign, the stronger England will be.'

'You speak well.'

'I speak true.'

'They are right though, Harold.' The king gripped his arm suddenly. 'I am not long for this world and in truth, I am ready to depart it. 'Tis only my fears for what I leave behind – or do *not* leave behind – that keep my feet tethered to this rough earth. You will take care of England, Harold, when I am gone?'

Harold looked nervously around. Servants were setting benches below them and showing the jury – twelve thegns rushed in from the local area – to their seats as the rebels moved closer to the gates. This was hardly the time for such a weighty conversation.

'Sire,' he pleaded, 'I have sworn too much on that already.'

'Duke William?' Edward waved this away like a dust mote and drew Harold further back on the dais. 'I absolve you of that false vow. You know as well as I that a king's final words are absolute. The heir I name in my passing is the heir God honours and where God leads, the people must follow.'

Harold glanced over at the great mass of rebels and his heart quailed.

'Sire, you are kind, truly, but I do not know how to rule.'

Edward just patted his arm, as if he had stated little more than apprehension at a new sword trick or the height of a horse's jump.

'You *do* know, Harold. Every part of you knows and always has. Now you just need to believe. That starts today. I wish you to lead this trial.'

Harold stared at him in horror.

'Sire, I cannot do that. The rebels seek your justice as God's representative on this earth.'

'And I will give it, Harold, through *my* representative on this earth – you.' He moved back to the throne suddenly and lifted the royal sceptre into his hand. It was heavy and they both watched it wobble in his frail grip. 'See, I am too weak to hold England.'

'Nay, Sire . . .'

'I am too weak, Harold. It is your turn now.'

He thrust the sceptre towards him and it shook so much Harold feared it would drop to the ground and shatter, but still he could not bear to take it.

'The rebels will not stand down, Sire,' he protested desperately. 'I fear we will lose my brother over this.'

'I fear, Harold, that we lost him some time ago. Now, please, take the sceptre for me as your king and, maybe more so, as your friend.' Gently he reached out his other hand and took Harold's, pressing it firmly onto the sceptre. 'I fought all my young life to rule England. It meant everything to me and I thank God every day that he granted me the honour of this great throne. It has not been the same for you, I know, but God calls us in different ways, Harold, and we must respond.'

Harold drew in a breath. To his left he could see Torr coming out of his bower in his richest clothes and heading their way in sharp, angry strides. To his right the great rebel army was moving through the compound gates, their collective footfall shaking the ground with giant determination. Dead ahead of him his king was waiting. He had no choice.

'As you wish, Sire.'

'As England wishes, Harold.'

'Look, our lords of Mercia approach.' Edward let go of the sceptre to point but Harold, feeling the weight of it in his hands, could not tear his eyes from its all-too-dazzling promise. 'Our lady too, if I am not much mistaken.'

At that Harold looked up and, following the king's wavering finger, saw Edyth walking towards them, flanked by her brothers. She was pale but she stood tall, holding her beautiful crown of Wales beneath her arm, and her eyes, when they met his, were steady. Harold could see no treachery in them, just calm, quiet support. And yet was she not here with enemy troops to force her brother into an earldom? Confused, he made himself step down from the dais and hold his arms wide, willing the sceptre not to shake.

'My lords, my lady – welcome.'

They all bowed. Harold was aware of everyone's eyes on the rod of justice but it took his own brother, stood to one side, to ask the question: 'What the hell are you doing with that, Harold?'

Harold turned to him.

'The king, *Earl* Torr, has asked me to wield it for him in this trial as he is still weak.'

Above them Edward bowed assent and sank onto his throne.

'We welcome your judgement, Earl Harold,' Morcar said, 'and ask leave to present our evidence regarding the rule of Northumbria.'

'Granted,' Harold agreed and waved the myriad rebel leaders

to the benches opposite the jury as their troops gathered in row after orderly row behind them. 'Earl Torr . . .'

He pointed to a chair set before the great crowd and saw his brother pale. For the first time in as long as he could remember, Torr looked frightened.

'Harold, for the love of God . . .' he started but it was too late for appeals, too late for anything personal between them. They were on England's stage now and must obey England's rules.

Harold took his own seat and the rebels stepped up with a list of grievances, carefully read from an elegant vellum by a composed young lord, Osric of Northallerton. The evidence was overwhelming. List after list of unattended problems, unfair judgements, tax frauds, abuse of the royal mints, and blatant favouritism were poured out into the soft autumn morning as the rebels paced before Torr's luxurious southern hunting lodge.

Lord Osric spoke eloquently and intelligently, a strong and passionate appeal for justice from a ruling elite. The jury listened intently but Harold could see from the way they looked at Torr that they were disgusted by him. It made him nervous. He was disgusted too but Torr was his brother; they had scrapped since they were little boys. What they were facing here was much more dangerous, for on this judgement rested the future of the whole kingdom.

'We present this evidence to the jury, to the king and to Earl Harold,' Osric eventually concluded, 'and ask for justice for the people of Northumbria who wish only to be ruled fairly and with due regard for their own interests and those of their country.'

Harold rose.

'Does anyone stand in defence of Earl Torr?' he asked.

Torr leaped to his feet.

'I do,' he spat. 'These people know nothing of the business of government and nothing of its costs.'

'Nay,' someone called from the back, 'we can see its costs right here.'

A bitter laugh rippled through the troops as all eyes roved around Torr's extravagant lodge.

'How dare you?! I am your earl. Do you expect me to live as you do, with your children in your bed and your animals at your feet and your . . .'

A great rumble ran around the crowd and instinctively Harold lifted his rod.

'Earl Torr, you will show respect for these people and for this court.'

'Why? They have shown none for me. I have done all I can to control their unruly land and this is how they repay me? It is spite.'

'It is,' Morcar agreed quietly, 'but it is you who spite us – and it must stop.'

Torr went for his sword and, without thinking, Harold leaped to face him, his only defence the jewelled sceptre of the realm. The crowd gasped and pressed forward as the two brothers stood up to each other.

'You would do this to me?' Torr hissed.

'You have done it to yourself, Torr.'

'You could stop it – you have the sceptre, brother dear, you have the power.'

'This is England, Torr; it is not a dictatorship. Our people have the right to speak and today they have spoken. An earldom is not a toy to play with but a child to care for, and it is all too clear that you have cared little for yours. Jury?'

He glanced across to the head of the jury, an elderly man, his back hunched but his eyes bright with understanding as he took in the rising tension around the arena. He shuffled forward and said in a loud voice: 'We find Earl Tostig guilty of failing to rule Northumbria in a just and fair manner.'

Harold knew what he had to do now but he felt as if he were screaming within. He could feel the sceptre pressing against Torr's sword with all the expectation of the crowd behind it but he could not form the words to condemn his brother to exile. What sort of a man did that?

He looked wildly round. He saw the king's ice-blue eyes boring expectantly into him, young Morcar's looking trustingly his way, and the troops, brows drawn, waiting. Then he saw Edyth, stood as firm and as sparkling as the damned sceptre. There was no doubt in her at all. Why? He had told her in Bosham that he needed unity, so why was she bringing him division?

He looked around the arena, confused, and suddenly saw that there *was* unity here, unity against Torr. Without him England would be stronger and she had seen that first. She might be standing opposite him but she was very much on his side and the strength of that crept through his spine, stiffening it. It was a rich, warm, energising feeling – it was, he realised, belief.

'Earl Torr, much as it pains me, as your brother, to do so, I must bow to the wishes of the people and the might of the great English justice system and pronounce you, for your own crimes, an exile of this land. You will surrender the earldom of Northumbria and you will depart from these shores with your family within five days. After that time, if you are caught in England your life will be forfeit. Do you understand?'

'Harold, no! You cannot do this to me. You cannot—'

'Do you understand?'

For a moment Torr increased the pressure of his sword against the sceptre but as the myriad nobles around him leaned forward he lost his nerve. Springing back, he lowered the weapon but his eyes stayed fixed on Harold.

'Oh, I understand, brother. I know treachery when I see it. Father would hate the man you have become.'

'Father would do the same.'

'You may think that, if you wish, but we both know otherwise. Family should stand together and you know it. You will pay for this, Harold Godwinson. God will make you pay for this and, believe me, so will I.'

In a flash of scarlet cloak, he flounced from the arena. Cheers erupted and men flung their hats in the air in celebration but all Harold could see was his father's face looking down on him. '*It is Torr that has done wrong,*' he told himself, '*Torr who has tarnished the family name,*' but even amongst the mass of men baying for his brother's exile it was hard to believe.

'You did right,' said a quiet voice at his side and he turned to see Edyth.

She put out a hand and he clutched at it.

'What is right?' he asked.

She had no answer but her fingers in his kept him upright and for now that seemed enough.

CHAPTER TWENTY-SIX

'*I* have brought you the north, Harold,' Edyth said softly. 'As I promised.'

'So it seems,' he agreed, drawing her away from the carousing rebels, before suddenly spinning round to trap her against an oak. 'I thought you were against me, Edie.'

'Against you? Never.'

'You led the Welsh against me.'

'A handful, no more, to ensure the correct result for us all.'

She forced herself to smile up at him. She did not want him to know that her Welsh troops had been bought with Billingsley, the town he had once gifted her. It had felt a sore price when she had negotiated it with Prince Bleddyn but it had been worth it.

'England will be secure,' she said now.

'With your brothers holding the north for me?'

'Exactly. They are true servants, Harold.'

'I doubt it not, Edyth, but the south will be uneasy with your family holding the balance of power.'

Edyth laughed.

'Hardly, Harold. Wessex is by far the most powerful earldom and your brothers hold all the riches of Kent and East Anglia.'

JOANNA COURTNEY

'The scales are even, perhaps,' he conceded, 'but the pans are not linked.'

'My lord?'

He was talking in riddles and her tired brain could not work them out. Now he leaned in so close she could see the moon curved in the dark blue of his irises like sideways silver smiles. Her heart pumped like a watermill in flood and she fought to quieten it.

'I came here in peace, Harold,' she protested weakly, 'to offer you my family's support and loyalty.'

'Which I accept gratefully but, as with all treaties, it needs ratification.'

'Ratification? You tangle me with snake words, Harold.' She pushed out at his chest but the solid muscle resisted her feeble protest and now he caught her hand and she felt his own heart beating hard against it. Her body pulsed treacherously. 'You cannot order me around,' she protested angrily. 'I am not yours to command just because you are sub-regulus.'

'Do not call me that!' His voice was sharp. He grabbed her shoulders, pulling her up against him. 'I'm sorry. This is hard, yes, but you *do* understand me, Edyth Alfgarsdottir. You have ever understood me. Your family and mine now hold England in our young hands and there is only one thing needed to make that alliance complete.'

'No!'

'Yes. You must marry me, Edyth.'

'No, Harold.' Edyth fought to hold back her tears. 'I have brought you the north,' she repeated, a plea.

'And in so doing have all but written our nuptial ceremony yourself. God help us, Edyth, but you saw what it's like out there. The country is not as stable as it was. It needs firm rule. Everyone is looking to me for that but I cannot do it without you.'

'I will keep the north to your cause, Harold, I swear it.'

He shook his head furiously.

'I know that. You do not understand, Edyth. I meant that I cannot do it without *you*.'

It was too sweet to bear. She tried to pull away.

'You are wed already.'

'You know that's not true.'

'Why not?' Fury flared in her, instantly hot as the deepest embers. 'Why did you not marry her properly, Harold? Why did you not spare us this?'

He shrugged helplessly.

'She would not let me. She does not believe in public conventions. She does not believe in rules and structures and titles.'

'Like queen?' Edyth whispered.

'Like queen.'

Edyth knew that much was true but she also knew that even if Harold was asking this of her to spare Svana, her own motivations were far baser. She pushed back against the tree but the bark of the old oak dug into her skin as if pushing her away.

'She will hate me,' she whispered.

'Nay, Edyth, she does not hate.'

'She should.'

'Your children . . .'

'Are still my children. I will explain the price of greatness to them.'

'I am a *price*?'

'No! Edyth, you are a jewel.'

'I am sick of jewels. I have four great rubies, Harold, do you know that? Four great rubies on the crown Griffin had made for me. They are beautiful, Harold, but they are of no *use* at all.'

'That's not true. They shine, as you shine, and the world needs that or it is too dull to bear.'

'You have an answer for everything.'

'I do not have an answer to my question – will you marry me, Edyth?'

My dearest Svana,

I write to you for mercy. You have never cleaved to the Roman church, I know, but I beg you to somehow find it in your heart to embrace their laws, at least outwardly, or we are both in peril. They want me to marry. You will know this. You have ever been wiser than I and ever purer of heart, though God knows that is not difficult now. I do not have the words for this and I know I stumble and make little sense. Forgive me. My pen is as confused as my heart.

I will say it. They want me to marry Harold, Svana. Your Harold. The court wills it so, the king wills it so, England wills it so. I will it not, but I have not your strength to resist the pulls of duty and expectation. Harold does not love me. Nay, he proceeds with this madness for love of but one woman – you. He seeks to protect you from the world he knows you despise and I, it seems, am to be the shield.

Preparations are afoot, Svana, and only one person can stop them. If you were to come now, if you were to stand before the altar in my place, the world would have to recognise you as Harold's true wife. You would be queen, Svana, and I would be your ever-loyal servant, not the viper at your breast.

I have delayed all I can, my dear friend, but the date is now set for two weeks hence. The king ails again and the court is in a panic that, it seems, only a wedding can calm. You told me the world was spinning and now it has spun me off my unwary feet. I know I can be queen, if so it must be, but I would far rather be your friend.

I hate to ask this of you for I know you see no reason in pandering to the foolish notions of those less trusting than your dear self. I fear you will despise me for this missive and blame you not, for I despise myself, but for our friendship at least, please come.

With unending love and sorrow,
Edyth

My dearest Edyth,

Save your spite for me, my dearest child, for I am the one at fault here. I am strong only in the awareness of my own weakness. Know this, Edie, I cannot and I will not come to Westminster to lie on the altar of Rome's insidious rules and the court's leeching fears. It would break my soul and even for you, my love, I cannot do that.

When I handfasted to Harold I knew I was taking on two men – the simple lover who pledged his troth to me barefoot in the grass at Nazeing and the earl who would always, sooner or later, have to put his boots back on and ride forth from my estate. I have treasured the former, and treasure him still, but his path has twisted too far from mine and I am not the right woman to carry him forward in these troubled times.

I am deeply sorry that it must be you who does so and yet I am also gladder than you will ever believe. For if there was one woman in this bitter world who I can trust to take care of the man who is dearer to me than my own self, it is you. We both know that Harold is not good alone and whilst I will ever be with him in my heart, he needs a woman to ride with him, to talk with him, to mount the throne with him. I have not the birth for it, nor the connections nor, indeed, the desire. It is too high a climb for me but you, Edyth, you have the spirit and the courage and the fire to climb higher than either of us. You always have.

I ask more of you, my dearest friend, than any woman should but you are more than any woman. Go safely, Edyth, and know that when your wedding bells ring out my heart rings with them.

Your Svana

CHAPTER TWENTY-SEVEN

Coventry, December 1065

oventry was ablaze with light. Edyth, staring out from her hastily refurbished 'bridal' chamber, felt as dazzled as if the devil himself were shoving his fiery torches into her face. The sun was not yet up and the city was still in the grip of one of the coldest nights of the year but already revellers were dancing around the braziers lit in every available space and gathering in clusters of vibrant shadows in the myriad pavilions all over the compound. The court, it seemed, was keen to begin its wedding celebrations early.

'I thought we agreed it would be a quiet service,' she protested to her mother, who was rustling through a mound of gowns behind her.

'You meant that?' Lady Meghan replied.

'You did not?'

'Clearly,' Godiva said drily, taking Edyth's arm to pull her away from the window opening. 'Come, my dear, we must prepare calmly for the day ahead.'

Edyth flushed.

'Calmly?!' she snapped. 'How can I be calm with this racket? I swear all of England is here.'

'And very good it is for the city too. I hear the market traders have taken more in a week than they usually do in a year. Is that not wonderful?'

'It is, Grandmother, truly. I'm just not comfortable with all this . . . pomp.'

Godiva wrinkled up her elegant nose.

'It is not there to make you comfortable, my girl, but to proclaim the honour and power of your family – as well you know if you stop to think about it. Besides, all this "pomp" as you call it is something you are going to have to become used to.'

'You are indeed.' Meghan leaped up. 'You will be the Lady of Wessex, second in rank only to Queen Aldyth herself. Your father would be so proud.'

Her eyes misted and, with a soft sigh, Edyth leaned forward to kiss her.

'Father used to tell me to steer clear of Godwinsons,' she said gently.

'Circumstances change. Alfgar would have embraced that. He was always very . . . adaptable.'

Edyth thought of their exile ten years ago. Alfgar had crept from Westminster like a squashed beetle but by the time they'd reached Rhuddlan anyone would have thought that a trip west had been his greatest wish. She smiled fondly.

'I wish he could be here with us now.'

'As do I, my dear. He would revel in all this – and you must revel in it for his sake.' She cast a look back across the room, worry creasing her plump brow. 'Have you enough gowns, do you think?'

'Enough gowns?! Mother, I have enough gowns to clothe half of England.'

'Nonsense. You must look the part, not just today but in the months and years to come, especially if you are to be—'

'Mother, hush. Do not say it.'

'Everyone else does.'

'Then they are foolish.'

'Or honest. Perhaps, Edyth, my love, you are the one deceiving yourself? The rest of the court sees the situation very clearly indeed – why do you think they are all here?'

As Meghan clucked back across the room to check the damned gowns again Edyth sighed. She thought back to her first wedding in an isolated hall on the stark Welsh coast – warm and raucous and easy. She had loved Griffin, had she not? Sometimes now, when her sharp, violent, guilty feelings for her new groom threatened to topple her, she wondered if her whole eight-year first marriage had been a sham.

'It was not,' she said fiercely.

'Beg pardon, my dear?' Godiva asked.

Edyth grabbed at her grandmother's arm.

'You said I would have a choice of who I married.'

'And you did.'

'Hardly. No one has ceased sermonising about how good this would be – for England, for the family, for the future, for everyone but me.'

Godiva looked at her, something of the old sharpness back in her all-seeing eyes.

'I think, my dear, that you do not despise this marriage as much as you feel you should.'

Edyth looked down. Godiva was right. She had tried to be noble about this, tried to approach her nuptials as the sacrifice she had pleaded it to be to her brothers, to Harold, to Svana, but the truth was far less worthy. The thought of sharing Harold's bed seemed to lurk like a flame between her legs and there were no words for her betrayal of Svana, not when every damned piece of her flesh willed her on in it. There was no sword point at her back, no hostage on the altar, no coercion save what was 'good for England'. Was that enough? Maybe, but tonight, in her marriage bed, would England be there then? Edyth doubted it and her skin prickled with shameful desire.

'Do not blame yourself,' Godiva said softly. 'In the end, my dear, you only have your own path to forge and yours is a good one. Truly. Now, shall we dress you? If the whole of England is indeed here, we had better not keep them waiting.'

Meghan needed no second urging and within moments Edyth was encased in her wedding outfit, a beautiful fine wool overgown in deepest green, artistically cut up the long sleeves and at the sides of the remarkably full skirt to show off an expensive cream silk undershift. The hem and cuffs were studded with so many jewels that Edyth marvelled at the seamstresses her mother must have pressed into service to have it ready in time and it was tied at the waist with a similarly studded girdle embroidered with the entwined emblems of Mercia and Wessex.

'Beautiful,' Meghan proclaimed. 'Now – shoes.'

She sniffed as she fetched them and Edyth hid a smile. With such an elegant dress she should be in light calfskin slippers but on that she had truly put her foot down. She was to process through the city on one of the coldest days of the year and she would wear boots. Meghan had grumbled but capitulated, rushing out to find Coventry's most superior tanner to create something worthy of her elevated daughter and as Edyth stepped out of her bower on Edwin's arm she was glad of the firm feel of the beautiful footwear. Even so, her legs shook as the gates were flung open and the first roar of the huge crowds rolled over her, and she had to lean heavily on her brother for support.

'Smile, sister,' he urged, squeezing her hand. 'Many have slept out all night to gain a position by the road to see you.'

Looking around her Edyth could see that was true. The men, women and children closest to her procession were bundled up in so many blankets that they looked more like bales of wool than people but they waved and cheered and reached out supplicating hands towards her and she felt warmed by their simple joy. Lifting her head, she let herself be led down through Coventry's winding streets to the door of the cathedral, smiling and waving and touching the hands of all she could as she passed. Ewan and Morgan walked proudly behind their mother holding her train and little Nesta followed, dressed in a cream gown that Edyth doubted would last the day, holding Morcar's hand and waving like a perfect miniature bride.

The crowds loved them all and by the time Edyth turned into the market square and approached the cathedral she had almost forgotten why she was here. The sight of Harold, however, stood tall and handsome in a rich scarlet tunic at the top of the steps, brought her right back to the union at the heart of all this celebration and she staggered.

'Steady, sister. I have you fast.'

Edwin's arm tightened, holding her firm, and she glanced up at him. He had grown into a strong young man, still as quiet and serious as he had been as a boy but with a calm authority that she knew must have been hard won.

'We have come a long way, Edwin,' she said.

'We have. I told you, I think, that it would be our turn next and here we are.'

'Here we are.'

'You will make a fine first lady, Edyth – the finest. I am so proud.'

Edyth's throat contracted.

'Nay, Edwin, you will make me cry.'

'At least, as bride, you are allowed. I, however, run the risk of looking a fool.'

He ran a surreptitious finger beneath his eye and Edyth

reached up to give him a swift kiss before together they mounted the steps to meet Harold, Earl of Wessex and subregulus of England. Edyth had no idea where to look but just then the great Coventry bells tolled out a joyous peal above them and she heard Svana's words: *know that when your wedding bells ring out my heart rings with them.* For a moment she cast her eyes east, as if she might see her dear friend standing there, but there were only leering courtiers so, lifting her chin, she looked straight into Harold's eyes as he took her hand and turned her to face him.

They were wed there by the Bishop of Coventry – another of Edwin's quiet commands – whilst the two great archbishops of York and Canterbury were left to jostle over singing the psalms at the blessing that followed. The service was kept short due to both the cold of the day and the squash in a Mercian cathedral that had never been built to take such a mass of nobles and royalty. Edyth almost laughed to see them all packed against each other like peasants and a glance at Harold told her he, too, was amused by the sight. She longed to speak to him about it but the demands of the ceremony left them with no chance to exchange anything more than a chaste kiss before they were back out on the streets as man and wife, the crowds screaming even more wildly than before.

'It seems we are better entertainment than any fair, you and I,' Harold whispered to her.

It was an apt summary. For the rest of the day Edyth felt as if she were indeed being whirled around like a maypole ribbon, wrapped up and displayed for all to see. At some point, though, she would have to be unwrapped and the thought of it sent shudders through her, making her maypole feast seem darker – both more thrilling and more fearful. Night came fast in midwinter and soon she and Harold would be ejected from the revels and left to the real business of marriage.

'Must we be publicly bedded?' she had demanded of her mother a few days back. 'I am a widow after all and he . . .'

' . . . is a great man with a great future, and a tricky past. The court must see this done properly.'

Edyth knew she was right but still, as the pyramids of honey-sparkled pastries were devoured and a golden goblet was passed around filled with rich, spiced wine to toast the marriage bed, she found her smiles draining away, taking her renewed confidence with them. By the time Meghan escorted her to the wedding chamber she was as shaky as an old ship.

She could hear the raucous noise of the men bearing Harold to her and she sat unsteadily down on the edge of the bed, heart skittering like an unbroken foal. Her mother clucked at her.

'Your shift, sweetheart.'

'Of course,' Edyth agreed but her fingers were trembling and Meghan had to lift it from her and tuck her, naked, under the sheets.

'We are ready,' she called and ran to open the door.

Edyth clutched at the heavy woollen blanket as Harold strode in with his men but before they could even strike up a song, he had gained the bed. He removed his rich robe and in a flash of flesh slid in beside her. Placing an arm around her shoulders, he nodded curtly to the crowd.

'You may go now.'

The men stood, stunned into silence, like young boys who'd had their pastries snatched away. They looked awkwardly at each other and Edyth felt Harold bristle at her side but then, thank the Lord, his brother Garth took charge.

'Let us not delay the groom, lads,' he said easily and, with a friendly wink at Harold, he hustled the men towards the door.

They bumbled and grumbled but moved away. Edyth saw

her own brothers hesitate and offered them a tight smile so that they too departed, taking Meghan with them. Suddenly all the pomp and ceremony of Mercia's great day was gone, but it left little peace in its wake for now the room was empty save for her naked groom and the thudding of her heart.

'You are fearful, Edyth?'

Was she? She dared not look at him but she could feel his body against hers and her own pulsing wantonly towards it.

'I am fearful, Harold.' She lifted her eyes and there he was, looking down at her with such concern. She had fallen into his arms again, but this time far, far deeper in. 'I am fearful,' she whispered, 'because I want you so madly.'

He caught his breath and she felt him stir and dared to run her fingers across his thigh. It was hard with muscle and soft with downy hair. His grip tightened and then he was up and over her.

'I want you too, Edyth.'

She could feel him straining against her and her legs parted beneath him. He kissed her, softly at first and then harder and she clutched at his back, arching towards him. Memories galloped across her mind: Harold catching her out of the tree in his strong arms; Harold gifting her Billingsley, his eyes dark as she stood on Griffin's arm; Harold accepting her surrender at Rhuddlan and keeping her safe from Torr's lascivious attentions when all the time, even before she realised it, it had been he who had tempted her; Harold twining his fingers in hers at Bosham and kissing her as if it was the only sanity in a mad world. Was it? Or was this, in fact, the madness?

'You said once that bedding me would be like bedding a sister,' she choked out, holding him off.

'I lied.' He spoke against her lips, grazing them. 'Perhaps to myself as much as to you. This is a strange marriage, Edyth, but it is a marriage all the same. *Our* marriage. We owe much to many, but this we owe only to ourselves.'

And then his mouth was devouring her and his body was pressing against her and Edyth cried out as he entered her, filling her up as if she had been empty all this time until tonight. There was no room for guilt; no room for duty, for families or countries or past or future, but room only for now and Edyth surrendered herself gladly.

CHAPTER TWENTY-EIGHT

Westminster, January 1066

The court stood silent. The great door to the royal chamber was tight shut and beyond that King Edward fought for his life. With him were the archbishops Eldred and Stigand, Queen Aldyth and her brother, Earl Harold. Everyone else waited in the chamber next door, separated from the mortal battle by thick wooden walls and falling snow. It was a bitter night and, despite the well-stoked fire, they were all wrapped in heavy furs so, to Edyth's weary eyes, they resembled scared little animals in the woodland.

Across the compound voices rose in the sweet tones of matins, welcoming in a day that would surely mark the end of Edward's twenty-four-year reign of England. It had been the longest and most peaceful reign since King Athelstan's over a hundred years before and it had done much to shape the prosperous, stable and highly envied country that he was now about to leave to the mercies of others. The monks' voices rang eerily around the great vaults of Edward's new abbey church, consecrated just yesterday, though Edward, after all his eager years of planning, had been too stricken to attend.

He had made it to Christ's mass only on a litter, weakened by the first convulsions that had struck him the night before.

292

He had lain before the altar, gaunt, almost spectral, with a beatific smile on his face, but the effort had drained him and he had not risen since. Now it was the feast of the epiphany but the matins psalms were muted, cautious – respectful. Listening to them, Edyth could not help but remember another Twelfth Night, years back, when Harold had brought fire to Rhuddlan and she had fled from him across frozen seas. She had not, in the end, got far.

The courtiers shifted tired legs, drawing her back into today's struggle. Edward had sunk into delirium yesterday evening and all had rushed to his deathbed but still he lingered.

'Can he speak, do you think?' Edyth whispered to Earl Garth.

'Can he name his heir, you mean? I do not know. He must, surely?'

'What if he names . . .' Edyth glanced nervously around but no one was paying attention, ' . . . Duke William?'

'Don't, Edyth! Why would he?'

'They say, do they not, that men regress as death approaches and the king spent his youth in Normandy.'

'Not until he was ten. He's English, Edyth, and he will name an Englishman. He *must* name an Englishman.'

'I hope he sees that as clearly as you.'

Edyth glanced to Edwin and Morcar, huddled together near the fire. Between them they ruled the north. Harold held the south and the link, the lynchpin, was Edyth herself. Her marriage held England together but if Edward did not name Harold as king it had been for naught. She rubbed at her temples, trying to ease the ache between them. She and Harold had been married a month. They had spent the days at court, flattering the lords and ladies who collected around them in a building frenzy as the king's health visibly faded, and the nights wrapped around each other in desperate, mindless passion.

Edyth felt as if she were existing in a state of disbelief that tonight's prolonged vigil had done nothing to ease.

Her children seemed content at least. Harold was kind to them, sparring with the boys and taking little Nesta on his shoulders or letting her scale him like a mountain so that she gazed up at him with open admiration much, Edyth feared, as her mother did. She wondered if the thought of his own children tore at his heart, as it did at hers, but did not dare ask. So much between them had to go unspoken.

Svana had not written again, nor had she come to the Yuletide court, but she had sent Godwin and Edmund with gifts – a new sword-belt for Harold and a pair of tiny, exquisitely crafted silver bells for Edyth. The significance had not been lost on her and she kept them with her wherever she went so that their teasing tinkles might drown out her fears. They rarely did and now, somewhere beyond the walls, another bell rang, low and sweet.

The courtiers raised their heads. Their shoulders rolled back beneath their furs. Their eyes blinked. The bell rang again, a soft call to the Holy Ghost to claim a soul – a royal soul.

'God have mercy.'

Garth crossed himself. Others took up the prayer but all eyes were fastened on the door. Eventually it opened, bringing Archbishop Stigand in on a flurry of snow.

'The king is dead,' he announced. 'May the Lord have mercy on his soul.'

'May He have mercy,' came the obedient response but everyone was waiting.

'King Edward named his successor in his dying breaths. His choice is sanctified by God who has now taken him to himself.'

Edyth felt Garth tense at her side and saw her brothers sidling towards her, creases in their young brows. The court held its breath.

'Even as we mourn the passing of a great king, we hail the rising of a new one.'

Morcar rolled his eyes and Edyth thought again of Svana and her hatred of Roman pomposity; she would see this cleric for the attention-seeking fool he was. She felt a treacherous desire to laugh and, struggle against it as she might, it burst forth in a tiny sob. The archbishop frowned but gathered himself at last.

'May God bless King Harold II.'

Edyth covered her face with her hands, all laughter gone. It was done. Relief crested through her but fear rode high on its back. It was not done; it was but begun.

'And God bless Queen Edyth.'

All eyes turned her way and, like skittles, the lords and ladies of England dropped to their knees before her. Even her stately grandmother bowed low and Edyth unpeeled her fingers and forced herself to stand tall and make her proud, though her knees were shaking and her breath seemed locked in her throat. She had been hailed as Queen of Wales with cheers and laughter and sloshing wine; it had done nothing to prepare her for the studied reverence of this awesome moment. Should she speak? What was there to say?

Panic began to rise inside her but now the door opened again and all eyes swivelled like frogs in a marsh as Harold stepped inside. Shoulders dipped instantly, as if trying to bow even deeper, as Harold crossed to Edyth's side. Their eyes met and his fingers laced tightly around hers, as once they had done in Bosham when this day still seemed a nightmare away. He faced the crowd.

'We thank you all for your loyalty. We will need it in the time ahead – England will need it. Rise, councillors, friends, we are joined in sorrow today.'

He sounded so noble; God surely had chosen him for a

reason and perhaps even chosen her too. It seemed hard to countenance but everything pointed that way, everything except her own conscience. That, though, was now a luxury she could ill afford. Stigand stepped forward again.

'King Edward will be buried on the morrow in God's holy sight before the altar raised to His glory by that blessed king. King Harold will be crowned the same day, his queen with him.'

Edyth turned to Harold.

'Tomorrow?'

'There is not a moment to lose, Edyth. The throne is far from stable and the sooner we make it so the better.'

'We should tour.'

He looked at her curiously and she spun round to grab his other hand in hers. 'We should tour the whole country – the north first. Let people see you, talk to you. It is what you do well, Harold, and people will trust a king they have seen with their own eyes.' He nodded thoughtfully and she pushed on. 'Griffin skulked at Rhuddlan. He thought he was safe, but it was an illusion – as you proved all too well.' Harold grimaced but now was the time for lessons, not recriminations. 'We only rode south when it was already too late – that is not a mistake you can afford to make.'

'You are right. You are so right, Edyth. See, I told you I needed you as queen.'

'Well, you have me,' she said shortly. 'And now there is work to be done.'

Edyth was crowned in Westminster in her wedding gown and again two months later in the astonishing minster at York. The great church could not match Edward's new abbey in artistic detail but with its soaring architraves and thirty separate altars, Edyth found it every bit as impressive. The ceremony was led by the down-to-earth Archbishop Eldred and for Edyth it was far more moving and meaningful than the service at Westminster.

Perhaps it was that she felt she belonged more completely in the north, especially with her brothers standing as her proud companions everywhere they went, or perhaps it was simply that she'd had time to accustom herself to her new title. Day upon day of being cheered through the streets had imprinted the goodwill of England firmly onto her strange queenship and, more than anything, she had enjoyed serving the country that was apparently now hers to rule. Sometimes she remembered Griffin's words way back when he had first asked her to marry him: '*You will be a great queen,*' he'd told her. '*You deserve to be a great queen – greater, perhaps, than a rough king like myself can offer.*'

Had he known? Had he somehow seen? That was ridiculous, she knew, but then so much about life felt ridiculous and she hoped that, in some strange way, her ferociously ambitious first husband would have been proud to see her here today.

York was a beautiful city. Some of the ancient Roman walls had been maintained for defence but they covered a huge area and much of the land within them was given over for grazing. The main town nestled in the rich area north of the confluence of the vast River Ouse and its smaller tributary, the Fosse. It had less of the excited bustle of progress that surrounded the ever-growing Westminster but in its stead it had the solid calm of a city sure of its place in the world. And sure too, it seemed, of its king and queen.

'You were right to make me come, Edyth,' Harold said the night of their northern coronation as they lay in bed together at the heart of the ancient royal palace. 'If this kingship does not last, if—'

'No ifs, Harold.'

'Well, let it suffice, then, that I shall treasure this time. I did not think I would ever feel truly a king but here I do. I have a surprise for you.'

'You do?'

He was smirking like a small boy and now he leaped out of bed and strode to the side table to fetch a small pouch. Edyth turned away. She was used to Harold's body against hers, inside hers, but still she was shy of looking at it and did not turn back until he was safety beneath the covers once more.

'See.'

He opened the pouch and drew out a penny, so shiny it had to have come straight from the mint. Edyth stretched out a hand and he placed it into her palm, face up.

'Harold, it's you.'

'It is but that's not the best bit. Here.'

He flipped it over to reveal a single word, stamped confidently into the silver: 'PAX'.

'Peace,' Edyth translated. 'That's perfect.'

He smiled awkwardly.

'Sadly writing it on England's coins does not make it come true but it is a start.'

'Have you heard any more?'

'Nothing from Scandinavia but Duke William is building ships. He will come, Edyth.'

'And we will be ready for him. We have the finest fyrd in Europe, with the finest leader.'

'I hope you are right. I'm told Torr has been turned away by Duke William but I will not believe it until I see it for myself. That Norman is capable of all levels of trickery and Torr is little better. He hates me for choosing your brother over my own and maybe he is right.'

'Hey.' Edyth took his chin and crawled up to straddle him. 'That does not sound like a man who feels like a king.'

He rubbed his fingers across one of her nipples, a thoughtless gesture, almost as if he were polishing one of his new coins, but it sent desire shooting through her. She was as hungry for him as a peasant at harvest time, determined to gorge herself for fear of famine ahead, and now she rolled her hips back, rubbing against him, rousing him.

'God, Edyth, I knew I said this must be a proper marriage, but I had no idea it . . . Edyth?' She jerked away, her lust collecting into a hard, hateful ball, rattling its way up from the wanton core between her legs and shaking tears from her eyes. 'Edyth, I'm sorry. Don't cry.'

'I should not pester you. You are not mine to command.'

'Nonsense. That's nonsense, Edyth. You are my wife.'

'To everyone else, yes, but we both know that is a lie, don't we?'

She scrabbled for covers, pulling them up and around herself. '*It's late,*' her head told her. '*It's been a long day, an amazing day. Don't spoil it. Don't fight him. Don't annoy him.*' It was no use. Sorrow was rising up, cresting high on a wave of guilt, and she could escape it no longer.

'Do you pretend I'm her?'

'Edyth!'

'Do you? Is that how you bear it?'

'No.' He grabbed her wrists, yanking her towards him so the covers fell away leaving her naked. 'It's different, Edyth. I don't know how to explain it. When I was in the Ottoman lands years back, I met men with more than one wife. It is their way, their law. I spoke to one of them about it and he said he loved them all equally. I did not understand it at the time but I do now.'

'You love us both.'

'Is that wrong?'

'But you love her best – as you should.'

He shook her gently.

'Best, Edyth? What is best? Which of your children do you love best?'

'None, but that is different, Harold.'

'Is it? Surely it shows the heart can be open? I know this is unusual, Edyth, but the times are unusual and it is we – you and I – who must carry them. Others may not understand but surely, if we are honest with one another, we can? Did you not love Griffin?'

'Yes, but he is dead.'

'And I am alive and so are you – alive and here with me.'

His hands held her wrists and now his lips found her neck, biting at it, teasing a flare from her body which her mind fought uselessly to resist. He was right. She was here with him and, intangible as that sometimes felt, it was all she had and she must make all of it that she could.

CHAPTER TWENTY-NINE

Westminster, May 1066

For what felt like months nothing happened. England busied itself with Easter. Harold and Edyth were cheered around the south and the blossoms opened. The lambs were born and it was possible to believe, if you did not look over your shoulder to the seas, that all was bounty and peace in King Harold's England.

'Begging your pardon, Sire,' Avery said one morning as he was helping Harold dress, 'but it's Trimilchi next week.'

'So it is.' Harold turned to Edyth, burrowed into the covers, not yet accustomed to being seen in the royal bed, even by servants. 'Shall we celebrate the May Day, my queen?'

Edyth considered. Trimilchi, or May Day as it was becoming known, was an ancient festival with its roots in paganism and it could get a little wild. King Edward had reined festivities back in the pious last years of his life but it was celebrated the length and breadth of the country and it would be an honour to mirror that in Westminster.

'I think we should,' she said. 'I shall set plans in motion today.'

Harold grinned at her.

'You will have to rise then.'

'All in good time,' she retorted primly. 'Avery can summon my maids when he is done with you.'

Avery bowed and backed away and Edyth looked around the sumptuous royal chamber with its richly hung bed, embroidered seats and expensively glassed windows. She might be still shy about being with Harold but, God help her, she was swiftly becoming accustomed to being a queen again. She scrambled up, grabbing her bedrobe, and Harold wrinkled his nose.

'Must you wear that, Edie? You look so much nicer without and is it not, after all, ancient tradition to go naked at Trimilchi?'

'In Wales it was certainly encouraged,' she agreed lightly and his eyes darkened.

'In Wales, as far as I can see, too much was encouraged.'

He advanced on her, his eyes flicking to the bed, but she ducked his arms with a smile.

'What's past is past. Come now, King Harold, we have a feast to prepare.'

Four days later, on the eve of Trimilchi, Edyth looked out across the Chelsea meadowlands and smiled with pride. Preparations had been frantic but the result was magnificent. The trees were hung with ribbons and coloured pastries. Two great piles of dry wood were set for bonfires and the royal tents stood, sides open to the soft spring air and trestles laden with food and drink to sustain the courtiers through a long night of celebration.

It looked a rich feast but in truth Edyth and her cooks had been forced to be creative for food was sparse and dry in this lean period before the crops began to yield. The ale, however, was plentiful and Harold's men had caught a boar in the forest this morning so at least there would be fresh meat. Besides, no one was here for the food. The joy of rekindling the ancient feast-night, designed to ward off spirits sneaking through the loosened boundaries between the living and the dead on the eve of the summer festival, would be enough to sustain them.

The courtiers were chattering excitedly as they flooded across the meadow. They were all dressed in green – the faeries' colour – and many, Edyth included, wore ribbons and flowers intertwined into their costumes, at odds with the usual more sombre, tight-lined fashions of the court. Even the adults skipped with the mass of overexcited children as they milled around the great oak that would be the centre of the festivities. They seemed stripped of their usual ranks and restrictive order out here in the open and something about their carefree muddle reminded Edyth of Griffin.

She had teased Harold about Wales's traditions but it was true that there Trimilchi had lingered firmly in its wanton Beltane origins. Griffin's court had paraded statues of the Green Man, clad in little more than leaves, and couples had jumped naked, or 'sky-clad', over fires for fertility before claiming the sparse shelter of the bushes. Edyth flushed to remember her own husband 'green-gowning' her little more than a sapling's length from other couples welcoming the summer in each other's arms. It was no coincidence that so many women had gone to their childbed in February and not all of them married either, not that anyone in Wales had concerned themselves with such 'Roman' scruples.

In England, however, things were more civilised, at least in the early part of the celebrations. Already today the court had crammed into Edward's new abbey to celebrate a mass for Mary, the bearer of Christ and therefore the queen of the May Day celebrations of fecundity and fertility. Her statue had been brought forth to the meadows at the end of the service and sat coyly beneath the great oak but already coloured eggs lay at her feet and love-token ribbons twirled in the branches above her head as the courtiers embraced more earthy traditions.

As the skies darkened forgivingly, the singing and dancing began and Edyth had little doubt that, even in Westminster, the bushes would not go unexplored once night was fully upon them. She glanced to the trees behind. The woodland was little more than a copse these days, so much had been cut back for housing, and she wondered if the tree she had climbed as an eager girl still stood. She would not recognise it if it did – her eyes had not been on the branches but on the couple beneath. She flushed as she recalled Torr's lazy sensuality when he'd claimed her as a dance partner and his dark pleasure in her foolish spying the next day. Thank the Lord Harold had been close or the naive episode could have ended very differently.

'Are you well, Edie?'

His voice spoke through her memories and she looked up at her then saviour, now, by some strange tangle of fate, her husband.

'Very well, Harold.' She shook the past away. 'The court is in festive mood.'

'As it should be. We must keep the spirits back with our good cheer tonight.'

'Such superstition, Harry, from the King of England?'

'Even kings are men before God, especially on nights like this.'

He touched his temporary crown, a simple plait of rowan, and Edyth's fingers went instinctively to her own. They had been crowned king and queen of the Trimilchi as soon as the party had deposited St Mary beneath the oak and were honorary faeries for the night. Edyth laughed at the thought.

'Come, Harry,' she teased, 'a civil man like you cannot believe in witches and sprites?'

'No,' he agreed and his voice was surprisingly sombre, 'but

there is more to this world, Edyth, than we will ever know. That's what . . .'

He caught himself.

'What Svana says?' Edyth asked and he nodded. She thought for a moment and then said, 'She would like tonight. Indeed. Harold, if the court were this way all the time she might like it enough to—'

'But it is not.'

'No.' Edyth pushed away her own ghosts and reached up to kiss his cheek. 'So we must make the most of it. Shall we dance?' She pointed to the spiralling figures around the oak, winding long ribbons round the great trunk to bless it and seal its fertility and their own. They were holding hands and laughing, their costumes melding into the green of the grass as the light faded. 'It looks fun, does it not?'

'It looks fun, Edie,' he agreed, 'but if you have not noticed, they are all women.'

'Then they will welcome a man.'

Harold laughed. He reached for her chin and tipped her face up to his. Someone had set fire to the tinder in the two piles of wood beyond the oak and she could see the first of the flames dancing in his pupils as he smiled down at her.

'Later, Edie. The men will dance later.'

'I don't doubt that, my lord. I have been green-gowning before, you know.'

'Edyth!'

'Harold? You don't need to play the innocent with me these days.'

He huffed.

'I remember a time when *you* were the innocent one, Edyth Alfgarsdottir.'

'I was thinking on that myself just now but it is a time, thankfully, long past. Torr is gone, praise God.'

'For now.'

'For now is enough, Harry, and if you will not dance with me, I will go alone.'

She took a step towards the dancers but he caught her hand and pulled her back.

'No green-gowning.'

'Only with you.'

He smiled and bent to brush a light kiss across her lips before letting her go. She ran to join the women who opened up their circle to let her within. The ribbons were wound to the ground now and the court musicians, who had earlier been grumbling about the effect of the night-damp on their precious instruments, seemed to have forgotten their complaints and were stirring up a jig. The notes of their lutes and pipes tripped across the soft air and tickled at the heels of the ladies. Several, Edyth noticed, had already shed their shoes and she was glad she'd remembered to send the steward's men out across these grazing lands with brooms and rakes.

She clucked at herself; it was a festival night and she should not be fussing about domestic trivia. She need not be queen now, just a girl in a rowan crown dancing by the firelight. She let her hands be clasped and picked up her feet to the music. The bonfires were burning high, throwing flames skywards as if they sought to be stars. Sparks thrust into the purpling sky and fell to the ground where children, squealing, pounced on them with their hard little boots. Edyth spotted Nesta clasping her Uncle Morcar's hand, heedlessly keeping back the older ladies vying for attention from the new earl. Ewan and Morgan were with a gang of the court lads playing tag in and out of the trees and she heard their voices calling to their new friends in swift, easy English with barely a whisper of a Welsh lilt.

'Catch me if you can!'

Their happy calls rippled between the notes of the jig,

warming Edyth's heart. 'For now' was indeed enough. Tonight, at least, the enemies over the seas could stay in the shadows with the other evil spirits; the English fires were burning high enough to keep them all away.

The woman to her left dropped her hand and new fingers clasped her own. They were warm and dry and something about their touch caught at Edyth's breath. She turned. It was almost dark now and the woman's face was lit only by the firelight catching in its contours but Edyth would know it anywhere. She gasped and her lips formed the name but the woman stopped her.

'Don't say it. If you do not say it then I am not here.'

Edyth stared at her old friend.

'You are a sprite, then?'

'Nay. Nay, not that, Edyth. Never that. I am all too human.'

Edyth drew Svana in against the rainbowed trunk and the circle of revellers danced on around them.

'I'm so sorry . . .' she began but again the other woman silenced her.

'No apologies, Edie. Not tonight. Not ever.'

'Then why have you come?'

'To see you.'

'To see if I am filling my role?'

'Nay! Not to test you, Edyth, truly, just to *see* you. To . . . know you are still here.' She looked down. 'You think me foolish.'

Edyth relaxed.

'I do not. I have been thinking the same myself, only not so clearly. Even when I was in Wales I never felt so far from you as I have done these last months.'

'It must be that way, Edyth, we both know that, but I thought that tonight, beneath the trees with the solid world in flux, I might creep between the gaps of "must be" for just a while.'

'You creep well. Come, we should find Harold.'

At that, though, Svana recoiled.

'I could not, Edyth. He is yours now.'

'But—'

'He is yours. Come, my love, the dance is turning without us. We must rejoin the circle.'

She indicated the women still moving around them and Edyth drew in a deep breath. The air was rich with the scent of earth and soot and spiced wine but beneath it all now ran a wisp of meadow flower – summer truly come at last. On an impulse, she grasped one of the myriad ribbons sewn to the waist-clasp of her gown and tugged it loose.

'Here,' she said. 'We must tie it to the tree for friendship.'

Her old friend pulled a ribbon from her own dress, green too but a far lighter shade, like a new leaf. She handed it to Edyth who twisted the two together and knotted them firmly closed at either end. Grasping a sturdy stem, she threaded the interlinked ribbon over it, looping it back on itself to keep it tight to the tree. It spun giddily as she released the branch and she watched, entranced.

'They look half-crazed.'

'Maybe we do too. Come, Edie, let's dance while we can.'

Edyth nodded and together they stepped out of their little space at the centre of the revellers and rejoined the circle. Night had fallen in earnest now and all around people had become their own shadows – shapes against the fire that held back the night. The great Thames rushed past to one side, eddying in pockets of froth like souls dancing in the moonlight, and beyond, torches burned on Thorney Island, illuminating the pale stone of Edward's beautiful abbey. Edyth half-expected him, too, to materialise on the Chelsea meadow but no such ghost came to seize Harold's crown, or her own. King Edward was dead but England lived on, strong and proud and certain.

In the shades of a night half-Christian and half-pagan it no longer seemed to matter who was who. Laughter sounded the same from lord or lowly servant and together the English court celebrated the arrival of another summer. Time became as formless as faces. The moon rose, silver-bright, and couples crept like beetles into the trees. Edyth danced on, entranced, until suddenly an arm caught her waist and she was pulled from the circle.

'There you are, Edie. I thought my queen had been spirited away.' She blinked up at Harold, then looked nervously around. 'Edyth?' His voice tightened. 'Edyth, where have you been?'

'Dancing, Harold. Here, with . . .'

She looked around again. Faces swam in the misty moonlight but she could not find the one she sought.

'With whom?'

'Are you jealous?'

'Should I be?'

'No. No, you definitely should not.' She pulled him closer. 'I have been with Svana.'

'What?' He leaped as if stung by an arrow-tip. 'That's not possible, Edyth. You have drunk too deeply of the wine.' Even as he spoke, though, his eyes flitted across the turning crowd.

'Truly, Harold, I have been with her.' Her own heart was doubting itself now and when she glanced to the oak, she was relieved to see the intertwined green ribbons swirling gently. 'She was here,' she insisted.

He frowned, blinked, put a hand to Edyth's forehead, but then there she was again – Svana, moon-pale but resolute just a few steps away. Harold's eyes widened like petals at dawn. He reached out but she moved back with a slight shake of her head.

'I'm sorry. I should not have come.'

Harold could only stare and it was Edyth who replied.

'I'm glad you did.'

'I will be gone by dawn.'

'You must not feel—'

'I will be gone by dawn, before the bells ring in the summer. I pray it brings us peace.'

'Pray rather,' Harold growled, finding his voice at last, 'for it to bring us victory, for that is the only way we shall have peace.'

She nodded slowly.

'So you always said.'

'Svana . . . !'

The name seemed to chime around the dark meadow and she put up a hand once more.

'And I am sure you are right. Truly. I came here out of love – for you both – and perhaps out of weakness of my own, but I came also with news. I'm sorry, Harry, but I must tell you. I have men on the eastern shores, fishermen. They have seen ships, far out yet but moving south. One . . . flew the sharpened spear.'

'Torr!'

'It seems so.'

Harold moved towards her again, but again she stepped back as if his touch might crumble her to dust. He flinched, then squared his shoulders.

'Then he is not with William at least,' he said. 'How many ships?'

'A handful, no more.'

'My brother has not found himself many supporters in any land then. I do not think a handful of ships need worry us too greatly.'

'That is true but, Harold, my men say they are Scandinavian in design.'

'Hardrada!' Edyth breathed and Harold turned to her.

'We must find your brothers, Edyth. If the Vikings are sailing with Torr they will need to look to their defences.'

They both scanned the meadow but the weak moon did not light up the young earls.

'How will we find them tonight, Harold?' Edyth asked. 'I am not hunting Marc down now. I followed a man into the woods once before if you remember and it gave me such a shock I fell from my tree.'

Harold smiled and glanced at Svana and for a flicker of time it was as if they were back in Westminster, back at the beginning. Then someone called 'Sire!' and Harold looked around and the past was lost.

'I must send messengers at least,' he said.

'You will call out the fyrd?' Edyth asked.

'I'm not sure. I shall send men to gauge the threat. We cannot afford to muster too soon, not with Duke William lurking over the narrow sea. What do your men say of . . . ?' He looked back to Svana but she had turned her face to the moon. He sighed. 'Warmongering,' he muttered.

'Harold?' Edyth asked but it was Svana to whom he replied. 'You have always hated my warmongering.'

She nodded.

'Yet can you not see that 'tis nights like this we fight for?'

Svana's eyes were upon him now but still she said nothing.

'That is true, Harold,' Edyth said quietly, 'but what is also true is that having fought for them we must enjoy them. Come now. The fyrd can wait until morning, surely?'

His fingers found hers. They were cold and she squeezed them tight, seeking to pump life into them from her own, even as she drew it from Svana's on her other side. The evil spirits had crept close but they had kept them back. The musicians played on and together, in the darkness, the three of them danced together.

*

Harold's men went forth next morning. The Trimilchi celebrations were cut short and the court dared not complain. The king was back on the throne they had elected him to, his diadem firm upon his head as his rowan wreath lay fading in the bushes. Svana had slipped away with the dawn mist, melting between the rumpled couples creeping from the trees as the abbey bell tolled out the arrival of summer, and leaving only a wisp of footsteps in the dew to show she was ever there at all. Harold was too busy with his council to mourn but Edyth crept to her bed and allowed herself to weep for them both. She knew that Harold felt that he had been elected for this duty – to fight England's fear, not to celebrate her riches – but she hoped he would at least hold last night in his heart as he did so.

The messengers were swift to return and it seemed that, although Svana's men had spoken true, the exiled earl had moved fast.

'Earl Torr has been sighted off the Isle of Wight,' they reported. 'Six ships are heading for the south-east coast. Earl Lane is monitoring them from Kent and he believes they mean to attack.'

'With six ships?'

Harold was scornful of his younger brother's intelligence but less so when the next men arrived to report that Torr's old deputy was sailing down the east coast with seventeen more, all, as Svana's men had reported, Scandinavian in design.

'The King of Norway is not aboard,' they assured them, 'nor his sons, but it seems the expedition has come from the Orkneys which he holds as his own.'

'An advance party?'

'Perhaps. And Sire, Earl Lane says to tell you Duke William has been holding a great service at his new abbey at Caen to bless his fleet. He has a banner from the Pope and is proclaiming a holy war.'

'Holy! There is nothing holy about the bastard duke, except perhaps that he is wholly determined to take my throne.'

Harold was defiant but when he turned to Edyth she saw his bright eyes clouding.

'It is starting, Edyth,' he said quietly. 'It is all starting.'

Edyth swallowed. She'd known this day would come, they had both known it, but until this moment there had been hope that they were wrong. Now there was no such hope, only faith – in God, in England, and in their own strength and right. Harold rose. He touched his hands, briefly, to his crown and to Edyth he seemed almost to swell with the demanding energy it gave him.

'I must call up the fyrd now,' he said. 'We must protect our southern borders.'

Edyth rose at his side, determined to prove herself worthy.

'I shall set the maids packing.'

She moved to leave but Harold reached out and clasped her arm, pulling her back to him.

'Do, please,' he said formally, 'but you know, my queen, that we must go our separate ways now.'

She stared at him.

'You are sending me away?'

'No! Lord, Edyth, of course not, but you know as well as I that we are under threat on all sides. I must protect the south and you . . .'

'Must go north. Of course.' Realisation fell onto Edyth's heart like a lump of lead. For six delirious months she had fooled herself into enjoying her marriage as a woman, but now, like the harsh dawn over the blissful whirl of their Trimilchi night, she saw the reality of her position. 'You married me for this,' she said dully.

'Not just for this, Edyth, truly, but, yes, our union has united the country, as it was intended to do, and we must exploit that now to keep it safe.'

'Is it because she . . . ?'

He kissed her, hard and fast, stoppering her words.

'It is not because of anything, my queen. It just *is*.'

His eyes were already darting sideways to his gathering commanders. She had become a part of the defence he had been elected to the throne to muster and she could not be petty enough to protest.

'Yes, my lord,' she said meekly and fled.

CHAPTER THIRTY

York, September 1066

It was a long summer, bright with sunshine and hot with nervous tempers. Even Ewan, Morgan and Nesta, who had at first treated the journey north as a great adventure, picked up on the mood and took to playing with the farm children as far from their mother's tense court as possible. Torr's ships full of mercenaries proved an uneasy fleet and scattered in rough winds that tore their sails and ripped up their resolve. They crept back up the east coast where Edwin and Morcar, positioned to catch any sign of Vikings, waited to pick them off. Harold mustered his fyrd at Chichester but contrary winds held Duke William in port and the camps grew as stale as the stifling air.

Alone and afraid, Edyth yearned to write to Svana. The magic of their snatched night of hazy-edged friendship warmed her heart but every time she tried to find words to express that they seemed to tangle the uneasy lines of their lives and, besides, it did not feel fair to burden her with the problems she had given Harold up for. Svana did not write either and Edyth's only letters were from Harold, terse, edgy notes about ship movements or rather the lack of them.

Edyth,

Why do they not come? My spies all say William's fleet is waiting in port and that he has nigh on eight thousand men camped up, yet still he waits. I am trapped here, useless. The troops are restless. Their fear is dulled and their sword skills with it. I run a fierce training programme but it isn't the same as real Normans to sink their blades into. Women are beginning to sneak into the camp and the men are becoming bawdy and complacent and all at England's expense.

Yours,

Harold Rex

It was a curt, impersonal missive and she could not help a stab of disappointment but she tried to understand. Harold was frustrated; frustrated and afraid and bowed down by inactivity and in that he had her sympathy. In the north, at least, they'd had more to do and she tried to put aside her peevish longing for endearments and respond in kind.

Harold,

I am delighted to report a great victory over the outlaw's fleet. My brothers tell me that they scattered like oats on the breeze and Torr has limped away to nurse his wounds in Scotland. The year marches on. Wild winds and driving rain have teased the leaves from the trees here at York and sent our enemies running for cover. Mayhap we will see out 1066 in peace yet? I pray that we can celebrate Christ's mass together with our borders intact.

With love,

Edyth Regina

Edyth,

You are right, autumn is indeed upon us. We have also had storms in the narrow sea, so violent that several of my ships have been wrecked and the bastard must have no hope of sailing. My spies say he has also lost many vessels and is disbanding his troops. I have, reluctantly, done the same. The men were rotting in the camp and the crops in the fields so I have despatched them to their homes and sent the fleet into the safety of the Thames.

I will ride to Westminster, Edyth, and pray for you and the children to join me there as soon as you are safely able. They tell me the harvest is a rich one, a blessing perhaps on our reign. Let us hope it sustains us through the winter so that we are fit to fight when our enemies come again in the new year.

Garth tells me my letters to you have been somewhat cursory. He tells me you are not a military leader to be briefed and ordered and I fear he is right but I also told him, Edyth, that you are you and that you would understand. I hope I am right too and thank you for your vigilance in the north.

I will see you soon at Westminster,

Harold

The letter was honest, if not eloquent, and Edyth held it close to her heart as she ran to order the packing of her household. Edwin was patrolling the Humber and Morcar the rough coastline around Scarborough and she sent messengers forth to ask them to return to York and disband the five thousand troops camped out around its walls. Two days later, one of Morcar's messengers skidded into the city and she ran to meet him.

'Is my brother on his way back?'

'He is, my lady, and with all speed.'

The man's words were hopeful but his eyes were fixed firmly on the floor.

'Why such haste?'

He coughed roughly.

'Scarborough has been under attack, my lady. It is the Vikings. Earl Morcar's forces have repelled the first wave but they are moving down to the Humber. The beacons are flaring all along the coast and they say more are joining the flotilla from across the northern sea.'

'How many more?'

He swallowed and scratched his dirty toe into the packed earth of the hall floor.

'They say there are nigh on three hundred ships, my lady, and they are heading this way. Earl Morcar says York has days at best.'

Edyth's foolish hopes collapsed around her. The enemy, it seemed, had not been driven away by the storms but had been hiding on the back of them and now they were descending like a tidal wave. Morcar had sent messengers to Harold who had kept his elite fighting force mobilised at Westminster but they all knew it would take days to reach them and even more for them to march north. For now they were on their own.

Hardrada's eyes haunted Edyth's dreams in the few hours of rest she snatched as the invaders drew closer and she rose regularly to check on the children, sleeping obliviously after their days in the hay. 'Ruthless' they called him and she knew it to be true. He could charm like a courtier but that was just a careful veneer stitched on top of a hardened and determined core. He proclaimed himself a Christian but had little regard for the sanctity of life, including his own, and Edyth suspected Valhalla was still a place he held in whatever heart he had. He would not surrender; this would be a fight to the death. She remembered Griffin's decimated troops crawling over the horizon after facing Earl Torr on the battlefield, women calling names desperately into the void, and her heart quailed.

'*Why must men ever make war?*' Svana's voice asked, creeping like a ghost into her head. Edyth tried to block it out but she longed too much to hear her old friend. They had both looked for a woman's year, but it had never come. Women, it seemed, were doomed to ever stand on the sidelines – of councils, of battlefields; even, perhaps, of their own marriages – and she'd had enough of it.

'I want to come,' she told Edwin when he announced they were marching to Fulford to meet the advancing Vikings.

'No.'

'I am the queen.'

'But you cannot fight and I cannot spare men to protect you. You have your children to care for and besides, sister, either you sicken more than most on war rations or you are carrying something very precious to England. Am I right?'

Edyth flushed and her hand crept to her belly, still flat beneath her gown, though it would not stay so for long. She had not told Harold. There had seemed little place for such womanly news amongst the sharp lines of troop movements and enemy positions but now the longed-for royal child might be threatened before his father ever knew he existed.

'You are right, brother,' she admitted, 'but please keep it to yourself. It is early days yet and I have not had the chance to tell Harold.'

'He will be delighted. An heir for England! *Everyone* will be delighted. Let me tell the men – give them something extra to fight for.'

'No.'

'But Edyth—'

'Queen Edyth.'

She felt ashamed of herself for pulling her tenuous rank on her brother but it worked.

'Later maybe,' he said mildly, before leaning in to drop a kiss on her forehead and add, 'but I am glad to know. Father would have been so pleased. A future king of our bloodline. King Harold III perhaps?'

Edyth felt tears threaten and turned to hide them.

'Let us not get too far ahead of ourselves, brother,' she choked out.

'No,' he agreed gently, 'there is much to do to secure all our futures, but we will do it. You must stay here, Edyth, and keep the city and prepare to accept Hardrada's surrender. Torr's too.'

Edyth's head snapped up.

'Torr is with him?'

'Of course. Treacherous bastard. It is good for us; the men are hot for his blood. He will not survive the day.'

Edyth clutched at her brother's arm.

'But you will, Edwin? Morcar too?'

'We will, Edyth.'

'How can you be so sure?'

He shrugged.

'I cannot afford not to be. A man can only pick up his feet to charge if he is certain of victory.'

Edyth watched him move away and considered his words. That, then, was how men fought; they did not truly think about it. Maybe if they did, they'd all stay at home and enjoy their lives as Svana had long advocated instead of sacrificing them to the battlefield like fools. Now, though, was not the time for such crazy wisdom. Her men were riding out and she had to see them go with a smile and then she had to wait and wait to see which of them returned.

They heard the clash of steel on steel even from York. Edyth sent the children to play with the others in the hall and huddled with the great women of the north, not so great now as they crouched, eyes shut against their luxurious bower so as better to hear the gruesome sounds of the battlefield floating in on a careless autumn breeze. Hours it endured. They were too far away to hear the suck and spurt of flesh being ripped apart but they cowered from even the imagining of it. As the day wore on, though, they became dulled to the sounds and sat fixed, mute, helpless.

In the afternoon the children crept in, seeking their mothers as the fear became too pervasive for even small minds to resist. Edyth drew Nesta and Morgan onto her lap as ten-year-old Ewan sat pale as a spirit at her side. And still they waited. Every so often someone would sob, as if being stabbed by proxy, and the others would cross themselves and pray their intuition was misplaced.

Edyth knew that in the city and in the villages all around, other women would be doing the same. She worried she should rise, speak stirring words, but the fools who listened to those were an hour's march away and their ears would be too full of blood to hear. She did not feel like a queen anyway, or like a wife, or even like a mother, just like a scared child. So she stayed, crumpled in amongst them, and prayed.

'Dear God, save my brothers.'

It seemed selfish but she could not pray for all the men out there; it was too great a task. The best they could hope for was that Hardrada lost more men than they did, but they would be lost men still. All over Norway women would be waiting too; they would mourn in a different language but it would sound the same. And still they fought.

The sun was dropping when the noise ceased. Light slashed red across the sky, like a mirror of the ground below, and the women and children raised their heads in desperate hope. A trumpet sounded a victory, shrill and arrogant but utterly without inflection to tell them the nationality of the trumpeter. Edyth clutched her children close and, beneath her overgown, ran her hands over her stomach again and again until she had to stop herself for fear she might wear Harold's babe right away, yet still the note rang round. She rose.

'To the watchtower.'

There was a tower above the main city gates, built into the Roman foundations some hundred years ago. It was not high enough to give a view all the way to Fulford but it would offer them early sight of whoever came up the road from the south. Leaving the children in the bower with their nursemaids, they spiralled up the steps and stood on the top in the dusk and looked to the horizon.

It was Hardrada.

He came riding high on a huge black horse, a lord striding before him waving his great banner. Edyth stared at the dark wings of the predatory raven and tasted defeat, sharp and bitter. In Wales she had known it too but in Wales the victor had been Harold, her Harold. The Harald who now rode towards them had no reason to favour her and they were in grave danger. Vikings were not known for their mercy. Edyth's hand flew to her belly. She had lost Harold the north and now she might also lose him his child – his heir.

'They will rape us all!'

It was so exactly an echo of young Alwen's cry way back in Rhuddlan that Edyth momentarily lost her place in time. For a heartbeat she was queen of a different country, a different race, but the thud of a thousand enemy feet on the great York road brought her to her senses. She was Queen of England now and she had to behave fittingly.

'Compose yourselves,' she told the women sternly. 'We are not peasant girls. Dry your eyes and stand tall – and quickly.'

She pushed her own shoulders back and stepped as far forward as the narrow top of the tower would allow. Hardrada drew up his horse below her and fixed her in his stormy eyes.

322

'You are defeated, my lady.'

'So it seems – for this day at least.'

He laughed.

'Your noble brothers are fled.'

Edyth's heart leaped; they were alive. The knowledge gave her courage.

'What do you want of us?'

'We seek entry into York which we claim as our own.'

Edyth bowed her head.

'I cannot oppose you, Sire, but I can ask that you honour me and all of my people.'

Hardrada glanced back at his men. Their heads were high but they looked weary and many were nursing wounds. He fixed on Edyth again.

'We come not to pillage, my queen, but to conquer. Today is but a step on our path.'

'A victory on the way to defeat.'

His eyes flashed.

'If it suits you to see it that way. It makes no odds to me. I seek food, I seek wine, and I seek terms – hostages.'

Behind Edyth the women whimpered. It would be their noble sons who would have to be turned over to the ruthless Viking king and Edyth's own heart squeezed in on itself at the thought of her own dear Ewan and Morgan going to Hardrada, but what else could they do? The men were fled, hiding so they could live to fight again, and the women were alone. There was only one thought in all of this that gave Edyth the strength to order the gates open and the Vikings inside – Harold would come. She had sent word and he would come but it was a long way with foot soldiers, perhaps too long. She had to stall Hardrada, and she had to pray, and above all she had to hope she was not simply luring more men to their deaths in the futile name of peace.

CHAPTER THIRTY-ONE

York, 23 September 1066

ardrada stayed in York just one night but it seemed to go on for ten. Edyth and her women were forced to serve their conquerors and whilst the Viking king kept a tight rein on his men, there were still plenty of presumptive hands and lewd threats. Far worse than such petty pestering, however, was the knowledge that within walking distance their own men might be lying mortally wounded and they could not go to them. Earl Torr, a gaunter, darker, even more predatory version of his previous self, prowled after Edyth and she was spared – if spared it was – only by Hardrada.

'I was so sorry to hear about your husband,' the Viking king opened as if this were no more than a social dinner. 'That is, your *first* husband. Do you make a habit of marrying your husbands' conquerors? I do hope so.'

'You are married already, Sire,' she replied stiffly.

'As was King Harold.' Edyth gasped and Hardrada looked at her curiously. 'You knew her? She was a friend perhaps? Ah, you women – you are so fickle.'

'At least we do not kill each other.'

'You think?'

His words were as sharp as his blade and he was a man who knew how to hunt down weakness. Edyth thrust her head up.

'I am queen of this country and the people love me. You would do well to remember that if you wish to rule them.'

'Oh, I *will* rule them and you, Edyth Alfgarsdottir, would do well to remember *that*. We will talk terms.'

'Now?'

'Do you have any better plans?'

His eyebrow rose and Torr leaned lasciviously in from his other side.

'No,' Edyth snapped. 'We will talk terms.'

The next day Hardrada took his troops back to his ships, anchored at Riccal. It was evident, despite the bravado, that they had suffered heavy losses and when Edyth and her women crept onto the battlefield it was apparent why. The open stretch of land was mired in bodies. They lay piled on top of each other like gruesome stepping stones across the oozing marshland. The water, forced out by the mass of flesh, flooded around the edges as scarlet as a dyeman's vat of madder and the stench of death was batted across the air by the black clouds of common crows feasting on Vikings and Englishmen alike.

'We cannot bury them all,' Edyth said.

'The bog will take them for us.'

'Dead or alive. We must hunt for any still breathing.'

It was a sickening, loathsome task but worthwhile. Even now men cried for help and each one they pulled from the filth felt like a victory all of its own. All too often, though, the cries were Norwegian.

'Do we leave them?'

Edyth shook her head.

'No. We save them. Hardrada can have them to swell the numbers of his precious hostages.'

It was sound politics but it masked a far more basic truth – leaving a man, any man, to die was like condemning your own soul. Edyth was strong, yes, but not that strong. All day they laboured, helping men, some almost twice their own weight and size, to the empty tents of the English battle camp. Edyth longed for word of her brothers but none came. She longed for word of Harold but none came. She was adrift in a bloody sea and could only walk on one bandage at a time.

She sent a message to Hardrada: '*We are treating 213 of your soldiers and offer them in place of half the agreed hostages.*' She longed to ask for more. Hardrada had demanded one hundred men and boys so it was hardly a fair swap, but she knew he needed surety and his own men would not offer that. She wrote on: '*Of the remaining fifty we have not yet a full quota and ask one more day to restore our own wounded to sufficient health to march into your keeping.*'

It was a miserable task to heal men only to send them into the jaws of the enemy but so far Hardrada had behaved honourably. If he wished to rule England as his ancestor King Cnut had done, he could not afford to lose respect and she could only pray that he would treat the hostages well. She sent the messenger and returned to the wounded. She could see those of her women who had retrieved husbands and sons looking daggers at her but she could do nothing.

'My boys go too,' she reminded them, her heart aching with the weight of her sons' young lives.

She longed to hide Ewan and Morgan away, protect them from this. They were Welsh princes, after all, not truly a part of this English battle. And yet, in marrying Harold she had made them a part of it and she could not hide from that, however much it hurt. She could only tell herself that it was not in Hardrada's interests to rip apart the families he sought to rule but it was small consolation for it was not just Ewan and Morgan who were in danger.

'If Hardrada wins again,' she added darkly, 'my husband will never be granted the chance of being hostage.'

It silenced the women but not her own fears. It was the first time she had ever dared to think of Harold as hers but it was bitter consolation. Besides, for all she knew he might be dead already. It felt as if the death of a king should echo instantly around the whole country but such a thing was not possible. The trumpet had not been crafted that could sound that far and her heart, whatever she might choose to wish, could not sense his – though Svana's perhaps could. She lifted another bandage and forced herself on.

Hardrada accepted her terms, praised her nursing and vowed honour to the Englishmen he would rule. Delivery of the hostages, along with more of York's ancient treasure than the weakened men and boys could carry, was set for the next day, 25 September, at a pretty crossing of the Derwent known as Stamford Bridge. Messengers crept in to say that Edwin and Morcar were hiding out with Morcar's fleet, stationed on the River Wharfe at Tadcaster. They were, the messengers assured them, seeking to raise resistance, but in truth they all knew there were not the men to be found to defeat the Vikings. Edyth sent more messengers south to find Harold but knew she had not won him enough time.

On the eve of the hostage-taking she took Ewan and Morgan aside in the beautiful bower she had last shared with Harold on their triumphant procession through the north.

'The time has come,' she told them, 'to stand as the princes I know you are.'

Eight-year-old Morgan obligingly adjusted his stance in a manner that would normally have had her laughing out loud but there was no place for laughter now. She put a hand on his little shoulder.

'You must go with the other men and boys of York for a little while.'

'Where?'

'To stay with the Vikings.'

Both boys' eyes opened wide.

'On their ships?' Morgan asked keenly.

'Yes.'

'Can I be on the one with the dragon at the front?'

'I don't know, Morgan.'

'And can you be on it with me?'

Edyth looked away, sucking in tears.

'It is men only, I'm afraid, my sweet.'

'Oh.'

Morgan looked bemused but ten-year-old Ewan was sharper.

'Will we be prisoners, Mama?'

'Not prisoners, Ewan, not really – hostages.'

'What's the difference?'

'The difference is . . . is . . .' She fought for composure. 'The difference is that when the kings have stopped fighting you will be released.'

'When will they stop fighting?' Morgan asked.

Edyth was losing her battle against tears and could not answer. Ewan, however, was there again: 'When one of them is dead.'

It was a stark, brutal truth and beneath it lurked an even starker one – only if Hardrada won would the boys gain their freedom. Once her precious Welsh princes were delivered to the Vikings it was them or Harold, and either way, Edyth would be torn in two.

That night she invited the hostages and those of their families still cowering in the city to the archbishop's palace to dine, presiding over the gathering with her sons either side of her. It was a sombre meal, salted with tears. They all fought to eat but too many platters returned to the kitchens untouched before Edyth caught sight of an arrival at the door – a man, armoured and travel-stained. A messenger! She rose and beckoned him in and he came forward until he was so close she could smell the sweat of his journey.

'I come from the king,' he said, his voice low.

'Harold!'

He put a finger to his grimy lips.

'He is at Tadcaster with your brothers.'

Edyth's heart soared. Tadcaster was but a few hours' march to the south-west of the city. Harold must have flown like Mercury to travel this far in so short a time and if he was with Edwin and Morcar they could surely form the resistance they had sought? The hostages might not have to be delivered; Edyth's heart leaped with a hope that seemed to ripple through the whole hall.

'King Harold is here. King Harold will save us.'

It was hard not to believe but their situation was precarious; they needed to be very calm.

'He has troops?'

'Some five thousand, my lady.'

'And Hardrada's force is decimated; most of them lie in Fulford's marshes.' Edyth looked round at the people crowding in, unable to hide her excitement. 'What does he plan?'

'To surprise them at Stamford Bridge on the morrow but to do that he must march through York. If he approaches from the south they will see him too soon. Harold says it is imperative the troops are kept hidden for as long as possible – they must pass silently through the city.'

'We can do that.' Edyth leaped up. 'Seal the doors!'

Guards pulled the great wooden doors shut and Edyth put

an arm round both her sons and beckoned her people in closer yet.

'We must go forth now, all of us. We must knock on doors and tell all householders to make no sound when the troops come through at dawn. Hardrada has a guard beyond the north gates. If they catch wind of anything they will despatch messengers to warn him.'

'Not if we reach them first.' It was Lord Osric of Northallerton. He had one arm in a sling but the other gripped his sword firmly. 'There are enough of us fit. We can slip round behind the camp and block them off. When Harold emerges from the north gates we will cut them down. No word will reach that bastard Viking if we have anything to do with it.'

'It will be risky.'

'Better to die putting Vikings to the sword than go to them with a yoke around our necks.'

There was a rumble of encouragement but Edyth hushed them.

'Lord Osric, I leave you in charge of that operation and I thank you for it on behalf of King Harold. For the rest of us, we have a long night ahead. Come!'

The dawn came all too quickly and they had to make haste to reach the last of the little houses at the bottom corner of the city but the citizens passed the word themselves and the sun rose on a startling sight. The winding main street of York was lined with old men, women and children; heads bared, hands clasped to their hearts, and mouths (even the smallest) closed tight. They turned their faces up to the king as he rode in and threw leaves and flowers in his path and he saluted their devotion.

Edyth stood at the far side of the city, her children at her side, her crown on her head and the whole world catching in her throat. She saw her brothers. Edwin had a jagged gouge across his smooth young forehead and Morcar a rough bandage around his shoulder but they rode tall, eager to prove themselves after their defeat. They blew her shy kisses as they passed and she held up her own hands in blessing but there was no time to talk and now Harold was coming. His eyes locked onto hers as he rode the last safe street and made for the north gates, pausing as they cranked open and turning to the city.

'I thank you, good people of York, for your help this morning and ask only now for your prayers. We will *not* surrender hostages to Hardrada; we will *not* surrender to him at all.'

The people raised their arms to him but still did not speak. He saluted them one more time, then leaned down, placing a solemn hand on the boys' upturned heads, before hooking an arm around Edyth's waist to pull her up against his horse's flank.

'God bless you, my queen. You have honoured me today and I hope to honour you in return with victory over the false challenger.'

'Ah, Harold,' Edyth said, ''tis me. I do not need speechifying.'

'Then take this in its place.'

He kissed her lips softly, a swirling moment of gentleness amid the mess, and then he released her and was gone. The men streamed past as outside shrieks of agony and rage told of a job well done by Osric's men. Harold, Edwin and Morcar were on their way to battle and Edyth – Edyth was waiting again.

It was longer, even, than Fulford and this time too far away to hear. There was nothing but silence and the sickening shriek of their own imaginings. Edyth sent her children into the safety of the bower whilst she and her women tended to the wounded men from the last battle and tried not to picture the many more being carved up as they did so. Those that could survive it had been carefully moved up into York but many others, including the Norwegians, were still in tents at Fulford and the stench of the battlefield pervaded everything, an ever-present shadow of death.

The sun arced over the sky and descended the other side with no news and it wasn't until the stars were bright and the moon winking from behind milky clouds that they heard anything. But when they did – what a sound! It was singing, not soft like the Welsh, but bright and forceful and run through with a deep, resonant, wonderful base: 'Ut! Ut! Ut!'

The women froze. They looked at each other in wonder.

'Ut! Ut! Ut!'

The meaning of it crept joyously under their skin and only then, at the drumbeat of English victory, did Edyth realise how little she had expected it.

'Ut! Ut! Ut!'

The women flew from the city, streaming out across the plain towards the marching troops and there, at their head, banner high and smile as broad as the moon itself, was the king.

'Harold!' Now Edyth was running too, tripping over her royal robes in a headlong rush towards him. 'Harold – you did it!'

She lifted her arms and he reached down and swung her onto his horse in front of him. She felt him quiver with the effort and saw, up close, how spent he was, but he was whole and he was victorious.

'You did it,' she said again, twisting in the saddle to look into his eyes.

'Did you ever think otherwise?'

'No! No, of course not.'

'Liar.'

'Did *you*?'

'Many times but I ignored it.'

Edyth thought of Edwin's words 'a man can only ride into battle certain of victory'; it seemed he had spoken true.

'My brothers?' she gasped out.

'They are bringing up the rear but they are well, Edie. They fought fiercely despite their injuries. You should be proud of them.'

'I am proud of you all. Is it over?'

'For now it is. Hardrada is dead.'

'You killed him?'

'No. Garth had that honour – he fought like twenty men.'

'And Torr?'

Harold's face clouded.

'He is dead too. I tried to save him, Edyth. Twice I offered him terms – before the battle and again when Hardrada was struck down – but he refused. We had no choice.'

'No choice,' she confirmed, running her hands up around his neck. 'You have done well, Harold. It is a great victory for England – one of the greatest ever.'

'It is, though at great cost too. Many noble men lost their lives today.'

'Then we must honour them tonight.'

They were at the city gates now and all those who had stood a silent guard over the troops that morning cheered them inside. Householders offered bread, ale, even precious meat to the soldiers and York erupted in celebration. Edyth fetched Ewan, Morgan and Nesta to her, covering them in kisses as the bells of the cathedral pealed out across the furthest reaches of the great north moors. Harold praised the boys' bravery and together the royal family led the way to the great hall. Barrels were opened and the people of the north were drunk at the very first sip – drunk on victory, drunk on joy, drunk, above all, on relief.

Stories flew around.

'We caught them lying like cats in the sunshine.'

'They wore no armour – insolent bastards.'

'And came with only half their force.'

'The rest came later but from too far and at too great a pace. They were sword-fodder from the start.'

After a while Edyth felt herself almost as sickened by it as she had been walking through the destruction at Fulford just a few short days ago and she clung to Harold. The details of the battle were as hideous as the last but at least this time the pain had a reward. England was safe from the invaders who had tried – and failed – to rip her apart. Whatever the horror, it was a blissful feeling.

Three days later messengers came: Duke William had landed.

CHAPTER THIRTY-TWO

Ware, 5 October 1066

'Harold, Sire – the men are weary. We cannot go on tonight.'

Edyth thought she would weep with relief at Garth's words. They'd been travelling for five days solid and even on horseback she was weary to her bones. Heart still aching from the pain of nearly losing her dear boys to Hardrada, she had sent them and little Nesta to the relative safety of Godiva and Meghan at Coventry whilst she rode south with her king, but parting with them had been hard. She could see now why Svana kept her own boys in Nazeing even though Godwin, at least, was old enough to fight. It sometimes felt as if the world were too dangerous a place into which to release anyone you held dear, especially this year.

She prayed her dear children would be safe with her mother, but she carried another to fret for now. She felt permanently sick and longed for respite but she had not told Harold why she was suffering for fear of him leaving her in some backwater abbey. A night's rest would be most welcome and, seeing him look longingly to the far-off beacons at the edges of Westminster, she stepped up to his side.

'We can go on at first light, Harold. It makes little difference where we sleep.'

He nodded reluctantly and gestured to Garth. The command rippled back down the long line of soldiers and the men parted, barely making the shelter of the woodland before hitting the ground and curling into it as if it were the softest down. As on so many occasions these last few days, Edyth was moved by their stoicism and their persistent cheer as they trod the long, long road to another battle.

'We will be in Westminster tomorrow,' she said to Harold, 'and you can muster your forces against the duke.'

'I am impatient to do so, Edyth,' he admitted. 'I want the bastard off our land before he poisons it with his evil ambitions. He has not the soul to rule England. He knows little of government or law; little of economics beyond collecting for weapons; little of art or music or poetry. He does not even own a hawk. He is a barbarian who covets only land and titles and he cannot be allowed to take our throne. We must drive him away.'

Those were words she suspected he said to himself over and over – a rite as strong and vital as the Lord's Prayer, but far less sustaining. His eyes were ever fixed on the horizon these days, his fingers ever tensed on his sword. He slept little and ate only for show. It seemed terrible to Edyth that his victory over Hardrada, the scourge of all Europe, had been so swiftly sucked into the fear of this hideous march. Had any man ever fought two such foes so close in time, and yet so far in distance? And if they had – had they won?

Doubt gnawed constantly at her but she feared it was eating Harold alive. So many times, she'd watched him striding between his men, praising them, reassuring them, tending to them, but who did the same for him? She'd tried, God knows she'd tried, but she had not the peace in her soul to soothe his. Only one person could offer that.

'Edyth is a marvel, Garth,' she'd overheard Harold tell his brother last night as they'd chatted beyond the tent where she was supposed to be sleeping. 'I am blessed to have her as my queen.'

'I hope you've told her that.'

'Many times – though she will never believe it.'

'Because of . . .'

'Yes.'

'Do you miss her – Svana?'

The name had driven into Edyth like a sword-point and she'd craned forward to hear the answer but there had been only a long silence before Harold had said: 'I must to bed.'

Edyth had heard the ashes being kicked out and forced herself to lie down and feign sleep but the missing answer had haunted her and now, as she looked out on the little town of Ware, so familiar to her from trips into East Anglia, she knew what she had to do.

'We are close, Harold.'

'To London, maybe, but Hastings is a long way yet.'

'Nay, Harold, not to London.'

He looked at her strangely and she turned her eyes east, up the road to nearby Nazeing. His whole body seemed to quake but he said nothing and Edyth touched a hand to his chest.

'You should go. Now. The men sleep – they will not miss you.'

'It wouldn't be fair, Edyth.'

'No, Harold.' On this Edyth felt very certain. 'It hasn't been fair for a long time but tonight maybe we can shift the balance.'

He placed a hand softly over her arm.

'You would have me go?'

'*No!*' her heart screamed. '*No, I would have you lose yourself in me and find the strength you need there,*' but that was not

337

fair. Svana had sent Harold into her care when the times demanded it and now she must do the same.

'I would have you go. Now. Take care and give her . . . No matter.'

'But you . . .'

'I will be quite well.'

His protests were token and there was a new light in his eyes that he could not hide. Edyth gave him a little shove and turned away and when she dared to look back, he was gone. She thought of Svana ducking his touch in the Trimilchi dawn and prayed she had not made a terrible mistake, but deep down she knew that at Nazeing it would be different. Svana would welcome the man she had handfasted beneath God's open skies and for one night Harold would be able to stand barefoot again. The bruise in her own foolish heart was as nothing to the salve that would offer him.

'We need to strike now!'

Harold pumped his clenched fist into his palm and glared round at the assembled council. Edyth watched him from beneath her crown. He was afire with energy and purpose, the Stamford Bridge victor again, not the weary leader he'd become on the march south. Perhaps it was being back in Westminster that had invigorated him, or perhaps it was scenting William, or perhaps – most likely of all – it was his night with Svana. He'd returned at dawn but had not joined Edyth in bed and she had kept her own distance, fearful she might catch the soft meadow scent of her old friend on his flesh.

'You are well?' she'd managed.

'I am well.'

'That is good.'

'And you, Edyth? Did you sleep?'

'Yes.'

They had both known it was a lie.

'She sends you her blessing.'

'She is too good, Harold.'

'And we must keep her that way. She knows you are as much a pawn in this crazy game as she, Edie. It is I who am at fault, yet she does not blame me either.'

'She loves you.'

'For all that has cost her.'

'It is better, surely, to know love whatever it costs?'

She had to believe that, not just for Harold but for herself. She'd longed to ask him more about his night, longed to know what they'd said to each other, done to each other, but known too that she must not. Even at Trimilchi Svana had been more a ghost than solid flesh and now it was almost as if Harold had crossed, for the space of a night, to the other side. If he had, though, he'd returned more alive than ever and Edyth was both grateful and shamefully heartsick.

'*You're here now*,' she reminded herself, glancing around Westminster Palace, but it felt like small consolation for Harold was very much the king again.

'Surely, Sire,' the Bishop of London was saying, 'we are better to wait until we can gather a greater fyrd? William does not seem to be moving from the coast.'

'No, but he is ravaging the lands all around – my lands; my people. And he might move at any time. One night he might mobilise the whole damned lot of them and suddenly we'll be on the back foot. He's a cunning bastard. I know. We need a battleground of *our* choosing and to gain that we must reach it first. We wait only for the troops from the west and the east and then we march. We can meet with the southern bands on our way through.'

'But Sire,' the bishop protested, 'the men from the north . . .'

'Are here already. They came with me.'

'And brave they are to do so, but there are only a thousand of them. Mercia and Northumbria are meant to provide five thousand.'

'Yes, and the rest lie dead below Viking swords, giving their life to destroy the greatest commander Europe has ever known so that you can sit safe in Westminster.' The bishop cowered and Harold moved closer. 'Despite their great losses, the earls Edwin and Morcar are marching with reinforcements, may the Lord bless them. In the meantime, however, we must look to our own men to fight. I hope your armour is well oiled, my lord.'

'I have no armour, Sire, save the grace of God.'

Harold snorted.

'Does that deflect a Norman blade?'

'I trust so.'

'Then you are a fool, Bishop. God's altar is for shining out his glory, not for hiding behind. You are concerned about the number of soldiers I take into the field, so arm yourself – all of you. We march in four days' time.'

'But Sire—'

'Do you not have better things to do than chatter with me? You'll find armourers in Steel Street but hurry, they'll be busy.'

The gathering broke up and the clerics scuttled from the hall, heads bobbing indignantly.

'Was that fair, Harold?' Garth asked.

'Of course it was. We're going to need everyone we can to defeat William. Have we heard from the north?'

'Not yet.'

'But they will come,' Edyth said, keen to speak up for her brothers.

Harold had left Edwin and Morcar in the north to muster more men. They had promised to follow their king south as soon as they had sufficient troops but as Edyth and Harold well knew it was a long and slow road.

'We must keep pressing forward,' Harold insisted now. 'We have defeated Hardrada and we will defeat William. Let them see that this island is not to be conquered.'

His spirit was infectious and it spread rapidly around the troops that filed endlessly into Westminster over the next three days. The Chelsea meadowlands on which they had so carelessly danced in May now burst with armed men, and the whole of London, it seemed, was an army camp. Soldiers huddled on every street corner or, if they dared, in every tavern. All were hot for Norman blood and the place was alive with eager swords, too eager sometimes, especially of an evening.

Harold spent all his time patrolling and Edyth was unable to find enough time alone with him to even tell him of the gift she was now certain she was carrying. On the morning they were due to ride out, she went with him through the makeshift camp. There was a smell of mingled mud and sweat, of leather and wool and rough stews. Everywhere holes in the trees told of sword and arrow practice but now the fires crackled gently and the men murmured to each other and Edyth caught snippets of wives and children, homes and villages, called up in words.

'Oh, she's a beggar about boots on the bed,' she heard one man say fondly.

'Mine too. Gives me a right tongue-lashing if I've not scraped 'em off.'

The second man sighed as if this were the greatest pleasure of his life and rubbed carefully at the rough leather jerkin that would be his only protection in battle. All around, men sharpened their weapons as carefully as they did their memories and the air rang with the scrape of stone on steel, honing blade edges and hammering dints out of shields. Sparks flew and men cursed and Edyth threaded between them, watching

Harold talking tirelessly to the nervous battalions. All faces turned up to his and all men listened intently, as to an oracle.

'Has he spoken like this with everyone?' Edyth whispered to Garth.

'Just about and he's not yet finished. I think he is waiting for someone to complain or to protest about his right to lead them but no one has.'

'Or will. They love him, Garth.'

'As they should. Never, I swear, has a king given so much of himself for his country.'

Edyth nodded and went to his side.

'Must you ride out tomorrow, Harold?' she begged. 'Can you not wait for my brothers to come?'

'I dare not, Edyth. Every day William's hold on the south coast gets stronger.'

'He has no hold on the coast, I swear it. His only true hold is over you.'

He winced and looked around his men as they lined up for the heavy march south.

'You think so? You think this battle is all for me?'

'No! This battle is all for England but it is exacting a heavy price on you. You have done so well, Harold.'

It sounded hollow, wrong, like something you would tell a child, not the King of England, and she was not surprised when he pulled away. He paced a few yards then suddenly spun back, his face pinched.

'I cannot pray, Edyth. I have tried but I cannot feel God any more.'

Edyth grabbed his hands.

'God blesses you, Harold, truly he does. He must or you would not have defeated Hardrada.'

'Hardrada had no right to England. William though . . .'

'William is nothing. *You* were promised the throne on

Edward's deathbed, Harold, a promise sanctified by God, so do not doubt it now. You have told me many times that Duke William can never be allowed to rule England and you must hold fast to that.'

'You speak true.' Harold clasped her to him. 'God, Edyth, I could never have come this far without you – you do know that?'

'Nay, Harold, I am but a substitute.'

'No!'

'Fret not. I am a willing one, too willing perhaps.'

'You are no substitute, Edyth. It is not that simple. It may look that way to others but we – you, me, Svana – we know. Tell me we know?'

Edyth thought back through the years, through the tumble of events and emotions that had carried them, somehow, from that innocent day when Harold brought her, ripped and scared, into Svana's pavilion through to here. They had been buffeted, all of them, by the tide of England's greedy needs. They had been thrown tight together and pulled too far apart but maybe Harold was right – through it all, in whatever strange patterns they had formed, they had been stronger for having each other.

'We know, Harold,' she said.

She glanced around. Harold's housecarls were taking their places around him ready to lead the men south and the commanders were mustering their battalions into marching order behind them. Time was running out. She drew in a deep breath.

'I have something to tell you.'

Harold pulled back.

'You are not riding to battle, Edyth.'

'No. No, not that. I, I am with child.'

'You are?' He looked down at her, eyes bright with joy. 'That's wonderful.'

343

Her heart sang at his simple response and only now did she see how much she had feared it.

'It should be born next Eastertime.'

'Easter, when Christ was born again. It is a sign, Edyth. Nay, more than that, it is an heir – an heir for England!'

'It is.'

She laughed as he lifted her into his arms and for a moment it felt as if the whole of Westminster looked up at the sound and smiled.

'An heir to fight for at last. Come, I must to my horse.'

He tugged her forward to where his great stallion awaited him at the head of the brave men of England. He reached for the reins but Edyth clutched him back.

'Please let me ride south with you, Harold,' she begged.

'No, Edyth.' His fingers found hers, tangling in them. 'I could not bear to have you that close to danger.'

'The moment I agreed to marry you, Harold, I put myself into the path of danger.'

'I know and I am sorry for it.'

'I am not. I have cherished our time together.'

'It is not over yet, Edyth. You will have to put up with me for many years but only if you do as I ask now. Once your brothers are here you may come if you must.'

'I distract you.'

For a moment she caught a smile flickering at the edges of his weary mouth.

'Yes, Edyth, you distract me. You are distracting me now, God bless you, and I need to marshal the troops.'

His fingers, though, stayed locked in hers.

'If you will not let me ride with you, you must promise me one thing.'

'I must?'

'Yes. Look after yourself as well as you look after everyone else.'

Now he truly smiled.

'You know me too well, Edyth Alfgarsdottir.'

'Promise?'

'I promise. Now, unhand me!'

He lifted their entwined fingers and kissed them, then he pulled away and mounted his horse to order his troops forward out of the city. Edyth wrapped her own hands into each other to hold onto the imprint of his touch but they were cold long before the main troops had even reached London Bridge.

She watched them surge across the great structure and head purposefully south, a coarse marching song floating back on the crisp October wind. She watched until even her churning belly grew still and the brave voices were just a mist hanging in the empty air. She had sent a husband to war again and, again, she was stuck waiting. She thought of Svana and her yearning for a year of peace and wished her dear friend were here with her, but Svana was in Nazeing on her lonely estate and Edyth was here in Westminster on her lonely throne and Harold, Harold was marching to a lonely battle with a man who had haunted him for far too long.

CHAPTER THIRTY-THREE

Senlac Ridge, 14 October 1066

'Hold the wall!'

It was all Harold had been shouting and it was all he would continue to shout. The shield wall stretched like a living turtle all along the ridge, writhing and shifting but never falling back. The Normans had been trying to breach it all morning and he could see the frustration in the eyes of those who came closest. It was a good sign. A frustrated soldier took risks, forgot orders, broke formation.

'Hold the wall!'

Harold could hear both his brothers bellowing the same command, hear the trumpets blaring the measured notes that told the mass of troops to stay tight.

'We are defenders,' Harold had told them last night. 'We will defend. It will be tough and it will be slow but it is the best way. Let them do the work. Let them labour up the incline to attack and let them roll back down it. Let us fill the valley with Norman corpses and let us keep our own men safe to return to the homes they hold dear enough to stand with us today.'

Now his eyes roved the field endlessly, wary of holes, but there were none. The Normans had come in wave after wave, great warhorses rushing forward, muscles rippling, jaws foaming, hooves pawing. Even Norman beasts, though, could not be forced to charge into walls and they had been repulsed time and again. Now, as the sun reached its apex, the ground was littered with corpses, making it harder yet for William's attack to penetrate.

'Hold the wall!'

He sounded like a fool but in the heat of battle men's minds could get lost and they needed simple instructions to hold on to. Harold could feel them pushing to charge the enemy and finish the battle, but a man stood far less chance in the loose than wrapped in tight with his comrades and now the Normans were retreating again. Water skins were swiftly passed forward as the sun shone mildly down on men and corpses alike. It was hot work weighed down by metal and men stretched their backs and flexed their shield arms and gritted their teeth for the next wave.

Harold glanced back, desperate for signs of the northern troops. He had been forced to draw battle lines without them when his spies had reported William was set to attack but a messenger had galloped into camp in the first pulse of battle to say they were on their way and he needed them sorely now. Reports said Queen Edyth was at their head with her noble brothers and he knew she would be pushing them furiously but sometimes there was only so much distance a man – or even a woman – could cover.

'Now would be good,' he muttered. 'Now would be perfect.'

A sudden furore over to the left of the field pulled his eyes back. A group of William's central Normans had stopped mid-attack, not far from the English line. They were in some chaos and shouts ricocheted along the shield wall.

'The duke is dead! The duke is dead!'

Harold felt his blood fizz in his veins. Was it true? How?

'Hacked down by an axe,' ran the whisper.

'Jabbed with a lance.'

'Shot by an arrow.'

The battlefield seemed to freeze, all eyes focused on the bumbling group. Avery stepped up to Harold.

'His standard was in that charge, Sire. I saw it, and look, isn't that his horse?'

A magnificent beast had broken in a panic from the group and careered away along the line of the shield wall before crashing into the trees at the far end, its head tossing and William's bright livery slipping from its bucking back.

'It is,' Harold agreed. 'It truly is.'

The shield wall pulsed and pushed forward as one.

'Hold the wall!'

Harold's cry was taken up by his commanders all along the line but the group of Normans was still in a tangle and suddenly at the far end, the English line broke as men flung themselves at the cavalry, axes scything the air and the great war cry breaking from their lips: 'Ut! Ut! Ut!'

'Hold the wall!' Harold cried again, more a reflex than a command for he, too, was fixed on the frantic conflict at the centre of the field.

Horses flailed and turned. Men screamed. The rest of the Norman attack was suspended. Harold saw Lane and his housecarls charge and felt his heart soar. They were going to win. William's troops were falling apart. His own men were straining to go but still he held them. Battles had turned on far less but surely here, today, God had spoken out against the bastard duke and saved England.

And then, like a phoenix from the flames, a single man rode out from the group, a little shaky in the saddle but tall and fierce. He pulled his helmet from his head and showed himself to his troops.

'*Le duc!*' they roared. '*Le duc, le duc, le duc!*'

William grinned. His eyes found Harold and fixed on his face so that for a moment he felt like a child again, caught in the tilting yard by a much bigger boy.

'Hold the wall!' It was all he could say now. He rushed to stop his left flank from bleeding away into the mass of oncoming Norman forces and the men, startled, pulled back. 'Shields!' he roared at them.

All around, Normans were hacking into the dispersed English ranks, carving up the crammed-in men. The English fought back fiercely and slowly the foreigners were despatched. The wall locked back down but much damage had been done and out on the slope the battle was bloody. Harold, helpless, saw Lane caught in the midst of the fiercest fighting and turned his head from his brother's inevitable slaughter.

For the briefest moment he felt a crazy longing to turn and flee the battlefield, to find Edyth on the road and pick her up onto his horse and ride away from all this royal madness – but where to? Nazeing, his heart begged, but he couldn't go there now, not with Edyth, and he could hardly leave her behind. He was stuck with nothing but a cold throne to support him. A cold throne and some five thousand huge-hearted Englishmen.

'Hold the wall! Hold the wall for England!'

His stomach rumbled, though more with sickness than hunger. The day was churning on. Time swirled around them, lost in a bitter, dragging fight for life but the sun was definitely reaching for the trees now. The men must be tired, hungry, thirsty. In that condition a man lost sight of noble concepts of right or victory and just fought to draw the next breath until even that became a struggle too far. Harold could see the whole wall drooping. Defending took its toll; it was more draining than attack. Where in damnation were the reinforcements? He turned to Garth.

'Can we hold, brother?'

'Yes, but we have to pray for night now. Surely Edwin and Morcar will come soon and tomorrow, with fresh troops, we will plough through what remains of theirs. They have taken heavy losses.'

'As have we.'

'But they have no one else to call on. Their backs are to the narrow sea and it is a merciless mistress. Stay strong, Harold – we can do this.'

The Normans were coming again, a great arrow-shaped attack led by William's own troops in the centre, with his Bretons pulling in on the right and his Flanders mercenaries on the left. The Norman had noted the light fading too and was throwing everything at them but the English were ready. Like skilled professionals to the last simple village soldier, they steadied their shields and Harold felt his heart swell almost beyond bearing. He had not asked to be king to these people but God knows he was blessed in it. They could hold. They *would* hold.

The great English war cry rumbled up from the wall: 'Ut! Ut! Ut!' It seemed to shake the very ground and the enemy horses faltered as if they, too, felt the tremor of hatred. Just to the right of William's core, one reared and its fellows skittered sideways. Harold's housecarls seized the opportunity to fling lethal lances into the confusion and horses fell, screaming and dragging their riders with them. The attack faltered. William's standard fluttered and sank in the crush of flesh.

The Normans were pulling back. Several turned tail. Harold ordered his archers to let fly with their last precious arrows. More horses fell and now the Bretons on the right flank were backing off, fleeing, their loyalty surely shaky at best, falling away in the panic. A long wail sounded out from the Norman trumpets.

'The retreat!'

The words fizzed through the English ranks. Shields were lifted.

'Hold the wall!' Harold bellowed but no one heard.

The battle cry was rising. Axes were banged on shields, lances were thrust into the air. The English strained to chase. Some of the commanders were chanting with their men and now a group of stocky Gloucestershire soldiers burst from the wall, the light of victory in their eyes, and made for the retreating Normans at full tilt.

'No!' Harold cried.

He looked to William's standard and saw the duke sitting stock still on his destrier, watching the charge with something like pleasure.

'Hold the wall!' he almost wept but it was no use.

His defence was tumbling apart as every man raced to spike the invaders down and charge them back to the sea from whence they had come. He could only watch in horror as the Bretons pulled their horses round, flight turned expertly into attack as they drew the bloodthirsty English into a circle of death. He glanced at Avery and saw his own nightmare in his squire's young face. They had seen this sort of feigned retreat before when they had ridden into Brittany at William's side. Why had he not remembered? Why had he not warned the men?

He looked back, hoping for his northern troops, hoping for a miracle, but none came. The skyline was resolutely bare of soldiers. All around, the remaining commanders were hustling their horrified back ranks into a hasty wall but all that was left were the barely trained men of the general fyrd – the young lads of England's villages whose only battles so far had been with each other. Their shields were brittle, their swords blunt with generations of sharpening, their only true weapon their courage but that, surely, must be crumbling now.

Harold felt his housecarls gather around him, Avery and Garth foremost amongst them. These men were highly trained, they were strong and ferociously brave, but they were few and they were tired and Harold could see from the set of their broad shoulders that they were here to die with him. He felt useless, unworthy.

'Flee,' he urged. 'Do not waste your lives for mine.'

A hand gripped his arm.

'We stand together, brother.'

Harold turned and looked into Garth's eyes.

'It wasn't meant to be this way.'

'No.'

'We've failed.'

'Not yet. If I die, I take twenty of the bastard's men with me. That's twenty less to terrorise England and I want one of them to be the bastard duke himself.'

Harold nodded grimly at this final spark of hope amid the dark horror of a battlefield falling apart. Some Englishmen were running for the shelter of the Andreaswald – the great forest behind the battleground – and Harold wished them luck. He took a last glimpse up the London road and thought he caught a wisp of dust rising into the darkening sky but nothing more. They were on their own. He turned back, set his feet in the muddy ground and lifted his sword.

'God bless you, brother,' he heard Garth say before the arrows came.

They flew in from nowhere – a devil's rain. Garth screamed out and Harold turned to grasp him but then Avery fell too, his neck lolling on exposed sinews, his body dragging Garth from Harold's arms. Harold stumbled and even as he found his feet, he felt pain drive into his cheekbone and sear across his whole body. He put up his hand and felt an arrow protruding from his skin. Blood flowed like scarlet tears but he forced himself to yank it out. His vision blurred. His knees buckled. He looked to God and saw only swords.

He thought of Edyth, riding desperately to reach him in time, with his son, his supposed heir, in her belly and hated himself for failing her. He had forced her to be queen and pulled her into grief.

'*I have cherished this time with you,*' she had said and he caught a glimpse of her smile before the first sword fell. The Normans drove into him like devils, driving their weapons into his flesh so that what was left of his world ripped apart and pure agony poured in. He tasted salt and mud and clutched at the air as red sucked into black and then spread slowly into searing white. He reached out and suddenly a hand clasped him and pulled him softly, tenderly to safety.

'Svana,' he whispered and let himself go.

CHAPTER THIRTY-FOUR

'**C**an we not go any faster?'

Edyth looked back along the ranks of men filling the road for as far as she could see. They had moved out of London two days ago but progress had been desperately slow. Edyth had had to continually pull Môrgwynt back into a walk though her every fibre ached to give her her head and speed south to Harold. The only thing stopping her was the knowledge that it was not her he needed, but the rank and file she brought with her. These were the men who would swell his battle lines enough to defeat Duke William and many of them were on foot. They walked stoutly, their communal foot-fall firm on the road south, but they walked all the same and Edyth's heart thudded, dull and painful, with every ground-out mile.

'It is not far now,' Edwin consoled her.

He was riding at her right, high on a magnificent stallion that chafed as much as Môrgwynt at the slow pace but he held it tightly in check. He had aged years in the last few months and now looked every inch the earl. He'd had his hair cut viciously short but his beard grew thick and new lines had been pulled out at the edges of his eyes. His Fulford scar ran down from beneath his helmet, a warrior's tear etched into his flesh, and Edyth prayed he need take no more. If they could just reach Hastings in time, just stand with Harold and defeat the bastard duke, peace would be secured. Not for long enough, perhaps, to erase the lines – Edyth knew now that life's experiences were never so easily wiped away – but at least to soften them.

'Listen!'

It was Morcar, on her other side. He, too, had aged but he was a handsome man yet and a spark lurked still in his brown eyes. If they survived this, Edyth vowed she would find him a worthy wife to make mini-Marcs with. They would be troublesome lads all right!

'Listen,' Morcar said again, pulling her away from her foolish woman's dreams. 'Seabirds. We must be close.'

They all looked up and sure enough birds were wheeling over the black mass of the Andreaswald ahead, stark white against the darkening sky.

'It grows night,' Edyth said.

'Good,' Edwin replied. 'We will arrive at Harold's camp under darkness and surprise the enemy on the morrow.'

'You will fight so soon?'

'If we are not too late.'

'You think they are engaged already?'

'It is possible. Harold was hot to attack.'

'But he will wait for us. Surely he will wait for us?'

'Surely,' Morcar agreed, 'if he can. Listen!'

His gaze was fixed on the horizon and, dread rising in her throat, Edyth strained to catch the sounds he was hearing. Edwin turned and signalled a halt with his arm. The commanders snapped to attention and the whole weary parade of men was brought to a stop. An uneasy silence fell, broken only by the shriek of the birds and then, far off, the cries of men.

'They are engaged,' Edwin said. 'God preserve them if they

have been fighting all day.' He turned to his troops, standing up in his stirrups to be heard. 'The king is engaged! He may have urgent need of us. All men on horseback fall in behind myself and Earl Morcar. Weapons ready. Those on foot follow at all speed.'

The response was immediate: chins jutted up, weapons scraped. Edwin and Morcar gathered their commanders and issued urgent instructions and suddenly Edyth was no longer part of a slow march but an active army.

'What about me?' she demanded.

Edwin glanced at her.

'You? You, sister, must stay safe.'

'Safe?!'

Edwin wheeled his stallion round and rode up tight against Môrgwynt's flank.

'Safe, Edie. You are Queen of England and you carry her heir. You must stay back.'

Edyth could see the sense of it but she was done with sense. She was done with waiting. She and Svana had craved a woman's year for so long but whilst women were left to 'stay back' it would never come.

'I *am* Queen of England, Edwin, at your desire and at Morcar's desire and at Harold's desire. I have done your bidding and now you will do mine. I ride with you.'

Her brother's eyes narrowed but there was no time to argue and he knew it.

'I will guard her,' Morcar assured him and Edyth just had time to flash him a grateful look before the Saxon horsemen spurred into action.

Môrgwynt, ever strong beneath her, sprang forward eagerly with the pack. Fleetingly Edyth thought of Griffin. He had given her this magnificent horse in an impetuous, generous gesture so typical of his fiery approach to life, and Môrgwynt had carried her much further than either of them could have imagined. She dug her heels in and drove on but within fifty paces they had to halt as a gaggle of men, eyes wild and limbs flailing, skewed up the road towards them.

'They're ours,' Morcar breathed.

The men fell to their knees before him, whimpering pitifully.

'Have mercy, my lord. We are not traitors. They have sounded the retreat. We must flee.'

Their eyes flickered desperately over their shoulders as they spoke and Morcar glanced back at his wall of troops.

'The battle is, then, lost?'

'The battle is lost, my lord, God help us.'

Edyth started forward.

'And the king?'

The men looked at the floor.

'I know not, my lady,' the first one offered. 'I'm sorry. He was with his housecarls when we fled but I fear . . .'

Edyth's whole body started to shake. Môrgwynt, feeling it, shied and she instinctively gripped the reins.

'We must go to him!'

'No,' the man cried. 'No, my lady, you cannot. They are coming. The Normans are coming.'

'Not any more,' Edwin said grimly.

'You cannot stand against them, my lord. There are too many. We must flee.'

Edwin regarded him coldly.

'We do not flee.' He glanced at Morcar. 'We must face them as cavalry. It is the only way.'

Morcar nodded, his eyes darting around. Already the men were fanning out, but they were not yet into the forest and the road was open with vast grasslands either side. Even Edyth could see that they were horribly exposed. '*We do not flee*' might be an honourable code but was honour wisdom? And yet, Harold might breathe still and, God help her, she would sacrifice every one of these soldiers – her own dear brothers included – to save him. She felt a strange calm creep across her flesh, stilling the shaking and stiffening her bones. She felt the future drain away and the present fill her up. Was this battle fervour?

'This way, my lord,' another of the fleeing men was babbling now. 'If you must fight come this way. There is a deep cutting at the edge of the trees, we call it Grim's Ditch. If you position yourselves above it the Normans may not see it in the fading light.'

'Is it a trick?' Morcar asked Edwin.

'It is a chance,' Edwin responded. 'And probably a better one than we have out here. There is little cover and they will surround us.'

Morcar nodded curtly and caught the man up onto his big chestnut's back.

'Follow me!'

There were some four hundred horsemen in their company but they were swift to turn aside. The man led them a little way east and, sure enough, the land sloped upwards to where the grass lost itself in shrub. Moving cautiously, they drew up on the edge of a great cut in the land, scattered with crumbling earthworks. Edyth strained to see the battlefield but it was beyond the first trees of the Andreaswald and she had no way of discovering Harold's fate.

'*Hold,*' she willed him. '*Hold but a little longer, Harold. We are coming.*'

They could hear Norman pursuers crashing up the London road, trumpets blaring, and suddenly they broke out of the trees, armour flashing in the last of the light.

'Sound the trumpets!' Edwin cried.

Their own buglers raised their instruments and blew, strong

and fierce. Below, the Normans reined in and their heads turned. A thrill ran through Edyth and she grabbed for her delicate eating knife, thrusting it into the air as fiercely as, all around her, the men did their great swords. The Normans let out a furious yell. Their leader raised his own sword and the whole storm of them swung off the road and onto the grass, spurring their huge, battle-dressed horses into a full canter as they surged towards the Saxons.

'Hold your position!' Edwin bellowed but no one needed telling.

They knew what lay at their horses' feet, but, as if someone had snuffed it out, the last line of light died away over the trees and the Normans had no such warning. The screams, when they came, were pitiful. Hundreds of horses plunged over the hidden edge, keening wildly, their riders shrieking with fury and sudden blind fear. In the darkness, Edyth heard more than saw the great mass of flesh crash through the little trees and tear against the jagged rocks below as man after man tumbled to his death.

The second line pulled back but many were moving too fast already and went over, crushing onto their comrades and mangling with their beasts. Edyth's brief bloodlust died with them. Around her, men were cheering, taunting the dying Normans, but all she could feel was waste. Surely no lives were worth losing so sickeningly for petty land squabbles? She slumped over Môrgwynt's neck, burying her face in her soft mane.

'They are retreating, Edie,' Morcar said softly in her ear.

'They are dying, Marc,' she flashed back.

He shrugged.

'Better them than us.'

'Better no one,' Edyth flared. 'Svana was right. It is all futile. Idiotic.'

'It is war, Edyth.'

He could not see; he thought she was the foolish one. Blood, it seemed, blinded.

'What now?' she asked.

'We must follow at first light. We must find Harold.'

Edyth shook her head.

'You will not.'

'We might.'

But she knew better now. Hundreds of Normans had fallen into Grim's Ditch and hundreds more escaped to flee back to their camp. Such vast numbers would not have been released from the battlefield if the king still lived.

'Harold is dead, Morcar,' she said, her voice grating on the vicious words. 'Whatever minor victory you have secured here, if you ride on, it will be to meet your new king.'

'You give up too easily, Edie.'

'Nay, brother, I should have given up years ago. I should have stayed in Coventry with Griffin's boys. I should have told Harold to retreat to Nazeing with his wife – his true wife – and let Duke William be king if he wanted it so badly. At least that way we would all be alive.'

'But dishonoured, Edie.'

She did not answer. Grief was whirling in on her, choking her heart in its coils. She tried to think of her children, safely back in Coventry with Meghan and Godiva, but dearly as she loved them she could not even picture their faces as anything more than ghosts. She, it seemed, like the hapless Normans, had fallen into an abyss. She had fallen off the side of the earth where there was only blackness and horror and a relentless icy wind sucking her ever downwards. Harold was gone and England was lost and all solidity and form seemed to have been taken.

'It cannot be true,' she said over and over, waiting for her words to gain a hold and stop her falling, but the wild-legged English soldiers scattering past told her it had to be. She slid from Môrgwynt's back and stood against her strong shoulder as, all around, men set guards and pitched rough shelters. Messengers were sent forth to spy on the battlefield and rode back to a solemn assembly but Edyth could not bring herself to be a part of it. She stood at the edge of the crowd, no longer a queen but a frightened girl once more.

'The king?' Edwin dared to ask.

'The king is dead.'

The words seemed to scream around the hollow woodland at their backs and be picked up by the wretched cries of the Normans still alive within Grim's Ditch. Edyth put her hands over her ears but such a petty barrier would never keep this horror out.

'How?' Morcar asked.

'How do you think?' Edwin snapped at him. 'Savaged by Norman swords. We were too late. We failed him in the north and now we have failed him again.'

Morcar sucked in his breath. Edyth knew she should step forward, should stop them squabbling as she always had when they were younger but she had no heart for it. Let them fight, all of them – nothing she said or did could make a difference anyway.

'It is not over yet,' Morcar insisted. 'If we retreat to Westminster we can regroup, defend. Harold may be dead, God rest his soul, but William is not yet king.'

It wearied Edyth.

'Will you have us all killed?' she demanded.

'Will you have us ruled by a tyrant?' he shot back.

'What choice do we have? It is over, Morcar, or it should be. Harold should never have been forced onto the throne. They made him king to stop the bastard duke riding roughshod over us but the duke has ridden anyway and now Harold is gone. England asked too much of him and she must see that.'

'Harold wanted Duke William kept from England's doors more than anyone,' Edwin insisted, stepping up next to Morcar.

'No,' Edyth said. 'That is what everyone else wanted him to want. In truth he just wanted peace in which to bring up his children.'

'One of whom rests in your belly now. Do you want him born into Duke William's rule?'

Edyth turned away.

'I just want him born safe.'

Silence fell between them and then Morcar said, 'I'm sorry, sister.'

He opened his arms and, after only a moment's hesitation, she crept into them. Edwin joined them and the warmth of their love cracked the hard surface of her grief. They were bigger than her now, her little brothers, and broader and tougher and so much more scratched by life than when they had crawled into her bed as children, but they were her little brothers still.

'I am done with fighting,' she whispered against their broad warriors' chests but they held her too tight to hear and now there came the sound of horses' hooves on the road.

Edwin and Morcar leaped back so that she tottered sideways and she clutched at a tree as the men ran out onto the road, weapons raised.

'Who goes there?'

The reply was faint but it stirred in Edyth's iced-up heart and she crept cautiously forward. The clutch of figures on the road held weapons but they were no band of soldiers. They walked with the rolling gait of farmers and at their head was a woman, a woman in a gown of softest primrose yellow, bright in the new moonlight.

'Svana? Svana!'

Edyth was out and running before anyone could stop her. The other woman looked up, frozen for a moment, and then she was down from her horse and running too.

'Edyth? Edyth, is it you? Thank God.'

They fell into each other's arms and for a moment Edyth lost herself in her old friend's embrace, but then the times rushed in on her again and she drew back.

'Why are you here?'

'I went to Westminster to find you. After I'd seen Harold I could not stand the waiting alone. It felt as if you were the only one who would understand and I longed to see you. It was presumptuous of me, I apologise.'

'It was not presumptuous at all, Svana.'

'Indeed it was. You are Queen of England.'

'I am not.' Grief rushed back in on Edyth and she grabbed for her old friend's hands as the men melted tactfully back into the scrub. 'He is dead, Svana.'

Svana's eyes, too, clouded in the moonlight and she nodded.

'I know.'

'You sensed it?'

'No! How many times must I tell you, there is no magic in me, Edie, especially not now. We met men on the road. Sad news travels fast. I'm so sorry.'

'Nay, Svana, the loss is yours. I never meant to take your place. I never meant to hurt you. I never meant . . .'

'Hush, Edyth, do you think I don't know that? Harold needed you. He needed something I could not give. If anyone forced you into this, it was me.'

'No! You have never forced anyone into anything.'

'Least of all myself. I should not have written to you as I did, Edyth. I asked so much of you, more than was fair. I'm so sorry.'

JOANNA COURTNEY

Edyth looked down. Guilt swirled around her, like the cries of the Normans still weeping for death in the ditch behind them.

'You have it all wrong, Svana,' she said quietly. 'You did not force me. I went willingly. I betrayed your position as his wife.'

'Because I asked you to, Edyth.'

'No! No, it was not for that, not truly. For so long I have tried to pretend that it was, to the world, to you, to myself even, but it was a lie. A lie, Svana. I married Harold because I loved him.'

Silence shuddered between the night shadows. Edyth looked miserably to the dewy ground but Svana's warm fingers clasped tightly at her own.

'I know that, Edie,' she said softly. 'I know that because looking into your eyes is like looking into my own.'

Edyth blinked, stunned.

'But I had no right to love him.'

Now Svana smiled.

'You had every right, my sweet. Love prefers to be free, and better, surely, an excess of love than all this hate?'

Edyth nodded slowly.

'They want us to go back to Westminster,' she said, indicating her brothers, hovering nervously nearby. 'They want us to find another man to force onto the throne to keep William from it and they want us to fight and to fight until all of us are gone.'

'Of course they do,' Svana said. 'And you, my love?'

'I am done fighting.'

'All done?'

'Svana?'

'I want to find him, Edie. I want to find Harold and bury him. *We* may not have peace, but I would like *him* to find it at last. Will you help me? Please?'

Edyth looked back to the soldiers in the scrub and to the

ditch of death behind them. She looked to the dark trees beyond which the bloody battlefield lay, swarmed over by Duke William and his carrion troops. Svana was right – they could not leave Harold to Norman mercies for there would be none.

'I can fight for that,' she agreed softly. 'With you, Svana, I can fight for that.'

CHAPTER THIRTY-FIVE

'*E*dyth Alfgarsdottir.' Duke William looked down his thin nose at her as if at some amusing curiosity before adding, almost as an afterthought, 'Queen of England.'

Edyth acknowledged the title with a curt bow of her head but William's thin lip curled.

'You're no queen. My Matilda, my wife . . .' He glanced at Svana, stood behind Edyth, and added sneeringly, 'My *one*, true wife, is queen now. She has been very supportive of my campaign to claim my rights. Very supportive. She commissioned me a magnificent ship, you know, to carry me over the narrow sea, and she dedicated an abbey to our cause and now God has smiled on her – as is only just. She will make a wonderful Queen of England – truly wonderful. I think you will like her. She is of very noble bearing.' He squinted at Edyth, dishevelled after her night in the wilds. 'Perhaps you could be her lady-in-waiting.'

'I'm no servant.'

The Norman lords looked at each other and sniggered.

'You Saxons,' William said indulgently. 'In a civilised society it is an honour to serve a queen.'

'That would depend on the queen.'

William growled and Edyth cursed herself; always she spoke too soon. She felt Svana's calm hand in the small of her back and stared at the ground, willing herself not to cry. Edwin and Morcar had begged her to retreat to Westminster with them but, with Svana at her side, she had been resolute. The men had ridden north before dawn had broken on their departure and at first light the two women had walked onto the battlefield alone.

William had stationed himself beneath a golden canopy on Senlac Ridge where only this time yesterday the shield wall must have held him at arm's length. He was sat on a golden throne he must have brought with him in arrogant anticipation and had thrown a fresh scarlet cloak over his still bloodstained chainmail. His men had cleared back bodies as roughly as they might have swept away rushes from a dance floor and Edyth could see them heaped all around the periphery of her vision. She fought to stay true to her mission.

'I seek the body of my, my husband.'

'How touching. You may find it, though, slightly . . . segmented.'

Edyth drove her nails into her thighs, digging down through the wool of her fine gown. She would not let him torment her.

'But I may look, my lord?'

'Sire.'

His eyes pinned her to the title. She thought it might kill her to speak it, but need drove her on.

'Sire.'

'King William – it sounds good, does it not? King William I, reigned the sixth day of January 1066 to . . . who knows yet?'

'The sixth day of January? That is not correct. That—'

'Oh, but it is, little Edyth. Harold had no right to be king. His reign must be wiped from the record – yours with it. No one will remember you as queen. Oh, and sadly that means that anyone who fought against me in that period is a traitor.'

'No! You cannot do that.'

'Harold's reign was false.'

'Like your birth.'

The nobles sucked in their breath and William leaped to his feet.

'My blood is true.'

'Blood does not make a man, still less a king.'

William snarled under his breath and then smiled, a slow, triumphant smile.

'Maybe not, but victory in the field does and victory, I believe, is mine.'

There was no more to say. Edyth dipped her head.

'May we search for his body – Sire?'

'*We?* You and his eastern whore?'

Edyth's head shot straight back up again.

'The Lady Svana is no whore.'

'No? Sweet. Let us settle on bigamist then, shall we? How very pagan of you all. No wonder God gave the victory to me; someone needs to bring virtue to this land.'

Only Svana's hand, still tight on Edyth's back, gave her the strength to ignore his jibes.

'May we search for his body?' she repeated.

'You may.' Thankfully Edyth threw a curtsey and turned. 'And when you have found it you may bring it to me.'

'But—'

'To me. I'm having no shrines, no made-up miracles around the tomb of an upstart pretender.'

Edyth's blood foamed. She spun back to retaliate but Svana placed a gentle finger on her lips and faced William in her stead.

'We will do as you ask,' she said, 'but know this – whatever else he may have been, Harold was no pretender. All he did was open and honest. He was King of England at the request of his predecessor and as the choice of his people, and even if you wipe him from their records you will never wipe him from their hearts. Good day.'

They fled, trembling. Edyth was certain William was going to send men to clap them into irons but he just sat and watched them go. She could feel his eyes driving into her back and held tight to Svana's hand as they moved out into the mutilated mass of bodies littering the grass of Hastings field. She glanced at her old friend and a thousand words passed between them – waste, greed, senselessness, madness – but they did not speak them aloud. There was no need; to them both they were as obvious as the scent of fresh blood was to the carrion crows scrapping noisily over the corpses at their feet.

There were few other women for Harold's brave soldiers had marched from all over England and many of their wives would not even yet have news of their loss. All around Norman foot soldiers were carefully retrieving their own dead and carrying them to be laid out in honourable ceremony, but most of the poor English would have to trust to their home soil to take them bit by putrefying bit to their final rest. Not Harold though, not whilst they lived to save him that ignominy.

They paced the field, seeking the clutch of armoured corpses that would signify the king's last stand but the robbers had been out in force. Already many were stripped of anything of value and all men looked the same naked before their Lord. Time and again they had to turn bodies over to look into the face of some other woman's loss or, worse, into faces too cut up for anyone to know who they were lost to. They moved fast, facing down nausea at the slashed and torn mess that battle had wreaked on Harold's people in their quest for his dear body.

'We will know him,' Svana muttered, over and over.

At first Edyth had believed her but now, with blood seeping up her gown and flesh beneath her nails and glassy eyes following her every frantic turn, her foolish confidence was draining away. They were where he had died, she was sure of it. The concentration of corpses was greatest here, to the east of William's fluttering canopy, and the bodies, even hacked apart, were clearly those of full-time soldiers – broad and hard. She turned one over and fell to her knees.

'Garth!'

He had an arrow deep in his neck and a single line of blood had congealed all the way down to his heart. His body had been slashed but his face was hardly scathed. Edyth stared into it and felt the truth of Hastings strike her full on, not a dull ache, not twists or knots, but a harsh, searing, battering agony.

'No,' she wailed, cradling him against her.

The Norman lords looked curiously over. They were eating and a sickening odour of elegantly cooked meat was threading itself carelessly amongst the stench of death below the barbaric new king, but they paused now, regarding the two women like some sort of jesters. Edyth looked nervously to Svana and pulled her grief inside. Surely where Garth lay, his brother would not be far away?

Laying him gently down, they moved on but the Normans who had cracked this last noble stand of England's finest commanders had cracked it with vicious ferocity. Limbs were mingled, eyeholes gaped, hair was matted with blood. What did it matter, Edyth thought bitterly, whose blood was royal when it ran into the ground?

Tears blinded her, making her task even more hopeless, and as they sifted uselessly through the gruesome pile she felt she might be best just to lie down amongst them and die too. Then Svana whispered, 'He is here.'

She peeled back a body and reached out to the one beneath.

It lay, one arm flung high, the fingers hacked away by blades hungry to feed on his poor face. A great wound gaped across one cheek. The nose was cut away and one eye was gouged out. The lips were ripped but curved up in a tiny, secret smile and the one remaining eye, though swollen, seemed to look deep into the very heavens.

'It is him,' Svana said, running a soft finger down the line of his shattered jaw.

'How can you tell?' Edyth whispered fearfully.

'His eyes are ringed with amber – see.'

She pointed and, sure enough, Edyth saw the palest ring of sunshine around the dark blue iris.

'Ringed with gold,' she corrected.

'With gold too precious for me to keep,' Svana said and sat back. 'I suspected the very first time I looked into them that he would not be mine for long but it was too late for that to matter, I had already fallen under his spell.'

'It was not you, then, who bewitched him?'

'Nay – quite the other way round.'

'And now you have lost him.'

'As have you, but, Edie, we cannot let the bastard duke claim him. We cannot!'

Her voice squeaked with grief and Edyth glanced over to the Norman camp. William had risen and was moving their way.

'We will not let him,' she said fiercely. 'This one is a woman's battle, Svana, and we will not lose it. Here.'

She tugged Harold's mangled body out of Svana's arms and pushed another into its place, then let her hair drop over it, weeping noisily.

'You have found him,' came Duke William's voice above them. 'Excellent. I will not have a martyr born of this insolent field.'

Edyth leaped to her feet.

'You cannot have him.'

'Oh, I think I can. I killed him after all. Stand aside.'

William pushed Edyth roughly out of the way and she stumbled to keep her footing as Svana stared up, her grey eyes awash. Edyth watched her nervously but Svana faced him unflinching.

'You have England,' she snapped, 'you do not need Harold.'

'But I will have him. Men!'

Two burly guards leaped forward. One wrenched the mangled body from Svana, the other clasped the women's arms.

'You bastard,' Edyth spat out, but William just laughed.

'How did you know him?' he demanded of Svana, seizing her chin and yanking it up. 'How?'

She pointed, slim fingers trembling.

'By the mole on his shoulder.'

William looked suspiciously down at the dark mark on the torn skin. He traced the tip of his eating knife around it and then, in one sharp, dry motion, slashed it straight across. A memory spun across Edyth's mind – herself walking into Harold's pavilion to find his steward, stripped to the waist to wash, his skin white in the gloom. She had been struck by the dark mole on Avery's muscular shoulder, a tiny personal dot on a man she had known only as Harold's servant. Now it seemed a gift from God but William still hesitated so she pulled forward, yanking her surprised guards with her.

'How dare you desecrate my husband further?' she demanded. 'You have his crown – is that not enough for you? That was *my* mole. I used to kiss it.'

William half-smiled. Svana glanced at Edyth and then she, too, sprang.

'I kissed it first,' she spat at her. 'You have no right to him.'

It was as much an act as her own, Edyth knew, but still she

crumpled and William leaped forward, a predator sensing weakness.

'Ladies, really!' he cackled. 'Little use fighting over a dead man.' He nodded to the guard holding the body. 'Bury the traitor on the cliffs so he can ever look across to Normandy where he swore to uphold me as king. And let these cats go – we need them no longer.'

The men shook Edyth and Svana to the ground and William looked down on them.

'I will expect you, Lady Edyth, to pay homage at my coronation. I can send men to accompany you if you wish it?'

Edyth shook her head.

'I will be there, my lor— Sire.'

'See you are.'

A trumpet sounded up the hill and William looked over. A richly cloaked rider was dismounting before his table and he smiled in thin approval.

'Forgive me,' he threw at Edyth and Svana. 'I have important guests to attend to and can waste no more time on women's business. You will not linger, will you?'

Then, with an amused sneer, he stalked off, dismissing them out of hand. The two women lay frozen until he was gone and then Svana reached out for Edyth's hand.

'We beat him,' Edyth said, though she was shaking with the emotion of the confrontation.

'We beat him,' Svana agreed softly, adding, 'you know I did not mean that you had no right to Harold, Edie? I had to make them believe it was him, that was all.'

'You succeeded,' Edyth said, forcing a smile. 'And I know you did not mean it, but I know also that it is true.'

'It is true indeed, for no one has the "right" to anyone. Harold loved me, Edyth, and Harold also loved you. Now he is gone let us please, at least, love each other.'

Edyth smiled.

'You have been such a friend to me, Svana.'

'And you to me but this friendship has only just begun. We will need it, I fear, in the years to come.'

She looked to the wiry body of Duke William, pointing arrogantly after the guard who had what he believed to be Harold's body slung carelessly over his shoulder.

'That was Avery,' Edyth whispered.

'He would be glad to do this final service for his lord.'

'He would.'

Quietly Svana waved over a cartman waiting keenly for a deathly fare. The two women loaded Harold in, laying Garth beside him and covering the two noble brothers with the tangled remains of their housecarls.

'We will take them to Waltham Abbey,' Svana said. 'Harold will be at peace there.'

Edyth nodded.

'And then? I will not go to his coronation, you know, Svana. I will not see him crowned in Harold's place; I could not bear it.'

'Nor I. Come to Nazeing, Edyth.'

'To Nazeing?' Pictures of the soft, faerie meadowlands flashed across Edyth's bruised mind like a flicker of hope. 'Could I?'

'Of course – your children too. We will be safe there, for a little time at least.'

She looked so earnest, but Edyth felt her innocent words like a new knife wound.

'My children?' Her voice rasped and her hand crept to her belly. 'You will not want me with my children, Svana.'

Svana, however, simply reached out and placed her own hand over Edyth's.

'You are carrying his babe?' Edyth nodded miserably. 'But

that is wonderful, Edie.' It was so much an echo of Harold's response that Edyth dared to look up. Svana smiled. 'It is a blessing – a babe to replace the one I lost; a babe for us to raise together.'

'You want me, truly?'

'Truly. You were his wife for me, Edyth.'

Edyth thought of a hillside wedding years ago. She had only been a child but already she'd had the wisdom to know, however much Svana denied it, that she had witnessed magic between two people.

'No, Svana,' she said. '*You* were his wife. I was just a girl who chased the sparks of your union.'

Svana sighed softly then reached out.

'He loved you too, Edie, truly – but neither of us need chase now. Come.'

Edyth took the proffered hand and together the two women followed the grunting cartman through the carnage of England's desperate last stand and up the barren road north.

EPILOGUE

Sometimes when she closes her eyes and pictures that night, Edyth cannot tell where memories end and dreams begin. She wonders if she was enchanted. She was only eight after all, her mind still shifting in and out of made-up worlds, but something about that night, played out in firelight beneath a million stars, still feels so solid, so very real as if, rather than being befuddled by it, her mind became truly clear for the first time.

He looked like a king that day, Harold. Even in a simple bride-groom's tunic of darkest green he looked like royalty as he stepped up to take the Lady Svana's hand. There was no gold in sight, just flowers; no parade of bishops, just a smiling monk in a sack-robe and bare feet. There was no betrothal contract, no formal prayers, no exchange of lands or elaborate gifts, just the linking of hands, joining two people for a year and a day.

'No longer?' Edyth had asked. Marriage was forever, everyone knew that – grumbled about it, jested about it, accepted it.

'Only if we wish it,' Lady Svana had told her. 'Ours is a marriage of hearts, not of laws. If we cease to love, it ends.' Edyth must have looked shocked because Svana had laughed and said, 'Fear not, this union will last to the grave – love prefers to be free.'

All love prefers to be free.

HISTORICAL NOTES

What fascinates me about history is the gaps between the dates – what the people, including the kings and queens, did on the non-headline days. In researching the rich and exciting Anglo-Saxon period I have often found far more gaps than dates and whilst for the earnest historian in me that is a frustration, for the cheeky novelist it is a joy to fill those gaps with my own imaginings.

The Anglo-Saxon Chronicle, our core primary source for this period, can happily cover a whole year of events in a single paragraph. In between the monks' carefully and sometimes rather randomly selected events, however, were hundreds of men, women and children, getting up every single day – feeling warm or cold, eating, drinking, going to the loo, arguing with each other, falling in love, and getting every bit as shy, embarrassed, excited and nervous as we do today. In the evolution of mankind a thousand years is a tiny length of time and although social customs and day-to-day experiences were certainly different back in 1055, I refuse to believe that core feelings have changed much and it is that connection to the people of the past – to their minute-by-minute existences – that I wish to capture in my novels.

In every instance I have tried my best to stay within the boundaries of the known facts but it is not my intention here to create a history as much as an interpretation. I am certainly not saying that this version of Edyth's life *did* happen, but I hope I have researched deeply and carefully enough to able to assert that it *could have* happened. There are several points in my story, however, that people might wonder about, so here are a few more details on some of the key historical customs, moments, people and places.

Customs and Terminology

Handfast marriages

Handfasting was the pagan way of cementing a marriage and involved a simple ceremony in which the bride's and groom's hands were literally bound with ribbons to symbolise their union. It remained popular in the Danelaw (Eastern England) into the eleventh century because, as the name suggests, this area was governed by Danish law. The Danes remained pagan into the 950s and even once they had converted to Christianity, they perpetuated old ways and customs for longer than central and southern England.

Handfasting was legally binding, accepted as such (if reluctantly) by ecclesiastic law, and remained so for a long time after the Roman church ceremony was introduced to England. Indeed, Shakespeare's signature stands as witness to a handfasting in 1604 and it wasn't actually until the 1753 Marriage Act that the need for an officiating priest or magistrate was made compulsory for a legally valid marriage.

The Normans stamped on the practice of bigamy but before 1066 having two wives was politically useful to prominent figures needing heirs and a number of northern European leaders in the Anglo-Saxon/Viking era, including King Cnut,

Harold of Wessex and Harald Hardrada had both a handfast and a 'Roman' wife.

Crownwearings

The formalising of this practice – literally a gathering at which the monarch wore his crown to be seen by all – is sometimes attributed to William the Conqueror but actually seems to have originated with King Edward to establish a core routine for his itinerant royal court. The Crownwearings marked the key points in the church's calendar and served to gather all the important people of England together three times a year. Except in unusual circumstances – Edward's own failing health at the turn of 1066 being one – these Crownwearings were always held at Gloucester for Christ's mass, Winchester for Easter and Westminster for Whitsun.

Pavilions

Royal and noble compounds were built to house a permanent household that was relatively small – approximately one hundred people. So whenever the full court gathered at Crownwearings or for big occasions such as weddings, families brought their own waxed-linen pavilions to house themselves. They did this all year round, including for Christ's mass when England must often have been deep in snow, so furs and blankets must have been vital to keep warm.

Yuletide

Eagle-eyed readers may have noted reference to the English bringing trees into their halls to celebrate Christmas and wondered at the anachronism, given that Queen Victoria's German husband Albert is widely credited with introducing the practice to our country. In truth, however, this was an ancient Scandinavian/Germanic practice which was lost to England across time and not so much introduced as re-introduced by Prince Albert.

Vikings

It is unlikely that Edyth and her fellows would have called Hardrada and his troops 'Vikings' as the appellation was not in use until later. They would more likely have called them 'Northmen' but for our purposes 'Vikings' more accurately conveys the sense of piratical fear that they would have inspired.

Hostages

Hostages were a normal and accepted way of securing an agreement and more often than not the people who served as such were treated as noble guests – unless, of course, the agreement was broken. We know that hostages, along with much treasure, were due to be delivered to Hardrada at Stamford Bridge but have no way of knowing who they were and certainly not if they included Edyth's two Welsh princes. Given that this was a vital agreement, however, the hostages would certainly have been important people so it seems quite possible that if they were with her in York (again, unknown) Ewan (Idwal) and

Morgan (Maredudd) would have been part of the terrible delegation.

Monarchs

William decreed that the numbering of monarchs would start with him so King Harold and all his predecessors have no numbers but rather appellations – e.g. Edmund Ironside and Alfred the Great. Many such names were given posthumously, notably Edward the Confessor, whose moniker was introduced only around two hundred years after his death as part of a PR move by the monks of Westminster to attract pilgrims to his tomb.

Key Historical Moments

William's visit to Edward's court at Christmas 1051

There is only one report of this visit but it is the largely reliable Anglo-Saxon Chronicle and the timing is believable. In 1051 the Godwin family had been forced into exile, largely due to the machinations of Edward's Norman adviser Robert of Jumièges, who was clearly working to pave the way for William's acquisition of the English throne. It is quite possible that William visited his cousin's court for Christ's mass and that he becoming Edward's heir was discussed, as it may have been discussed with others (in much the same way that Elizabeth I was later to dangle promises of marriage). There is, however, no record of a formal agreement.

The Kingship of Wales

King Griffin can honestly claim to be the only man in history ever to have been King of all Wales. Although there were some leaders who'd controlled vast areas before him – notably Rhodri the Great, who ruled all of Wales bar Deheubarth from 844–878, and Hywel ap Cadell, who ruled all bar Glamorgan from 910–950 – none of them, until Griffin, controlled all four key principalities (Deheubarth, Powys, Glamorgan and Gwynedd).

After Griffin's death, English overlordship was asserted, so although there were sovereign princes – notably Rhys ap Gruffydd, 1155–1197, and Llywelyn Fawr (Great) *circa* 1200–1240 – there was never again a full king. In 1282 King Edward I of England conquered the country fully and from that point on the title of 'Prince of Wales' became an honorary one for the heir apparent, as it still is today. This means that Edyth was the only woman ever to be Queen of Wales and, indeed, ever to be Queen of both Wales and England – a fact for which she surely deserves recognition.

Harold Hardrada's visit to Rhuddlan

I have taken some artistic licence with this visit. There is documented evidence that Vikings travelled to Wales and invaded England from that vantage point, though sources (notably the *Brut y Tywysogyon* or Chronicle of the Princes) suggest that they were led not by Hardrada himself but by his son, Magnus. Harald, however, did travel widely around the North Sea and the Atlantic – including quite feasibly to the legendary 'Vineland' (Newfoundland in America) – so it is perfectly possible that he could have been part of such a landing.

Harold's trip to William in 1064

It is documented that Harold's ship was wrecked at Ponthieu and that he was rescued from Count Guy by William himself and thereafter spent some time in the ducal court, fighting with William in a successful Brittany campaign and making some sort of oath before he left. What is not documented (as it did not interest contemporary chroniclers) is *why* he went. Theories range from him being blown off-course on a fishing trip, to him trying to rescue his hostage brother and nephew, to him being on a diplomatic mission from King Edward. We will never know but I hope my version is consistent with my characters.

King Edward's deathbed

There is no formal recording of King Edward bequeathing his throne with his final breaths, simply a deliberately mysterious report in the far from reliable *Vita Edwardi Regis* (the 'Life of King Edward' commissioned as a medieval PR exercise by Queen Aldyth) that he commended 'to Harold's care the queen, the kingdom and the foreigners who had served Edward well'. Harold, however, was crowned the next day and given that he had long been recognised in formal documents as 'sub-regulus', or under-king, there seem to be few grounds for dispute regarding Edward's intentions.

In Anglo-Saxon times having royal blood was only one of the criteria for becoming king and definitely not the most important one, that being the ability to defend the country against enemies. There was no rule of primogeniture – a Norman introduction – and the Witan, or Council, held the right to elect the man that they saw most fit to rule. Harold, in 1066, was undoubtedly that man.

Northern Reinforcements at Hastings

If history does not record why Harold travelled to Normandy in 1064, it also fails to document why he chose to march on Hastings before his northern reinforcements made it to London. For such an experienced and battle-hardened warrior it seems a reckless and impatient mistake – one that cost him his life and kingdom – so why did he do it?

William was ravaging the lands around Hastings which were in Harold's patrimonial earldom of Wessex so he would have felt a duty to defend his people there as soon as possible. It could also be true that as speed helped him defeat Hardrada, he wished to persist in pressing forward. William's troops do seem to have suffered from severe dysentery so he may have been hoping they were still weak. Plus, so many troops milling around London would have been costly and violent and keeping them moving would have been a sound strategy. Harold must also have been on a high from defeating Hardrada, exhausted from a summer of waiting and the long march north, and desperate to get rid of this final invader. Once in the south he would have had less control of timings, being at the mercy of William's advancing army, but it certainly seems likely that fighting the battle a day or two later would have been wiser.

We do not know for sure that the men who apparently lured a large number of pursuing Normans into a ravine after the battle existed or that, if they did, they were Edwin and Morcar's troops. The brothers were in London defending Edgar Atheling very shortly afterwards, however, so they definitely did ride south and it seems more than probable it was their troops. If so, it can honestly be said that Harold may have lost England in the last hour of the Battle of Hastings and that had the northern men made it a little sooner (or if Harold had waited for them before going into battle) history could have been so very different.

Harold's burial

There is no hard evidence of where King Harold is buried. Two stories exist: the first is that his body was rescued by Svana (or in some versions his mother) and taken to Waltham Abbey. The second is that William scornfully had him buried on a cliff somewhere on the south coast to look out at the dukedom that had 'reclaimed' the English throne from him. What seems to be fairly well established is that his poor hacked-up corpse was identified by Svana because of a mole on his shoulder. I simply took these reports and transposed the mole onto Avery to create a dramatic and hopefully credible ending.

After the battle

In 1067 Edyth gave birth to a baby boy whom she named Harold and who could, had history only been a turn of a battle different, have ruled after his father. We do not know what happened to Edyth in the aftermath of 1066 but she may well have escaped to Ireland with Svana's three elder sons who launched abortive rebellions against William in the south-west in 1067, 1068 and 1069, possibly to try to put the young Harold on the throne. Edyth's brothers also attempted rebellion in the north in 1068 and again in 1070, when Edwin was killed and Morcar imprisoned for life.

The young Harold reappears thirty years later at the Norwegian court. It seems that he may have been welcomed by Magnus II,

Harald Hardrada's son, because Harold had treated him so well in letting him retreat with his ships after the Battle of Stamford Bridge. He could also, of course, have been a possible inspiration for a further attempt at invading England but, if so, that never happened.

Edyth, Edwin, Morcar and Nesta may have gone with the royal child to Norway, but there is a clear record of Nesta marrying Osbern FitzRichard, son of the Norman lord who built Richard's Castle (one of the few stone castles built in England before the conquest) near Ludlow. As this is very near to the border of Wales it is tempting to consider the possibility that Edyth at some point returned to her first husband's country but we have no concrete evidence of this.

People and Places

Westminster

Readers will note that Westminster is portrayed here as being on Thorney Island. This is a well documented fact and shows the significant changes London's landscape has seen over the centuries. Thorney Island was created by the Tyburn river which came from the hills of South Hampstead and divided between what is now St James' Park and Buckingham Palace, cutting Thorney Island off from the 'mainland'. The Tyburn, along with various other ancient rivers and streams, still exists but it was sunk into brick sewers in the early nineteenth century and now flows well beneath London's pavements and buildings.

Earl Torr

I may have been harsh on the character of Earl Tostig in that there is some evidence to suggest that far from being the woman-iser of my story he was a pious and faithful man. The nickname 'Torr' – the Anglo-Saxon word for 'Tower' – is of my own making and I have borrowed some of his reputation from that of his wild older brother Svein who died in 1052 before this tale begins. Earl Tostig was, however, undoubtedly known to be hard on his northern subjects and inclined to spend as much of his time in the south as possible which led to the very unusual civil rebellion of 1065. The key facts of the northern rebellion as used in this story are well documented and lend weight to the idea that he was a hard and unpopular man.

Macbeth

Lovers of Shakespeare will, I hope, be pleased to see the real Macbeth make an appearance in this story. He ruled Scotland between 1040 and 1057 with his son Lulach then succeeding him for a year. Malcolm fled to England where he seems to have been fostered by Earl Ward (Siward) of Northumbria and brought to court where King Edward – who was himself an exile in Normandy for years – supported him. It was English armies who helped Prince Malcolm win back his throne, a process which took several years between 1054 and 1058 and which came at considerable cost to Earl Siward as his adult son, Osbeorn, was killed in battle. Osbeorn's death meant that there was no natural successor as Earl of Northumbria when Siward died of old age the following year – thus opening the way for Earl Torr and the chain of events this story explores.

Edyth's sons

Whilst Nesta is almost certainly Edyth's daughter, there is some confusion in texts about whether Ewan (Idwal) and Morgan (Maredudd) were actually hers or Griffin's sons from some previous mistress, perhaps Lady Gwyneth. Given how long Edyth was queen, however, it seems likely that they were hers.

Svana and Edyth's friendship

There is, I must confess, absolutely no historical evidence about a friendship between these two women (and certainly no letters), but friendships were not something Anglo-Saxon chroniclers were interested in. It is true, however, that Edyth would have been in East Anglia during her father's rule as earl between 1051 and 1055 so would more than likely have met Svana (Eadyth Swanneck), a key landholder within the area, a number of times. The rest is my own fancy and I hope readers enjoyed it.

CHANGED NAMES

Given that some of the original names of the characters are either hard to pronounce or confusingly common I have made some changes to help the flow of the story for the modern reader. For the curious, however, here are the original names:

	ANGLO-SAXON/ WELSH	MY VERSION
	Eadyth Swanneck	Svana
	Earl Siward	Earl Ward
Earl Godwin's children	Harold	Harold
	Eadyth	Aldyth (Queen)
	Tostig	Torr (Tostig used occasionally)
	Gyrth	Garth
	Leofwine	Lane
	Aelfgifu	Emma
	Gunnhild	Hannah
	Wulfnoth	Wulf
Earl Alfgar's children	Burgheard	Brodie
	Eadyth	Edyth
	Eadwin	Edwin
	Morcar	Morcar (Marc)

CHANGED NAMES

Edyth's children	Idwal	Ewan
	Maredudd	Morgan
	Nesta	Nesta
Svana's children	Godwin	Godwin
	Eadmund	Edmund
	Magnus	Magnus
	Gytha	Crysta
	Gunnhild	Hannah

ACKNOWLEDGEMENTS

I have so many people to thank for getting me this far. Writing a book is a crazy thing to do and whilst for me it's been largely a joy, I can't say it's made me a joy to be around for the other poor souls in my life and I cannot thank them enough for being there for me.

Firstly I need to thank Stuart and our children for their patience, love and tolerance of my endless interest in Anglo-Saxon facts. In particular Hannah for telling everyone I 'only write about the Battle of Hastings', Alec for keeping my feet on the ground by reminding me 'football is so much more important than books', Rory for being an example of endless studiousness, and Emily for being my fellow history-lover and Welsh reader-in-residence. They're so proud of having a 'writer' for a mum and I very much hope this book will live up to their loving and trusting expectations.

Then there's my brother, Sandy, and my sister, Lindsay, for being so damned successful in their own spheres that I've had to fight and fight to try and keep up! And of course, along with their lovely families, for being my confidants, supporters and drinking buddies. My dad for reading my work, providing honest and valuable feedback, and, particularly, for always picking up accidentally rude or foolish words (never will anyone in my books 'stoke' someone's thigh again). My stepmum for vital childcare in the early years when I was trying to become 'a writer', and my mum for chocolate, emotional support and the lovely message recently left on my whiteboard stating: 'Keep going – I sense a breakthrough coming'. How right you were, Mum!

Then there are my friends. Maggie and Jacky and all the Cambridge girlies who have insisted with impressive consistency that I am not totally mad for trying to be a writer. My Supper Club ladies for boosting my confidence with my waistline and for keeping me sane (well, almost sane) through the perils of working as a self-employed mum. Brenda and Jamie for editorial wisdom and vital hot tubbage, Tracey for nononsense encouragement and quality snacks, and my writerly mates Tracy Bloom and Julie Houston, both of whom I met through the RNA, and with whom I have been privileged to share some of the trials and joys of becoming published.

And finally the pros. A big thanks to all my editors at the women's magazines for their backing and advice over the last fifteen years. To the Open University for employing me as a Creative Writing tutor – work that I love and that has brought me the income that enabled me to continue writing as a 'proper job'. Emily's Welsh friend, Aled, for verifying my clumsy use of his beautiful language; the fantastic Anglo-Saxon House; the British Museum; and the lovely ladies at Mickleover Library for their endless help and patience.

And then of course I have to say a huge thank you to Kate Shaw, my fantastic agent, who first showed belief in me as a writer way back in 2004 and who has stubbornly persisted in that belief and finally persuaded somebody else to agree with her. And finally to that somebody – Natasha Harding at Pan Macmillan – for being the one who loved my novel enough to take it on and bring it to the world, as well as for her enthusiasm and astute editing.

ACKNOWLEDGEMENTS

I've wanted to be a writer since I sat up in my cot and read picture books to myself. I thank every person listed above and no doubt a thousand more besides for all they've done to help me get this far and I look forward to sharing the next part of the journey with them too.

BIBLIOGRAPHY

I am indebted to the creators of many, many books, websites, museums and exhibits for bringing this murky period of history to life for me. Here is a list of just a few sources that readers might enjoy if, having read this work of fiction, they wish to dig for more facts.

Historical Events

Campbell, James, *The Anglo-Saxon State* (Hambledon and London, 2000)

Davies, Wendy (ed), *From the Vikings to the Normans* (Oxford University Press, 2003)

De Vries, Kelly, *The Norwegian Invasion of England in 1066* (Boydell Press, 1999)

Freeman, E.A., *The History of the Norman Conquest of England* (Cambridge University Press, 2011 [1867])

Harvey-Wood, Harriet, *The Battle of Hastings* (Atlantic Books, 2008)

Higham, N.J., *The Death of Anglo-Saxon England* (Sutton Publishing, 1997)

Hill, Paul, *The Road to Hastings* (Tempus, 2005)

Huscroft, Richard, *The Norman Conquest* (Pearson Education Ltd, 2009)

Huscroft, Richard, *Ruling England 1042–1217* (Pearson Education Ltd, 2003)

BIBLIOGRAPHY

Reston Jnr, James, *The Last Apocalypse – Europe at the Year 1000 AD* (Anchor Books, 1941)

Stenton, Frank, *Anglo-Saxon England* (Oxford University Press, 1989, 3rd edition, [1943])

Trow, M.J., *Cnut, Emperor of the North* (Sutton Publishing, 2005)

Wardle, Terry, *England's First Castle* (The History Press, 2009)

People

Bates, David, *William the Conqueror* (George Philip Ltd, 1989)

Davis, Michael and Sean, *The Last King of Wales – Gruffyd Ap Llywellyn* c. *1013–1063* (The History Press, 2012)

Marsden, John, *Harald Hardrada, The Warrior's Way* (Sutton Publishing, 2007)

Mason, Emma, *The House of Godwine: The History of a Dynasty* (Continuum-3PL, 2004)

O'Brien, Harriet, *Queen Emma and the Vikings* (Bloomsbury, 2005)

Stafford, Pauline, *Queen Emma and Queen Edith* (Blackwell, 2001)

Walker, Ian W., *Harold, the Last Anglo-Saxon King* (The History Press, 2010)

Life and Times

Jessup, Ronald, *Anglo-Saxon Jewellery* (Shire Publications Ltd, 1974)

Lacey, Robert, and Danziger, Danny, *The Year 1000* (Abacus, 1999)

Mortimer, Ian, *The Time Traveller's Guide to Medieval England* (The Bodley Head, 2008)

Quennell, Marjorie, and C.H.B., *Everyday Life in Roman and Anglo-Saxon Times* (Jarrold and Sons Ltd, 1968, [1959]

Reynolds, Andrew, *Later Anglo-Saxon England* (Tempus Publishing Ltd, 1999)

Q & A WITH
JOANNA COURTNEY

1. Have you always wanted to be a writer?

Yes, ever since I can remember. My mum says that as a toddler I used to be happy in my cot for hours, as long as I had plenty of books in there with me, and I've always been a voracious reader. I loved Enid Blyton and was writing my own boarding-school books by the time I was about ten. English was always my favourite subject, with History close behind.

I did Creative Writing as part of my Duke of Edinburgh Award and always kept writing privately: both long, angsty diaries and short stories. I studied English Literature at Cambridge University and then, when I was working in a wonderful Lancashire mill town and had loads of time on my hands, I started writing again. I discovered that short-story writing really helped me refine my ability to create a narrative. I've had over two hundred stories published in women's magazines and I still love writing them, but bit by bit I've crept back to longer fiction – first serials for the magazines and, increasingly, novels.

My children are now thirteen and ten, which has helped me find time to devote to my writing, but I still can't quite believe that it's actually happening. All my life I've dreamed of having a book on the shelves of a bookshop and now that I'm there, it's wonderful.

2. Why do you write historical fiction?

I've always been fascinated by the past. I remember, as a child, visiting Holyrood Palace in Edinburgh and standing over the (presumably re-touched) bloodstain where David Rizzio was murdered by Lord Darnley, and being forcibly struck by the reality of standing on the same spot – the very same boards – where the killing had taken place.

That sense of the layers of human experience through time has remained with me always, and as I moved on in my study of English Literature, I found myself gravitating towards Medieval and Arthurian Studies because I was fascinated by the idea of context – of the cultural lives that surrounded these stories. A story told out-loud to a post-feast crowd of Vikings would have been aimed at creating drama and mood to rouse a live audience, who might well have been about to try and emulate their heroes in battle so needed courage as well as entertainment. In comparison, a nineteenth-century novel, designed to be read in private, would seek to provoke quieter emotion and thoughts for serious discussion later. I wanted to understand more about those differences and inevitably, I guess, that led me into learning more about the way lives were lived in the past. The more I learned, the more I was gripped and I wanted to explore the people who might have lived in those past times in my fiction.

3. How long did it take you to write The Chosen Queen?

That's a hard question to answer because I think all the years of writing, both as a child and as a short-story writer, have gone into making me the person that could craft this book. Writing the actual novel probably only took a few months, but so much else goes into it – not the least, my research.

Before *The Chosen Queen* was accepted by Pan Macmillan

I wrote another novel set in 1045–52 about Aldyth Godwinson, wife of King Edward. Much of the research for that I used for *The Chosen Queen*, but all the Welsh history was new to me and had to be carefully studied.

Then of course there's the editing – I reckon it takes almost twice as long to edit a novel as it does to write the first draft so, in total, a solid year went into creating this particular book.

4. Can you tell us about your book deal moment?

I vividly remember my agent, Kate, sending me through an email from my current editor Natasha, saying how much she loved the book. It was full of the most lovely praise for *The Chosen Queen* and I printed it off to keep with me as it was so close to my heart. We were going on holiday with good friends the following week, and I remember my friend Brenda reading it aloud on a blowy beach in Wales for all the world to hear. Even hearing it out loud (very loud), it was still hard to believe, but it was true and the contract followed shortly afterwards.

5. How did you come up with the title of the book?

I didn't. I find titles really difficult – they either come first time or they're almost impossible to hunt down. The book was initially called *The Half Year Queen*, which I rather liked because it sounded so poignant, but it didn't really reflect all the amazing time Edyth spends as Queen of Wales so it wasn't quite right.

In the end, the lovely team at Pan Macmilllan came up with *The Chosen Queen* and when we then thought of the titles of the other two books in the trilogy (*The Constant Queen* and *The Conqueror's Queen*) – it all seemed to fit beautifully.

6. Are you writing a new novel at the moment?

I've just finished editing Book Two of the trilogy – *The Constant Queen* – and am now researching the Normans for Book Three – *The Conqueror's Queen*. I'm really enjoying the research and it's going to be a fascinating challenge to turn Duke William 'the Bastard' into a romantic hero.

THE CHRISTMAS COURT

JOANNA COURTNEY

Christmas 1051: King Edward's royal court has gathered to welcome William of Normandy to England. But as the ambitious Norman duke takes his place amongst the English lords, rumour and speculation are rife. It appears that William has an ulterior motive for making his timely visit to his childless royal cousin . . .

For Freya, however, who is new to the court, the enticing entertainments of the burgeoning Wessex city of London are far more intriguing than the political machinations which surround the gathering. Enchanted by the wassails, evergreens and crowds of the Christmas celebrations, she and her friend Alodie see the Normans as more of an enticement than a danger.

Even in the daytime, the vast Christmas markets along the sprawling banks of Chelsea village offer endless delights – until a pickpocket cuts through their happiness and throws Freya into the arms of an unlikely saviour. As the feasting and dancing begin, Freya finds herself falling for a man from the wrong side of the Narrow Sea and, with the help of a little mistletoe and wine, 1051 becomes a Christmas to remember . . .

The Christmas Court is perfect for cosy, winter reading. Sumptuous meals, roaring fires and a touching romance will transport you through time to the magic of the medieval Christmas markets.